FATE

REWRITTEN

DONG XI

Translated by
John Balcom

SINOIST

Published by Sinoist Books (an imprint of ACA Publishing Ltd)
London - Beijing

info@alaincharlesasia.com ☎ +44 20 3289 3885
www.sinoistbooks.com

Published by Sinoist Books (an imprint of ACA Publishing Ltd), translated
with the permission of the author and the Shanghai Literature & Art
Publishing House, Shanghai, China

Author: Dong Xi **Translator:** John Balcom
Editor: Susan Trapp **Cover Art:** A. Bodrenkova

Originally published in China as 篡改的命 (cuan gai de ming)
© Copyright Dong Xi 2016

English Translation text © 2024 ACA Publishing Ltd, London, UK. A catalogue
record for *Fate Rewritten* is available from the National Bibliographic Service of
the British Library.

Paperback ISBN: 978-1-83890-571-2
Hardback ISBN: 978-1-83890-573-6
eBook ISBN: 978-1-83890-572-9

Supported using public funding by
**ARTS COUNCIL
ENGLAND**

*Sinoist Books is honoured to be supported using public
funding by Arts Council England.*

PROLOGUE

— • ONE

WANG CHANGCHI ARRIVED at the appointed place ten minutes early. He had been early all his life because in the end, he didn't want to be labelled as "late". His clothes were neat and clean, and he had had a haircut and a shave. He had considered buying a brand-new pair of leather shoes, but after working out that the five hundred yuan was enough to put a new glass window in his dad's farmhouse, he swallowed, wrung his hands and gave up the idea. He was wearing a pair of cloth People's Liberation Army shoes bleached out from washing and was standing at the railing in the middle of West River Bridge. It was the highest point above the water from which the loudest splash would be made if a person fell. After a lifetime, a person either disappears quietly or leaves with a bang, he must choose. The sky was particularly blue and the clouds were of the purest white, as if the sky were putting on its best just for him or to give him a final memento. The sunlight on the water's surface was broken by the wind into waves of varying intensity, blinding for an instant here, then there. The roar of the traffic was not as disagreeable as in the past, almost pleasant now, even the exhaust fumes seemed fragrant. Seeing the successive rows of orderly multi-storey buildings, he thought, That person must be hidden there behind a window, observing me and my every move through his binoculars...

1

KOWTOWING
DESPERATELY

二 · TWO

WANG CHANGCHI WANTED TO MASK THE STINK of the news before giving it to Wang Huai. Having a drink when he heard the news, Wang Huai felt as if he had just swallowed a rotten egg and immediately wanted to puke. News was just news and not enough to make a person vomit. As a result, all he could do was stifle the urge, almost to the point of injuring himself internally, before taking a breath and saying, "Weren't you at the top? How could you qualify in the upper percentile and not be admitted?"

Wang Changchi lowered his head and replied, "They said I failed to write down my choices correctly."

"What did you write down for your choices?"

"First Peking University or Tsinghua, then whatever they'd assign me."

Pop! Wang Huai crushed the cup in his hand and said, "You're a real bold one – not since 1949 has a single person from the county managed to get into Tsinghua or Peking University."

"I just wanted to say that I'd do what they allowed me. For someone with my score, I should be able to get into any rotten university."

"Not everyone who looks down sees money. Obviously, you

were made for a rotten university, so why dream about going to a renowned one?"

"I just wanted to have some fun with them."

"What kind of fun can you have other than laughing away your own chances? You're just a Three-No's Person: no power, no influence, and no savings. Every step you take is like walking on a steel cable, and you want to joke around with your fate!"

The Three No's Person sank his head lower and lower, like an ear of grain in heavy rain. He dared not lift it all night, as if such a gesture would prove that he was mature like the ripe grain in the fields. He watched as Wang Huai tottered on his legs and Liu Shuangju moved on hers with trepidation. The broken bits of the wine cup shimmered whitely, and the dog scuttled back and forth under the table. The wind swept in recklessly, blowing away the stuffy air. He felt the cold on the back of his neck like a moist pain-killing plaster stuck there. Wang Huai and Liu Shuangju didn't want to talk to him, they all understood in their hearts that silence is a cruel punishment. The idea of committing suicide flashed through his head, and he even decided where and how, but it was a passing notion that was soon erased.

As night deepened, he heard the sound of someone bathing and a door closing, but he didn't hear the creak of the plank bed. The usual squeaking of the bed was absent tonight as if it were restraining itself out of sorrow for him or as if it were halting all pleasurable activities. Only when he heard Wang Huai snoring did he venture to squat and pick up the pieces of the broken cup. Picking up the pieces, he cut his right forefinger. Blood oozed out, but he felt no pain.

The following morning, Wang Huai woke from his stupor. He wanted to go with Wang Changchi to talk sense into the University Admissions Office. Wang Changchi lay in his room, not daring to come out. Wang Huai kicked open the door with one foot. This was the final, brilliant performance of his foot. Wang Changchi's shoulders heaved as he sobbed like a girl. The towel in his hand was wet with tears. Wang Huai asked, "Will crying solve anything?" Of course, Wang Changchi knew that crying wouldn't solve anything, but at least it relieved the pressure for him. He tried to stop, but the harder he tried the more he cried, so he covered his face with the towel to hold back the flood, but his repressed sobs broke the dam, and his sobs became bitter tears. Standing at the door, Wang Huai watched as if he were witnessing the performance of a tragedy. Wang Changchi wept loudly for a while and, feeling embarrassed, he slowed down, the sound of his crying tapering off until finally he forced himself to stop. But after calming down, he still felt a lingering fear and his body jerked from time to time.

"Can we go now?" asked Wang Huai.

"I cut my finger."

"You don't walk with your finger."

"I didn't sleep all night."

"When your mother had you, I didn't shut my eyes for two days and two nights."

Wang Changchi rubbed his eyes and said, "Who's to blame for me not filling out the form correctly?"

"Blame them. They're a bunch of swindlers."

Wang Changchi asked to wash his face first. Wang Huai waited at the front door. Washing slowly with both hands, Wang Changchi vigorously scrubbed his face from his forehead to his chin and from his chin to his forehead, up and down like a woman massaging her face, wishing he could focus on that and nothing else his whole life. However, a cough from Wang Huai resounded sharply, like an alarm clock, reminding him that patience had its limits. Wang Changchi thought it would be better to run away rather than go with him and make a fool of himself. He headed towards the back door, not realising that Wang Huai was standing outside. In a split second, he had gone from the front door to the back. Wang Changchi was about to pull his right foot back over the threshold but couldn't, and was stopped dead in his tracks by a look from Wang Huai. Wang Huai asked, "Do you want to use the toilet?" Wang Changchi shook his head.

They walked towards the road with Wang Huai in front and Wang Changchi following. Wang Huai carried a soft bag on his back that clattered with every step. It was the sound of water. He had packed an army canteen in the bag. A full canteen never makes a sound, just a half-full one. The aroma of cooked corn on the cob wafted at every moment from the bag. After walking a distance, Wang Changchi was covered with sweat.

"Are you hot?" asked Wang Huai.

"No, my sweat is cold," said Wang Changchi, wondering how he knew he was hot without turning around.

"Want a drink?"

"No."

"Are you hungry?"

"No."

Actually, Wang Changchi had not eaten, drunk or slept in eight hours, so everything he said was a lie, as if just to be contrary on purpose.

The two of them fell silent. The plodding of their feet on the long road was audible. Wang Changchi saw a flock of birds cut across the limpid blue sky above his head, resembling so many sesame seeds scattered among the trees or small fry tossed into the sea. Wang Huai walked faster with each step and after twenty metres he discovered Wang Changchi was no longer with him. He stopped, removed his canteen and took a swig. From a distance, Wang Changchi got a whiff of alcohol. So it wasn't water in the canteen. As Wang Changchi approached, Wang Huai thrust the canteen at him and asked, "Want a drink?" Wang Changchi shook his head. It was then that Wang Changchi noticed Wang Huai's dirty and messy hair. The sweaty grime on his collar looked like rust, and his bag had a palm-sized patch on it. Was Wang Changchi really going to try to reason with the University Admissions Office accompanied by an alcoholic with dishevelled hair, and messy clothes, who couldn't speak standard Mandarin?

Looking at Wang Huai's small silhouette from the back, he felt increasingly negative, and the future looked ever vaguer as he walked. Passing a tea plantation, he took off through the tea trees, running like crazy as if he wanted to run through the earth. The branches smacked his face, boxing his ears again and again.

Unable to run any farther, he leaned against a tea tree, gasping for breath. Panting, he heard Wang Huai's scolding drifting through the air, "Wang Changchi, you're spineless and no son of mine! You're a rotten egg and deserve to be swindled..."

That scolding voice circled above his head. The wind blew and set it trembling, making it sound bleak and solemn. Wang Changchi hugged the trunk of the tree, tighter and tighter, as if it were his mother, hugging it until his arms ached. He actually fell asleep hugging the tree and when he woke, his arms and legs were numb. His limbs felt as if they had separated from him and had turned to wood. He sat on the ground, slowly regaining consciousness and only after he recovered the feelings in his hands and feet did he stand up and walk back.

When he returned home, Liu Shuangju asked, "Why are you back?"

"I forgot my ID," said Wang Changchi.

Glancing towards the street, Liu Shuangju said, "So you're OK with him going alone? With his temper, he'll end up in a fight."

"That's his own fault."

"Where's your heart? He went on your account."

"He's an embarrassment."

Liu Shuangju stood there distracted, and it was a long time before she came to herself.

The following day, Wang Changchi assumed that Wang Huai had returned. However, by nightfall there was still no trace of him. Night deepened, but still no footsteps were heard. Wang Changchi pricked up his ears but didn't hear what he hoped to hear. Liu Shuangju was so anxious she couldn't sit still, and every day she pressed Wang Changchi to go out and help Wang Huai. Wang Changchi pretended not to hear. On the fifth day, Liu Shuangju said, "If you don't bring him back, the grain is going to rot in the fields."

Wang Changchi sat in a chair in front of the house looking at the distant mountain range. Liu Shuangju gave him a shove, but he budged no more than a heavy piggybank, tilting briefly before settling upright again. Regardless of which angle she pushed from or how much strength she used, his backside seemed fixed to the chair with superglue, and she couldn't budge him.

Liu Shuangju then suggested, "Perhaps your dad has been arrested. How can you just sit on your arse? Are you a stone? You don't have to help him, but you must go and get him – even if he's a corpse."

Liu Shuangju wiped her eyes as she spoke. Her eyes were red, and she started to cry. Wang Changchi was unmoved. Liu Shuangju put the book bag on her shoulder and said, "If you won't go, I will."

Wang Changchi finally moved. With so many things to do at home, he was afraid to stay on his own. He tightly grasped the chair as if it were part of his body. Holding the chair, he took a few steps, but finding it awkward, moved the chair from under his backside to his shoulders. Shouldering the chair, he set off.

"Why are you taking the chair?" asked Liu Shuangju. "Do you plan to go somewhere else and do nothing?"

"If you don't understand, don't pretend to," replied Wang Changchi.

Liu Shuangju hung the book bag around his neck. He strode off, shouldering the chair with the bag around his neck.

It was a winding mountain road. The forest was vast. He felt as minute as an ant, and the road was as fine as a strand of white hair.

三 · THREE

WHEN HE CAME OUT OF THE BUS STATION, Wang Changchi headed straight to the Bureau of Education. He saw Wang Huai sitting cross-legged on the playing field, holding a cardboard protest placard in both hands. The placard read, "The top-notch are not admitted. Who will give me justice?"

The only thing seen on the otherwise empty playing field was Wang Huai's silhouette. The sun shone so brightly that his neck was clearly delineated. His whole body was like half a rice shoot sticking out of the dry ground and his lowered head and stooped shoulders resembled an unmoving tree stump. Wang Changchi put down the chair and went over to help him up. He was very heavy, many times heavier than Wang Changchi had imagined. On his first try, he was unable to help him to his feet. On his second try, he still couldn't get him up, despite exerting more strength. Having gone numb himself a few days before, Wang Changchi knew that Wang Huai was so heavy because his legs had gone numb and were of no use, so he massaged his legs. After rubbing for half an hour Wang Huai was, with one hand on the ground for support, able to get up and sit in the chair. He said, "In a city the size of the county town, there isn't an extra wooden stool to be had." Wang Changchi handed him his bag. He fished out a glass bottle, twisted off the cap, and glug, glug, glug, gulped down one third of its contents. It was his own home-brewed rice wine, the taste of which reinvigorated him.

"The grain is ripe and Mum says for you to come home for the harvest," said Wang Changchi.

"What does grain matter? It's fate that's most important," replied Wang Huai. With his right thumb, he wiped the corners of his mouth, moist with rice wine.

"Even if you sat on a concrete floor and wore it out, you wouldn't be able to change their minds."

"What am I doing here if I can't change their minds? Don't I have anything better to do? I'm telling you that the issue has already attracted the attention of the leaders, and they are investigating. Sit with me for a few days more, and we might just get a special dispensation."

"I'd rather go home and be a farmer than lose face here."

"You're qualified, so why be a farmer? You ought to be like them and work sitting in an office."

It was a four-storey office block with twelve offices on each floor. Exterior corridors graced the building, and the doors and window frames were painted green, which was no longer the same green it had once been. It had faded into a mottled surface after long exposure to the elements. Moss and water stains were visible at the foot of the wall, the exterior face of the corridors and even in some corners of the top floor. A number of neatly trimmed Chinese holly trees were planted in a row in front of the building.

Pointing at the building, Wang Huai said, "The bureau director's office is in Room Five on the second floor with two assistant directors in Rooms Three and Four, and the Admissions Office is the first one on the third floor. Wang Changchi observed someone poke his head through the window and very quickly withdraw it.

"I'll wait for you outside. When you come to your senses, we'll go home."

"I won't come to my senses unless they include you in the quota," shouted Wang Huai.

Heads poked through a number of windows and stared for a long time, as if hoping to see a change in the situation, however slight.

"Know why they are so nervous?" asked Wang Huai. "Because they have guilty consciences. Every time I raise my voice, the first head to appear is the one from the Admissions Office. When have I, your dad, ever had such power and prestige? Only when I grasp the truth and champion justice, that's when."

The heads were still there. Some of the people held teacups and sipped tea as they watched, some tapped on their cups, and others lifted cameras.

"How about I kowtow to you?" whispered Wang Changchi.

"That won't do," Wang Huai replied loudly. "If anyone kowtows to me, it will be them."

"Why don't I take the test again next year after more study?" Wang Changchi almost begged.

"If they don't admit you this year, they'll cut you down like chives just the same next year," replied Wang Huai, his voice as resonant as ever.

A burst of laughter came from the building, someone whistled, and someone else snapped their fingers. Wang Changchi felt he was attacked from both front and rear. He wanted to run but was afraid that the people in the building would laugh at him for failing to enrol. He had to harden himself and take the sarcastic, disdainful and gloating looks. Perhaps half an hour of silence or stillness and they would lose interest in surrounding him and watching. Standing there quietly, Wang Changchi was anxious lest a sneeze break the equilibrium. Now there were two slanting shadows on the playing field, one standing and one sitting. The sunlight shone from the west, making his scalp tingle. One after another, those watching disappeared. Wang Changchi wanted to slip away while they were not watching when suddenly a bell rang. It was the bell announcing the end of work. One after another the doors and windows were closed, and talking and laughter could be heard from the corridors of the building. The office workers were seen approaching, but they suddenly turned, skirting them as if they had encountered a reef or plague. Wang Huai stood up on the chair and raised the cardboard placard high. Wang Changchi couldn't bear to look, so he pressed his chin to his chest as if he were a nursing sow, burned by the eyes around him. He lifted his head only when the sound of many footsteps vanished, at which point he turned and ran. Wang Huai jumped down off the chair and said, "Wait for me."

They arrived under a concrete bridge. Wang Huai climbed up the bridge pier and from an opening removed a rolled mat and tossed it down, where Wang Changchi caught it. As the mat unrolled, a plastic bag fell out. Wang Huai slid down the bridge pier to the ground, picked up the bag, opened it and took out a *mantou*, and handed it to Wang Changchi, who shook his head. Wang Huai stuffed the steamed bread into his mouth as if to swallow it whole. His cheeks were briefly puffed up. Judging from the amount of time he spent chewing and the movement of his cheeks, it must have been a hard *mantou* that had been in the plastic bag for some time. Wang Changchi's nose tingled slightly as if in sympathy for Wang Huai or himself.

"You've been staying in the opening under the bridge?" he asked.

Wang Huai was unable to reply immediately because he was still chewing on the *mantou*. Wang Changchi's ears were filled with the loud and protracted sound of chomping.

Wang Huai took a swig of rice wine when he had finished

chewing and said, "It doesn't cost anything to stay there and besides it's cool."

"Just like a beggar."

"Of course now that you're here, I'll have to move."

"Move where?"

"Wherever makes you happy."

At the hotel, Wang Huai took a standard room. With both hands, he pressed on the mattress, exclaiming, "It's so soft and white, let's go to bed early tonight."

After washing, they turned off the light and got into bed. As soon as Wang Changchi closed his eyes, his brain, like a powerful generator, took his exhausted body wandering all over the place. His body and thoughts seemed to rise and fall in weightless space, never coming down to earth. As he drifted and swayed, his brain faintly ached and felt swollen. Five days before, he had been able to fall asleep while standing and holding a tree but tonight he couldn't fall asleep for the life of him, despite being so tired. By midnight, he couldn't stand it any longer, so he got up and turned on the light and discovered that Wang Huai was gone. He looked again and saw him sleeping on the floor next to the bed. In the bright light, Wang Huai covered his eyes with his hands, and said, "I've slept on a hard plank bed for decades, so I'm not used to this soft one."

"Let's go home. Why suffer here?" said Wang Changchi as he got dressed. Soon he was almost fully clothed in his trousers and socks, and sitting on the chair he had brought.

"What time is it?" asked Wang Huai.

"Two o'clock," he replied.

"Two o'clock. It's a long time till daybreak, so there won't be a bus home."

Wang Changchi pulled opened the curtains. It was black as ink in the distance. He moved the chair over, sat down and looked east, without moving, as if by looking at the sky it would grow light sooner. Wang Huai got to his feet and went into the bathroom where he took a long piss, then came out and sat on the edge of the bed.

"I'm even more against you retreating now," he said, "because it's like a battle in which victory or defeat can be decided in the last five minutes. We'll wait till the key moment when the charge is sounded. Whatever you do, don't weaken."

Wang Changchi didn't believe in any call to charge and kept his eyes fixed straight ahead beyond the window, hoping the sky would hurry up and grow light so they could catch the early bus home.

Wang Huai seemed to read his mind and said, "If you don't go to university, you'll spend your whole life stuck in the village, so why are you in such a hurry to get back? Twenty years ago, I applied for a job at the cement factory and, despite being qualified, I wasn't taken on. Only ten years later did I learn that the nephew of the deputy township head had replaced me. If you don't protest, they'll cheat you. What's more, all the Toms scoring twenty points lower than you have been admitted and all the Dicks who weren't even listed have been admitted. So why not you?"

Whoosh! Wang Changchi pulled the curtains closed, but because he used too much force, one of the curtain rings fell to the floor with a ding, echoing throughout the room.

"If you find this to be too much trouble," said Wang Huai, "then go home. But I have to see it through. Watching you grow up, I knew you had a cadre's fate, and it's impossible for you not to pass the university exam..."

"Where's all this nonsense come from?" asked Wang Changchi. He quickly stood up and lifted the chair to go.

"The earliest bus is at seven," said Wang Huai, "and the station is still closed."

"Can't I go out and vent first?"

"Tell your mum if I don't get you admitted, I won't be coming home."

Wang Changchi opened the door and walked out, the chair banging against the door frame. Wang Huai closed the door and lay down on the floor to sleep. Soon he was snoring.

四 · FOUR

THE FOLLOWING MORNING, Wang Huai slung his canteen of wine over his shoulder, picked up the chair in the room, went downstairs and bought several *mantou*, and then went to the Bureau of Education. Unexpectedly, Wang Changchi was sitting ramrod straight on the playing field. Overcome with joy, Wang Huai set the chair next to him, patted him on the shoulder, sat down and held up the cardboard protest placard. Now, father and son sat shoulder-to-shoulder. They left early and returned late, without resting over the weekend. They sat for five days in a row and the new semester began.

The sound of a bugle was frequently heard from the nearby campus, like a sharp point pricking Wang Changchi's nerves. When the callisthenics commands were broadcast over the playing field, Wang Changchi stood up and followed: one-two-three-four, two-two-three-four, three-two-three-four... in doing a series of callisthenics. When the commands for a series of eye exercises came during the class period, he followed suit and completed them too. On the broad playing field, he was the only person waving his hands and kicking his feet and pressing the acupressure points for his eyes. Seeing him alone, Wang Huai would sometimes join him, but his movements were stiff and inaccurate, resembling a trained monkey, frequently eliciting laughter from the building. Wang Changchi no longer dreaded the mocking laughter. He believed that as long as he stood on the playing field doing exercises, then he was a student.

One afternoon, the light above grew weaker until it all but disappeared. The sky darkened, and they felt a few scattered raindrops fall on their necks. Waves of heat rose from the concrete, and the smells of dirt, paint and lime wafted toward them. Gradually, the raindrops fell more heavily. Everyone in the vicinity took off at a run, and even the dog staying cool in the shade of a tree ran away. But they continued to sit motionless in their places. The rain poured down from above, the varied smells disappeared, and the slightly salty rainwater trickled down around the corners of their mouths after washing their hair and faces. The characters on the cardboard protest placard that Wang Huai held up grew indistinct, and the cardboard finally grew limp and was ruined. The rain enclosed them like a wall. They couldn't clearly see the office building or the Chinese holly trees a few metres from them. Their sandals were submerged under the water that had accumulated on the ground. They were soaked to the bone, the only thing staying dry were the thoughts in their heads. Their shirts and trousers clung tightly to their skin and couldn't be pulled away. Their hair was plastered down, their fingers wrinkled from the soaking.

The pattering of the rain was heard.

Half an hour later, the heavy rain lightened to a moderate rain, and after another thirty minutes, it became a light rain. Everything reappeared. The rain stopped, but their soaking wet clothes continued to drip, and the two of them were shivering with cold. It took several tries before Wang Huai succeeded in twisting off the cap of his canteen with his trembling fingers. He took several large gulps before his body gradually stopped shaking. Wang Changchi, however, continued to tremble fiercely, even his teeth were chattering. Wang Huai passed him the canteen. Wang Changchi hesitated a moment before taking it. First he took a sip and then he took a big gulp. His stomach instantly burned like an oven, and his whole body felt much warmer.

"Aren't we pitiful?" whispered Wang Huai.

"They're no longer interested in watching us," replied Wang Changchi.

"I admit our protest has gone down in defeat."

"Let's go home."

"Then have we been sitting here the last ten days or so for nothing?"

"Would you care about a couple of ants on your doorstep?"

"We have to give it one more chance."

"Forget it. We can't beat them."

"There's hope for you." Tapping Wang Changchi on the head, Wang Huai got to his feet and entered the hall of the building, leaving a trail of water behind. When he arrived on the first floor, he looked back once. Wang Changchi was still sitting on the playing field. He started for the second floor. Wang Changchi thought he was going to the director's office, but unexpectedly he climbed up on the railing along the outside corridor.

"Dad..." Wang Changchi shouted as he ran towards the foot of the building.

The director came out as did the assistant directors. The recruiters on the third floor ran down to the second floor. A group of cadres stood in front of Wang Huai.

"All you have to do is get down and I'll see that your son has free tutoring for a year," said the director.

Not persuaded, Wang Huai asked, "How about my life for a place in the university quota?"

The director exchanged glances with the assistant directors and said, "OK, but come down first."

Seeing them exchange winks, Wang Huai suspected a trick, so demanded that they first provide him with the letter of admission.

"We have to coordinate with the universities to make sure the quotas haven't been filled," the director explained.

"Then go and coordinate," said Wang Huai.

The director put his hand to his chin. With great urgency, the recruiter turned and ran to the third floor, and slid and spun on his legs because of his speed. When they did so, Wang Huai did the same.

"The section chief is going to coordinate," said the director, "so come down."

Wang Huai shook his head. The director took out a cigarette and handed it to him. He shook his head again. No one dared utter a word, and time seemed to stop temporarily. On the third floor, the section chief's telephone conversation was as clear as a bell. The cigarettes in the director's hand were all crushed.

After more than ten minutes, the section chief came running down from the third floor.

"Regrettably all the universities I'm more familiar with have filled their quotas," he said.

"I hear you," said Wang Huai, "but there was one yesterday."

"But this is today," replied the section chief.

"Then why didn't you coordinate for me yesterday?" asked Wang Huai. "Was it because I didn't intend to jump off the building?"

The section chief was tongue-tied.

"I've only just heard it too," said the director. "The quota had not been filled because a student had failed to show up when classes started. The whole province will be trying to grab a single opening, but we come from a remote county and don't have the reach."

"You have no intention of trying to grab it," said Wang Huai, "and you have treated the two of us sitting below as if we were cured meat – didn't you notice we have been curing for more than ten days?"

"If anyone is to blame it's your son," said the section chief. "His file was sent to Peking University and Tsinghua University, and when it came back to us all the university quotas had been filled. If your arse isn't big enough, then don't try to sit on such a big stool."

Wang Huai's heart seemed to stop. He wanted to say twenty points, a full twenty points above the standard. But before he could say a word, everything went black, and he teetered forward on the railing. Everyone shouted in alarm. Wang Huai tried to right himself and seemed to do so, his hands hanging over the railing. But the concrete railing was too wide and slippery with moss growing on top. Unable to secure his grasp, he fell straight down. Amid the cries of alarm, Wang Changchi caught him in his arms, but Wang Huai fell through, sending them both tumbling into the trees. A loud bang was heard, drops of water flew everywhere, and then the world fell silent.

Wang Changchi stood up among the trees and discovered people all around him, but there wasn't a single familiar or friendly face among them, they were all wearing cold and curious expressions. Moving to Wang Huai's side he felt his nostrils and seemed to detect his warm breath, and so shouted, "Dad, Dad...", each time louder than the last, each time more heartrending. After shouting more than a dozen times, Wang Huai seemed to hear him and opened one eye before closing it immediately. Opening his eye that way startled the surrounding onlookers, forcing them to step back as if he were more frightening alive than dead. Wang Changchi tried to stand up and was surprised he could get to his feet. He looked himself over and found that his clothes had been torn in many places by the tree branches and that some of those places were stained and soaked with blood. Only when he saw the blood did he feel his body burning all over. He bent down and lifted Wang Huai by the shoulders in an attempt to get him up. Each time he used a little strength, Wang Huai would cry out in pain. So he dared not apply any force – all he could do was hold him.

After holding him a while, he asked, "Can someone call an ambulance?"

No one replied and a third of the onlookers disappeared in a flash. He searched Wang Huai's pockets from his jacket downwards, until he finally pulled a plastic bag out of his trouser pocket, inside of which he found a wad of cash.

Peeling off one note, he held it out and asked, "Can someone help me and call an ambulance?" A boy stepped out of the crowd, took the money and ran off.

"Dad, someone has gone to call an ambulance, just hang on," said Wang Changchi.

Wang Huai gritted his teeth and nodded slightly, his forehead covered with beads of sweat. For a long time, Wang Changchi managed to control himself, but unable to hold back any longer, his tears flowed copiously, falling on his father's face.

The ambulance finally arrived. Two men in white coats placed the stretcher beside Wang Huai.

"You had the courage to call an ambulance," said one of them. "Now d'you have the money to pay for it?"

Wang Changchi handed over the money and the man in the

white coat removed a hundred-yuan note and stuffed it in his pocket. After that, they lifted Wang Huai from both ends and tossed him on the stretcher as if they were throwing a dead dog. He cried out in pain, his whole face twisted like a fried dough crisp. They placed the stretcher in the ambulance and Wang Changchi squeezed in as well.

五 · FIVE

WITH NO MONEY FOR THE HOSPITAL, Wang Huai's stretcher was dumped in the hallway. Wang Changchi suddenly recalled a classmate.

"Dad, hang on, I'm going to borrow some money," he said. Wang Huai nodded.

Wang Changchi reached Little River Street and located his classmate Huang Kui, who had also failed to pass the university entrance exam. Hearing that he wanted to borrow five thousand yuan, he turned and looked at his dad. His father had a small store selling an assortment of goods for daily use.

He asked Huang Kui, "How did he treat you in general?"

"He usually let me copy his homework," replied Huang Kui.

"Can you pay back the money?" asked Huang Kui's dad.

"Yes," said Wang Changchi. "At home we have two oxen and two pigs."

"Write me out an IOU," said Huang Kui's dad.

Wang Changchi did as he was asked.

"We have to go to the bank," said Huang Kui's dad.

The three of them arrived at the bank entrance. Huang Kui's dad suddenly stopped and pulled out a cigarette to smoke. He puffed vigorously and, even though it was broad daylight, the butt still glowed brightly. Quite absorbed in smoking, he threw the butt down when it burned his fingers and crushed it underfoot, leaving a mark like a comma on the ground.

"I shouldn't have smoked that cigarette," he said.

Wang Changchi had a bad feeling. Sure enough, Huang Kui's dad fished two "old guy's heads" out of his pocket and offered them to Wang Changchi, saying, "I'll give you these two hundreds, but I won't lend you the money."

Although he'd expected something like that to happen, Wang Changchi was still stunned.

"Two hundred isn't enough to save his dad's life," said Huang Kui.

"I just remembered that there's no money in the account – your mum took it out to pay for a shop," said Huang Kui's dad.

Wang Changchi bowed, turned and walked away. As he walked, he tore up the IOU. Huang Kui's dad stuffed the two hundreds in Huang Kui's pocket, saying, "Village people are so pitiful. Go and buy something for his dad to eat."

Huang Kui turned and caught up with Wang Changchi.

"I asked my dad and there really is no money in the account, please understand," he said.

"If you can't pull shit out of the ground, don't blame the ground for being hard, blame yourself," replied Wang Changchi.

He flung the paper scraps in his hand away and they fluttered down, covering the ground like paper money burned for the dead.

Huang Kui bought a case of bottled water, a bag of *mantou* and a bag of toilet rolls and placed them beside Wang Huai's stretcher. Wang Huai constantly gnashed his teeth and knitted his brows, as if he were making a strenuous effort to control his pain. His lips were white and dry. Wang Changchi opened a bottle of water and carefully gave him some to drink. He forced a smile several times. Suddenly his eyes closed, and his head fell to one side. Wang Changchi thought he had died and checked to see if he was still breathing. He was. He fetched a bucket of hot water, soaked a towel and wrung it out, and then wiped his face. Slowly he wiped lower with the towel – from his face to his neck and to his chest. When he got to his waist, Wang Huai cried out several times in pain. Wang Changchi wiped around his waist and then continued wiping downward.

Sitting to one side, Huang Kui asked, "With no money, what do you plan to do?"

"Rob a bank," said Wang Changchi.

Suddenly Wang Huai lifted his right hand a little and struggled to grasp two of Wang Changchi's fingers.

"Dad, what is it?" asked Wang Changchi.

Wang Huai squeezed his fingers more tightly.

"Are you afraid I'll do it?" asked Wang Changchi. "Don't worry, I'd never steal, I was just blowing off steam."

Wang Huai released his grip and his hand fell to the floor. Wang Changchi changed Wang Huai into some clean clothes and bought a round mosquito net in which he covered his father.

"Dad, can you hang on for a couple of days?" asked Wang Changchi.

Wang Huai nodded slightly. Wang Changchi asked Huang Kui to look after his father while he took the evening bus home.

Wang Changchi returned home at midnight. All the lights were out in the village. He didn't knock straight away but rather stood at the door thinking about his lines. The yellow dog circled him, back and forth, whining happily. The sound of the dog woke Liu Shuangju, who turned on the light and opened the door.

Seeing Wang Changchi standing there, she gasped and asked, "Has something happened? During today's heavy rain, I felt like a knife was being plunged into my chest several times."

At first, Wang Changchi had meant to deceive her, but having no talent for theatrics, the tears welled up in his eyes.

"I knew something would happen to that stubborn father of yours," said Liu Shuangju. As she spoke, she doubled over as if she had a pain in her stomach, and slid down along the doorframe until she was sitting on the threshold. She heaved a long sigh and beat her breast. Wang Changchi walked over and sat beside her.

"Is he still alive?" she asked.

"Yes," Wang Changchi replied, and she burst into tears. She cried loudly, seemingly happy then sad, starting deep down and rising, growing longer and circling up and away, setting off the dogs nearby howling.

The following day, they sold the two oxen, one bull and one cow to Second Uncle, his father's younger brother. When Second Uncle arrived, he opened the cattle pen and went to lead out the bull. The bull planted its legs firmly on the ground and then shifted its body backwards, unwilling to leave. Growing impatient, Second Uncle pulled at the halter as if playing tug-of-war with the bull. Yet regardless of how hard he pulled, the bull wouldn't budge. Eventually, the ridge of its nose was rubbed raw and bloody by the halter. Wang Changchi squeezed into the cattle pen and put his shoulder against the bull's rump to push it out. Even with one person pulling and one pushing, the bull still wouldn't budge.

His uncle tossed a wooden club in and said, "Changchi, prod him with that." Wang Changchi picked up the club and tapped the bull softly.

"That's too soft, hit him harder," said Second Uncle. Wang Changchi raised the club and struck but to no avail.

"Where has all your book learning got you?" asked Second Uncle. "You hit a bull as if you are tickling it."

Closing his eyes, Wang Changchi raised the club and brought it down hard with a thud on the bull's back, but the bull still didn't budge.

Liu Shuangju spoke to the bull. "Second Bull," she said, "you have to go, we can't take care of you. Your dad was injured, and we need money for the medical bills, so do us a favour and go home with Uncle. Fortunately, Second Uncle is part of the family and also surnamed Wang, so you'll still be the Wang family ox at his house".

The ox seemed to understand, flexed its four legs and walked out of the cattle pen, his eyes brimming with tears.

"And Miss Three, you go with Second Bull," Liu Shuangju added.

Eyes also brimming with tears, Miss Three hesitated a moment before leaving the cattle pen and going with the bull.

"Second Uncle," said Wang Changchi, "whatever you do, don't sell them to a butcher. After I've made some money, I'll buy them back from you."

Second Uncle replied that he understood. Liu Shuangju only

had one child, so she always treated the bull as her second child and the cow as her third.

After selling the two oxen, they sold the two pigs to Guang Sheng, who came with two cages and four helpers. The pigs squealed all the way as they were carried through the mountain gap. At noon, Liu Shuangju stared absentmindedly at the rice in her bowl.

"How will you make it all the way to the main road if you don't eat something?" asked Wang Changchi.

Dumping the rice into the dog's bowl, Liu Shuangju asked, "What about the dog?"

Wang Changchi called the dog several times, but there was no trace of it.

"It saw us sell the oxen and the pigs," said Liu Shuangju, "so it was probably afraid we'd sell it too."

"They are more sensitive than people," agreed Wang Changchi.

六 · SIX

TOWARDS EVENING, WANG CHANGCHI and Liu Shuangju hurried off to the County Hospital. Wang Huai was still lying in the hallway. His eyes were wide open, the eyeballs so large they resembled artificial grapes. The moment Wang Changchi appeared, he started to close his eyes, but they didn't close smoothly. His eyelids moved slowly over his eyeballs because he didn't have enough tears, and his eyes were dry and even covered with dust.

"He's been waiting with his eyes open ever since Wang Changchi left," said Huang Kui. "Each day he had only a few bites of *mantou* to eat and sipped a little water because he couldn't go to the bathroom."

After the money was paid, Wang Huai was carried into the hospital. He was examined and in addition to many small wounds caused by the tree branches, he was found to have one major injury – his fifth lumbar vertebra had been broken.

"He could end up paralysed for life if it's not handled properly," said the doctor.

"It's a miracle he's still alive after falling from such a height," said Wang Changchi.

"He didn't die because he managed to grasp the railing for an instant," said the doctor, "and Wang Changchi was there to catch him, and the trees broke his fall."

According to the doctor, Wang Changchi's hands were not injured because Wang Huai had slipped through them in an instant. In other words, the gravitational force had not impacted his arms for more than a second or two. If the impact had been more sustained, his arms certainly would have been broken.

A week later Wang Huai spoke. "Take me home," he said.

"You're not well enough yet," said Wang Changchi.

"This will never heal," asserted Wang Huai.

"Even if there's no way for it to be healed, it still has to be healed."

Wang Huai lost his temper and demanded, "Are you made of money? What business does a poor man have showing off how rich he is in a hospital? If we don't go home, we'll have to part with the family fortune. If we do that, you'll have no way to study, and if you don't study you'll never have any prospects."

As Wang Huai spoke, beads of sweat broke out on his forehead, but Wang Changchi and Liu Shuangju pretended not to hear. They were like two diligent machines: every day they bathed him on time, massaged his legs, fed him and emptied his bedpan. After three more days, Wang Huai closed his mouth and refused to eat and drink. The rice porridge ran out from the corners of his mouth and down his neck, not even water passed between his teeth.

Liu Shuangju heaved a sigh and said, "I feel bad about spending all this money, but if we return before your back has healed, and you slip and fall, you'll be hurt again."

Wang Huai closed his eyes and didn't reply but his breathing grew heavier.

"Moreover," continued Liu Shuangju, "the doctor would never agree to discharge you."

Opening his mouth a bit, Wang Huai asked, "Why believe a doctor?"

Wang Changchi and Liu Shuangju retired to the courtyard to discuss the matter but couldn't come to a decision. Dejected, the two of them sat on a stone soaking up the sun's rays. Insects chirruped in the trees. Curious pedestrians turned to look, but looked away at once, feeling embarrassed.

"How much money do you have on you?" asked Liu Shuangju.

Wang Changchi fumbled in his shirt pocket and two trouser pockets, pulled out a wad of odd notes and placed them on the jacket Liu Shuangju had spread out. Fearing he had missed something, he turned his pockets inside out. The three pockets looked like the stomachs of three hungry tramps. Liu Shuangju took the money she had and placed it on the jacket as well. Wang Changchi smoothed out the notes and handed them to her.

She counted them twice. "Altogether one thousand and fifty-three yuan and six mao," she said. "Enough for five more days."

"Then one day at a time."

"Your dad's not going to improve markedly in five days."

"Then you think we should go home?"

"I don't know, you're the man, you decide."

Wang Changchi put his head in his hands. His head was filled with the screeching of the insects, which was like boiling water, or like the pounding of thousands of little hammers. His scalp numb, he raised his head. Liu Shuangju handed him the uneven stack of notes. He didn't take it, he didn't dare to. Liu Shuangju thrust the money into the palm of his hand. The notes were moist, with beads of water on them as if Liu Shuangju had twisted tears out of them.

A shout came from the hospital. Listening carefully, they heard a call for the family members of the patient in bed number two. They stood up and ran. A circle of patients were standing in the hallway. Forcing his way through, Wang Changchi saw Wang

Huai crawling on the floor. He was pulling his stiff lower body along, his legs leaving two tracks.

"Where are you going?" asked Wang Changchi.

"Home," said Wang Huai.

"Can you crawl twenty kilometres?"

"I can at least crawl to the bus station."

The surrounding onlookers applauded. They kept pace with Wang Huai as he pulled himself along as if they were watching an animal show. Liu Shuangju laid the stretcher in front of him. Wang Huai raised his head and looked, again and again. Liu Shuangju's eyes were red and glistening with tears. Wang Huai lowered his head and climbed onto the stretcher.

After taking care of the hospital discharge paperwork, Wang Changchi and Liu Shuangju, carrying Wang Huai, walked towards the bus station. The plastic bucket, dinner pail, army canteen, bags of food and soft packages all swished together. Wang Huai looked up at the sky, which was a clear, vast blue stretching for miles. Half an hour later, they reached the bus station and bought three tickets. The stretcher was folded and placed in the aisle. Wang Huai had to sleep half reclining on his side. The bus jolted along the mountain road for more than an hour before reaching the road to the village in the valley.

They carried Wang Huai off the bus and carefully opened out the stretcher. Wang Huai heaved a long sigh, rejoicing that he could finally lie down. Only then did they notice a dog waiting by the road. It was Ah Huang, the yellow dog. It was scrawny and its fur was covered with grass and dirt. It looked at them as if they were strangers. Or perhaps every day it had leapt at every person who got off the bus, only to be disappointed and now it had become quite calm. Wang Changchi called, "Ah Huang..." Tentatively, it sniffed at their trouser legs, then it leapt onto the stretcher and licked Wang Huai's face. Wang Huai held it tightly. It struggled free and circled Liu Shuangju and Wang Changchi and then returned to the stretcher to play with Wang Huai. All three were family, and it didn't know who it should stand next to, so it circled around, dilly-dallying.

Wang Changchi and Liu Shuangju picked up the stretcher. The yellow dog ran ahead to lead the way. They passed through the forest, where the afternoon sun flickered through the trees. They passed the reservoir, Longjiawan and the terrace, and finally saw the tea trees and their own house.

"Don't think I'm useless," said Wang Huai, "I still have two kidneys. If Changchi will listen to reason and study, I'll sell one of them. Did you hear that, Changchi?"

"Yes," said Wang Changchi.

"Your fate is for wealth and honour," said Wang Huai. "I had someone tell your fortune when you were little. As an official, you'll rise to the rank of department head, and in terms of wealth, you can make a million. If you don't listen to me and get some tutoring and retake the university exam, then you'll be just another Wang Huai, who falls to his death and no one cares."

The yellow dog stuck out its tongue. Wang Changchi and Liu Shuangju were panting while Wang Huai spoke continuously. At first, they took in everything he said, but as fatigue set in, the meaning vanished and all they heard was a jumble of sounds. Suddenly the yellow dog's body contorted, and it fell prone on the ground. Gently, Wang Changchi kicked it. It struggled on for a few more steps, but it contorted and fell on its belly again.

"I know what's the matter," said Liu Shuangju. "It hasn't had anything to eat or drink in days."

They put down the stretcher. Wang Changchi gave it some water to drink and a *mantou* to eat. It seemed to revive a bit, but it didn't move. Wang Changchi picked it up and placed it on the stretcher. Wang Huai held it tightly. Once again the stretcher was lifted.

"No wonder it wasn't excited to see us," said Wang Changchi. "It was so hungry it had no strength."

七 · SEVEN

RETURNING HOME, WANG CHANGCHI ran to their rice field. The field was on the slope below the village. Everyone else had harvested their rice, but only in their field did the wind still blow waves of grain. From a distance, it was a stretch of yellow, which the sun painted with gold. But as he got closer, he could see that the stalks of grain were bent and askew. They had been rained on and dried by the sun several times, the heads of grain were already mildewed and rotten, and some of the grains had fallen to the ground and were sprouting. The household's unharvested rice had become fertiliser. Wang Changchi squatted and picked up a few fallen grains and didn't stand up again until after nightfall.

There was no point in harvesting as most of the grain was ruined, so Wang Changchi and Liu Shuangju gathered the grain that had not rotted by hand. They plucked and picked up the grain and threw it into the small baskets tied to their waists. When those were filled, they dumped the small baskets of grain into the big baskets on their backs. It was still hot during the day, the sun just as scorching, especially when they squatted to pick up grain and were surrounded by the stalks, which blocked the movement of the air. Their faces, necks and hands were streaked red, cut by the leaves, and burned like fire when moistened by sweat. In the surrounding forest, the insects took great pains to utter their noisy cries, making the atmosphere tenser and tenser.

Wang Huai, who had been lying at home, couldn't stand it any longer, so he hired Liu Baitiao and Wang Dong to carry him halfway up the mountain for twenty yuan. They came to a large flat rock, surrounded by oak trees. Wang Huai lay prone on the rock and looked down on the family field from above. Wang Changchi and Liu Shuangju looked like two grasshoppers crawling through the yellow waves of grain. They squatted, stood up and frequently wiped away their sweat. Each movement pulled at his heart, even interfering with its beat. He watched in a daze.

"The time has come," said Liu Baitiao.

"Normally you sleep until late in the morning," said Wang Huai, "so why are you so on time today?"

"More time will cost extra," added Wang Dong.

Reluctantly, Wang Huai withdrew his gaze. Liu Baitiao and Wang Dong carried him home.

Wang Changchi hired a carpenter to construct a wooden wheelchair for Wang Huai. When the wheelchair was finished, Wang Changchi tried it out and thought it was fine. He then put an old bit of clothing on the seat and carried Wang Huai to the wheelchair. The normally recumbent Wang Huai could now sit up. Wang Changchi pushed the wheelchair to the main room and handed Wang Huai a stick of bamboo. Pushing the bamboo stick against the floor from the left made the wheelchair move right. Wang Huai tried it again from the other side and made the chair move left. Although he could move, Wang Huai wondered what to do when he hit the raised threshold. As the thought entered his mind, he looked and saw that openings had been cut in all the thresholds. He poled his way out of the main door and saw the roofs of the village houses, high and low, and finally his eyes rested on the eaves of Second Uncle's house. Wang Changchi supposed that he wanted to speak with his Second Uncle, so when he had time, he cleared the surface of the road to Second Uncle's house so that the wheelchair could freely make its way.

Once the road surface was fixed, Wang Huai was apparently in no hurry to visit Second Uncle. Close to evening one day when Wang Changchi and Liu Shuangju were busy with household chores, he quietly slipped out of the front door and rolled over to Second Uncle's cattle pen. As soon as Second Bull and Miss Three caught sight of him, they stretched forward and licked his fingers. He lifted his hand to pet them, but they were too high. Second Bull and Miss Three seemed to understand what he wanted, so they knelt down close together. He petted their chests until his hands were warm. Wang Changchi hastened over just in time to observe the scene. He stood at a distance.

"Changchi, push me home," said Wang Huai.

Wang Changchi approached and pushed the wheelchair back towards home.

"Do you know what I was thinking today?" asked Wang Huai.

"No idea."

"I'd like to become a huge, round boulder and roll down the slope."

"That would hurt. Why bother? Old Man Heaven has tormented you enough. Maybe he'll do something good for you."

"In my heart I am not resigned, I just don't want you to repeat my life."

"Didn't you repeat your father's life?"

"There are limits. You need to go and get some tutoring."

"Where'll the money come from?"

"The director said you can get tutoring for one year for free."

"Who'll take you to the bathroom? Who'll do the harrowing and the ploughing?"

"You don't need to concern yourself with that. All you have to do is pass the university exam and I'll stand up right away."

The wheelchair moved with a creak. Wang Changchi didn't utter a word.

"Since the day you were born," said Wang Huai, "I just wanted you to do something different. I just want to see it. Don't give up."

"I don't really have that ability."

"You could read when you were four and could use an abacus when you were five. Everyone said you were a genius."

"If I left, Mum would be exhausted."

"Having a child with a good future would be reward enough for any parent who is a little tired of suffering."

"But I'm not the genius you think I am."

"You're looking for an excuse. You feel bad that I broke my back for you." As he finished speaking, Wang Huai stuck his bamboo pole into the ground and stopped his forward progress. Beyond the road was a pit that looked about five metres deep.

Pointing at the pit, Wang Huai said, "If you're not willing to be tutored, then I don't have anything to look forward to."

Wang Changchi pushed the wheelchair more vigorously, but Wang Huai stopped it dead with his bamboo pole. The pole bent into an arc. The harder Wang Changchi pushed, the more the pole bent, to the point where it looked like it would break. Wang Huai suddenly loosened his grip and the wheelchair plunged forward.

As the pole came out of the ground, the wheelchair turned and started down the pit. Wang Changchi rushed over and grabbed it. The wheelchair hung on the brink. Wang Huai struck Wang Changchi's hands with the pole for all he was worth. Each blow pierced the heart.

He was about to lose his grip, when Wang Changchi pleaded with his father, "Don't hit me, I agree to what you want."

Wang Changchi was packing his bag. Liu Shuangju repeatedly reminded him not to forget his ID like last time. After packing, Wang Changchi handed over the thousand yuan he had on him.

Liu Shuangju removed five notes. "This money is for your meals when you are studying," she said. Wang Changchi took one note.

"One hundred is only enough to cover your bus ticket and food for a single month," said Liu Shuangju.

"I'll think of something," he replied.

"You can't steal or rob. What are you going to do?" said Liu Shuangju, thrusting the money at him. He pushed it away.

Around midnight, Wang Changchi was awakened by a rustling sound. On the other side of the mosquito net, he saw Liu Shuangju stuffing money in his pack. He immediately closed his eyes and pretended to be asleep. The next day he shouldered his bag and set off. Wang Huai and Liu Shuangju saw him off at the door. Liu Shuangju ordered him to keep an eye on his bag and not let it be stolen. Wang Huai gave Wang Changchi a thumbs up. Wang Changchi set off happily. Wang Huai, Liu Shuangju and the yellow dog watched until his silhouette vanished through the gap.

Three days later, Liu Shuangju was going out to pick corn and had to change into a pair of rubber shoes. As she placed her right foot in the shoe, she felt a hard mass in the toe. She pulled out a plastic bag with four hundred yuan inside.

Alarmed, Liu Shuangju shouted, "Old Man, Wang Changchi didn't take the money with him."

Wang Huai sighed. "It would be a pity if the child didn't study," he said.

"Didn't he go to study?" asked Liu Shuangju.

"Without money, how can he focus on studying?"

八 · EIGHT

AT THE COUNTY TOWN, WANG CHANGCHI looked up the director of the Bureau of Education. The director regarded him as if he were from outer space.

"I'm Wang Huai's son," he said.

"Who's Wang Huai?" asked the director.

Wang Changchi was taken aback and replied, "He fell and nearly died in front of you, don't you even remember his name?"

"Oh," said the director as if he remembered. "What is it you want?"

"I came for the free cram class at the county town," he said.

"The classes are full to bursting and there's no room," said the director. "You want to do it for free? That's a good one."

"That's what you agreed to at the time."

The director didn't recall any such thing. Wang Changchi swore up and down that he did.

"Even if I did," said the director, "it was to save your dad, and you shouldn't have taken me literally. There are only two high-school cram classes set up for the entire county and all the parents have their sights set on them, so I can't be that brazen and corrupt."

In a fit of anxiety, Wang Changchi's legs nearly gave way, and he broke into a sweat. Leaving the director's office, he went downstairs where he suddenly realised he still had a chair there. He looked around and saw the chair sitting in the security office. He explained the situation to the comrade guard, picked up the chair and left. He went straight to the county high school and sought out the teacher in charge of the cram classes. The teacher in charge of the classes had heard about the case of his father leaping from the building. He clasped his hands tightly and then patted him on the shoulder. "I came for tutoring," Wang Changchi said. The teacher in charge of the classes took him to see the school principal. The school principal had heard about the case of his father leaping from the building. He also clasped his hands tightly, patted him on the shoulder, and then escorted him to the cram classes. Two classrooms were filled, but there was an open spot in the back row of the second class. He put down the chair he was carrying and sat down for class.

His classmates all called him "Mr Chair" on account of his having only a chair and no desk. Even if he'd had a desk, it wouldn't have fitted in. He had a piece of cardboard in his book bag and when it was time to do homework, he'd pull out the cardboard and place it on his knees to serve as a desk. Because his "desktop" was high at the back and low at the front and his eyesight was poor, the characters he wrote tended to be big at the front and small at the back. He had to crane his neck to write and after two weeks his neck was stretched longer.

One afternoon, a crash was heard in the classroom. All the students turned to look in the direction of the sound and discovered that Mr Chair was gone but looking again they saw him curled up on the floor. Four boys carried him to the school clinic.

The doctor asked, "Where do you feel ill?"

He forced a single word from between his teeth. Even though he listened carefully, the doctor had to listen twice before he heard the word "hungry" and then quickly gave him an infusion. The liquid dripped into the tube one drop at a time.

The previous few weeks all Wang Changchi had had to eat was gruel cooked in salty water just once a day. When he was hungry, he drank tap water. Tap water wasn't very effective, so he added some sugar. He carried one bottle of his brew to class each day. He became more and more dependent on the water and would drink a whole bottle during each class. Drinking a lot of water, he had to urinate, and urinating a lot seemed to make him weak as if all the nutrients were carried away in his urine. At the very beginning, he thought he would be a person of some talent and that all difficulties would just put him to the test. So, regardless of how hungry he was, he would study one hour longer than all the other students. After the lights went out in the dorm, he'd go down to the street and read under the street light. In the first week, the words on the page were still words and he could remember their meaning. But in the second week, the words became white bugs, black bugs and rainbow-coloured bugs, flying back and forth before his eyes. Not only was he unable to recall the meaning, but the mere recollection of their shape would make him sweat. The ideal abounds; the real is felt in the bones. Every day he had to fight off dizziness, loss of memory, yawning, dozing off and being dog-tired. To conserve his strength, he didn't do the callisthenics or the exercises to keep his eyes healthy when they were broadcast. During the breaks between classes, he would usually close his eyes and try to refresh his spirits. Every time he blinked, the colour of the blackboard would change – blink, it was green, blink, it was red, like the non-stop colour changes at the stock market. Sometimes the entire classroom had a golden glow, sometimes it went black as if the electricity had gone off for a split second. He fainted because the times the electricity went off increased in frequency and in length.

He was awakened by a heady aroma. It emanated from a small stall at the school gate and had gone up the twenty steps, across the playing field, and skirted the flower bed before finally coming to a halt in front of his nose. Opening his eyes, he saw his class-mate Li holding a bowl of rice porridge with minced meat in it. Inhaling deeply, he was as excited as if he saw Wang Huai and Liu Shuangju. Li, his classmate, wanted to feed him, so he sat up, took the bowl and polished off the porridge in a few large gulps. As if allowing his stomach to adapt, he held that final gesture of finishing the bowl for a while. Li reached over to take the bowl, but he clutched it tightly, refusing to let go of it. After a few seconds, his hand trembled and the bowl fell clattering to the floor. He came to himself and apologised. The doctor asked him if his family was suffering from hardship. He looked at his class-mates. They blinked, waiting for him to reply. He hesitated a moment and said no.

"If they are not suffering hardship," the doctor said, "why are you so hungry? You're as skinny as a pole, are you trying to lose weight?"

His yellowish face flushed red as he hung his head in shame and said, "I'm OK, I'm no longer dizzy."

With the nourishment from the meat porridge and the glucose solution, his brain cells burned, and he finally realised that all ideals are nothing without the support of protein, fat, carbohydrates, vitamins, minerals and water, and were nothing but nonsense. Now he'd seen the light, he went in search of Huang Kui. Huang Kui allowed him to stuff himself. He ate two bowls of rice noodles and two eggs, before leaning back in his chair with satisfaction. Huang Kui asked if he was willing to work with him. He had no idea what he did, but he agreed.

Huang Kui was the general manager, and the company was set up in a store on Little River Street. Huang Kui used half the store for his office, and his father used the other half to sell his goods. The sign hanging there read: "Circum-Pacific Trade Company". It had nothing to do with the Pacific, but by stretching the point, it referred to the little river in front of the store, because it eventually did flow into the Pacific. In terms of trade, there was none but the goods his father sold, which brought in about two hundred yuan a day including costs. Huang Kui's line of work was as a bill collector for other people. Collecting bills was a matter of chasing debts, the successful pursuit of which produced a percentage for Huang Kui.

"I don't understand the business," said Wang Changchi.

"It's simple," said Huang Kui. "When they throw me off a building, you be there to catch me."

"How tall is the building?"

"That doesn't matter."

Frightened, Wang Changchi hurriedly looked at his arms.

Huang Kui went to collect a lot of bills. Decked out each time in a Western-style suit and leather shoes, he looked like a salesman. He never took Wang Changchi, but always came back with something. Receiving his percentage, he'd invite Wang Changchi out to eat and drink. Wang Changchi ate and drank, but when he compared himself to Huang Kui, he felt he was totally lacking in any merit, simply useless. As soon as Huang Kui left, Wang Changchi would help Huang Kui's father sell his goods.

When Huang Kui saw this, he asked, "Don't you have any other prospects?"

Wang Changchi had no idea what kind of prospects he had. In any event, he didn't have anything to do, so he continued helping Huang Kui's father.

"Don't listen to him," said Huang Kui's dad. "He's a know-nothing with no respect for groceries. But how was he brought up? Depending on his dad's store and nothing else."

Wang Changchi spent nights at the company, looking after the store and doing business. Huang Kui and his dad would go home, while Wang Changchi sold goods and reviewed his homework. Sometimes, Huang Kui would stay and chat and drink with Wang Changchi. Late one night, Huang Kui had too much to drink and threw Wang Changchi's textbooks out of the door. They went flying across the five metres of road and into the river. Wang Changchi dived into the water and fished out his books. His clothes were soaking wet, as were his textbooks. He placed his clothes and books on the spring bed and turned the electric fan on them to dry them.

"If you manage to get into a college," said Huang Kui, "the best thing to do after graduation is to be a cadre. But these days, even the cadres are going into business to make money, so why bother taking a test?"

"I don't want to give up," said Wang Changchi. "I have to do it for my parents."

"If you want to take the test, go and study and don't waste your time here."

Wang Changchi turned off the fan and the flapping pages of the books grew still.

"When you're hungry you want to eat," said Huang Kui, "but when you've eaten your fill you start fantasising."

"I don't think studying affects selling goods," said Wang Changchi.

"If this is as high as you aim, how much money can you make selling stuff like this?"

The following day, Huang Kui took Wang Changchi to the barber to have his head shaved.

"Can't I have a crew cut?" asked Wang Changchi.

"It has to shine," said Huang Kui.

While his head was being shaved, he couldn't hold back his tears. He felt like it was a hair-cutting ceremony to join a monastery, and it wasn't even his own choice.

九 · NINE

EVERY DAY, WANG HUAI SAT in his wheelchair gazing towards the gap in the mountains. After a long time, the sight of the maple tree in there was like a colour photo stamped on his brain. The shape of the tree's crown, the spacing of its limbs and the density of the foliage were all clearly visible to him when he shut his eyes. He was worried that Wang Changchi didn't have money for food and had entrusted Second Uncle with going to the town and posting him five hundred yuan. Second Uncle handed him the receipt, which he put in the left-hand pocket of his jacket and would take out to look at when he had nothing better to do as if it were Wang Changchi's exam paper, which the teacher marked with five 100s. Other than eating, all he did was gaze into the distance. The idler Liu Baitiao would often scrounge cigarettes from him. Although his goal was to get a cigarette, he wouldn't bring it up directly. He'd always start with, "Brother Huai, what are you looking at?"

"I'm watching Changchi."

"Can you see him that far away?"

"It's just like he's right here in front of me."

"What's he up to?"

"Studying."

"How are his studies going?"

"He's number one in his class."

"If I had a son who excelled so, I'd be treating people every day."

At that point, there was an eighty to ninety per cent chance that Wang Huai would pull out his cigarettes and even light one for Liu Baitiao. They would smoke and talk about Wang Changchi. On more than one occasion, Liu Baitiao said he dreamed he saw Wang Changchi in a high official post despatching a plane to bring Wang Huai and Liu Shuangju to the big city. Wang Huai cracked a smile and said that a plane was going a bit too far but that a limousine would be more reasonable.

"When it comes, you'll have to send me a carton of cigarettes each month," said Liu Baitiao.

"That's nothing," said Wang Huai, "I'll get him to give you a high road."

"I can't afford a car, so there's no point in giving me a road. A carton of cigarettes would be better."

Wang Huai would take out his pack of cigarettes and say, "This is for you in advance." Liu Baitiao would pretend to refuse.

Angry, Wang Huai would say, "So you look down on others because it's only one pack?" Liu Baitiao would then happily accept.

All the Wang Baitiaos or Zhang Baitiaos who wanted to smoke his cigarettes and drink his rice wine would resort to this ploy and begin by offering their praise to Wang Huai. Wang Huai would never grow tired of listening to them praise Wang Changchi. That's all they had to do, and he would grin from ear to ear. Liu Shuangju told him that she heard people laughing at him behind his back for being crazy.

"It's just like reciting scriptures", said Wang Huai, laughing foolishly. "The more you recite, the more spirits come and protect you. Why at festival time does everyone talk about good fortune and favour or why do people paste couplets on the door frame that say, 'open the door to good news' and 'taking steps for wealth'? It's the same principle in Wang Changchi's case."

Every day, Wang Huai would offer three sticks of incense, not to wish that his back would get better, but that Wang Changchi would get into a university and someday be a high official. Sometimes he would wake up laughing because he had dreamed that Wang Changchi was a county official. Whoever showed up the next day to cadge a cigarette or drink, he'd relate his dream to them. So the male villagers would tell each other and then take turns listening while drinking and smoking. At such times, he'd forget the pain in his back along with his misfortune. It was as if the dream were real. Even though that was not yet true, he believed that sooner or later it would become a reality.

The colour of the maple underwent a slight change, its crown taking on a pale yellow hue. No one else noticed except for Wang Huai, who looked at it every day. That evening, the postman came to the village, returning the money order his uncle had posted. On the money order was stamped: "unable to locate recipient". Wang Huai took the money order and examined it and examined it some more. The address was correct and the name was correct, so the only possible explanation was that Wang Changchi had evaporated. His hopes were immediately dashed, and he went limp as a cooked noodle. He couldn't see the maple in the gap, or Second Uncle's tile roof, everything was black, so black he couldn't see his fingers in front of his face. There were no stars, no lamplight, not even a sound. Liu Shuangju called him to eat, but he didn't hear. Liu Shuangju pushed him into the main room.

Staring at the electric light, he asked, "Why is it so bright?"

"Hasn't it been this light all along?" asked Liu Shuangju.

He made Liu Shuangju close the front door and took out the money order. "Tomorrow you have to go to town," he said. "We can't delay another moment."

Liu Shuangju stared at the words "unable to locate recipient" and thinking of how she kept house and worked in the fields day and night, she cried sadly.

"If you cry like that, Liu Baitiao will hear you and then the whole village will know," said Wang Huai.

Liu Shuangju restrained herself. Swallowing her tears, she asked, "Do you want me to take something for him to eat?"

"If I give the bastard anything, it will be a horsewhipping," Wang Huai replied.

At midnight, Wang Huai shook Liu Shuangju awake. Liu Shuangju asked him what he was going to do.

"I can't sleep," he said. "Maybe it would be better if I sat up."

Liu Shuangju helped him to the wheelchair and then went back to bed. Wang Huai poled the wheelchair out of the bedroom to the kitchen where the aroma of leftover food and rice filled his nose. He lifted the lid off the wok, and it fell to the floor with a clang. He leaned over to pick it up but couldn't bend far enough and struggled to reach it with his right arm. The handles on the wheelchair pressed into his armpits till they hurt, and even then he could only touch the edge of the lid with two fingers. Trying to pick it up with the tips of his fingers sent it sliding across the floor. The wheelchair followed. Once again, he reached out determinedly, and two fingertips touched the lid again. He got them under the lid and finally managed to pick it up. Trying to get the lid from the ends of his fingers to the palm of his hand sent it to the floor again with a clang. Unwilling to admit defeat, he reached out to hook it again, once, twice, three times... He spent nearly an hour before he managed to pick it up. At once a feeling of joy swept through him. Excited, he lifted the lid as if it were an Olympic gold medal. Struggling with the lid for over an hour, he was able to rid himself of thoughts about "unable to locate recipient".

When she entered the kitchen the following morning, Liu Shuangju found Wang Huai sound asleep in his wheelchair, his head tilted to one side. In front of him sat a basketful of boiled sweet potatoes and hardboiled eggs.

"Oh my," said Liu Shuangju, "how did you manage to do that?"

Wang Huai woke with a start and blinked his eyes.

"Didn't you say not to take him anything to eat?" asked Liu Shuangju.

"Maybe we're accusing him wrongly," said Wang Huai. "Perhaps he had gone to the Second High School or someone had picked on him, anyway, I have to go with you."

"How can you go to the city in your condition?"

"I've figured out a way."

They couldn't bring themselves to eat a single egg and ate only a few sweet potatoes. Wang Huai got Wang Dong and Liu Baitiao to fix a bamboo pole on either side of the wheelchair, and off they went. Liu Shuangju shouldered a bag and led the way. Wang Dong and Liu Baitiao lifted Wang Huai and followed carrying him. Creaking, they carried him past the terrace, Longji-awan and the reservoir, reaching the main road, by which time they were covered with sweat. They waited two hours before they saw the bus on its way. They carried Wang Huai and his wheelchair onto the bus. The bus was off in a flash, raising a long column of dust behind. As the bus turned, Wang Huai looked out of the window and saw Wang Dong and Liu Baitiao were blocked from view by the cloud of dust, even the mountain road to the valley was obscured.

十 · TEN

AFTER WANG CHANGCHI'S HEAD WAS SHAVED, Huang Kui bought him a Western-style suit and a pair of dark glasses, and then told him to go to the bathroom and have a look at himself in the mirror. Wang Changchi spent a long time in there looking before coming out.

"What d'you think?" asked Huang Kui.

"I look like a criminal," he said.

"Well that's the whole idea," said Huang Kui. "The way you looked before, you wouldn't even frighten a mosquito."

Considering how long he had been eating and drinking for free, Wang Changchi finally started collecting bills.

As expected, Huang Kui assigned him the duty of accompanying him to go and see someone. Someone owed Party A more than 1.3 million yuan and had put off paying it back, so Party A entrusted Huang Kui with pursuing the debt.

"All I have to do is stick close to your backside?" asked Wang Changchi.

"Yeah, but you also have to carry a cleaver," said Huang Kui.

Wang Changchi broke into a sweat. "I won't kill or commit arson."

Huang Kui pulled a bright, shiny cleaver out of his drawer. "It's not that big a deal, but one of his fingers must come off," he said.

"Do you cut or do I?"

"You do, of course. No manager does the cutting himself."

He passed the cleaver to him as he spoke. Wang Changchi didn't take it. Even his legs were trembling, and he wanted to wet himself.

"Why does a wasp sting?" asked Huang Kui. "Why does a dog bite? Because they are forced to. In this world, those who are cruel and ruthless are successful."

Wang Changchi's mind went blank. The person standing here was now a stranger to him and he didn't dare look him in the eye. Huang Kui thrust the cleaver into Wang Changchi's hand. He felt like he was clasping a piece of ice, and a shiver ran down his back to the soles of his feet.

Huang Kui removed his dark glasses. "Your eyes have to be like bullets and filled with hate," he said.

Wang Changchi put on an angry look, frowning, tightly knitting his brow.

"Look crueller." Wang Changchi's eyeballs drew closer.

"Even more." Wang Changchi almost went cross-eyed.

Huang Kui placed his hand on the desk. "Now I'm your enemy," he said.

Looking at that plump and familiar "bear paw", friendly and loving, that had rubbed his head countless times, Wang Changchi couldn't bring himself to raise the cleaver.

"I'm not asking you to hack someone to death," said Huang Kui.

"Forget it," said Wang Changchi. "I'm not cut out for this."

"Don't give up so easily. Close your eyes and give it a try."

Wang Changchi closed his eyes.

Huang Kui moved his hand away and said, "Chop."

"You really want me to chop?"

"Stop mucking about."

Wang Changchi gritted his teeth, raised his hand and brought down the cleaver, leaving it stuck at an angle in the desktop.

"Hacking or not is your problem," said Huang Kui. "Dodging or not is my problem."

"Looking threatening will be enough," said Wang Changchi.

"No, sometimes you have to draw blood, or they won't pay up." Wang Changchi nodded, seeming to understand.

"Huang Kui..."

A familiar voice suddenly drifted in. Wang Changchi headed towards the door, hurriedly putting on his dark glasses. "Shh," said Huang Kui, signalling him not to make a sound. With a bag and chair on her back, Liu Shuangju wheeled Wang Huai in like an ant moving house. Huang Kui stepped forward to take the luggage. They heaved a sigh, their eyes sweeping the office, pausing on Wang Changchi for a moment, and finally settling on Huang Kui's face.

"We checked County High and Second High, but all we found was this chair. Do you know where he is?" asked Wang Huai.

"He went to work," replied Huang Kui.

"Why didn't he tell us?"

"He hasn't made any money, so he didn't want to."

"Where is he working?"

"The provincial capital."

"Do you have his address?"

"No."

Wang Huai sighed, his face was ashen, and his chest rose and fell. Liu Shuangju rubbed his chest and gave him some water to drink. He choked and started coughing. Liu Shuangju began patting him on the back. By then, Wang Changchi's legs were about give way under him and his nose tingled. But he bit his lip and stood up straight, wanting to see how hard-hearted he could be.

"Bastard!" Wang Huai cursed. "I asked the brute to study and he doesn't. I'm so pissed off."

"Li Jiacheng didn't study," remarked Huang Kui, "and he got rich all the same, didn't he?"

"One is named Li, the other's named Wang. There's no comparison."

Liu Shuangju opened her bag and took out the eggs and sweet potatoes and placed them on the desk.

"Our chickens laid the eggs, and we grew the sweet potatoes," she said. "We wanted to give them to him to eat, never expecting he wouldn't be here."

Huang Kui peeled an egg and took a bite. The special aroma of a free-range egg suddenly spread, carrying the scent of home to Wang Changchi's nose. He swallowed his saliva and controlled himself.

Wang Huai also swallowed his saliva. "Normally we wouldn't eat them ourselves, but save them all for him," he said.

"You were his best friend at school," said Liu Shuangju. "Seeing you is like seeing him. If you eat them, it'll be the same as him eating them."

Huang Kui smacked his lips and ate with bits of food flying from his lips. Tears formed at the corners of Wang Changchi's eyes.

"Your aunt begs that if he gets in contact, please encourage him to come back and study," said Liu Shuangju.

Huang Kui nodded.

"I slop pigs," Liu Shuangju said, "feed chickens, carry water, cook, chop firewood, peel corn, move stones to build walls and never once have I complained – I can bear anything when I think of the good future he might have."

Both sides of Wang Changchi's face itched, from his eyes downwards, almost to his chin. He quietly wiped his face and found his hand all wet.

"I've raised the boy who has failed to meet our expectations," said Wang Huai. "I should disown him."

"Should I relay that as well?" asked Huang Kui.

"No," said Liu Shuangju. "Tell him we miss him. If he really is unwilling to study, then he should come back and farm with me. It can be tough working outside, and he's got no money or family in the city. I wonder how he gets by. We don't know if he's dead or alive..."

Wang Changchi dropped to his knees and cried out, "Mum", and then wailed. Liu Shuangju and Wang Huai were stunned and looked on with confusion. Wang Changchi removed his dark glasses and with tears streaming down his face said, "Mum, it's me..." Liu Shuangju burst into tears.

"Such wickedness!" Wang Huai closed his eyes and didn't open them again until Wang Changchi and Liu Shuangju had nearly stopped crying and then said, "Change your clothes."

Wang Changchi found his old clothes, went into the bathroom and changed out of his suit, and then came out.

"Pack your things," said Wang Huai.

"Why should he pack his things?" said Huang Kui. "He works here."

Wang Changchi looked at Huang Kui, then at Wang Huai.

"Get moving," said Wang Huai.

Wang Changchi packed his old clothes and his dried textbooks.

"Where are you taking him?" asked Huang Kui.

"To where he ought to be," said Wang Huai.

Wang Changchi picked up his bag.

"You're nuts, you'll soon be making lots of money," said Huang Kui.

"Sorry," replied Wang Changchi.

"If you listen to them, you'll never amount to anything."

"I want to study."

Huang Kui was disappointed and brought his fist down on the desk.

"Let's go," said Wang Huai. Together the family left, pushing and pulling their things. Surreptitiously, Wang Changchi looked back several times.

They arrived at the tree on the County High School playing field.

"If you hang out with Huang Kui, you'll be in trouble sooner or later," said Wang Huai. "If you just concentrate on your studies, we'll borrow money to provide for you."

Wang Changchi bit his lip and nodded, took his chair and set off. He crossed the empty playing field and entered the hallway and came out from an opening on the first floor, and turning right, walked down the corridor to the last door. He waved to Wang Huai and Liu Shuangju, and then put down his chair and entered the classroom. He returned to the same spot by the back door from where his silhouette could be seen through the door frame. Wang Huai and Liu Shuangju stood there watching for ages as if they were looking at a photograph.

All at once, the classroom was filled with the sound of the students reading aloud.

十一 · ELEVEN

THE FOLLOWING SUMMER, Wang Changchi's university entrance exam score fell even lower, not even reaching the mid-percentile for admissions. At home in the doorway, his knee joints gave way and he fell to his knees before Wang Huai. Wang Huai closed his eyes, opening and closing his hands, opening and closing them as if he wanted to squeeze water out of the air. Wang Changchi was so ashamed that he wished he could place himself in his hands and have his life squeezed out. Flexing his hands, time passed extremely slowly, so slowly as to be suffocating. The wheelchair smelled strongly of urine. Looking down, Wang Changchi saw that Wang Huai was wearing shorts, cut-offs which had two large holes and countless small ones. The big holes were where the fabric had worn through, the small holes were from cigarette burns. His legs were more bone than flesh, withered away and looking like two tea trees. His bare feet were speckled with mud, his toenails long and black. Eventually, he stopped flexing his hands and opened his eyes.

He heaved a long sigh. "Why is it the more you try the worse you do?" he asked.

"The questions were more difficult than last year."

"No matter how hard they were, you couldn't drop a hundred points."

"I didn't skip class, I went to bed late and rose early. I memorised everything, I tried everything."

"Then it means you're thick in the head."

"Perhaps. There's just too much crammed into my brain, so I can't remember anything."

"Nonsense," Wang Huai said, turning to look at the gap in the mountains. "What are your plans?"

"To come home and work."

"Then you just stay on your knees like that forever."

"I'm not as smart as you think I am. I'm not that capable."

"Yes you are. If you keep studying, you'll get it."

"But... I don't want to study."

"Then you've let us down."

So saying, Wang Huai pushed with his bamboo pole and the wheelchair creaked away. The four wheels were caked with mud, dry grass, hair and tree leaves, making them turn slowly and with difficulty. Wang Changchi stood up, turned his head and looked into the distance. The trees on the mountain were a lush green, the large leaves shimmering in the sunlight. The fragrance of the trees and the green grass wafted toward him, the cries of the insects rose and fell, and the paddy field on the mountain slope was a stretch of golden yellow.

Wang Changchi and Liu Shuangju harvested the grain. Liu Shuangju cut, and Wang Changchi threshed. Taking a break, they would sit in the cool under the oak tree beside the field. Liu Shuangju told him about the many things that had happened in the village that year. Liu Baitiao had a gambling debt of more than a thousand yuan, and his wife had nearly burned the house down. Tian Daijun's two oxen had been stolen, and some people said the theft was pulled off by Zhang Xianhua with the help of some outsiders. Zhang Wu's daughter was working in the provincial capital and sent money home every month, and they had already built a concrete house with two and a half storeys. Wang Dong's wife Wang Dong had a female complaint for which she was taking medicine. She had thrown away the boxes and directions so that all the children in the village had seen "cervical erosion" and "irregular menses".

Liu Shuangju took just two days to tell all the village news, but the field was only half harvested. Since there wasn't a whole lot to talk about in the muggy, lonely valley, Liu Shuangju talked about herself.

"One evening while I was beside the well preparing to water the vegetables," she said, "Wang Dong, who was passing by, tried to take some liberties with me."

"Did you give in or not?" asked Wang Changchi.

"I threw a ladle of night soil on him, making him stink from head to toe."

"Does Dad know about this?"

"I told him."

"What was his reaction?"

Liu Shuangju wiped away her tears

"My reaction was the same as his," she said. "He said that before you passed the exam, we couldn't do anything impure. He said that if you passed, I could do anything I wanted. He knows I'm not a loose woman, but he still said that. Every day we burn incense, and worship the gods and ancestors, fearful lest the slightest evil thought would make you meet with retribution. We didn't dare step on ants, kill birds, and always gave in to others. Zhang Xianhua seized the ground next to your grandma's grave, but we didn't argue about it. The ancestors and the gods were all watching... Even if you passed, I wouldn't do any such thing. We can't help you write essays or memorise your lessons, but we can give you merit in this life with our good deeds."

Wang Changchi felt distressed, never imagining that his university entrance exam would be linked to his mother's sex life and the ants beneath his parents' feet. He said nothing for several days, and Liu Shuangju seemed to have finished talking. Wang

Changchi picked up the cut stalks of grain and fiercely struck them against the inside of the threshing box, and the grains fell as the threshing echoed. The valley seemed lonelier than ever.

In his wheelchair, Wang Huai was able to cook now. Every day upon returning home, Wang Changchi and Liu Shuangju could eat the hot dishes he prepared. In addition to cooking, he could peel corn, sweep the floor, shell peanuts, feed the chickens and make tea. Every evening after dinner, Wang Huai would try to get Wang Changchi to study.

"I want to study," said Wang Changchi. "Can the two of you afford it?"

"No problem," said Wang Huai. "Didn't we make it through this year?"

Wang Changchi was sceptical. The cost of his food, clothes, school supplies and other things, when added together, totalled twelve hundred yuan. They had no oxen to sell, and the one pig was for the New Year. There was no other source of income apart from selling chickens, eggs and the yellow dog. In the end, they did sell the yellow dog. They had no new clothes. Wang Huai had stopped taking his painkillers. He said his back throbbed with pain on rainy days.

Wang Changchi secretly went and asked Second Uncle, "Did the family borrow money from you?" His uncle said no. Wang Changchi thought it strange, so when nobody was watching, he ransacked the drawers and chests at home. One day, he found a sheet of paper stuck in Wang Huai's pillow on which was written:

> Owe Second Uncle 300 yuan.
> Owe Zhang Xianhua 200 yuan.
> Owe Wang Dong 150 yuan.
> Owe Zhang Wu 100 yuan.
> Owe Liu Baitiao 16 yuan.

Goodness! They even wrote an IOU to Liu Baitiao! The paper shook in Wang Changchi's hand. After trembling for a while, he folded it up and shoved it in his pocket. His pocket suddenly felt heavy, as if it were a piece of steel dragging down the shoulder of his shirt. He took the paper and went to see the creditors.

"Your dad repeatedly said it was not right to bring up the matter as it might affect your studies," the creditors claimed.

Wang Changchi collected the old IOUs and wrote five new ones, with himself as the borrower in place of Wang Huai. Wang Huai knew nothing of this change, encouraging Wang Changchi every day to study. To Wang Changchi he was like a drunkard speaking defiantly, spittle flying, but who never really considered his own strength.

Once the harvest was finished, Wang Changchi gave Wang Huai's feet a thorough scrubbing with soap and trimmed his long, black toenails.

"From the look of things," said Wang Huai, "you're going to study, right?"

"I want to go to town to work," said Wang Changchi.

"Criminal," scolded Wang Huai. "You won't study, you just want to sell your labour, snuffing out the hopes of the family. If you don't go and study, then put my nails back and return the dirt you washed away. I want you to study, not wash feet."

"I'm not cut out for studying," said Wang Changchi. "I'm just a mediocre person like everyone else."

"No, you're a genius, you're the liberator of the Wang family."

"You're exaggerating. I'm nothing but a piece of dog shit."

十二 · TWELVE

WANG CHANGCHI SLIPPED AWAY BEFORE DAWN. Bag on his back, canvas shoes in his hands, he walked barefoot down the muddy road. The surface of the road was ice-cold and as he walked, a well-known metaphor came to mind: "The dust on a muddy road is the ashes of the ancestors." The dew on the grass moistened the bottoms of his trouser legs, and he frequently heard the strange cries of animals coming from the forest. The stars twinkled in the dark sky. When he reached the foot of the maple tree in the gap in the mountains, he turned and looked back to find the village still shadowy and indistinct, with houses and trees a patch of inky black. Everything was vague and murky as if his eyes had cataracts, as if this were his very last glimpse. After some time, the colour of the sky seemed to change gradually from a deep black to a dark blue. The houses had outlines and the trees had shapes, the black colour melted off the roofs and the tree branches. He rubbed his eyes, then turned and departed. The sky grew light. Looking down, he noticed that his canvas shoes had been washed to a wretched white, white as a city wall.

Wang Huai woke up in bed, the morning light shining on his scrawny backside. He shouted "Changchi" twice, but no one answered. Liu Shuangju came in and helped him into his wheelchair.

"I overslept," he said. "Where's Changchi?"

"Changchi went to the city," said Liu Shuangju.

Wang Huai poled his wheelchair to the door and, looking at the lush green in the distance, he began to scold.

"Wang Changchi, you've got no gumption or fighting spirit, you won't study, and all you want to do is go to work. You won't think of being a cadre, just a labourer. You won't give your ancestors face, you just disgrace your parents, you're no child of mine, I expected too much from you..."

Although he did not shout very loud, he pronounced each word at the appropriate frequency and so they carried with penetrating strength, gusted over Second Uncle's rooftop and brushed the treetops in the village. Wang Changchi, who sat dozing by the main road, seemed to respond as if he was awakened by someone. The mountain's shadow fell over the fields and the sound of the water was mixed with the chirruping of the cicadas. The bus approached along the ashen road and stopped in front of him. The door opened and he boarded, bag on his shoulder. Wang Huai, who was shouting from the doorway, abruptly shut his mouth, like the bus door closing.

Everyone knew Wang Changchi had left. Liu Baitiao was the first to become uneasy.

He took the IOU to Wang Huai and said, "I thought he was a filial son, not a swindler."

Wang Huai took the IOU and looked it over. "Since he wrote it, he'll pay it back," he said.

"He's disappeared," said Liu Baitiao, "so who'll pay it back?"

"I'm still here, aren't I?" said Wang Huai.

Liu Baitiao looked him over, re-evaluating him. "I can't believe you don't even have sixteen yuan in the house."

"Why don't you take the two hens?"

Liu Baitiao didn't want two old hens, and he went inside to search the house. Lifting Wang Huai's bed mat, he saw a purse, but it was empty. He opened the trunk and found some worn old shirts and trousers, but nothing of value. He opened the cabinet and found only an earthenware jug of lard.

He removed the jug and said, "I'll take this as payment."

"Fool," said Wang Huai, "once you eat the lard it's all gone. You'd be better off taking the hens because they can lay eggs, and eggs hatch more chickens, and chickens lay eggs, so you're bound to see an increase."

"You keep the hens and see an increase yourself," said Liu Baitiao. "I like lard, and it's been six months since I've seen nice white fat. Even the wok is rusted."

"If you take it then won't our wok rust?" asked Wang Huai.

"That can't be helped, debtors can't be choosers. My creditors treat me the same way. They even broke up my plank bed and considered digging up the top three inches of soil on my land."

Hanging his head in shame, Wang Huai tore up the IOU.

Carrying the jug of lard home, Liu Baitiao ran into Zhang Wu. Although Zhang Wu had an IOU in his possession, if Wang Changchi didn't make any money, then it would become worthless, a scrap of paper with no value. Was there any guarantee he'd make money? How long would it take before he did? The more Zhang Wu considered the matter, the longer time seemed to grow and the more his doubts seemed to increase, so he spun around and went home to get the IOU and go to see Wang Huai. Wang Huai agreed to pay interest, but he asked Zhang Wu to give him an extension of several months. Zhang Wu wouldn't give him an extra minute because he thought he was being cheated. He said that when Wang Changchi took over the IOU, he never said anything about going away to work, so the information didn't conform to what he said, which meant he was being cheated.

"Wang Changchi isn't that sort of person," said Wang Huai. "He will definitely make money and he will definitely pay off the debt."

"For you everything is definite," said Zhang Wu, "which means it definitely will not happen. At first, didn't you say he would definitely pass the exam?"

Wang Huai was at a loss for words. Zhang Wu went inside and looked once around the house and decided to cart off the old wooden cabinet.

"If you don't believe me, then take the cabinet," said Wang Huai. "I don't have anything to put inside it anyway."

Zhang Wu handed over the IOU. Wang Huai rubbed it and rubbed it until the palm of his hand hurt. It was as if the words had grown teeth.

Wang Dong happened to see Zhang Wu carrying the cabinet home. Wang Dong then had a crisis. He quickly located his IOU and went to Wang Huai, demanding to be repaid.

"There's nothing of value left in the house," said Wang Huai.

"Isn't there a coffin upstairs?" asked Wang Dong.

"That's for me when the time comes. Young as you are, you won't die before me."

"It's not a matter of dying, but a matter of whether or not I'll get my money back."

"My character is my guarantee. Changchi will definitely repay the money."

"These days character isn't worth a fart."

"OK, then take it for now. When Changchi has money, I'll come and redeem it from you."

Wang Dong asked Liu Baitiao to help him. They slid the coffin down the stairs, and with one person on each end, they went out through the front door. Wang Huai was heavy of heart as if oppressed by death and watching his own funeral.

A light went on in Zhang Xianhua's head when she saw Wang Dong and Liu Baitiao carrying away Wang Huai's coffin. She immediately got her IOU and went to the Wangs' house.

"Wang Huai, Wang Huai," she said, "I'm your biggest creditor. Why didn't you inform me first before declaring bankruptcy?"

"I didn't declare bankruptcy, but they don't trust Changchi," said Wang Huai.

"If they don't trust him," said Zhang Xianhua, "why should I?"

"Didn't you watch Changchi grow up?"

"They watched him grow up too."

"From the time he was little till he grew up, did he ever tell a lie?"

Zhang Xianhua shook her head.

"Did I ever borrow money and not repay it?"

Zhang Xianhua said no.

"To each seed its sprout, to each vine its melon, so just believe in us this once," said Wang Huai.

Zhang Xianhua looked at the IOU, slowly folded it and went to stick it in her pocket. Wang Huai was all tensed up and even clenching his fists as he watched the IOU going towards her pocket when suddenly her hand paused as if someone had stopped her.

"Changchi never lied to me, but he was in the village then," she said. "Now he's in the city, and that's a different environment. Who can guarantee that he's the same as he was before? There are so many swindlers in the city, all he has to do is meet one and he'll be corrupted."

"Even if you dropped him in a vat of dye," said Wang Huai, "he'd come out as white as ever. He's not one to go back on his word."

"Is that what you told Liu Baitiao and Wang Dong?" asked Zhang Xianhua.

Wang Huai said no.

"Then why are you only telling me?"

"Because there is really nothing in the house to pay off the debt."

Zhang Xianhua looked around the house twice, but in truth found nothing of any value. She patted her head and said, "Don't you have some fir trees on the other side of the mountain?"

"Those are being saved for making roof beams," said Wang Huai. "Look at the beams of my house – they are rotting and won't last many more years."

Zhang Xianhua looked up and saw that the beams were half black, the result of too much rainwater seeping in. She softened a bit but hardened at once.

"I'm only concerned about collecting my debt and couldn't care less about your beams," she said.

"The wok can go without fat," said Wang Huai, "I can die and not have a coffin, but if a house beam gives way, I'll have no place to live. Can't you even forego a few fir trees? Are you that cruel?"

Zhang Xianhua suddenly grew angry and said, "I loaned you money and that was so your son could study, but now he's gone off to work, so why don't you want to repay me?"

"He's such a good boy," said Wang Huai. "Why don't you believe in him?"

"Because he's not my son," said Zhang Xianhua.

Wang Huai sighed. "What if I write you another IOU?"

"For what?"

"If Changchi doesn't send the money to you in six months, the debt will double."

"You can't even pay the current one, so how can you repay twice the amount?"

"If I can't pay when the time comes, this house and garden are yours."

"You'd actually dare to put that on paper?" asked Zhang Xianhua.

Wang Huai did put it on paper and also affixed his thumbprint in red. Zhang Xianhua took the promissory note and left. She showed it to anyone she met.

Seeing the paper, Wang Dong was incredulous. "You only

loaned him fifty yuan more than I did and you get the house and garden in exchange," he said.

"That's capital at work," said Zhang Xianhua.

Everyone was discussing that piece of paper. Liu Shuangju felt distressed. Her throat narrowed, her shoulders became inflamed, her stomach ached, she suffered from insomnia, lost her appetite and as a result, her immunity weakened.

Comforting her, Wang Huai said, "If you can't trust your own son, who can you trust?"

2

WEAK IN THE EXTREME

十三 · THIRTEEN

WANG CHANGCHI WAS NOW EMPLOYED as a mason at the County Town Meeting Hall project at a monthly wage of three hundred yuan, including room and board. For breakfast he had *mantou*; for lunch, rice and vegetables; for dinner, rice and vegetables with some cubes of fatty meat. When there was no meat, everyone ate quietly, but when there was, everyone became more animated. Wang Changchi always pushed the meat beneath his rice, eating the rice and vegetables first, saving the meat for last. This way of eating was termed first the bitter then the sweet, allowing him to savour the flavour of the meat for a long time, much like a lingering melody. But one had to be ever vigilant when employing the method, otherwise a co-worker might reach over and snatch the meat with their chopsticks. When burying the meat under the rice, Wang Changchi experienced the elation of squirrelling something away. With his last few bites, entirely of meat, he felt as though he were concentrating his resources to do something big. He found dodging his co-workers' chopsticks as fun as playing a game. If no one eyed his bowl, he felt deeply disappointed, unable even to flaunt his greasy lips. As a result, he'd sometimes tap his rice bowl and loudly chomp the meat, trying to entice his co-workers to attempt to steal the meat.

He spent his nights in the workers' shed in which there were bunk beds nailed together out of new planks, the scent of pinewood filling the air. Each shed housed forty workers. Wang Changchi occupied bed seventeen in workers' shed two. At night when all was quiet, someone would suddenly shake their bed. The shaking would spread until everyone was affected. The creaking of the beds would fill the shed, making the married men think of home and keeping them awake all night. Others, including Wang Changchi, would never wake up regardless of how the beds shook. Exhausted, they slept like concrete blocks.

Wang Changchi's job was transporting mortar, pushing a full, wheeled mortar pan from the mixer to a simple lift. A bloke by the name of Liu Jianping teamed up with him, taking turns pushing the mortar pans. Once there were four pans of wet mortar in the lift, they'd close the door of steel bars and release the brake. The lift would clank as it rose, the mortar jiggling ever so slightly. Reaching the first floor, the lift would screech to a halt, and some of the mortar would spill out, falling with a plop to the floor each time the lift ascended and descended. Wang Changchi would listen closely as the sound reminded him of his father's wooden wheelchair.

He had found the job himself. After leaving the bus station, he'd walked a distance and looked around the area. His target was to find the long boom of a crane, and he went to every place he saw one. He then looked for scaffolding and did the same. Then he listened for the sound of piles being driven. He visited every place he heard a pile being driven. Then he smelled wet cement. He asked at every one of the dozen or so dusty construction sites in the small county town, and the foreman at this site was the only one willing to take him on. The foreman's name was He Gui. His head was pointed, he wore a spotless white shirt, was soft-spoken and even offered him a cigarette. That day, he moved his bag over from the space under the bridge. He figured that if he could hold on, grit his teeth and last for three months, he could pay off the family debts.

The time to collect wages came at the end of the first month. They received nothing, so they went to see He Gui about their money. All smiles, He Gui said that wages were paid once every three months and they needn't worry. Some expressed doubts and demanded cash. He Gui pulled out a stack of notes and slapped them against his palm and said anyone who wanted to could take their money and leave. A number of them did and took their bags and never looked back. They didn't even change their mortar-spattered clothes, making it look from a distance as if they were wearing camouflage. Most of the workers stayed put, unsure of He Gui's intention.

He Gui said, "This is what's called management. When I train a worker, I expect him to help me for three months, otherwise constantly changing workers are like the rotating shadow figures on a carousel lantern and will severely impact the progress of the project."

Everyone stood there for a while, then went back to work regardless of whether they knew what he was talking about or not.

Liu Jianping complained as he pushed the cart, saying, "That bloke He Gui might be a swindler."

"That's unlikely given the size of the project," said Wang Changchi.

He felt that receiving wages every three months wasn't a bad thing because it would force him not to spend money, and was just like putting it in the bank, the only disadvantage being he received no interest.

Three months later, He Gui vanished. The workers broke into his office. Someone stole the computer, the television, the water dispenser, the office desk and the Simmons mattress. Most of the workers stole nothing. Gathered at the work site, some swore, some broke the machinery to vent their anger; others played chess or cards and forgot the troubles before them; a few squatted at the foot of the wall, and without blinking eyed the exit as if waiting for a miracle to occur. Wang Changchi lay in bed catching up on lost sleep, trying to recover from ninety days of strenuous labour. The smell of the pine boards had already faded, and the din made by his co-workers seemed near at hand, then far away. He Gui still appeared in his mind as he dozed. He was so eloquent, his teeth white and straight, he always carried a pack of name-brand cigarettes and a disposable lighter in his pocket, which he would offer to whoever he met, and the moment they took a cigarette, his lighter would flick on. Handing out cigarettes and lighting them was performed smoothly and expertly, like a seasoned smoker, but he himself never smoked, at least Wang Changchi had never seen him. How could such an urbane foreman just up and disappear?

He thought for a while and slept for a while and only got up when his empty stomach was growling with hunger. Walking out of the workers' shed, he discovered he had slept for a day and a half. A stretch of burning clouds floated in the evening sky. The work site was much quieter. Some of the workers had left, some sat at the foot of the wall, smoking, chatting and staring into space. Wang Changchi drank some tap water and his stomach gurgled.

He sat down next to Liu Jianping and quietly asked, "Have you eaten?"

"Yes," he replied.

"Can I borrow some money?"

Liu Jianping stood up and took a new seat twenty metres away. Wang Changchi looked to his left and then to his right. His co-workers stood up one after another, brushed off their backsides and either went back into the workers' shed or moved away. Everyone was avoiding him as if he were a stinky fart. Then he understood. Friends and co-workers could talk about anything but couldn't ask to borrow money. He lowered his head and looked at the grass growing in the cracks and the ants coming and going over the ground. He picked up an ant and placed it on the back of his hand, allowing it to walk back and forth and up his arm, and watched it crawl to his shoulder. He picked it up between his thumb and forefinger and placed it on the back of his hand once again. The ant climbed diligently, thinking it would find a way out, but not knowing that all ways were blocked. Doing this again and again, he temporarily forgot his hunger. The sky gradually grew dark, and the electricity was off at the work site. The ant on the back of his hand was swallowed by the darkness. He couldn't see it, but he could feel it. His stomach started growling again and grew bloated with gastric acid. He slapped the ant and felt the moisture in his palm. He wiped the spot dry, rubbed his hands, stood up and left the work site.

十四 · FOURTEEN

WANG CHANGCHI HAD SUSPECTED that Huang Kui had been jailed, but he went to Little River Street all the same. Not only was the Circum-Pacific Trade Company sign still there, it was even more polished than before. The storefront was broad, and the light inside shone out through the window, across the street and over the river. It was no longer a place selling everyday items, the storefront had been upgraded to that of an office. Huang Kui and two others were drinking beer. Some plates and dishes were placed on the table and the aroma of salted pigs' feet and salted duck feet wafted through the air. As if seeing a long-lost relative, he called out excitedly to Huang Kui. The three of them turned their heads, all with a look of amazement on their faces. Huang Kui in particular looked amazed. He stopped chewing and his brow wrinkled. Then his mouth moved.

"Did you take the university entrance exam?" he asked. "I thought you didn't want to be seen with me. Didn't your parents consider me a bad person? When you lot left here, you all acted like you were number one in the county and didn't want to dirty yourselves with me, so gallant and superior, all high and mighty never turning back all the way to the south wall."

"As Heaven and Earth are my witnesses," insisted Wang Changchi, "I did glance back several times, feeling that I'd wronged you."

"I'm one to bear a grudge," said Huang Kui. "The way you paused with that look of having turned over a new leaf is deeply impressed here."

He pointed to his head as he spoke.

Wang Changchi swallowed a couple of times and said, "I'm willing to help you cut off fingers."

"You're too late, I've already done it myself."

"Then can I help you with something else?"

"You haven't got the guts to do anything."

"No one's born with courage, it's forced on you."

"Well said. If you've got the guts, then take off your trousers."

Wang Changchi did take off his trousers, exposing his buttocks and legs to the cold wind. Their eyes fixed on him like searchlights. The bottom half of his body was pitch black, except for the part covered by his underpants. His dick seemed to have withdrawn up into his belly as if it were shy. Huang Kui suddenly recalled the days in junior high school when they went swimming naked in the river. In those days, Wang Changchi's skin was as white as his, and without their clothes on, you couldn't tell who was from the countryside and who was from the city. But now there was a vast difference between them, and without their clothes on the difference in their lives was plain to see.

Huang Kui felt a twinge of sympathy and said, "Come on in."

Bare-arsed, Wang Changchi came in.

"Put your trousers on," Huang Kui said angrily.

Only after eating his fill did Wang Changchi's fear subside. His legs no longer trembled, and he had no more cold sweat. He stood firmly on the ground. It was then that he discovered Huang Kui and his friends had been watching him eat.

Wiping his mouth, he said, "Sorry, I was really hungry."

"Would you be willing to go to jail?" asked Huang Kui.

"As long as I don't have to kill anyone, I'd consider it."

"A bloke beat someone up and went to jail yesterday to serve fifteen days. You take his place tomorrow and you'll be paid one hundred yuan for each day, which makes a total of fourteen hundred for fourteen days."

"How can I take his place if he's already in jail?"

"Don't worry about that. When someone calls Lin Jiabo, all you have to do is say 'present' loud and clear and everything will be OK."

"Who's Lin Jiabo?" asked Wang Changchi.

"That's not important," said Huang Kui. "What is important is that you can make some money."

Returning to the workers' shed, Wang Changchi retired early. Unable to sleep, he tossed and turned. As he digested the food, his hunger disappeared, and he no longer felt a sense of urgency. He discovered that a hungry person acts differently from one who is full. A person will agree to anything when they are hungry, they have no shame, not even with their dick hanging out. But after eating one's fill, one is more akin to being a member of the bourgeoisie, overcautious and indecisive. So what am I? An idiot who takes off his trousers? A criminal? A bad person? Wang Changchi? Lin Jiabo? The more he thought about it, the more he was filled with regret, and the more he scorned himself. Deeply saddened, he saw himself like the ant he smashed in his hand. It could go in plenty of directions but had no way out.

As he was thinking, the sky grew light. Wang Changchi grabbed his bag and set off briskly for home. He saw the reservoir, the tea plantation, the big maple, the village and his house with the door shut tight. He knocked on the door and it opened with a creak. Huang Kui was standing inside.

"Why so early? It's only six," said Huang Kui, still half asleep.

Startled, Wang Changchi felt he was dreaming; his mind was filled with home, but his feet had brought him here.

Huang Kui offered him morning tea and ordered a whole table full of food.

"The more you order, the less I eat," said Wang Changchi.

"You feel sorry about the money?" asked Huang Kui.

"I feel like a prisoner having his last meal before facing the firing squad."

"You're thinking too much about it. Inside you've got three

squares and a place to stay. It's safe from earthquakes, so when you go inside think of it like a holiday."

"My mind has been numb ever since last night. If I wasn't honest and a man of my word, I'd have been out of here like greased lightning."

"Don't be nervous. Inside they train people, also toughen 'em up, testing them, like a furnace or a school."

Yeah, a poor person's school, thought Wang Changchi, but he said nothing. He tried to eat a little but couldn't swallow a thing.

Pulling out a piece of paper he said, "This is my address. I want you to send a thousand yuan to my dad and keep the other four hundred for me. Don't put your address on the money order or my dad will show up here again. If something happens to me... look after my folks, make sure they have food and clothing, and a coffin when they die."

"You're making this into a big deal," said Huang Kui, "a matter of life and death. If something does happen to you, I'll move your parents to the county town and care for them as if they were my own mum and dad. They'd have a car and a house, they could see a doctor, buy insurance, have their feet washed, eat at restaurants, go dancing and fully experience the advantages of the system."

Wang Changchi knew he was saying this because he was sure nothing would happen to him, but still he had to ask, "Will you really do that?"

"Talking big is not my thing," said Huang Kui.

"It would be hilarious if they had a son as outstanding as you."

Before going in, Wang Changchi needed to spend ten minutes silently committing things to memory like a spy: Lin Jiabo, male, thirty-three years of age, single, son of an official, chairman of the board of Huihuang Real Estate Company, address: Longteng District, 1 Dong, Unit 2, Room 508. At ten o'clock on the first, while speeding in the 8888 to take girlfriend Wang Yanping out for an evening snack, I hit and knocked over the fruit stall of Sun Yiping. Not only did I fail to compensate Sun for damages, I struck him and broke two of his ribs. I was held by the angry bystanders.

Wang Yanping, aged twenty-three, is a singer and actress in a song and dance troupe and the daughter of Director Wang.

Huang Kui drove Wang Changchi to the door of the lockup for prisoners. All the way there, Wang Changchi kept making mental suggestions to himself. As the door to the lockup slowly opened, he had already become Lin Jiabo. In a mere thirty minutes, he went from being a poor slob to a rich bloke with an official for a father, a good car, a high-rise suite and a beautiful woman.

十五 · FIFTEEN

WANG HUAI RECEIVED THE MONEY ORDER for a thousand yuan, with the address of a PA Company in the provincial capital.

"Shuangju," called Wang Huai loudly.

Liu Shuangju came out.

"What's the matter?" she said.

"Is your blood pressure normal right now?" asked Wang Huai.

She looked him over and asked, "Is yours OK?"

"Are you in a calm frame of mind?"

Liu Shuangju's expression changed, and she asked, "Has something happened to Changchi?"

Wang Huai handed the money order to her. Liu Shuangju took it and looked at it, her eyes blurring. She wiped away her tears.

"I never expected Changchi to make his mark so quickly," she said.

"I've already calculated it," said Wang Huai. "Changchi needs money for food and rent plus some spending money. So, to be able to send us this much, he has to make at least five hundred yuan a month."

"He's not a manager," said Liu Shuangju, "so how could he make that much?"

Wang Huai pointed to the "PA" on the money order and said, "See that? Those are foreign letters. Only foreign companies would be that stupid. They probably mistake dollars for renminbi."

Liu Shuangju smiled broadly and said, "If they're really that stupid, then our Changchi has got himself a great deal."

The news that Wang Changchi had sent money spread, and everyone came to offer their congratulations. First of all, Wang Huai made tea for them but then discovered that tea and cigarettes weren't enough to get rid of them. So Liu Shuangju had to provide food. Not having anything decent to serve, she bought some cured meat from Zhang Wu on credit. Zhang Wu was afraid she wouldn't be able to pay for it, so Liu Shuangju took out the money order and showed it to him. It had already passed through the hands of many people and was full of tears, mud, fingerprints and kitchen grime. Zhang Wu took it to examine it and added streaks of grease. Liu Shuangju cooked the cured meat for everyone who came to offer their congratulations. Wang Huai felt that the meat ought to be accompanied by wine.

So Liu Shuangju took the money order and went to see Second Uncle.

"As soon as we cash the money order, we'll repay our debt and pay for the rice wine at the same time," she said.

Second Uncle took the money order to have a look and stained it with distiller's mash. The money order resembled a credit card, swiped here and there all over the village, swiped until Liu Shuangju's heart ached. Those who came to offer congratulations ate the cured meat as they praised Wang Changchi and drank rice wine while they tried to guess what Wang Changchi was actually doing. Someone said PA Company makes mobile phones; someone said they make televisions; another said they make computers. Wang Huai said, "Maybe they make cars."

Despite all their conjecture, no one guessed that Wang Changchi was in jail. Every day he curled up in a corner, trying to picture Lin Jiabo's extravagant lifestyle. He had imagined on the day he entered, Huang Kui would make a single trade with the lock-up, as if they were exchanging prisoners of war, but what he didn't expect is that as one entered here, the other exited there. He never even saw Lin Jiabo's back. One day he recalled that the construction site where he was working was being built under contract from Huihuang Real Estate, so the man who owed him back wages was none other than Lin Jiabo. Although Lin Jiabo was paying him fourteen hundred yuan this time, if he subtracted the nine hundred he owed him, he was making only five hundred. That was really unfair! He felt that someone like Lin Jiabo, who owed people money for their sweat and blood, ought to be given the maximum punishment, and ought to be taken out and shot, but here he was, Wang Changchi, doing jail time. If Lin Jiabo were taken out and shot, maybe only his name would be shot. So long as the price was high enough, there would always be someone to die in his place. When he imagined Wang Yanping, Lin Jiabo's girlfriend, Wang Changchi felt he had been taken advantage of. He imagined her singing voice, her voluptuous bosom and white legs, imagined them sleeping in the same bed...

During Wang Changchi's days of wild fantasies, Liu Shuangju's younger sister brought a girl to the Wangs' place from the village where their mother lived. The girl's name was He Xiaowen, and she was tall and quite pretty. As soon as she entered the gate, she took the water buckets from Liu Shuangju's shoulders and went to draw water from the well, which was five hundred metres from the house. As she carried the water back, she supported the carrying pole with one hand while the other swung free, her body swayed to and fro, the carrying pole bobbed up and down, her two braids swung back and forth, and her whole person seemed to dance. The five-hundred-metre path seemed to be her catwalk. All the villagers watched her. Wang Huai watched her.

Shuangju's sister asked Wang Huai, "Is she to your liking?"

"She's a nice girl," said Wang Huai, "but she has no education, and with no education, she'll not be able to go to the city. If she can't go to the city, she'll never be able to make a life with Changchi in the provincial capital. Changchi is working for a foreign enterprise and he's making big money, so he has no reason to come back to the village for a wife."

"Girls as pretty as Xiaowen are rare," said Shuangju's sister, "and she's the only one left in the village. If she had an education, she would've married a cadre a long time ago."

"A village cadre isn't necessarily better than a worker in the provincial capital, so you might as well take her home."

"You only want to dream. You never think about the real difficulties at home – my big sis is ready to collapse from exhaustion. If Xiaowen were to help out, she could catch her breath and you'd sit at ease in that wheelchair of yours."

"Don't exploit or harm others. We can't take Changchi's place in this matter."

Meeting obstacles from Wang Huai, she went to Liu Shuangju to seek a solution. After conferring, the two sisters decided to keep Xiaowen around for a while to let Wang Huai assess her so that he could see her outstanding qualities.

The day Liu Shuangju went to town, she took her personal seal, her ID and Wang Changchi's money order and cashed it. She didn't buy anything for herself, just a set of lightweight clothes as a gift for Xiaowen. Although Xiaowen wasn't family, Liu Shuangju already looked upon her as a daughter-in-law. With the rest of the money, she paid off the debts. After Wang Dong got his money, he returned Wang Huai's coffin. After Zhang Xianhua got her money, she tore up the IOU and the promissory note. Liu Shuangju also paid what was owed to Second Uncle, including the money for the wine. Zhang Wu was also paid for the cured meat. There was still a little money left over. After Liu Shuangju and Wang Huai discussed the matter, they bought two pigs.

He Xiaowen did everything, cooked, carried water and fed the pigs. Wang Huai discovered that when she fed the pigs, the pigs ate with more zest, and the sound of their grunting as they ate filled Wang Huai with happiness. After working all day, Xiaowen would bathe and then dress in the clothes Liu Shuangju had purchased for her and sit sewing in front of the Wangs' house. She patched and mended all their clothes and secured all the loose buttons. One after another, the women came to enjoy dropping in on the Wangs, and the men soon followed. Wang Huai and Liu Shuangju were very aware that everyone was coming for no other reason than to see He Xiaowen and to chat with her.

Xiaowen filled a basin with warm water and washed Wang

Huai's feet and trimmed his nails.

"Why didn't you go to school?" asked Wang Huai.

"My brother was already in school," said Xiaowen, "and I was an extra child so the family was fined heavily, and I couldn't go. Later, my parents had yet another extra child, a little sister, which made things more difficult, so I helped with the farm work."

"Have you seen Changchi?"

Xiaowen shook her head and said, "No, just a photo."

"I'm much obliged for all that you've done, but you should go home because the longer you're here the more I'll owe you."

"My big brother and his wife are really afraid I won't be married off."

"They underestimate you."

"Several matchmakers have come, but I didn't take a fancy to any of the proposed matches because they were so ugly or they had no money. I just want to marry someone like Brother Changchi and leave the village."

"You're illiterate so how can you leave?"

"I taught myself a few hundred characters. I can write my name, read street signs, make phone calls and do sums."

"What if Changchi is unwilling?"

"Then I'll give up hope."

"You'll hate us then."

"I help you work, and you feed and clothe me, so that means I'm working for a living."

Towards nightfall, the slope was reddened by the evening clouds on the horizon, and white kitchen smoke curled upwards above the tile roofs of every home. Wearing a brand-new shirt, Zhang Wu whistled, just back from his hometown. Before entering the village, he noticed He Xiaowen cutting plants in the Wangs' field for feeding the pigs. Zhang Wu hesitated on the road before stepping into the Wangs' sweet potato field.

"Uncle Zhang," He Xiaowen called out.

"Can you keep a secret?" asked Zhang Wu.

"What kind of secret?"

"I'll tell you."

"As long as it doesn't harm anyone, I can keep it."

Zhang Wu took a piece of paper and asked, "Ever seen one of these?"

"It's a money order. Did Changchi send it?"

"Look at the name on it."

He Xiaowen, half-guessing and half-knowing, said, "Is it for you?"

Zhang Wu said, "Look at the amount."

"Three thousand."

"My daughter Zhang Hui sent this to me from the provincial capital. Don't tell a soul."

"Then why are you telling me?"

"I went to town today and called Zhang Hui and mentioned your situation. She said if you're willing to work where she does you could make at least three thousand to five thousand yuan a month."

"What kind of work does she do?"

Zhang Wu lit a cigarette and said, "Can you keep a secret?"

Xiaowen nodded.

"She works in a big hotel, where she washes people's feet and massages their legs and the like."

"Someone already asked me and said I could go to the city and help give massages, but I turned them down flat."

Zhang Wu sighed and pointed to the slope.

"All pretty village girls are like those trees," he said. "Sooner or later, someone from the city will come and buy them and take them away. It's only because I see you're bright and pretty and your family is having a hard time that I recommended you."

"Thank you, Uncle Zhang."

"Changchi doesn't make as much as my girl. You'd be better off making your own money than marrying him."

"If she made even more money, you still wouldn't dare tell anyone."

"That's right. I'm the richest chap in the valley. If you want to make big money, come and see me."

"Only if Changchi doesn't want to marry me."

"Foolish girl," said Zhang Wu. "With money, why be afraid of not finding a husband?"

"Wait till Changchi gets home," said Xiaowen, "and see what his attitude is before anything else."

十六 · SIXTEEN

After Wang Changchi was released from the lock-up, he sat down on a rock beside the river. The sun was intense, and his joints were soon warmed. He flexed his four limbs and with a splash, he jumped into the river and swam around as he took off his clothes and washed them by rubbing them in his hands. After washing his clothes, he spread them out on the rocks to dry in the sun, then he once again leapt naked into the river where he washed his hair and picked the muck from between his toes. In the light of the sun penetrating the water, he could see the filth he scrubbed from his body floating like a cloud of dust. Feeling thoroughly clean, he lay down on a rocky shoal in the river and rested. When his whole body felt hot, he waded into the water. He waded for a while and sunbathed for a while. When his clothes on the rocks were half dry, he climbed up on the shore, turned them over and steam started to rise. Again, he waded and sunbathed a while until his clothes were completely dry. He sat on the shore until the sun had dried the drops of water from his body before putting on his clean clothes. He sniffed his sleeves and they smelled of ultraviolet rays.

Returning to Little River Street, he found that Huang Kui was not at the company, just an assistant. Wang Changchi waited until evening before he saw Huang Kui come staggering along drunk with a mobile phone the size of a brick.

He patted Wang Changchi on the shoulder.

"Did anyone pick on you?" he said.

"Now that I've been in jail," said Wang Changchi, "I feel dirty, just like a girl who is no longer a virgin that no one wants to marry."

"You still care about your reputation?" said Huang Kui, as he pulled open his drawer.

"So poor people aren't entitled to a good reputation?"

"I care about this." As he spoke, Huang Kui took an envelope from the drawer and tossed it over. Wang Changchi took it, opened it, and saw four hundred yuan inside along with the stub from a money order.

He looked at the address on the stub and asked, "What's this PA Company?"

"I haven't the slightest idea," said Huang Kui. "It was a deception concocted by my assistant when he sent the money."

Holding the stub in his hands, Wang Changchi said, "Thank you."

"So, what are your plans now?" asked Huang Kui.

"First, to go back to the worksite."

"I don't have any work suitable for you here, and the chance to take someone's place in jail doesn't come along every day. If someone needs a person to take their place, I'll contact you."

Wang Changchi offered his thanks once more, shouldered his bag and left. Arriving at the worksite, he got a whiff of the smell that comes when water and electricity have been turned off for some time. The muddy road had turned to a solid crust and the tyre tracks, potholes and depressions were all hardened. The weeds had grown tall in the vacant ground and there were more mosquitoes. As he entered the worksite, Wang Changchi saw more than a dozen workers sitting at the foot of the wall. He wasn't sure if it was the light playing tricks on their eyes or just that their reactions were slow, but it took a while before his co-workers recognised him.

"Where have you been the last few days?" they asked.

Wang Changchi made no reply. They poked around in his bag looking for something to eat. The bag contained nothing but a few articles of clothing. They searched his clothes to see if they could find any money. Wang Changchi knew what to expect before he arrived, so he had hidden his money in a small bag in his trouser pocket. Finding nothing, they went back to their places and sat down, disappointed.

"When a bloke comes back," complained Liu Jianping, "he at least brings a few potatoes or at worst a few peanuts. You didn't bring anything. What'd you come back for?"

"To borrow some money," said Wang Changchi. Everyone avoided him when they heard these words.

Actually, he came back to find a place to sleep. That night he slept very deeply and the following morning he went to a roadside stall and ate six large *mantou* and a bowl of egg-drop soup. After having his fill, he returned to the workers' shed to sleep. He discovered that half an hour before eating, his co-workers who had been chatting energetically would fall silent as if a thirty-minute transition was needed to change the familiar bloke before them into a stranger. One by one they would sneak off, each one going to a nearby *baozi* shop, rice noodle shop or a fast-food place. Before entering one of the small eateries, each of them would turn and look around, afraid that one of their co-workers had come for a share. Once they had crammed their bellies full, one by one they'd come back again to gather at the foot of the wall to chat, as if their absence had gone unnoticed. Wang Changchi stayed away as much as possible, but on the third night when he hurried into a rice noodle shop, Liu Jianping suddenly appeared in front of him.

"Wang Changchi," said Liu Jianping, "You have no shame, hiding your money in your pocket."

Looking outside, Wang Changchi saw that no other co-workers were there, so he ordered a bowl of rice noodles with meat for Liu Jianping. The two of them ate outside.

"Where'd you get the money?" asked Liu Jianping.

Wang Changchi made no reply but kept his head lowered as he wolfed down the rest of his rice noodles. He felt like having another bowl but restrained himself since Liu Jianping was present.

"Why don't you go out and make some money?" he asked.

"I worked for a hundred and fifty days," said Liu Jianping, "and I've worn out three sets of clothes, two pairs of shoes and lost four layers of skin. Can I just keep my mouth shut and leave?"

"Then you'll be waiting for He Gui to find his conscience. I don't think he'll be coming to pay us."

"A lot of co-workers are protesting, so the relevant department will have to sort it out."

"I've been to the door of that department," said Wang Changchi. "It used to be crowded and noisy, and now there is hardly anyone there. After a few of the riotous workers had been arrested, most got afraid and came to sit quietly under the trees along the street, calmly reminding the officials entering and exiting: someone owes the rural workers their wages. But the officials entering and exiting the main door have become oblivious to it. Those taking cars roll up their windows and those riding bicycles pedal with more force. As long as no one up above looks into the matter and the county holds no important meetings, they just let them sit by the roadside, with everyone minding their own business.

"I heard that a leader made an appearance and said that the matter was being looked into and they would quickly arrive at a solution. But it's been more than twenty days, why is there still no solution? Either it's a complicated issue or it's being obstructed. The longer this drags on, the fewer workers come, because no one can afford to. With no money for food, everyone has to leave, and now there are just a few left and the whole matter will just blow over."

"Since you have no hope," said Liu Jianping, "why did you come back to the worksite?"

"To build up my strength," replied Wang Changchi.

A week later, Wang Changchi felt he had regained his strength, and could lift a concrete block with one hand. That night he went round to the Longteng District, 1 Dong, Unit 2 and saw that the lights were lit on both sides of the fourth floor, and quietly went upstairs. When he reached apartment 508, he stopped and took a deep breath, and then rang the doorbell. After a minute or so, he could see a light from the peephole in the steel door, and then it went dark again. Seeing no alternative, Wang Changchi rang the doorbell several times. The steel door opened a crack and a young man in pyjamas showed his face.

"Who are you?" he asked.

"Lin Jiabo," said Wang Changchi.

"You are?" said the man.

"I'm the bloke who took his place in jail."

"Lin Jiabo isn't here," said the man, frowning, and then closed the door.

As the door shut, Wang Changchi tried to force his way in, but the door chain was fastened, and he couldn't push the door open. Wang Changchi rang the doorbell again several times, but there was no response. He sat down on the floor, staring at the steel door as if he were afraid it would run away.

Less than half an hour went by before Huang Kui arrived. He told his two assistants to pick up Wang Changchi and take him downstairs, stick him in the jeep and take him to the door of the Circum-Pacific Trade Company on Little River Street. The door opened and Wang Changchi was dragged inside the office.

"Do you have a death wish?" asked Huang Kui.

"Is the site where I work Lin Jiabo's?" asked Wang Changchi.

"If so, what of it?"

"He owes blood and sweat money to a hundred workers, shouldn't he pay?"

"Don't forget, we signed a secrecy agreement."

"But," said Wang Changchi as he pulled out a contract, "I also signed an employment contract."

Huang Kui took the contract and looked at it, brandished it about and then tore it. Wang Changchi grabbed but only got half and then reached forward to grab the other half.

Huang Kui pushed him away.

"Isn't it only for nine hundred yuan?" he said. "I'll give it to you, but you must promise not to let him set eyes on you again."

"I want my wages. What business is it of yours?"

"What proof do you have that anyone owes you money?"

Wang Changchi held up the contract.

"Take a good look," said Huang Kui. "Is there an official seal?

Has it been signed?"

Wang Changchi looked at the contract and discovered that the other half that had been torn away contained the seal and signature.

He pointed at Huang Kui's face and said, "You... you have to pay me."

Huang Kui took out nine hundred yuan and placed it on the desk.

"All you have to do is write one line and you can take the money," he said.

"Write what?"

"That you'll disappear from the county town."

"Is this his territory?"

"More than that."

"Then I don't want the money."

"What do you want?"

"I'm going to tell all the workers to go to his house and get what they're owed."

So saying, Wang Changchi turned and left.

Huang Kui told his two assistants to bring him back and hold him. Wang Changchi fought free of them but they held him again until he stopped struggling, then they let him go.

"You took the man's money to replace him and then you go and harass him," said Huang Kui. "Can you still be trusted?"

"If it's a matter of trust," said Wang Changchi, "then everyone will have to agree to it, not just me."

"Take your wages."

"Do I have to write an affidavit?"

"If he doesn't owe you wages, then it's a matter of trust. He trusts you, you trust him."

"What about what he owes the others?"

"Why are you sticking your nose into everything?"

Wang Changchi shut his mouth at once, and Wang Huai and Liu Shuangju came into his mind along with that dilapidated house and their difficulties. In truth, he wanted to seize the nine hundred yuan, but at the same time he didn't want to back down.

"How can he not pay what he owes?" he said.

"Because his dad is Lin Gang."

Wang Changchi hesitated. He knew he couldn't beat Lin Jiabo, much less care for anyone else, and he did need the money badly, so he reached for it.

"You have to disappear if you take the money," said Huang Kui, "otherwise no one will be able to guarantee your safety."

His hand suddenly shook as if it had touched fire and he pulled it back in a flash.

十七 · SEVENTEEN

LATE AT NIGHT, WANG CHANGCHI was walking back to the worksite. There was no electricity in the place, and it was pitch-black. Entering through the gate, he was set upon by two men who beat and kicked him. Wang Changchi shouted for help as he fought back. He hit one of them on the nose four or five times and even heard the crunch as the bridge of his nose broke. But all at once, he was clubbed twice on the head and stabbed twice in the belly. His strength vanished in an instant. By the time Liu Jianping and the others came running out of the workers' shed with torches, he was already lying in a pool of blood.

Liu Jianping and the others reported it to the police, who took Wang Changchi to hospital. He received immediate attention because he had been brought in by the police. That night, Officer Wang of the Township Police Station received a call from the duty office of the police station in the county town. That same night, Officer Wang went to the village in the valley and beat on the gate of Wang Huai's place till it opened. The following morning, Wang Huai asked Second Uncle and Liu Baitiao to carry him up to the roadside. The Wang family, including He Xiaowen, boarded the bus for the county town.

Wang Changchi was woken by the sound of weeping. Off and on for a week, the sound of weeping had been a companion to his ears. The sound was like wind in the trees, flowing water, chirruping cicadas, sometimes there sometimes not, sometimes weak sometimes strong. On the seventh day, he clearly heard Liu Shuangju crying. He called, "Mum". Tears welled up in his red eyes and rolled down his face to his neck. He Xiaowen turned her back to secretly wipe away her tears. Wang Huai did his best to restrain himself, but moisture appeared at the corners of his eyes. The hospital room erupted with the sound of weeping. After crying themselves out, they rested. After resting a bit, they resumed crying. They had no better way to express themselves. In addition to crying, they wiped each other's tears away. Liu Shuangju wiped away Wang Changchi's tears; Wang Huai wiped away Liu Shuangju's tears; Wang Changchi wiped away Wang Huai's tears; He Xiaowen wiped away Liu Shuangju's tears; and Liu Shuangju wiped away He Xiaowen's tears. Wet with tears, their fingers were like salted meat.

Liu Shuangju pushed Wang Huai to the police station on Little River Street.

"Have the perpetrators been caught?" they asked the policeman there.

"It doesn't happen in the blink of an eye," replied the policeman. "There's no way it can be done so quickly."

Wang Huai and Liu Shuangju sat in the duty room and were still sitting there when the shifts changed at noon. When the night shift left, they were still sitting there. All they each had to eat the whole day was a bowl of rice noodles.

"So you think this is a hotel?" asked the policeman.

"We don't have the money to pay for Changchi's hospital stay," said Wang Huai, "so we beg you to arrest the perpetrators as quickly as possible."

"We don't even know who the perpetrators are," replied the policeman, "so how can we arrest them?"

"Is he conscious?" asked another policeman.

"He has been for days," said Wang Huai.

When night fell and the street lights went on, they were still sitting in the duty office.

"You can go," said the policeman. "When there's any news, we'll let you know."

"We don't have any place to go," said Wang Huai, "so we'll wait here."

"I'm getting off work," said the policeman, "so wait outside the door."

Liu Shuangju pushed Wang Huai to the doorway and the policeman shut the door with a thud.

The following day, two policemen showed up in Wang Changchi's hospital room. One was surnamed Lu and the other Wei. Lu asked the questions while Wei took notes. Wang Changchi explained what had happened the night of the attack and, based on their strength and the way they held him and their smell, he was certain that the perpetrators were Huang Kui's two underlings. This was because two hours before he was attacked, the pair of them had held him fast in Huang Kui's office. The memory was fresh in his mind, shoulders, legs and nose. The policemen asked him not to jump to any conclusions.

"I broke the nose of one of them," said Wang Changchi. "All you have to do is check and see if one of Huang Kui's underlings has a broken nose, and everything will be cleared up."

The policemen offered no comment but tried to make him think if he had any enemies among his co-workers. Had he borrowed money from anyone? Had he stolen someone else's girlfriend? As they asked this, they eyed He Xiaowen. They asked her where she was from and if she had ever had a boyfriend before. They asked far and wide, even asking about Liu Baitiao, Wang Dong, Zhang Xianhua, Second Uncle, and He Xiaowen's older brother and his wife. Since Wang Changchi felt they were intentionally avoiding Huang Kui, he didn't feel like saying anything.

"If you're not willing to answer our questions," said the policemen, "it'll be hard to break the case."

"I've said everything that needs to be said," said Wang Changchi. "The only thing I've left out is the perpetrators' names."

Officer Lu stood up and Officer Wei closed his notebook.

Every day, Wang Huai and Liu Shuangju kept watch at the door of the police station, observing as the policemen came and went and asking, "Have the perpetrators been caught?" As it had become an everyday occurrence, their questions elicited not a single response from the police, regardless of any looks, expressions or nods of the head. Hearing the question so many times, they had worked out how to shield themselves from it. But Wang Huai and Liu Shuangju continued to hope desperately, thinking there would be an answer. When the policemen were discussing a case inside, Wang Huai and Liu Shuangju would hold their breath and listen carefully. The fragments of speech that drifted out through the cracks in the windows had nothing to do with Wang Changchi's case. Not once did they hear them speak of it. One day at noon, Wang Huai latched onto the trouser legs of Officer Lu.

"When will the case finally be solved?" he asked.

"For the moment, there are no clues," replied Officer Lu.

Wang Huai rolled out of his wheelchair and, lying prone on the ground, kowtowed.

"Will kowtowing bring out the perpetrators?" asked Officer Lu.

Wang Huai continued to bang his head, each time with more force, so much so that the floor ached. Officer Lu pulled his legs from Wang Huai's grip, got on his motorcycle and left. Liu Shuangju went to help Wang Huai up, but he pushed her hands away. Wang Huai just lay prone on the ground, kowtowing to anyone who came or went, saying to each and every one, "Please help us". Wang Huai kowtowed until his head was covered with blood. Liu Shuangju wiped his face with a paper towel, and each time she wiped, his face would quiver.

With nothing left to do, Wang Huai pointed at the other side of Little River Street with his bamboo pole. Liu Shuangju knew what he meant and proceeded to push him to Huang Kui's office. Huang Kui was there, as were his two underlings, one of whom had a purplish-black nose, indicating it had been fractured and the blood had clotted.

Staring at Huang Kui, Wang Huai said, "You even attack your classmate. You really are mean."

Huang Kui did not respond but just looked coldly at him.

"Why?" asked Wang Huai.

"Ask him," said Huang Kui.

"Did he offend you?"

"Worse than offend."

"So you sent your underlings to kill him."

"If that were the case, would he still be alive? It was just a warning."

"Don't you have any respect for the law?"

"Sure. The police station is right there. Get them to come over and arrest me."

"Fuck your mother. Do bullies like you really exist?"

In a fit of rage, Wang Huai thrust his bamboo pole at Huang Kui's face. Huang Kui dodged. The pole slashed wildly, but because he used so much force, Wang Huai ended up sprawled on the floor.

"Don't be such a fool," said Huang Kui. "If you have what it takes, get up and take two steps."

Liu Shuangju helped Wang Huai back into his wheelchair. Furious, Wang Huai trembled all over and was ready to spit fire. He clenched his fists intending to stand up, but his legs refused to cooperate. Since his fall, his legs had completely atrophied, his thighs were no bigger than his calves, and his calves were as thin as his arms. Now, even though he wanted to eat his opponent alive, his mouth wouldn't reach. Even though he wanted to flatten him, his arms weren't long enough. In a matter of seconds, his anger drained away, as if in desolation his throat had been cut. His hands went limp, his backside settled heavily, his chest rose and fell, and he even had trouble breathing and coughed without stopping.

"Given your condition," Huang Kui said, "you should behave yourself and take Wang Changchi back to the village and not be out causing a ruckus."

Wang Huai coughed vigorously and spat a mouthful of phlegm in Huang Kui's face. Huang Kui swore and even boxed his ears several times. Liu Shuangju charged at Huang Kui with her head. The two underlings pulled Liu Shuangju away and threw her out of the door. Before Liu Shuangju could pick herself up, she saw the wheelchair come flying out of the room and, describing an arc, land in front of her, shattering into a pile of wood. Wang Huai landed on top of the pile.

"Murderer," cursed Liu Shuangju, "demon, son-of-a-bitch, heartless, worse than an animal, you deserve to be hacked to pieces..."

The roll-up door came whooshing down with a crash.

Wang Huai lifted his finger and pointed across Little River Street. Liu Shuangju carried him across on her back. They went from this side of the street to that and back. Officers Lu and Wei both happened to be in.

"Huang Kui admitted to it," said Wang Huai. "Go and arrest him for me."

Officer Wei took out his notebook and flipped it open.

"We questioned Huang Kui," he said, "and he didn't admit to it and there is no proof."

"Isn't the bloke with the banged-up nose proof?" asked Wang Huai.

"We questioned him," said Officer Lu, "and he said Wang Changchi was beaten after he injured his nose and because Wang Changchi saw that his nose was injured, he fabricated everything to frame him."

"Why would he frame him?" asked Wang Huai.

"He said that Wang Changchi was afraid if the perpetrators weren't arrested, no one would pay his hospital bill," said Officer Wei.

"Crap and nonsense," said Wang Huai.

"They also said that Wang Changchi is paranoid on account of persecution."

"Was Changchi really beaten or not?"

"He's in the hospital."

"Was he really stabbed twice or not?"

"The wounds are there."

"Then is the persecution real or is it paranoia?" asked Wang Huai.

Lu and Wei replied simultaneously, "It's real."

"I swear to Heaven," said Wang Huai, "Changchi has never told a lie."

"The problem is that we can't prove that Wang Changchi broke that bloke's nose," said Officer Wei. "Everyone has a different story, so we can't form a judgement."

"Huang Kui just admitted to it," said Wang Huai.

"Who heard him?" asked Officer Lu. "Was he recorded?"

"You've got to be joking. How can someone like me afford a recorder?"

"Then again," said Officer Wei, "if you had a recorder, he wouldn't have admitted to anything."

Pointing at Liu Shuangju, Wang Huai said, "She can bear me out, she heard him too."

"You're all from the same family with a common interest," said Officer Lu, "so you can't testify on one another's behalf."

"So is the case solved or not?" asked Wang Huai.

"Up to now, there hasn't been a breakthrough in the case," replied Officer Wei.

"Maybe solving another case will help us break this one," offered Officer Lu. "What we need is luck."

Wang Huai's mind snapped. It was hopeless, so hopeless he wanted to smash his head against the wall, but he couldn't, because everyone in the family, young and old, was waiting for him to decide what to do.

十八 · EIGHTEEN

THE NIGHT BEFORE GOING TO THE CITY, Wang Huai had borrowed two thousand yuan in emergency funds from Second Uncle and Zhang Wu. They couldn't bring themselves to spend any of the money and it had remained sewn inside Liu Shuangju's pocket. Every day, the hospital had pressed him to pay the medical expenses, but Wang Huai and Liu Shuangju had said they had no money and that the perpetrators could pay after they were caught. Angered, the hospital cut off Wang Changchi's medicine. Fearing

Wang Changchi might be in pain, she tore open the pocket and pulled out the money as if she were pulling out a breast to feed a baby.

"Once we hand over this two thousand yuan," said Wang Changchi, "the hospital will assume we have the wherewithal to pay, and once they assume that, we will have to go on until we can no longer pay."

Liu Shuangju didn't understand and turned to look at Wang Huai.

"What he means," said Wang Huai, "is that you should hide the money and not hand it over."

"Will Changchi be able to bear the pain?" asked Liu Shuangju.

"The big wounds have already healed," said Wang Changchi, "so it's not that painful."

Wang Huai lifted Wang Changchi's gown and examined the two knife wounds.

"The redness and swelling are gone," said Wang Changchi, "and the wounds are dry, so they won't become infected."

Wang Huai pressed gently on the wounds with a finger. Wang Changchi secretly gritted his teeth.

"Can you really bear the pain?" asked Wang Huai.

"When I was little and injured myself and bled," said Wang Changchi, "didn't it always heal on its own?"

"I can't do much," said Wang Huai, "so you'll have to learn to grit your teeth."

Wang Changchi gritted his teeth and nodded.

After Huang Kui and his cohorts destroyed Wang Huai's wooden wheelchair, Liu Shuangju had to carry him on her back whenever they went anywhere. Her back was soaked in sweat and scarcely had a chance to dry. Wang Huai felt ever heavier and harder to carry, more like a burden, so she pulled three notes from her pocket and bought a metal wheelchair. The wheelchair had tyres, an imitation leather seat cushion and brakes, and the person sitting in the chair could turn the wheels with their hands. When Wang Huai took his seat, his backside stung as if he had sat on a globular cactus, and he even felt constipated, all on account of having spent so much money.

Every night, Liu Shuangju spread two mats on the floor of Wang Changchi's hospital room, one for Wang Huai to sleep on, and the other for her and He Xiaowen. At first, the hospital was opposed and forced them to leave the room, but though the world is big, they had no other place to go and would slip back in around midnight. Once it had happened several times, the hospital just silently accepted the situation. After stopping Wang Changchi's medication, they were frequently startled awake by him talking in his sleep. The one thing that Wang Changchi shouted most often was, "Huang Kui, I'm going to kill you." Hearing Wang Changchi shouting about killing, they couldn't go back to sleep. Liu Shuangju got up off the floor and gave Wang Changchi water to drink and soup to eat and wiped him with a moist towel. Wang Changchi had a slight fever for several days, and Liu Shuangju was so concerned she wanted to go and pay for the medicine in secret, but as she started to walk out of the door, Wang Changchi woke up, as if her feet were linked to his nerves.

"If you pay," he said, "you're no mother of mine."

Unable to do anything else, Liu Shuangju rubbed him constantly with cold water until the fever broke.

Even though his temperature was normal, Wang Changchi continued to talk in his sleep, as if doing so would reduce the pain. Unable to sleep, Wang Huai would climb into his wheelchair and listen. Still, the words he uttered most frequently were, "Huang Kui, I'm going to kill you." It was like a cassette recording playing the same thing over and over again. Sometimes as he spoke, he would make a hacking motion. Wang Huai thought he was awake and shook him only to find he was asleep. Worried, he shook him awake. Wang Changchi opened his eyes and looked at Wang Huai in his wheelchair.

"Why aren't you in bed?" he said.

"Do you know what you just said?" asked Wang Huai.

"I know. Sometimes what I say in my sleep wakes me up," said Wang Changchi.

"Don't shout it again. Just accept it."

To Wang Changchi, that didn't sound like something Wang Huai would say. Never had he admitted defeat or lowered his head in anyone's presence. Wang Changchi couldn't see his face, just the top of his head, on which there was a good deal of grey hair.

"Go to sleep," said Wang Changchi. "I won't be any trouble."

After saying this, he closed his eyes. Wang Huai knew he was only pretending to sleep and trying to comfort him. So he turned out the light, climbed out of his wheelchair and lay down on the mat to sleep. They all pretended to breathe regularly and fall asleep, allowing the others to relax, but a train seemed to be chugging around in their chests... After dozing for a while, Wang Changchi rolled over on his side and stole a glance at Wang Huai resting on the floor. Even though Wang Huai's eyes were closed, he could still feel those burning eyes on him, but he didn't move, pretending to be asleep. Wang Changchi looked at the three shapes on the floor for more than a full minute before rolling over. Quietly, Wang Huai opened his eyes and looked at the grey outside the window, the faint light of the street lights on the trees and the individual leaves vaguely discernible. Wang Changchi rolled over again. In the dark, their eyes met but immediately looked away, each unwilling to acknowledge the other and to be considerate of the other's feelings.

"If all you think about is revenge," said Wang Huai, "your recovery will be slow."

"I swear I won't talk in my sleep again," said Wang Changchi.

But the talk in his sleep of killing people continued from deep in his subconscious. Late every night, Wang Huai would sit beside his bed and the moment he heard a "Huang...", he would poke him to wake him. Wide-eyed he'd look at Wang Huai, swallow a mouthful of water, bite his lip, close his eyes and start all over again. Wang Huai was like a faithful night watchman, sitting in his wheelchair and occasionally dozing off. Even if Wang Changchi bit his tongue, it wouldn't stop him from talking in his sleep. But each time Wang Huai poked him, it would cut him off.

Gradually, he spoke less in his sleep until he stopped completely. His health got better by the day, improving the quality of everyone's rest. Late one night, they suddenly heard Wang Changchi call out to Xiaowen in his sleep. "Xiaowen, Xiaowen..." Hearing him call out in this way, they were elated. He Xiaowen stood up immediately, her teardrops falling audibly.

"I've cared for him all this time," she said, "and he finally calls my name."

During the day, while Liu Shuangju and He Xiaowen were out, Wang Huai closed the door and asked, "What do you think of Xiaowen?"

Looking at the ceiling, Wang Changchi replied, "She's a fine girl."

"Are you willing to marry her?"

"Why would she ever consider me in my present state?"

"If she didn't like you, she would've left a long time ago."

"What does she like about me? My troubles?"

For a moment, Wang Huai made no reply and turned his head to look out of the window. Beneath the trees was a lawn over which two colourful butterflies were fluttering.

"Give her a little hope," he said.

"But I have nothing."

"Tell her about the PA Company and that after you are well, you'll take her to the provincial capital. She likes the city."

"The PA Company was a lie."

" If I hadn't deceived your mother at first, she never would've married me."

"I'm not that low."

"So you plan to waste your life in this little county town?"

Wang Huai turned back. Fearing to meet his eyes, Wang Changchi turned to look out of the window. The two butterflies had already flown over the treetops. He thought, If only I had wings too, then I'd fly away and not have to pay the hospital bill.

"Xiaowen could go with you to the provincial capital and work. You could get married and start a career," said Wang Huai.

"You think too much."

"At the very least you want to be nicer to her. No one else would be willing to sleep on the floor with us."

Wang Changchi asked Liu Shuangju to buy a small blackboard, which he hung on the wall at the head of the bed. Every day, he taught He Xiaowen ten characters. Wide-eyed, she learned from him, character stroke by character stroke. She learned 吃, the character for "eat"; 穿, the character for "wear"; 住, the character for "live"; and even 行, the character for "walk". He could teach her some characters many times, but she wouldn't remember how to write them. He'd call her stupid, but she wouldn't give up. She'd think for ages, her head tilted, and then write 料 for 科 or write 渴 for 喝. Occasionally, she'd get angry, and throw the chalk to the floor and say, "I'm not your match when it comes to writing, but I am your match when it comes to cooking and slopping the pigs." So saying, she'd squat and cry, cry saying she wasn't smart, cry saying her family was too poor to send her to school.

"If you want to move to the city," said Wang Changchi, "you'll have to know a thousand characters."

He Xiaowen's mouth fell open and she said, "That many?"

"It's like saving money," said Wang Changchi. "If you save ten yuan a day, you'll have a thousand yuan in a hundred days.

"My brain's not that big."

"If you don't know a thousand characters, you'll be cheated when you get to the city."

"I might not know them, but you do, right?"

"You won't be able to hang onto my shirttails every day, will you?"

He Xiaowen thought about it and saw that he was right, so she stood up, bit her lip, and read and repeated after Wang Changchi:

"I..."

"I."

"Want..."

"Want."

"Revenge..."

"Revenge."

十九 · NINETEEN

DURING THE DAY, WANG HUAI AND LIU SHUANGJU did not stay in the hospital room, giving some space to Wang Changchi and He Xiaowen. They even thought about pasting a "double-happiness" character on the window. Liu Shuangju would only wheel Wang Huai back at night. For all his stoicism, Wang Huai looked exhausted, and before Liu Shuangju could finish sponging him, he'd fall asleep in his wheelchair.

Wang Changchi felt guilty and asked, "Why do you leave early and come back late every day?"

"If we stay here," said Liu Shuangju, "we'll affect Xiaowen learning characters."

"It doesn't matter," said Xiaowen. "I'm always at the same level whether you're here or not."

"Actually, Xiaowen and I don't have all that much to say in private," said Wang Changchi.

"We have our own business to take care of," said Liu Shuangju.

"Did you go to see Huang Kui?" asked Wang Changchi.

As if jolted awake by an electrical shock, Wang Huai said, "No, no, we went to the police station."

Wang Changchi and Xiaowen looked at them as if those were two new words that had to be looked at over and over again until they were understood.

"If we don't go and push them," said Wang Huai, "they'll forget about the case. If they forget, no one will solve it. And if no one solves it, then no one will pay the hospital bill."

"Has any progress been made on the case?" asked Wang Changchi.

"I even kowtow," said Wang Huai, "but still they just shake their heads."

Although weak, Wang Changchi dragged himself sneakily out of the hospital and went and stood under a tree on Little River

Street, diagonally across from Huang Kui's company. The door was open, and the jeep was parked out in front. Although it was autumn, the sun was scorching and bright, making the shadow of the jeep resemble liquid black oil. The air was as stuffy and oppressive as that of summer. People came and went on the street, and the sounds of sellers and bells were constantly heard. Wang Changchi's eyes were fixed on the jeep. He wanted to get close to it, become familiar with it, and even make use of it, but now lacked the nerve to approach it. He had to do it stealthily. Thinking of the result made his pulse rush, his mind go wild and his whole body delight. For two full hours, his pulse was quickened by the jeep, giddy, sweat soaked through the back of his clothes, and the ground spun so that he couldn't regain his balance even by sitting. He sat, leaning against a tree, squinting for a while. When he felt somewhat improved he stood up, still leaning against the tree, steadying himself before slowly heading back to the hospital.

Lying in bed, he started thinking about that jeep, remembering with longing its doors, tyres, steering wheel, gear stick, headlights, engine and brake pedal... He thought until his head was ready to explode, but he still couldn't come up with a plan to start. He found it strange and too technical, so, slipping out of the hospital again, he went to a car repair shop near the bus station. He sat on a stone in front of the shop, watching the mechanics with their greasy hands remove tyres, dismantle engines, take off brake pads, and then reinstall the repaired parts.

After he'd watched for two afternoons, Master Tu the mechanic asked, "What are you thinking of doing?"

"I'd like to be your apprentice," said Wang Changchi.

"You can be my apprentice," said Master Tu, "but can you lift two tyres at the same time?"

Wang Changchi stacked one tyre on top of another and tried to lift them, but before he had them an inch off the ground, he was already huffing and puffing.

Master Tu gave him a kick and said, "Get out of here."

"Wait till I'm fully recovered," explained Wang Changchi,

"and it won't be a problem."

Master Tu ignored him. Wang Changchi poured tea for Tu, swept up, wiped the table and helped him wash his clothes.

Every afternoon before slipping out of the hospital, Wang Changchi told Xiaowen, "I'm going to borrow money from my teacher and classmates."

Only Xiaowen was left in the hospital room. She couldn't go anywhere except the bathroom because the nurse would look in from time to time to make sure someone was in the room, otherwise they might suspect Wang Changchi of trying to run off without paying the bill. Xiaowen became a hostage and each time the nurse poked her head in, she'd always say Wang Changchi has gone to borrow money. Although this is what she said, she was in a panic, because each time Wang Changchi returned, he had no money in his pockets. She had her doubts, so one day she climbed out of the window and followed him all the way to the repair shop. She watched as he assisted the master, sometimes handing him a nut, sometimes handing him a hose and sometimes some rubber, sometimes quietly squatting and watching from the side.

The next morning, Wang Huai and Liu Shuangju left. Xiaowen started to pack her things. She neatly folded her clothes and placed them in a soft bag. After packing the clothes, she packed her toothbrush, toothpaste, hairbrush, mirror and even rubber bands.

"Don't forget your towel," said Wang Changchi.

Xiaowen removed the towel from the hook and put it in a plastic bag. Wang Changchi took out two hundred yuan and handed it to her. Xiaowen reached out to take it and saw that his hands were black with grease. Xiaowen was touched and tears fell from her eyes. Wang Changchi wanted to wipe them away but pulled his hand back as he reached out.

"You've been away from home such a long time," he said, "you really should return."

Xiaowen wiped her eyes several times, turned her back and asked, "Do you plan to be a mechanic?"

Startled, Wang Changchi asked, "How do you know?"

"I followed you."

Wang Changchi's face instantly went pale and he asked, "Did you tell anyone?"

Xiaowen shook her head.

"Don't tell anyone about it."

"You know so many words," said Xiaowen, "why not go to the big city and work your arse off?"

"Because..." Wang Changchi stuttered.

"Because?"

Xiaowen turned around, tears streaming down her face. Looking at her reddish face, fair skin, jet-black hair, limpid eyes and long eyelashes, he didn't have the heart to deceive her. She bit her lip as if waiting for the answer.

"Can you keep a secret?" asked Wang Changchi.

"Why do men always want me to keep secrets?" she asked.

"Because they want to tell you the truth."

She nodded.

"I've been going to the repair shop because I want to learn about technology so I can ruin Huang Kui's jeep in a car accident and get revenge for being knifed twice."

"You're not afraid of being caught by the police?"

"I won't admit to it."

"Then they'll interrogate me."

"You won't admit to it either."

"What if they use torture?"

"That's why it's best if you left. You won't know anything."

Xiaowen lowered her head and asked, "You can't be a filial son, get a wife or pass your days in peace unless you do this? Uncle Wang and Auntie Liu are pitiful with nothing left but bones. Do you have the heart to make them even more pitiful with nothing left but a few broken bits? Think about it, if you end up sacrificing yourself, who will support them? Who will hold and comfort them on their deathbeds?"

"But I can't swallow this crap," said Wang Changchi.

Xiaowen grabbed his trouser leg and asked, "Will that relieve the anger?"

"Sorry, Xiaowen, sorry..." said Wang Changchi, trembling all over.

Xiaowen took out the damp towel and hung it back on the wall. Wang Changchi asked her to let him leave for a bit.

"This time I'm really going to borrow some money," he said.

Xiaowen pleaded to accompany him. They went to Huang Kui's office. Huang Kui never expected to see him again and was stunned.

"You're still alive?" he said.

"Barely," said Wang Changchi.

"Your girlfriend's good-looking," said Huang Kui.

"If you pay me the wages owed me," said Wang Changchi, "I'll leave right away."

"You can ask whoever owes you wages for them," replied Huang Kui.

"You tore up my contract, so who can I ask?"

"Why were you so shy at the time? For a bit of stupid dignity, you made me so miserable."

Wang Changchi and Xiaowen both found Huang Kui's words a little unexpected. Xiaowen lifted his shirt and pointed at the knife wounds in his belly.

"Are you as miserable as him?" she asked.

Huang Kui lifted his hand. "To smooth out your case cost me five digits," he said. "That's not miserable?"

Wang Changchi stood up angrily to hit Huang Kui. Xiaowen clung on and stopped him.

"Doesn't everyone have some hatred and want revenge?" Huang Kui asked. "But first you need the capital."

Wang Changchi struggled free of Xiaowen, picked up a bench and was just about to hurl it when he suddenly heard Wang Huai shout, "Changchi..."

Wang Changchi's arms trembled as he turned his head and saw Liu Shuangju push Wang Huai in unhindered through the front door.

He was holding a pile of brand-new renminbi in his hands.

"Don't fight," said Wang Huai. "The PA Company sent the

money for the hospital bill."

Knowing the PA Company was fake, Huang Kui laughed grimly. Wang Changchi smashed the bench on the floor, breaking three of its four legs and sending splinters flying.

"If the bench were insured, you could break it," said Huang Kui.

The entire family tried to get him to leave. They pushed him, rubbed him, and just like kneading dough, they made his hard body pliant. Heads lowered and feeling disheartened, the four of them returned to the hospital. Wang Huai handed the money to Xiaowen and got her and Liu Shuangju to go to the business office to settle accounts. Wang Changchi and Wang Huai faced each other in the hospital room. Dark-faced, Wang Changchi sat on the bed.

"I lifted both hands in surrender," Wang Huai said, "so why are you still blowing the bugle charge?"

"By the laws of Nature, it's unacceptable," said Wang Changchi.

"There are no laws of Nature. We've been losers from birth, we lost at the starting line."

"I was stabbed, and I have to pay for it myself. Damn! Is this how I encourage domestic productivity?"

"It's not all bad. Some nice people gave us the money."

"Where'd the money come from?"

"Can you keep a secret from Xiaowen?"

"Don't tell me you stole it?"

"Day after day I got that money by begging."

Wang Changchi's expression suddenly changed, startled like a prostitute being arrested in the act.

"You became a beggar?"

"I begged and got people's spare change. I was afraid that Xiaowen wouldn't believe me, so I exchanged it all for big bills at the bank."

"Don't you feel ashamed?"

"Ashamed or not, we had to stay in the hospital. Do you know how much it costs to act like that?"

Wang Changchi lowered his head in shame, saying, "I was the one who brought you to this."

"If you want to blame anyone, blame your grandfather. Blame him for not joining the revolution back then."

二十 · TWENTY

THE VILLAGE IN THE VALLEY IN THE MIDDLE OF AUTUMN, red and yellow up and down the mountain. The wind blew, the trees rustled, and the ground was covered with fallen leaves. High skies, pale clouds, cool temperatures. Pure white kitchen smoke rose above the roofs, like milk squirting towards, the sky. In twos and threes, oxen grazed on the slopes. Zhang Wu's black horse sported in the paddy field. The Wang Dongs, husband and wife, sat on the rooftop drying floor peeling corn, the yellow cobs piled high as their chins. A row of clothes was hanging in front of Zhang Xianhua's window drying in the sun and flapping in the wind. Although the water in the well was low, the sound of flowing water was more audible, like someone playing a musical instrument. The garden at Wang Huai's house was already bare. A single cabbage, which looked as if it were made of jade, stood in Second Uncle's garden. The windows were full of cobwebs. On the door was written one line, "Wang Huai, where have you gone?" The words were written using a white stone and had faded due to the wind, sun and rain. The writing looked like Guang Sheng's from the neighbouring village.

They pushed open the door, swept, chopped firewood, carried water, lit a fire, washed the dishes, aired the quilts and retrieved the two piglets they had entrusted to Second Uncle. Life resumed. Wang Changchi discovered a few dried fruit on the plum tree at the corner of the house. He climbed the tree and picked them and put them in Xiaowen's mouth. Biting down, Xiaowen found them sweet and sour, and just like in the advert, they tasted astounding.

Wang Huai got someone to choose the day and prepared a feast for twenty tables, thus making Wang Changchi and He

Xiaowen legal. That night Xiaowen and Changchi sat on the marriage bed.

"Are you really going to take me to the provincial capital?" asked Xiaowen.

"And if I say we aren't going?" asked Wang Changchi.

"Then you're a cheat."

"Why did you want to marry a cheat?"

For a moment Xiaowen didn't reply. She sat on the edge of the bed, covering her buttons with both hands.

"Perhaps after entering the nuptial chamber we won't want to go anywhere else," suggested Wang Changchi.

"Impossible," said Xiaowen.

"If you haven't done it before, how do you know it's impossible?"

Xiaowen blushed deeply.

Moving her hands away, Wang Changchi said, "The wedding banquet has ended, the procedure is done, and it's too late for regrets."

Xiaowen poked his nose and said, "You're bad."

"For this life, I'll only be bad to you."

"You're a cheat."

Wang Changchi raised his hand and promised to be good. Xiaowen undressed. Actually, even if Changchi had not promised, she still would have got undressed. She waited for him to do so first because she wanted him to pay a little attention. She had undressed as he expected, but after she did that whiteness, that size vastly exceeded his expectations. Her whiteness illuminated the room and her size for the moment made the bedroom seem cramped. Wang Changchi looked for a long time before he reluctantly extinguished the light.

Each time Wang Huai heard the wooden bed creaking in the next room, he'd tap Liu Shuangju to wake her so that she could also listen, for if he didn't get her to listen it was like eating alone and couldn't be enjoyed. Late at night the two of them would listen intently, once, twice, three times... It was even more exciting than counting money. The sound gave them hope and they longed to have a grandchild soon, to the extent that every morning after getting up Liu Shuangju would examine Xiaowen's figure to see if there was any change. When she was looked over in such a way, Xiaowen didn't lift her head.

Wang Huai quietly reminded Liu Shuangju, "Have you forgotten? The change doesn't start with the figure but with vomiting."

Slapping her thigh, Liu Shuangju said, "Look at me, I'm so anxious I've totally forgotten how it was."

They used the cash gifts from the wedding to pay off Zhang Wu and his Second Uncle. Second Uncle didn't want the money back. All he wanted was for Wang Changchi to help him build a multi-storey house. Every day, Wang Changchi went over to Second Uncle's place to do masonry work. The house rose a bit each day. When Xiaowen had some free time, she'd go over and make tea, pour water and carry bricks.

In the evening Xiaowen would ask, "When are we going to the provincial capital?"

"We have to at least finish building Second Uncle's house," said Wang Changchi.

"I'm stuck in the house every day," said Xiaowen. "I haven't seen a car in ages."

Wang Changchi felt guilty so he asked his uncle for a day off to take Xiaowen to town to go shopping. They bought oil and salt, clothes, perfumed soap, cosmetics, laundry detergent and canvas shoes. They also sat on the roadside watching the cars coming and going. While Xiaowen was absorbed in watching the cars, Wang Changchi went to the post office to make a phone call. After that, they both ate a bowl of rice noodles and then they started back, singing popular songs all the way home.

In the afternoon, three days after visiting town, Wang Changchi and Second Uncle were working on the house when suddenly they saw two policemen appear under the maple tree in the gap. Their build and gait seemed familiar to Wang Changchi. As they approached, they reached the village well where they bent over and drank for a while, after which they walked past Zhang Wu's house, the Wang Dongs' place, their figures blocked from view for a moment by a house only to reappear at the corner of Zhang Xianhua's place. Sure enough, it was Officer Lu and Officer Wei. Wang Changchi figured they had solved the case, so he quickly slid down off the scaffolding and headed toward them. Wearing serious expressions, they watched Wang Changchi for a long time as if they were looking to see if he had lice. Wang Changchi apologised and then bent over and brushed off his trousers. A cloud of cement dust rose from his trousers to enshroud him like fog. The two policemen pinched their noses and turned away, waiting for the wind to carry away that cloud of dust before approaching.

"Let's find somewhere to chat," said Officer Lu.

"Come to my house," said Wang Changchi.

Officer Wei nodded. Wang Changchi took them to his house. Wang Huai, Liu Shuangju and Xiaowen all expected that they had come bearing good news and hurried off to the kitchen to prepare some food.

"Let's find a quiet place," said the policemen.

Wang Changchi led them to the bedroom. They inspected the door and the window and found they could be overheard, as more and more villagers were piling into the house and heading to the bedroom to have a look, some even pressing their ears to the wall.

"Let's find another place," said Officer Lu.

Wang Changchi led them to the tea plantation behind the house. They took a seat under a tea tree. The curious villagers gathered behind the house. Officer Wei dispersed them. The conversation began.

"What have you been doing recently?" they asked Wang Changchi. "Where have you been? Who have you been in contact with?"

Wang Changchi answered each of their questions, but they did not seem satisfied.

"Have you or have you not been to the county town?" they asked him repeatedly.

"Once and for all, no," said Wang Changchi. "I'm not making anything up."

Halfway through the questioning, Wang Changchi realised they hadn't come to deliver good news. So in responding to their questions, he seemed to figure things out and came across as if he didn't care. He even wanted to stop Liu Shuangju and Xiaowen from cooking for them, but it was too late. The smell of rice and meat wafted from under the eaves of the house. The aroma of the meat seemed to distract them.

Taking a deep breath, Officer Lu said, "The air in the village is really good."

"That's enough questions for today," said Officer Wei, closing his notebook.

"What are you guys really investigating?" asked Wang Changchi.

"I'll tell you when the time comes," said Officer Lu, "but you must keep today's conversation a secret, otherwise you will suffer the consequences."

"Have you arrested the men who stabbed me?" asked Wang Changchi.

As if prearranged, they both shook their heads at the same time.

Wang Changchi ate lunch with them, assuming they would leave, never dreaming that they would inquire individually of Xiaowen, Wang Huai, Liu Shuangju and Second Uncle. After asking questions of the Wang family, they still did not seem satisfied and then went and questioned Zhang Wu, Zhang Xianhua, Wang Dong and Liu Baitiao. They asked the same thing, which was, Has Wang Changchi been in the village all along? Everyone testified that Wang Changchi had not left since returning to the village. Fearing they did not believe him, Second Uncle pointed at the half-built brick house. They looked and saw white bars drawn on the wall, next to each was written a date, indicating the amount of work Wang Changchi and Second Uncle had done that day. They counted the white lines and discovered that one day had not been recorded, so off they went to ask Wang Changchi about it.

"Xiaowen and I went shopping that day," said Wang

Changchi.

Officer Lu was furious. "Why didn't you tell us you went shopping?" he asked. "Were you intentionally hiding something?"

"Do I have to inform you of every fart I made?" Wang Changchi retorted.

"Of all the people we questioned, not one mentioned you went shopping."

"No one said anything, because no one saw any connection between shopping and what you are investigating."

"Of course there is a connection."

"What connection?"

"The day after you went shopping, someone took Huang Kui's life."

Wang Changchi was dumbstruck as if hit over the head with a club, his head suddenly seemed to explode, and just as suddenly returned to normal, and the pain vanished.

He abruptly laughed and said, "So he's finally dead! You wouldn't take him, so Heaven did."

"Are you in any way connected with this?" asked Officer Wei.

"How I wish I was," said Wang Changchi, "but I don't have what it damn well takes, I don't have the damn guts, I'm too damn timid and weak, and I'm a damn sorry excuse for a human being."

Officer Lu watched his every move and listened to every word he said, but without discovering anything out of the ordinary. Officer Wei flipped through his notebook.

"Xiaowen said that you once thought about murdering him," he said.

"I not only thought about it," said Wang Changchi, "but would've done it if they hadn't stopped me, and if I hadn't been afraid no one would look after my parents."

"How did you plan to do it?"

"I thought of tampering with his brakes so that he'd die in a crash."

"That's exactly how Huang Kui died. How is it that his death and what you thought match perfectly?"

"People who pay a debt of gratitude are all different, but people who want revenge are all the same."

White clouds floated on the horizon, the sun was already falling in the west, and the shadows of the tea trees were growing longer.

Looking at the mountains far off in the distance, Officer Lu said, "You'd want to take personal revenge if he sent someone to stab you twice, smash your father's wheelchair, insult you and bully you."

"Which only goes to show that I'm not human," said Wang Changchi, "not even an animal, because even animals feel hatred. Only trees don't feel hatred, but that doesn't include living trees, only dead trees, so I'm just a wretched piece of dead wood."

"Judging from your anger, you're not a piece of dead wood, but rather you're a manic genius who loves to shoot his mouth off. There'd be no problem sending you to seize the bloody Diaoyu islands."

"Unfortunately, you've heaped snow on my hot blood."

"What's that got to do with us?"

"You've always denied that Huang Kui was the perpetrator," said Wang Changchi, "and claimed you didn't have enough evidence to arrest him. Now, in order to prove that I killed him, you finally admit that he was the perpetrator behind my stabbing. If you knew it was him, why didn't you arrest him back then?"

"We are simply reasoning," said Officer Wei.

"Even the Old Man in Heaven would not condone this sort of harmful reasoning."

As Wang Changchi spoke, a gust of wind blew, rustling the tea trees. Compared with the same time the previous year, the cold wind blew more gloomily. The three of them trembled.

In fact, Officer Lu and Officer Wei were both under pressure. They knew there was some conflict between Huang Kui, Lin Jiabo and the people whose fingers Huang Kui had cut off, but those people were all "somebody", who couldn't just be arrested. They whispered under the trees, thought for a while about life, and then decided to take Wang Changchi away.

Wang Changchi didn't want to go and clung to a column in the main room. They pulled and the column seemed to sway a little so that even the tiles on the roof were alarmed. Burning with anger, they detached his tightly clasping fingers one by one, but as soon as they detached one, he'd replace it with another. Impatient, they lifted a bench and smashed it on the column. In pain, Wang Changchi let go of it at once. They put him in handcuffs and then, with each one taking an arm, they forcefully dragged him outside. Liu Shuangju rushed forward and latched onto Wang Changchi's left foot. Xiaowen rushed forward and latched onto his right foot. Wang Changchi was pulled taut like a rope in a tug-of-war match with two men on one end and two women on the other.

Facing the village, Wang Huai shouted, "Second Uncle, get over here quick, our Changchi is being treated unjustly. Zhang Wu, come and help Changchi. I, Wang Huai, am kowtowing to you. Wang Dong, you've seen the world, come and talk sense into them. Baitiao, if you don't help our Changchi today, then they'll come and take you away as a suspect tomorrow. Relatives and neighbours, I implore you to come and stand up for justice. Don't let them take Changchi away. If they take him away and torture him, then sooner or later he'll be killed like a murderer. I kneel before you, my fellow villagers…"

As Wang Huai shouted, he rolled out of his wheelchair and knelt on the ground. The villagers came running in twos and threes and formed a wall blocking any exit.

Officer Lu took out his pistol and, pointing it at everyone, said, "If you interfere with official business, I will shoot to kill."

He pointed the gun for a while at Zhang Wu, then at Wang Dong, then at Liu Baitiao, and then turned, pointing at everyone as if using a handheld inventory scanner, until the lot had been checked.

"Changchi didn't have time to commit the crime," said Second Uncle, "any idiot can see that."

"But he made a phone call when he was in town," said Officer Wei.

"I called the class director," said Wang Changchi, "and asked him to collect the chair I left in the classroom."

"Is the chair that important?" asked Officer Lu. "That's clearly a lie, you're all lying, and this is a village of liars."

Everyone felt insulted and someone started to shout, "Get them."

Back to back, Officer Lu and Officer Wei raised their pistols.

"Calm down," said Wang Huai, "everyone calm down, be reasonable and don't fight."

"All you have to do is ask the teacher to find out if he is lying or not, right?" said Second Uncle. "Why arrest him without checking?"

"I'm afraid that by the time we ask the teacher and come back," replied Officer Wei, "Wang Changchi will already have emigrated."

"I'm no corrupt and rotten lawbreaker," said Wang Changchi, "why should I run?"

Someone shouted, "Put away your guns or you'll be sorry".

Officer Lu discharged his pistol into the sky. Chafed by the bullet, the air seemed to solidify. The villagers were furious. They rushed forward, took away their guns and removed the handcuffs from Wang Changchi.

"Infuriating people," said Officer Lu. "Sooner or later I'll be back to take you all in."

The villagers raised their fists and said, "Get him, get him."

"Stop! Keeping Changchi here is enough," shouted Wang Huai. "Whatever you do, don't offend them."

The policemen squeezed out of the crowd.

"Second Uncle," said Wang Huai, "return their guns to them."

Someone shouted, "No, don't."

"If they're not returned," said Wang Huai, "there'll be trouble."

After thinking about it, Second Uncle tossed the guns towards them. They hurriedly picked them up and wiped them off with their hands.

"Get the hell out of here," shouted Liu Baitiao.

They stared at Liu Baitiao until his flesh was seemingly cooked, and then they turned and walked away.

The neighbours glared and struck their chests, swearing that Wang Huai's bones were made of straw.

"Don't think being tough is always tough," said Wang Huai. "sometimes it's just holding in piss."

They all agreed, so they watched as the policemen left the village and disappeared through the gap.

By then it was almost dusk, and under the red evening clouds the village seemed to sit in a lake of blood.

二十一 · TWENTY-ONE

EVERYONE EXPECTED THEM TO RETURN WITH REINFORCEMENTS. Wang Changchi packed clothes, shoes, a torch, crackers and money in a soft bag. His tactic was to grab the bag and run the moment he saw them, aiming to avoid them while not offending them. Second Uncle's house rose ever higher, and from time to time Wang Changchi would stand up straight and from high above look into the distance, scanning like a radar, fearing they make a surprise attack.

Everyone in the village was a bit nervous, even Second Uncle absent-mindedly dropped bricks on several occasions, almost injuring his aunt. When Wang Changchi looked down at the brick wall they were building, Second Uncle would look up to check. Only when Wang Changchi stood up again did Second Uncle lower his head. Watching them rising and stooping, Wang Huai, who was sitting behind the house, was determined to speak.

"Keeping watch is making you two nervous," he said. "I'll keep my eyes peeled, OK?"

Although Wang Huai talked tough, he was nervous inside. His eyes were open wider than anyone else's, his ears more alert. Every day he sat in his wheelchair looking at the mountain gap, watching endlessly the way he did when he was thinking about Wang Changchi in days gone by. He even borrowed a brass gong from Zhang Wu and placed it beside his wheelchair.

"The moment I bang the gong," he said, "you'll know they're here and that it's time for those who should run to run and for those who should gather to gather. Anyway, no one wants to come to grief."

Late one night, someone knocked on Wang Huai's door. Wang Changchi rolled out of bed, grabbed his soft bag and ran out of the back door. Liu Shuangju and Xiaowen got Wang Huai into his wheelchair, and together they went to the main room.

"Who's there?" asked Wang Huai.

"Baitiao," came the reply.

Liu Shuangju opened the door and said, "You devil, waking people in the middle of the night and scaring us to death."

"Wang Huai, do you still remember the day I cursed them?" said Liu Baitiao, his face ashen.

"So what?" said Wang Huai. "What are you afraid of?"

Liu Baitiao raised his hand and slapped his hand over his mouth.

"Retribution," he said. "I just dreamed they came and arrested me, handcuffed me, and announced that I had been sentenced to ten years and stripped of my political rights."

"I never thought a dream could scare you enough to piss yourself," said Wang Huai.

"To tell you the truth," said Liu Baitiao, "I've been having nightmares every night, and my hair is falling out by the handful."

Wang Huai told Liu Shuangju to ladle out a cup of rice wine. Liu Baitiao gulped it down and wiped the corners of his mouth.

"I cursed them on account of Changchi," he said. "If they show up, don't say it was me who cursed them."

"Don't worry," said Wang Huai, "just tell them it was me who cursed them."

"Good enough," replied Liu Baitiao, "otherwise I won't help you next time."

"We all appreciate your support," said Wang Huai.

Liu Baitiao drained the wine in his cup to the last drop.

"In wine is courage," he said. "Let's have another."

Xiaowen took his cup and refilled it. This time he sipped it instead of gulping it. As the three of them looked at him, he felt uncomfortable.

"Drinking alone is no good," he said. "Why don't you have one?"

"I'm not in the mood," said Wang Huai. "Get Changchi to drink with you."

Xiaowen went to the back door and clapped three times, and Wang Changchi came out of the tea plantation carrying his bag. He cooked a plate of peanuts and filled a jug with wine and slowly drank with Liu Baitiao. The others went back to their rooms. The more he drank, the more excited Liu Baitiao became. "Isn't Uncle Liu lots of fun?" he said.

"Yeah, sure..." said Wang Changchi, nodding and bowing.

"If you get rich... get rich, you won't forget your Uncle Liu, will you?"

"If I forget, may I be in a car crash."

"When the time comes, how will you thank... thank me?"

"I'll give you cigarettes and wine."

Liu Baitiao grunted and nodded with the satisfaction of an official in charge of an interview. His face and neck were red from drinking, and his head felt heavy.

"Why don't I see you home?" asked Wang Changchi.

Liu Baitiao wasn't ready. He wiped his face and put his head down on the table.

"Changchi, you've made me miserable," he said, with tears in his eyes and a runny nose. "What good are cigarettes and what good is wine? If they take me away, my old lady will find herself a new husband and my kids will be forced to change their surname."

"You didn't break the law, why would they come and arrest you?"

"Didn't I curse them and say, 'Get the hell out of here'?"

"But didn't my dad just agree to take responsibility?"

"It won't work. They stared at me for a full two minutes, and they know who cursed and who didn't."

Wang Changchi moistened a towel and wiped Liu Baitiao's

face.

Slapping the towel to the floor, Liu Baitiao said, "If you really want to be good to me, then all you have to do is go to the county town and give yourself up. That way they won't come back. Otherwise, we're all in danger and everyone in the village will treat you with contempt."

Wang Changchi thought to himself, I committed no crime, why should I turn myself in?

However, a few days later he discovered what Liu Baitiao said wasn't drunken maundering, but rather yeast that had slowly fermented in the village to become reality. The first to reveal himself was Zhang Wu. He summoned Wang Changchi to his house, shut the door, closed the windows and carefully sounded him out.

"You know, Changchi," he said, "our Zhang Hui is a masseuse in the city. It's a complicated profession, you can say it's beneficial for health or you can say it's immoral. Anyway, in short, as long as they leave you alone, it's legal, but when they want to get you, there are plenty of ways to do so. It's not easy for a villager to make money in the city, especially a woman."

"Uncle Wu," said Wang Changchi, "if you've got something to say, just come out and say it."

Zhang Wu opened a window. Wang Changchi thought he wanted to speak frankly, but instead he looked outside in both directions and then closed the window again.

"It would be terrible if by some chance they took it out on Zhang Hui," he said in a mysterious whisper.

"Isn't Elder Sister Hui in the provincial capital?"

"It would only need one phone call to take care of that."

"So massaging someone's feet and hands is illegal?"

"Who knows what she massages?"

"Uncle Wu, you're making too much out of this."

Zhang Wu started walking around the room, round and round he went, ever more worked up.

"What do you want me to do?" asked Wang Changchi.

Suddenly coming to a halt, Zhang Wu said, "You know."

"I don't know," replied Wang Changchi.

"I didn't start out thinking this way," said Zhang Wu, "but I had no other choice because I was the one who took their guns away that day. Even though they were returned, it's still something, and if by any chance they hold a grudge, the first ones they'll remember will be me and Second Uncle. I shouldn't be blamed for this, maybe I should be blamed for rushing in, but the matter is unsettled, and I can't sleep at night. All night long, my eyes are as big as brass bells, I cough and I'm constipated. If you have any thought for your Uncle Wu, you'll raise both hands and surrender to them, and say a few conciliatory words. Then and only then will everyone sleep soundly, and the sound of snoring will return. In the past when in bed at home, I could hear Liu Baitiao, Wang Dong, Daijun and Second Uncle snoring. But now, I hear nothing. Snoring has disappeared from the village – it's extinct like the dinosaurs. Can a village without snoring be a safe village?"

Wang Changchi couldn't ignore the opinions of Zhang Wu and Liu Baitiao, nor was he willing to surrender to curry favour, so he was all tied up in knots inside. During the day when he was laying bricks, he relaxed a bit, but by evening, his mind was unusually active in trying to come up with a solution. The more he tried to find one, the more agitated his brain and nerves became, so much so that he couldn't sleep. Afraid of waking Xiaowen, he gently tossed and turned. With each turn, the bed creaked softly. Normally the creaking sound was easily ignored, but with insomnia, it sounded more like an earth tremor. So he took even greater care to move as little as possible. But by not moving, his limbs and body felt tied down, tight here and tight there, every muscle felt tight so that he perspired lightly. What did he think insomnia was like? It was as if his body was suspended in mid-air and never coming to rest on the ground, like a knife circling his forehead, the sound of scraping bone reverberating. He was exhausted in mind and body, but he rejected the exhaustion. His mind was piled high with rubbish, but he kept dumping more in.

He thought Xiaowen was already sound asleep, so he gently got out of bed and went to the kitchen where he scooped up half a ladle of cold water and gulped it down as if to suppress the internal heat of his body. Unexpectedly, Xiaowen got up and followed him for a drink of water – she had been pretending to be asleep. They finished drinking and heard a movement in the house. They thought it was a thief, so they both picked up a cleaver, turned on the lights and discovered it was Wang Huai and Liu Shuangju. They had been sitting in the dark with their eyes open as if they were advocates for the night.

"Why aren't you asleep?" asked Wang Changchi.

"For the last few nights," said Wang Huai, "we've been sitting like this until the sun comes up."

"So you've been suffering from insomnia too?" asked Wang Changchi.

"It's not just us. The Wang Dongs, Daijun, Xianhua and Second Uncle all have insomnia and sit and watch all night," said Wang Huai.

"I didn't think everyone'd had their backbones removed."

"You can't blame them, everyone has their own weak point. Second Uncle, for example, is afraid they'll go to the county town and check. You know bribes were paid so that your cousins could go to the county junior high school, and if that's discovered, they'll have to come back and go to the village junior high school. And Xianhua, she's afraid of the taxman because she trades and often doesn't pay or report her taxes, not to mention being suspected of being a cow thief. If they were to look into Daijun's oxen that were stolen, Xianhua would... and Wang Dong, his wife has a female ailment and they can't partake in conjugal life, so he often goes to the county town to the hair salon for some wild fare. He's afraid they'll crack down on illicit activities and illegal publications and pull the radish with mud on it out of the ground. Daijun isn't any better – he often goes to the county town to gamble, and quite a few people suspect that those oxen of his were actually gambled away and, to hide it from his wife, he had someone come and take them to cover his debts. If they find out about the gambling, then Daijun will be spending his time in jail..."

"Why don't I make a trip to the county town?" suggested Wang Changchi.

"Aren't you afraid they'll arrest you?" asked Liu Shuangju.

"If they want to arrest me, then they'll arrest me, otherwise the villagers will curse me."

After thinking the matter over, Wang Huai said, "Go and stay for two days in the county town and when you get back tell everyone you went to see them, and then no one will be watching and waiting. Only then will the heavy stone be lifted from their hearts."

"What if they come to investigate who was responsible?" asked Wang Changchi. "Wouldn't that be self-incriminating?"

"Since it's been several days and they haven't come back yet," replied Wang Huai, "that means they're not coming back."

In the morning, Wang Changchi and Xiaowen set off. Before they left, Liu Shuangju repeatedly warned Wang Changchi not to go and see them and be arrested as that would be a pity.

For added protection, Liu Shuangju secretly admonished Xiaowen.

"Keep an eye on him and don't let him do anything foolish. On the face of things, you're going to give yourself up to the police, but in fact, you are going on your honeymoon."

Xiaowen nodded a dozen times or so before Liu Shuangju felt reassured.

As he walked, Wang Changchi shouted, "Uncle Zhang, Uncle Liu, Second Uncle, Brother Dong, Sister Xian, Brother Daijun, I'm going to give myself up, so you can catch up on your sleep."

One after another the insomniacs opened their windows and doors, watching as Wang Changchi and Xiaowen departed into the distance. They breathed long sighs of relief. Wang Huai lit three sticks of incense and stuck them in front of the door. Smoke rose from the three sticks like Wang Huai's three hopes: one – nothing bad would happen; two – nothing bad would happen; and three – again that nothing bad would happen.

3
THE LOSER

"Let's check out the department store," said Xiaowen, so Wang Changchi went along.

They started on the ground floor and made their way to the third floor, spending three hours looking at almost everything in the store, but in the end, Xiaowen bought only five buttons.

"Let's have our picture taken," said Xiaowen.

"OK," said Wang Changchi.

They went to Wooden Tower Photo Studio beside the big river and had their photo taken with three different backgrounds: Tiananmen, the Great Wall and the Shanghai Bund.

Coming out of the photo studio, Xiaowen asked, "What do you want to eat this evening?"

"I'll take you out for some river fare," said Wang Changchi.

Xiaowen was worried about money. "Fast food is fine," she replied.

Wang Changchi disagreed and insisted on taking her to a restaurant.

For the meal, Wang Changchi ordered a wild grass carp weighing three *jin*, or 1.5 kilos, a plate of braised pork and preserved vegetables, a dish of peanuts, a crushed and marinated cucumber salad, a bottle of sorghum wine and four bowls of rice. Arms akimbo, the two of them dug in and polished off everything from pot, plate and bottle. While eating they didn't notice anything, but after finishing, they felt full to the point of bursting and found it difficult to even stand up.

"I've never been so full," said Xiaowen.

"From when I was little to when I grew up," said Wang Changchi, "I dreamed most of eating. The hungrier I was, the more I wanted to eat, and sometimes I'd dream of being so full that my belly was like a ripe, split-open pomegranate."

He patted his belly as he spoke, his face suffused with satisfaction.

"I'm so big I look pregnant," said Xiaowen, rubbing her abdomen.

The following day they slept in and didn't get up till around noon.

"Is there anything else you want to do?" asked Wang Changchi.

Xiaowen shook her head and said, "We have to pick up the photos."

They arrived at the studio and the photographer told them they would have to wait another three hours. They stood at the studio door and watched the flowing river below the tower. The water was blue, and from time to time a small whirlpool or two would appear on the surface. It was so clear, the rocky bottom was visible. The mountains and trees on the opposite shore were reflected in the water, and red and yellow leaves floated on the blue water. Sometimes they looked at the mountains. Sometimes their eyes followed a leaf as it floated off into the distance until the red or yellow had vanished entirely from sight before they looked away to follow another floating leaf. Tired of watching the leaves, they looked at their own reflections against the railing. Wang Changchi took aim at his reflection and spat as if he were spitting on himself.

"It's still early," said Xiaowen.

Wang Changchi took her to a place to watch videos. The

doorway to where the videos were shown was covered with two layers of heavy curtains, which blocked out light and sound. As they entered, day immediately became night. Four people were sitting there, and the video was half over, an adult video from Hong Kong. To avoid anyone seeing the backs of their heads, they sat in the back row. The man and woman in the video were wearing less than paupers and constantly moaning, "Oh, oh...". Xiaowen flushed red to her ears and stood up to leave.

Wang Changchi held her back.

"Two tickets cost four yuan," he said, "about what I make in a day. It's paid for, so watch it. If you don't watch it, the money's wasted."

Xiaowen struggled to free herself but to no avail, so she sat down again.

As Wang Changchi watched, he whispered, "Wrong, we got it all wrong."

Annoyed by his shamelessness, she slapped his mouth.

After the video, they left the dark and returned to the light. Feeling awkward, they avoided looking at each other and didn't speak a word as they walked. When they had picked up the photos, they returned to the hostel. Unable to restrain himself, Wang Changchi performed as he had seen it done in the video. Xiaowen let herself go and shouted, outdoing the female star of the video.

Afterwards, Wang Changchi offered a summary. "This honeymoon trip was the first time I had my picture taken alone with a woman, the first time I ate until I almost burst, the first time I slept in, the first time I saw a dirty movie and the first time I did it in broad daylight. Altogether, that's a total of five firsts."

As he summarised, he lifted five fingers. Xiaowen thought that some of the things could be done, but best not summarised. Once summarised, they only disgusted. But Wang Changchi was not at all fed up and proceeded to count them off again. Xiaowen reached out to pinch him, but he pinned her arms and her body down. Xiaowen was unable to move and apparently exhausted, her breathing soon became even.

Wang Changchi released his grip and looked for a while at the soundly sleeping Xiaowen. Then he gently got up, dressed, took one of the photos of them together and placed it in his left shirt pocket, and left a note before quietly leaving. He arrived at the police station on Little River Street, where the duty officer told him that Officers Lu and Wei had been transferred to the Criminal Investigation Division at the County Police Station. Sweating, he made his way to the station, where the duty officer told him to take a seat while he made a phone call.

About two minutes later, Officer Lu entered, ramrod straight. With a straight face, he eyed Wang Changchi without uttering a sound.

Wang Changchi was scared. "Sorry, I came to apologise," he said.

"That's impossible. Do people like you apologise?" asked Officer Lu.

"A person has to admit when he's wrong."

"And what about the others? Why didn't the two men who took our guns come?"

"I was the cause of everything, so I'm here to represent them."

"If there's an arrest, will you also represent them?"

Wang Changchi nodded.

"OK, when I have time on my hands, I'll lock you up."

"Can't you lock me up now?"

"Who has the say around here, you or me?"

"I just wanted... to discuss it with you."

"Is there any room for discussion in the matter?"

"I... I thought there was. Anyway, sooner or later, I'm going to be arrested. Being arrested sooner is better than later. Also, after the New Year, I want to take my wife to the provincial capital and go to work, and I want to make sure I'll have the time available. Can you help me out and lock me up since I have the time now?"

"You really want to go in?"

"I'll feel uneasy if I don't. It's sort of like having a debt and not paying it. I don't enjoy eating or sleeping, afraid all day in case someone comes and arrests me."

"What if I say I'll let you off?"

"That's impossible. You mean you can have sympathy for others?"

"Fuck, what sort of person do you think I am?"

"Don't fool around, my nervous heart might not be able to take it."

"Stupid cunt, if I were you, I'd turn around and leave."

Wang Changchi looked at Officer Lu. Officer Lu turned and looked out of the window. Wang Changchi stood up.

"Can I really leave?" he asked.

Officer Lu didn't move.

"Has the Huang Kui case been solved?" asked Wang Changchi.

"Solving it has nothing to do with you."

"That means your suspicions about me were wrong?"

"Where do you come up with all this nonsense?"

"If you hadn't handcuffed me, they wouldn't have taken away your guns."

"Any more trouble and I will handcuff you."

"Don't..."

Wang Changchi turned and ran, wiping away his sweat as he looked back, afraid someone was pursuing him or that he would suddenly hear the command, "Come back". But nothing happened, the blank space behind him only grew longer and quieter. Even when he arrived outside the main door, he couldn't believe it was true.

On his return to where they were staying, Wang Changchi quietly opened the door only after making sure that no one was in pursuit. Xiaowen was woken with a start.

"Where've you been?" she asked, her face filled with suspicion.

He told her everything that had just happened.

"When we get back to the village," said Xiaowen, "just fib in the same way, otherwise Second Uncle and Uncle Zhang Wu won't be able to sleep."

He said he wasn't making it up, that it was true.

Xiaowen reached out and felt his forehead.

"You don't have a fever," she said.

He brushed her hand aside and handed her the note he had left at the head of the bed.

She read it word by word. "I've gone to turn myself in. You go home first."

After reading it, she asked, "Did you really go?"

Wang Changchi nodded.

"That's impossible," she said. "If you did, why would they let you go?"

When they returned to the village, Wang Changchi told everyone, "There's nothing to worry about. They're not pursuing the matter."

But no one believed his lies, including Wang Huai. In order to comfort the nervous insomniacs, Xiaowen confirmed that everything he said was true. Since Xiaowen didn't believe it herself, every time she went to confirm it, she struggled. For example, her speech broke off, her eyes wandered or the details varied. As a result, the villagers were even more sceptical. Nothing could convince them that the police were so decent or that they would be so polite to Wang Changchi. Who the heck did he think he was?

Still no snoring was heard in the village as everyone was trying to figure out what Wang Changchi was trying to hide. All night long, Wang Huai never shut his eyes. Then at dawn, he heard snoring coming from Wang Changchi's room, which to him seemed like a timely rain on a spring night. But at once he was on his guard because he suspected that Wang Changchi was trying to comfort him by snoring on purpose, as they had all done in the hospital. He tapped Liu Shuangju, and she pricked up her ears and listened carefully. Listening for a while, Wang Huai couldn't lie still and got Liu Shuangju to help him into his wheelchair, and then asked her to quietly fetch Second Uncle and Zhang Wu. The four of them sat in the main room, without turning on the lights or saying a word, their ears pricked up as if they were listening to the voice on an enemy radio station or the leader's voice amid a trumpet fanfare. It was a sound that they hadn't heard in ages. It came through the cracks in the wall. As they listened, they became nostalgic and even couldn't help imitating it.

"It doesn't sound like he's pretending," said Liu Shuangju.

"If he was pretending," said Second Uncle, "he wouldn't have that rhythm, nor would the pauses be that natural."

"If he can keep it going for that long," said Zhang Wu, "I'd believe it even if it was fake".

"The boy doesn't have an iota of deception in him," said Wang Huai. "If he were scheming at something, he wouldn't be able to sleep so soundly."

They continued to listen for ages, unwilling to leave, because Wang Changchi's snoring seemed to have the power to ease the pressure and cure them of their nervousness, anxieties and cowardice.

二十三 · TWENTY-THREE

EVERY MORNING, SECOND UNCLE'S RESONANT VOICE could be heard shouting from the top of the brick wall, "Changchi, it's time to work." His voice was like a cockcrow, like an alarm clock, spreading in the faintly lit sky, rousing the soundly sleeping people. In the beginning, Wang Changchi would rise with the call, but since he and Xiaowen had returned from the county town, he became a procrastinator. After hollering, Second Uncle would wait for ages without seeing a trace of him and then holler again. In the beginning, Second Uncle would bellow just one more time, and he would come. But as time went on, the number of additional times he had to shout increased, from one shout to two, then two became three, and three became innumerable shouts. Wang Changchi came out to work later and later, sometimes the sky was already bright, and sometimes after the sun was well up. Each time Second Uncle shouted, Wang Huai dropped a basin or banged a pot to remind Wang Changchi it was time to get up. But Wang Changchi would simply say, "I know", and then go back to sleep. He'd lifted the back of his head ever so slightly off the pillow, only to let it down heavily, as heavy as a pile of bricks.

Liu Shuangju believed that Wang Changchi was wearing himself out building Second Uncle's house. Wang Huai would have none of it.

"Just listen to them at night," he said. "You'd know why he's worn out if you counted the number of times they do it."

Liu Shuangju raised her fingers and counted, admitting that Wang Changchi and Xiaowen were doing it too frequently, three times more than she and Wang Huai had the year they were newly married.

"If it were to go on this way," said Wang Huai, "even a precious diamond blade would wear out."

Liu Shuangju told Wang Huai to have a talk with Wang Changchi. Wang Huai felt it would be too difficult to talk about, and suggested that Liu Shuangju talk to Xiaowen. Liu Shuangju's face flushed red, and she asked, "How can I talk about that?"

Second Uncle's house rose higher. Wang Changchi stood working above the second storey. Wang Huai sat below on the bank looking up, constantly shouting, "Careful." Each time he shouted, Wang Changchi would be roused. But he was afraid if he shouted too often, Wang Changchi would get upset and that others would laugh, so he started singing folksongs. He didn't sing them for real as the content was obscene, and they were delivered an octave too high and out of tune. When he got tired of singing, he'd throw stones at the chickens till the chickens flew and the dogs barked all around. Those who didn't know how things stood thought Wang Huai had gone mad, but Wang Changchi knew that these strange sounds produced by Wang Huai roused him from his sleepiness and kept him from falling off the scaffolding.

Wang Changchi grew skinny and dark, his eyes sunken. When dishing up the rice at mealtime, Liu Shuangju would pack as much as she could in his bowl. Occasionally, she'd fry several eggs or cook a plate of meat, most of which she would press into Wang Changchi's bowl. But Wang Changchi remained skinny and dark, and he was either yawning all day long or he couldn't get up on time.

Liu Shuangju was worried. "He can eat and sleep," she said, "so why is he so skinny?"

"A body is like an account book that doesn't tell you how much you save but how much you spend," said Wang Huai.

"You must find a way to give him some advice. He's our only son and if he ruins himself, he can't be replaced."

One evening when Xiaowen went to the well to wash clothes, Wang Huai took the opportunity to slip Wang Changchi a wrapped package slightly larger than a box of matches.

Feeling it, Wang Changchi asked, "What is it?"

"It was given out for free ten years ago by the family-planning cadres," said Wang Huai. "I put it in the bottom of a trunk and never used it."

Wang Changchi opened it and found a box of antique condoms. He kneaded one with some force and found it had lost its elasticity and so was about to throw it away. Wang Huai stopped him and said, "As long as it doesn't leak, you can use it even if it's out-of-date."

"You're not anxious to have a grandchild?" asked Wang Changchi.

"When sowing seed you still need to find a propitious location," said Wang Huai, shaking his head. "Your granddad fathered me here and I fathered you here, and as a result, we have all failed. Our failures are failures, but I won't have my grandson fail too. It's my hope that he can go to school in the city, work in the city and not suffer or be cheated and not be marked at birth."

"Even Xiaowen has temporarily stopped mentioning it, but you are still bringing it up."

"I think you two are partners in sinking low and have no ideals at all."

"How can someone who flunked the university entrance exam, a bricklayer and a villager, have any hopes?"

As he spoke, Wang Changchi tossed the box out of the window.

"So you want to spend your whole life in this crappy place?" asked Wang Huai.

"You've stayed, why can't I?"

"Then you'll never amount to anything."

"If you wanted me to amount to something, then from the very start why didn't you have me in the city?"

"If someone else hadn't taken my place when I was recruited for the job, I'd at least have had you in the county town."

"There's no room for hypotheticals, just reality."

Wang Huai had nothing more to say, so in shame he turned his wheelchair around and rolled straight out of the door. It was growing dark and the distant mountains and the trees near at hand were indistinct. A daub of light hung over the black horizon, the final struggle of day. He turned his eyes away and searched below the window for the box of condoms Wang Changchi had discarded. He looked all over but couldn't find it. It was getting darker, and he was soon unable to distinguish the stones, twigs and dirt. Carrying a basket of washed clothes on her back, Xiaowen stopped in front of the door.

"Dad," she asked, "what are you looking for?"

"I'm looking, looking for a reason," said Wang Huai.

Before going to bed, Wang Changchi discovered the box of condoms at the head of the bed.

"What's that?" asked Xiaowen.

"A family heirloom," replied Wang Changchi.

As he spoke, he opened the box and pulled out a condom. Heavens, it had become a lump like a mud cake, like a wart. To Wang Changchi, it looked like it could be eaten rather than used.

"Quick, throw it away," said Xiaowen.

Wang Changchi looked at it for a long time and seemed to see Wang Huai's abundant hopes. That night their bed didn't creak. In the next room, Wang Huai breathed a long sigh of relief.

"See," he said, "having a talk created a chemical reaction in Changchi's body."

"I took a torch to look for the box," said Liu Shuangju, "but couldn't find it. Where did you find it?"

"In the hibiscus," said Wang Huai, "it got caught in a branch. It's a case of Heaven protecting Wangs."

Liu Shuangju pinched Wang Huai and said, "You devil."

Work finished on Second Uncle's new house. Wang Changchi slept for three straight days to allow his exhausted body to recover, and then he sat absent-mindedly at the door of the house. The weather grew colder and in addition to turning his nose red, it grew desolate all up and down the mountain, everything was a dreary grey. The tree branches resembled iron bars and seemed to gesture threateningly, with scarcely a leaf left. The north wind howled, blowing into the house through holes in the windows and cracks in the door and walls, making the interior behind him sound like a musical instrument. Blown by the wind, his house was the most resonant in the entire village.

Wang Huai and the others retreated indoors to sit close to the fire. Xiaowen stuck her head out of the window.

"Are you doing martial arts training?" she asked.

Wang Changchi didn't move.

"Come inside," said Liu Shuangju. "You've got chilblains on your hands."

Only Wang Huai didn't disturb him, as he knew that he was thinking. The year Wang Huai failed the test for the job, he sat in exactly the same place and let the cold wind blow until he was stiff. In fact, Wang Changchi was admiring Second Uncle's new house. It was the loveliest house in the village, thoroughly surpassing Zhang Wu's, especially the side facing Wang Changchi's place, which he had built. The lines were straight, the bricks level, the windows square. There were no mistakes, and the entire house was as handsome as if it had been drawn using an angle ruler on white paper. He wondered if it looked lovely only because he had built it himself, but he dismissed the thought immediately, inordinately enjoying his own handiwork, secretly crying out in admiration for the man who had done such fine work! At the height of his admiration, he thought, Will I ever build such a beautiful house for my family? The answer was "no" because they had no money, and even if he were frozen by the wind, they'd still have no money, and even if flowers sprouted from the wall, it would still be just an illusion.

二十四 · TWENTY-FOUR

A FEW DAYS BEFORE THE NEW YEAR, the north wind stopped blowing and the temperature rose. There was a succession of sunny days and clear skies. The tree branches shimmered as if gold bars were hung out. The sunlight warmed the ground and the dry grass and dead leaves, producing a sour aroma. Everything took on a transparent quality, including the five viscera and six hollow organs of the people, and the quilts, sheets and clothes airing in the sun. Wang Huai sat at the door looking at the gap in the mountain, yelling from time to time, "Baoqing is back, Jiangpo is back, Yilong is back..." His yells were sending out invitations as if those returning were relatives. Hearing him shout, his neighbours to the right and left came out to look. Family elders rushed out and, also facing the gap, shouted names. The footsteps of those who heard their names called got briefly muddled as the folk lugging suitcases, or with bags on their backs, or carrying small children flew towards home. Some were seen to rush through the front door only to take a tumble, thus fumbling things. Wang Huai only stopped shouting after Xingze and his family appeared in the gap, or perhaps all his shouting had been a prelude to this moment of silence. He got Liu Shuangju to carry him on her back to Xingze's house, where he insisted they must come to his house and have a simple meal.

Xingze was the son of Tian Daijun and a junior high school classmate of Wang Changchi. He was now working in an electronics factory in the provincial capital where he assembled television parts. The following day, he brought his wife and child to Wang Changchi's house. His wife was not from the village and also worked in the electronics factory. Their child was fair-skinned and pudgy. Xiaowen instantly fell in love with him and wouldn't let him go.

"Only city kids are so clean," said Wang Huai.

While they were eating, Wang Changchi asked, "Should I leave this place or not?"

"If you leave, you might be able to change things," said Xingze. "If you stay, you may end up with nothing."

Hearing what he said, Wang Huai was so happy he drank three cups of wine in a row.

Zhang Hui returned two days after Xingze, and as soon as she put down her luggage she went to see Xiaowen. The moment the two saw each other, Zhang Hui was silent for at least five seconds. Xiaowen flushed red at being examined in such a way.

"What a waste," said Zhang Hui. "A fresh flower stuck in cow dung."

Scared, Xiaowen quickly covered her mouth, not sure if she or Zhang Hui had uttered those words. By chance, Wang Changchi heard the remark.

"Who's a fresh flower," he asked. "Who's cow dung?"

"Do you need to ask?" replied Zhang Hui. "She's the fresh flower... you, you're not the cow dung, the cow dung is this crappy place. Oops, by crappy place I don't mean your house but our village, not just our village but all villages in general. Do you understand? All villages."

"That about sums it up," said Wang Changchi. "I thought you were calling me names."

Patting Wang Changchi on the shoulder, Zhang Hui said, "Who'd dare call you names?"

Xiaowen deeply admired that pat on the shoulder. Zhang Hui's gesture was utterly charming as well as being both gentle and rough, both affectedly sweet and harsh, coquettish and serious. She reached out, flicked her wrist, applied the lightest pressure with her fingertips and immediately withdrew her hand. Her entire figure turned on that gesture, even the sound was pleasing. Xiaowen wondered how crazy she could make Wang Changchi if she moved in such a fashion.

Perhaps it was in order to prove that Xiaowen was a fresh flower that whenever Zhang Hui had a moment to spare, she'd come and teach Xiaowen how to apply makeup. She even cut her long hair short and dressed her in her own clothes. Each day Xiaowen changed. At first, she looked like a private-school teacher, and then gradually came to resemble a state-school teacher, a township cadre, an actress in a county troupe, a female spy in a movie and finally a white-collar professional from the city.

Seeing herself in the mirror, Xiaowen said, "It's a shame I can't read many words."

"Knowing lots of words is useless," said Zhang Hui, "but beauty is worth money."

Xiaowen looked absent-mindedly into the mirror, wondering where a fresh flower ought to be stuck if not in cow dung. Being polished this way, she felt nauseated, and then she wanted to throw up.

Before going to bed, Xiaowen said, "I think I'm pregnant."

Wang Changchi was so startled he nearly spat out his teeth.

"Why didn't you ask my opinion about getting pregnant?" he said.

"What measures did you take?"

Wang Changchi thought, That's right, no measures, there was no room for discussion. She was bound to get pregnant sooner or later.

"I'm not grown up yet and now I'm going to be a father," he said.

"Don't you want to be a father?" asked Xiaowen.

"I do. It's just that I'm sorry the kid has to grow up in this crappy place."

"Then where should the child be born?"

Wang Changchi reached over and caressed her belly and suddenly felt his hand had grown large, so large that he could contain her belly in his hand. And Xiaowen's belly no longer seemed smooth but started to hurt the palm of his hand.

"The child should be born in a room that isn't draughty," he said, "where the lightbulbs are brighter, where the windows and doors are all glass and the windows have curtains, where there is a crib, a wooden horse, where the quilt smells of new cotton, where the floors are tiled and so clean that we can see our reflection."

"You're dreaming, you –"

"And lots of toys, baby dolls, model cars, transformers, a football, a plastic gun, a bicycle, a dog, a kitten, jigsaw puzzles, kids' books, cartoons and music, everything that one should have."

"Are all these things just going to fall out of the sky?" Xiaowen looked up at the exposed floorboards above. Wang Changchi did the same and saw that they were water-stained and the corners filled with cobwebs. Mice could be heard scampering upstairs, and the cold wind howled outside. Wang Changchi returned to reality and placed another layer of cardboard over the window to help lessen the draught.

"Can you keep your pregnancy a secret for the time being?" he asked.

"Why do you always want me to keep secrets?"

"Because I want to take you away from this place."

"Take me away to live in poverty? I've got enough here."

"Don't you have me?"

Xiaowen shook her head. She doubted Wang Changchi would be able to feed two mouths, or more accurately, three, if they went to the city. She didn't know what nerve she had mistakenly touched, but Wang Changchi actually vowed to look after her, allow her to have regular check-ups, have three meals a day, go for strolls, listen to music, eat fruit and enjoy how a pregnant woman is treated in the city.

Hearing this, Xiaowen cried. "I'm not an empress, so how could I enjoy such a wonderful fate?" she said.

"City women with money," said Wang Changchi, "stick out their bellies and go to the United States or Hong Kong to give birth. If we don't go to the city to have the baby, then in the future the kid loses before it even starts."

"What about money? Having no money is like making a report and never getting to the point because of all the nonsense."

Wang Changchi had no reply and started pacing in the room, seven steps this way and seven steps that way, as if he wanted to compose a *Poem of Seven Steps*. Xiaowen figured he'd come up with a solution, but a minute passed, then ten minutes and Wang

Changchi more and more resembled a hypnotic pendulum, which finally put her to sleep.

Liu Shuangju noticed that Wang Changchi was looking after Xiaowen. In the past, Wang Changchi had never helped Xiaowen fetch water for washing feet, and now he was not only helping her fetch the water, but he also secretly transferred the meat Liu Shuangju had pressed into his bowl to Xiaowen's bowl. He wouldn't let her carry water, nor would he let her go to the well to wash clothes. He also went with Zhang Hui to buy a scarf to cover her head and neck. If the two of them left the house at the same time, he would get between her and the wind to protect her from the cold. Liu Shuangju couldn't figure out what was going on and even felt a little at a loss.

"Why has Changchi become Xiaowen's mum?" she asked Wang Huai.

"Is Xiaowen pregnant?" asked Wang Huai.

Liu Shuangju slapped her head and said, "That's possible."

Sighing, Wang Huai said, "That's fate. You want them to go to the city to lay their eggs and all they want to do is lay them in the village, as mysterious as being confronted by a bald man with a ton of pubic hair."

After the New Year, Wang Changchi and Xiaowen started packing in preparation to leave for the city. Wang Huai took Wang Changchi to one side. "Is Xiaowen pregnant?" he asked.

"Didn't you say we have bad feng shui," said Wang Changchi, "so why would she dare get pregnant?"

Wang Huai fixed his eyes on him as if he could determine whether it was the truth or a lie from his eyes.

"Really," he said, "she's not pregnant."

"If you take a pregnant woman to the city," said Wang Huai, "you'll face twice as much pressure, and not only will you end up worn out, but Xiaowen will also suffer. All I ask is that you tell the truth. We can still talk about it."

Wang Changchi had met with a challenge and there was no way out.

"Why not first have the baby first," said Wang Huai, "and then go to the city to work?"

"Then won't he be just another Wang Changchi? Don't talk about having a baby. Even when it comes to breaking wind, I would rather hold it back and do it in the city."

Wang Huai raised his thumb in approval.

二十五 · TWENTY-FIVE

WANG CHANGCHI HADN'T EXPECTED XIAOWEN would cry until her eyes were red and swollen. When they left home, her mother cried, Liu Shuangju cried, and Wang Huai's eyes and those of her father grew moist as if they were on the verge of tears. But she seemed like an outsider, who, smiling broadly, said, "We're not involved in a pyramid scam, so why this outpouring of tears?"

Passing through the gap, she was optimistic, and after boarding the bus she didn't sleep a wink, asking about everything she saw along the way, as excited as if she had been injected with chicken blood. But a week after arriving in the city, her tears flowed copiously.

One evening, before Wang Changchi had returned from looking for work, she was in the kitchen cooking. Off in the distance firecrackers popped, down below cars roared, and steam sputtered from the vent in the electric rice cooker. These sounds together suddenly made her think of home. She missed the noises of New Year in the village; she missed her mother's chatter; she missed chopped spring onions and cabbage in the fields and the piglets in the pigpen; she even missed the cold wind in the mountains and the freezing well water. She mused as she cut vegetables, lean meat, carrots, tomatoes and green pepper, but as she cut the onions, her tears fell, plopping on the cutting board. She kept wiping her tears away but never quite wiped them dry, so she put down the cleaver and cried properly. The sound of the sputtering rice cooker was lost in the sound of her crying. The buildings across the way darkened, and the cut vegetables on the counter gradually grew indistinct, until nothing could be seen in the room. As night fell, the unfamiliar scene was covered in darkness, until here and there were alike and undifferentiated, which gave her the illusion of returning home. So she didn't turn on the light, and simply sat in the dark, shuddering for a spell and crying for a spell, crying for a spell and shuddering for a spell, as if they were her only bodily functions. She cried and shuddered. Wang Changchi returned and heard her crying but couldn't see her.

"What's wrong?" he asked.

"I want to go home," she replied.

That day, Wang Changchi had just got a contract and was humming as he walked up to the first floor, but not anticipating the tears waiting for him. He turned on the light and gave the contract to Xiaowen.

"Haven't you always wanted to come to the provincial capital?" he asked. "Your seat isn't even warm yet, so why do you want to go home?"

Xiaowen looked at the contract but didn't understand one line.

Taking her in his arms, Wang Changchi said, "Don't cry, don't cry. If you keep crying, the child will shake."

Suppressing her sobs, her shoulders continued to shudder, and as if she had not cried enough already, cried to the fullest.

"I swore an oath," said Wang Changchi, "that the child would be born in a room with no draught, with glass windows, with curtains and a tile floor. All of these conditions have basically been met. Wait till I get my first month's wages and I'll take you to the B Supermarket."

"Every time I see chopped spring onions," said Xiaowen, "I think of home. At home, I give them away by the bunch, but here each stalk goes on the scales – that's just taking advantage of people."

"Then from now on, don't buy any spring onions."

"But when I see cabbage, I also think of home."

"Don't buy cabbage either."

"What'll we eat?"

"We'll eat whatever doesn't remind you of home."

"There's no such thing. Even when I feel cold and hungry, I think of home."

"Then eat meat. Will eating meat make you think of home?"

"Yeah. Each bite reminds me that my mum and dad can't afford to eat it, that your mum and dad can't afford to eat it, and that my big brother and his wife can't afford to eat it. So what good does it do to eat it?"

Staring blankly, Wang Changchi hadn't thought that Xiaowen was so emotional and looked for a hole to crawl into.

He sighed and said, "We'll be ruined if we go back, even the child will be ruined. If the child is ruined, will we have anything to look forward to?"

"Can't we come back to the city when the child is old enough to go to school?"

"Will he be able to adjust?"

"But I'm so unhappy – there's no one to talk to all day long."

"Talk to the child – he understands."

"The city is nothing like I thought. It's no fun."

"Without money, no place is fun."

Wang Changchi massaged Xiaowen's shoulders. Xiaowen got up, went to the bathroom and washed her face. Wang Changchi went into the kitchen and cooked.

"What kind of work is the contract for?" asked Xiaowen while they were eating.

"Concrete work."

"The hardest and the most tiring job again."

"There's no money in it if it's not tiring."

Wang Changchi was working on a construction site just two junctions from their apartment. He set off every morning before Xiaowen got up. Downstairs, he bought three steaming-hot *mantou* and ate them on his way to work and finished them by the time he arrived. He drank a glass of water at the office and then put on his hard hat. It was his job to lay brick walls for the hallways and rooms inside the framed building. Thanks to the experience he had gained working on Second Uncle's house, he laid walls that were plumb and level, unlike those of other workers. As a result,

Andu the foreman praised him many times. They were provided with two meals a day at the construction site, lunch and dinner. Every evening he'd carry the dinner back to the apartment and eat with Xiaowen. Xiaowen would prepare a soup and fry some vegetables to go with Wang Changchi's boxed meal. The two dishes and one soup were placed on a small table and the two of them would begin to eat in a civilised way, munching and chatting, until gradually there was a feeling of home. If the construction site added more food to the boxed meal, Wang Changchi would pick the meat out with his fingers and give it to Xiaowen. Xiaowen didn't have the heart to take it, so put it back. They passed the meat back and forth, neither one of them willing to eat it.

"You work hard, if you don't eat meat, you'll fall apart."

"You're going to have a baby, if you don't eat extra meat, the baby won't have enough nutrition."

The one who gave way and compromised was usually Xiaowen because she agreed with his viewpoint that the child was more important than anything else.

Slowly, Wang Changchi became less talkative. Returning every evening, the only thing he did in addition to eating and bathing was to lie down. After washing the dishes, Xiaowen would return to the side of the bed and find him already snoring. Xiaowen would pinch him, then pinch him again, but he didn't respond. All his muscles were tight. Unable to wake him by pinching him, Xiaowen sat on the side of the bed looking at him. She looked at his deeply sunken eyes, his coarse, dark skin and the hairs in his nose moving ever so slightly. When his nails grew, she helped him trim them; when his ears were stopped with wax, she removed it. Even when she removed the earwax, he didn't wake up, as if he had no sensations.

When most tired, he said three things to Xiaowen, "Everything OK?", "Have a little more to eat" and "I'm going to bed".

As things went on this way, Xiaowen said nothing, but group after group of words steeped in her heart, steeped until they got stuck in her throat.

She didn't feel like going anywhere other than where Wang Changchi was working, because only there did she have a connection to anything. She came to the construction site and sat in the shade of a tree opposite and watched as the workers raised the building. The building was very high, already having reached fifteen storeys. A slogan was hung on the scaffolding at the tenth storey which read "Time is money, speed is effect". The machines roared, dust flew, and the boom of the crane moved back and forth. When the boom was overhead, she wondered if those stuck in the prefab building units would fall. If they did, would they crash on top of her? At first, she was very worried. As soon as the boom moved, her heart would contract, but after several times, she got used to it and didn't think about it. High up on the scaffolding, seven or eight figures would sometimes appear, none of whom were Wang Changchi.

One afternoon, Wang Changchi left the construction site to buy some cigarettes for Andu. Xiaowen assumed he had seen her from the building and had come out expressly to see her, so she stood up and waved and excitedly called, "Changchi, Changchi." Wang Changchi ran across the street.

"What are you doing here?" he asked.

"I was bored to death alone," replied Xiaowen, "so I came out to have a look."

"It's cold and dusty here. Do you want the kid to grow up to be a concrete worker?"

"Why not a foreman? Or maybe a property developer."

"That's impossible because property developers rarely come to construction sites. You should go and walk around the school and let the kid hear the sound of people studying."

"But I want to be close to you."

"We can't let the child be like me. You should get as far away from here as possible. Hurry up and get going."

Wang Changchi waved her away as if he were brushing away flies.

"You nutcase," said Xiaowen, "you can't even tell that your

wife misses you. From now on that won't happen, I won't think of you."

Wang Changchi continued to wave her away.

"Hurry up, get going, the air here is bad," he said. "If you want to think about me, wait till I get home."

"Don't you get off in another two hours?" asked Xiaowen.

"Then go to the park, the square or the shops."

"I have no money, so why go to the shops?"

"Go wherever it's clean, just don't come back to this place."

Xiaowen didn't want to leave. She looked at Wang Changchi the way a dog might look at its master after being driven away. Her pitiful look melted Wang Changchi and his bodily fatigue vanished immediately. He realised he was so fortunate to have someone who would stick to him this way.

"Working in the building we all wear masks," he said, "otherwise our lungs would turn black."

As he spoke, he wiped his hand over Xiaowen's hair, which was immediately blackened with a fine layer of dust. This is what was known twenty years later as particulate matter 2.5, which public intellectuals could get everyone worked up over. Xiaowen wiped her hands over her hair, and they too were filthy.

"Go home," said Wang Changchi, "otherwise your lungs and the kid's lungs will all be black."

"The air in the village is good," said Xiaowen. "Let me go back there."

"Having lungs with no knowledge is no good," said Wang Changchi.

"Having knowledge with no lungs is also no good," countered Xiaowen.

Wang Changchi took a mask out of his pocket and helped Xiaowen put it on. Xiaowen tried breathing through the mask and immediately pulled it aside.

"I'm suffocating," she said.

二十六 · TWENTY-SIX

AFTER DINNER, WANG CHANGCHI WENT TO BED and lay stretched out ramrod straight, looking for all the world like a wooden pole. Xiaowen rubbed a little essential balm at the corners of his eyes. It felt so hot, he sat bolt upright immediately.

"I'm going to go see Zhang Hui," said Xiaowen, "otherwise I'll go crazy with no one to talk to."

Wang Changchi washed his face, got an old newspaper and started drawing on it.

As he drew he explained, "Go out of the door, turn right and go fifty metres where you'll see a bus stop called Wangshan Stop. Take the number twenty-two bus. Remember, it'll have two 2s written on it."

Xiaowen nodded.

"You go five stops," Wang Changchi continued, "and that will put you at the junction of Qiyang Street."

Not recognising the character for "qi", Xiaowen read it several times before she mastered it and asked, "And then?"

Wang Changchi drew a street on the newspaper.

"Then you cross the street," he said, "and find the sign marked Qiyang Stop and there you take the number seven bus. You got that? Go three stops and that will put you at the junction of Chaoyang Street and Minzhu Road. Get off there, walk three hundred metres and you'll see a tower block that says Hongdou Hotel. Inside the hotel, take the lift to the second floor and you'll see Phoenix Foot Spa. Tell them you're looking for Zhang Hui and they'll take you inside. Clear?"

Pointing at the newspaper, Xiaowen asked, "What did you draw?"

Wang Changchi looked and the map he had drawn, squiggled all over the place like a tangled ball of hemp. Wang Changchi tore up the newspaper, unzipped a suitcase, opened the drawers and pulled back the bed mat, but he couldn't find a single piece of white paper. Xiaowen felt around the top of the cupboard and found an account book. Wang Changchi tore out the first two pages and redrew the maps, one page for going and one page for the return journey.

The following morning after eating breakfast, Xiaowen took the two drawings and set off. Just before noon, Wang Changchi, who was laying a brick wall, heard someone shouting for him. Sticking his head out from the fourth floor he saw Rongrong, who looked after the phone, shouting through a megaphone. He flew down the stairs where Rongrong told him that He Xiaowen had been rushed to the emergency department of the First Hospital. The hospital had called and requested that he hurry over. Wang Changchi's legs nearly gave way.

"Was she hit by a car," he asked, "and does she still have the baby?"

"I'm not sure," said Rongrong, "they didn't say."

Wang Changchi felt around in his pockets and then rushed out.

When he arrived at the emergency department, he saw Xiaowen with her eyes closed, leaning against a bench. Thank goodness she seemed uninjured.

"Xiaowen," he called.

Xiaowen opened her eyes and immediately shut them again.

"Changchi," she said, "I'm so dizzy."

He touched her all over, especially her belly and as he felt, he asked, "Where are you hurt?"

"Nowhere," she said, "I'm just dizzy, the bus was crooked, the ground kept shifting, the tower blocks were all leaning and all the faces were blurred…"

"Who brought you here?"

"I don't know."

"What did the doctor say?"

"He wants to have me examined."

Wang Changchi felt his pockets.

"Well, let's go," he said.

Xiaowen shook her head. Wang Changchi tried to help her up.

"Don't move," she said, "just let me sit here a while and maybe the dizziness will go away."

Wang Changchi stopped and said, "Maybe you're malnourished. I'll go and buy something for you to eat."

Xiaowen nodded. Wang Changchi bought a bowl of chicken soup and carried it back, where he slowly fed Xiaowen.

"You have some," said Xiaowen.

Wang Changchi tilted the bowl and made a slurping sound as if he were drinking the soup.

"You're drinking air," said Xiaowen. "Don't think I can't tell the difference."

"I'm not the one who's dizzy," said Wang Changchi, "so why should I have the chicken soup?"

After resting a while, Xiaowen opened her eyes. Supporting her, Wang Changchi helped her walk a few steps, but she sat down almost immediately, feeling that the whole world was spinning. Wang Changchi put her in a wheelchair and told her to close her eyes, and then he wheeled her away.

"Where are we going?" she asked.

"To get you examined."

"We only have enough food money for seven days."

"Don't worry about money."

Wang Changchi wheeled her to gynaecology, neurology and the ultrasound room.

"The child is normal," said the doctor, "and everything is normal with the mother."

"If everything is normal," said Xiaowen, "then why am I dizzy?"

"In the early stages of pregnancy," replied the doctor, "some women get dizzy, but a village girl like you ought not to be so delicate."

Hearing this, Wang Changchi was furious. "So village girls have no right to be dizzy? There was I thinking she was too weak to withstand the wind. She looks pale and complains all day long about her aches and pains."

"You're far too sensitive," said the doctor, pulling a long face. "All I did was tell you a fact."

"Villagers are people," said Wang Changchi, "and they get ill just like city folk."

The doctor repeated himself several times, yes, yes, yes... and with a sudden wave of his hand said, "Get out of here."

Wang Changchi wheeled Xiaowen out and from behind him came the comment, "That country bumpkin is a loudmouth. Hearing him shout a few times will make the other pregnant women miscarry."

"Did you hear what he said?" asked Wang Changchi.

"Don't piss them off," said Xiaowen, "we still have to come back for more check-ups."

Wang Changchi helped Xiaowen onto a long bench in the lobby and got her to lie down. She fell sound asleep. Afraid she would get cold, Wang Changchi took off his coat and covered her with it. Because Wang Changchi sweated so heavily at work, he wore only a pair of long johns underneath. Now, having removed his coat, he felt chilly. To stave off the cold, he paced rapidly around the lobby, stopping only after he began to perspire. When he felt cold, he walked, when he got warm, he stopped. He walked and stopped until evening when Xiaowen woke up. By then there were few people in the hospital entrance hall and the sky outside was already dark. Xiaowen felt she could breathe more easily, and she didn't feel that dizzy.

Xiaowen had difficulty finding Zhang Hui. She tried several times, but each time, the bus made her dizzy and she almost didn't make it back to where they were staying. The more trouble she had finding her way, the more nervous she became, and the more nervous she became, the dizzier she got. Sometimes when she went to buy groceries, she would faint. But after fainting several times, she grew more experienced and whenever she felt dizzy, she found something to lean against until she steadied herself and waited for the dizziness to pass before getting up. Every day after work, the first thing Wang Changchi would ask her was, "Are you still dizzy?" Afraid he would worry, she'd deceive him and say, no. But the dizziness had a serious impact on her sleep. Every night when she lay down, the whole bed seemed to spin, the ceiling spun, and one moment she seemed to float in the air, the next to fall to the floor. She wouldn't sleep all night long, just like Wang Huai and Second Uncle when they were worried about the police turning up. Because of her insomnia, she felt not only dizzy but also ached. Wang Changchi noticed she had grown thinner.

"It's nothing," she said, "all pregnant women are like this."

After a dozen or so bus trips, Xiaowen finally succeeded in locating Zhang Hui. Like a bullied child, she cried and poured out her heart to Zhang Hui.

"Too bad," said Zhang Hui, "too bad, your beauty isn't coupled with an understanding of how to make money."

"What is coupled?" asked Xiaowen.

"If you came here and massaged people's feet," said Zhang Hui, "you could make four or five hundred yuan a month."

"Really?" said Xiaowen, her mouth falling open. "Changchi makes that each month doing concrete work."

"If you lower your standards, sometimes you can make two or three hundred in a single night."

"What do you mean by lower my standards?"

"That when you accompany..."

Xiaowen gasped and her face flushed red.

Zhang Hui patted her face and said, "People like the shy and modest ones like you. They think it's purity, and the purer it is, the more they'll pay."

Shocked, Xiaowen trembled all over as if the person who just touched her was a strange man.

"Your face is rough," said Zhang Hui. "How long has it been since you last had some skincare?"

"Buying vegetables, I have to watch the cost. There's no money for skin care products."

"Then you have to make some."

Stuttering, Xiaowen said, "But I'm... I'm pregnant."

Zhang Hui told her to lift up her clothes. Xiaowen lifted them up.

"You're just a little over a month and not showing," said

Zhang Hui. "Just don't say anything to the clients."

"Then I'll miscarry."

"Miscarry and make some money, and once you've made enough money, get pregnant again."

"Changchi would kill me."

"So why tell him?"

"But I'm dizzy."

"Poor people can't make any conditions. Do you know where the money came from for your check-up?"

Xiaowen shook her head.

"When Wang Changchi went to the hospital," said Zhang Hui, "he dropped by here first to borrow a couple of hundred. Money isn't all-powerful, but nothing is possible without it."

Xiaowen sighed and said, "Can I just wash feet and not sleep with them?"

"If I were you, I'd get rid of the child and make money while I was young, then go and live a life waiting for death."

Xiaowen pulled her lapels tightly together and looked frightened as if someone were going to snatch her child away.

二十七 · TWENTY-SEVEN

IT WAS TEN O'CLOCK AT NIGHT, AND XIAOWEN was not in bed when she should have been. The soundly sleeping Wang Changchi suddenly awoke. Normally, even if Xiaowen talked to him, pinched his nose, pushed him or teased him, he wouldn't wake up. But this time he actually woke up without any of this happening. He turned on the lights, but Xiaowen was not in the room. He instinctively stuck his head out of the window, but the ground at the foot of the building was all clear, apart from the occasional passing of human shadows. Cars went along the street. In the past, he automatically screened out the noise, but now it came louder than ever in a deafening roar. Two rows of street lights stretched out with neat regularity, the light was filled with dust, making the distance a haze. Smoke was rising from the stalls grilling meat nearby, and the air filled with a fragrant aroma.

Groups of people sat around the plastic tables, drinking and talking, with the sound of swearing rising through the air.

Wang Changchi got dressed and took the bus to the Phoenix Foot Spa. Zhang Hui pulled back a corner of the curtain, and Wang Changchi could see Xiaowen and five other girls working inside. Xiaowen clenched her fists and massaged the feet of a middle-aged man. Her fists were like rollers, rolling back and forth over the soles of his feet so that the man's mouth stretched from ear to ear. Wang Changchi wanted to enter and call Xiaowen but was blocked by Zhang Hui. Zhang Hui took him to the office and shut the door.

"Do you know that she's pregnant?" asked Wang Changchi.

"Being pregnant makes earning money all the more important, otherwise in the future, the kid won't even be able to afford to stay in hospital."

"It can affect the baby."

"What village girl doesn't work up until she gives birth? Didn't your mum have you in a cornfield?"

"That's why I have no prospects."

Gloating over his misfortune, Zhang Hui said, "If you hadn't rejected me back then, you might have passed the examination."

"At the time I didn't like it that you were only a junior high school graduate."

"Now you've married a girl who's never been to school."

"Xiaowen is a good person."

"So that means I'm bad?"

Zhang Hui refused to back down and thrust her finger at Wang Changchi's face. Wang Changchi dodged to one side. This subconscious reaction seriously upset Zhang Hui. She felt that Wang Changchi had always looked down on her. A concrete worker with rough skin and whose trousers were spattered with mortar actually looked down on her! She forced him into a corner, and with both hands tilted his face upright as if to make him take a good look at her. She was no longer a village girl. Her hair was permed, and she was lightly made up. She wore perfume, her skin was white and delicate, and her figure was slender. She wore designer brands, spoke with proper pronunciation, and in her purse she had bankcards from the four largest banks, each card with a big credit limit. Wang Changchi had eyes but failed to see the substance, he only saw a motionless corpse. Zhang Hui pressed close, teasing him with her chest. He suddenly came to life, panting heavily, and a surge he hadn't felt in ages passed through his body. But he controlled himself, just as he had when he was a child competing to hold his breath underwater or when he was squeezed into the same bed, pressed close against his uncle. Zhang Hui kissed him; he bit his lip. Zhang Hui caressed him, and his pectoral muscles tightened.

"Don't you have even a little desire to do it?" asked Zhang Hui.

"Of course," he said, "but I can't."

Her nose at his chest, Zhang Hui took a deep breath and said, "You're the only one who still smells of home."

He rubbed his nose as it was filled with the fragrance of makeup. She continued caressing him.

"This is like Back Slope," she said, "this is like Big Field, this is like Yangxi Bend, this is…"

Watching her, he was about to collapse.

"Stop fooling around," he said, pushing her away. "I don't have any money."

She slapped him across the face and said, "Peasant, who do you think you are?"

"Aren't you a peasant too?"

Zhang Hui laughed loudly and said, "I'm a new person."

As she said this, she whipped out a brand-new ID. Wang Changchi could see that it was an ID for the provincial capital. Her name and age hadn't changed, but her address was 8 Jianzheng Road.

"Do you see?" she said. "This old girl is now a city person, different from you. I can seduce you for free because there've been lots of clients today and I'm in a good mood. Do you still think I'm that foolish junior high school graduate? In the past you could look down on me, today the boot is on the other foot."

"If you look down on me," said Wang Changchi, "why do you

want to seduce me?"

"Get out of here."

Wang Changchi waited in the foyer until Xiaowen got off work. He wanted to have a talk with her, but she didn't give him any time to speak and went straight out of the door and flagged down a pedicab. As he sat there, Wang Changchi again wanted to talk to Xiaowen, but once seated, she leaned against his shoulder and fell asleep. When they got back to their place, it was already one in the morning. Xiaowen was so tired that the moment her head hit the pillow, she went off to sleep. Wang Changchi still felt like chatting, but he couldn't wake her. That night Wang Changchi lay still, his mind in upheaval. He closed his eyes, but sleep refused to come. He lay dazed until the sky grew light, and as Xiaowen still hadn't woken up, he set off for work. That evening while eating dinner, he again wanted to talk but instead kept everything bottled up in his belly in case he spoiled their appetite.

After eating, Xiaowen said, "You wash the dishes, I have to get ready."

As Wang Changchi washed the dishes, he turned to look at Xiaowen. She put on some new clothes and then applied makeup in front of the mirror. It had been ages since she had done this.

"It's already dark," said Wang Changchi, "who's the makeup for?"

"Clients. Don't you know that the client is god?"

"It's the middle of the night. Aren't you tired?"

"I don't feel tired, but can you support me financially?"

"Save a little and it's no problem."

"Can you raise a child? When it comes, we'll be spending money every minute."

"I'll think of something when the time comes."

"What solution do you have apart from borrowing?"

"The problem is that... other people's idea of prenatal education is listening to music, while yours is washing someone's feet. How will the child compete in the future?"

Xiaowen threw her lipstick on the bed and said, "Then I'll stay inside and listen to music every day."

"That's it," said Wang Changchi. "You mustn't tire out the child or make the next generation suffer."

"What about the music? Can you buy music? Do you have any? Where are the discs?"

Wang Changchi walked over and coaxed Xiaowen into sitting on the bed. He then pulled a bench over and sat down. His head was facing Xiaowen's belly. Xiaowen was panting with rage. Wang Changchi snapped his fingers and said, "Music." Xiaowen looked around for the music. Suddenly Wang Changchi started to sing. It was a popular number titled, *So Long as You Live Better Than Me*.

"So long as you live better than me, there are no difficulties that can put me off..."

He sang it again. Xiaowen listened and half of her anger dissipated.

"In the past, after eating you'd sleep," she said. "How come you're so lively tonight?"

"I was wrong in the past," said Wang Changchi. "From now on, I'm going to sing to the baby every night."

"Can we eat your songs?"

"At least it'll make the baby a little smarter."

"It would be better to teach him to wash feet rather than this nonsense."

"Put it out of your mind."

Wang Changchi got up and locked the door and then hung the key on his belt.

Looking at the swinging key, Xiaowen said, "There's money to make and you won't let me. Serves you right if you stay poor all your life."

"Intelligence is instilled in the embryo," insisted Wang Changchi. "From now on, you mustn't go to those dirty places."

Xiaowen had no choice but to bathe and go to bed. Wang Changchi went to sleep but she found she couldn't. In terms of sleep, they were like two gourds in water, push this one down and the other bobs up. It was as if the Old Man in Heaven had deliberately arranged for one to keep watch for the other at night. Xiaowen once again began to feel as if the bed were spinning, the ceiling began to spin, the light bulb overhead began to spin, and spinning became a foot, then a myriad of feet. The more feet there were, the more excited she became as if each one were a banknote. But the door key was clenched tightly in Wang Changchi's hand and even though he was snoring, it was still tight in his hand. Xiaowen prised open one finger at a time until she managed to open his hand. Quietly she got out of bed, looked at the clock, and saw that it was nine o'clock and she could still put in three hours at work. So she dressed neatly and left.

After dinner the following day, Wang Changchi wanted to rebuke Xiaowen but was afraid of frightening the child, so he managed to squeeze out a fake smile.

"Do you have to go?" he asked.

"If I don't go, I'll just get dizzy and not be able to sleep. If I go, I'll sleep till noon."

"Why is that?"

"I can make money, so my mind can be at ease."

"So your dizzy sickness is caused by having no money and not because you're pregnant."

"To tell you the truth, I'm dizzy with poverty."

Wang Changchi could only let her go. After dinner every day, he'd accompany Xiaowen to the Phoenix Foot Spa and then sit in the hotel foyer and wait for her. As he waited, he drifted off to sleep.

The security guard woke him with a tap of his foot and said, "Hey, you can't sleep here."

"There's no one else on the sofa, right?" said Wang Changchi.

"Your appearance will frighten away the guests."

"You look like you're a villager. How about showing a little compassion?"

The security guard pointed to a passageway. Wang Changchi entered it and sat down with his back against the wall. The security guard peeked in, afraid he might be up to something.

"When my wife gets off work," said Wang Changchi, "please

tell her I'm here."

The security guard withdrew. A few seconds later, Wang Changchi resumed his interrupted sleep.

二十八 · TWENTY-EIGHT

XIAOWEN DISCOVERED WANG CHANGCHI sleeping in the passageway.

"Zhang Hui has an office," she said, "why don't you sleep there?"

"She used to be a country bumpkin," said Wang Changchi, "now she's the boss. The situation has changed, so it's better if I sleep here."

When there was a lull in the work, Xiaowen told Zhang Hui that Wang Changchi waited for her every night in the passageway and that it was quite pitiful.

"He brought it on himself," said Zhang Hui. "Don't you know the way here? Why does he have to bring you to work and take you home every day?"

"He doesn't think it's safe."

"If he can last a whole month waiting in the passageway, it'll prove he really cares for you."

Each time she finished massaging a pair of feet, Xiaowen would step out into the hall for a breath of fresh air and then go from the second floor down to the ground floor to see Wang Changchi as a way to exercise and relax. Hearing Xiaowen's footsteps, Wang Changchi would immediately wake up. He would hug her, kiss her, pat her shoulders and say, "Be good, Child, your ma is making money for you."

After several minutes of affectionate contact, Xiaowen would feel completely revived.

"Go to sleep," she'd say, "you still have to lay brick walls tomorrow."

Wang Changchi closed his eyes. Xiaowen went back upstairs. As her footsteps were sounding in the passageway, Wang Changchi was already fast asleep. A serious shortage of sleep meant he had to grab what he could and not waste a second.

To relieve her burden a little, he moved from the ground floor to the second floor. The moment Xiaowen opened the door to the hallway, she could see him. He now carried a bag with an insulated meal box containing the chicken soup Xiaowen had cooked during the day. The moment Xiaowen appeared, he opened the meal box and fed her. The various levels contained pickled turnips, sweets and biscuits. He would hand Xiaowen whatever she felt like eating. If Xiaowen had the time, he'd massage her shoulders and loosen up her arms. He'd massage her and she'd go and massage the clients. He was like her refuelling station, and she was an extension of his fingers, extended all the way to the clients' feet, like a massage relay.

One night, Zhang Hui called Xiaowen to her office and gave her two weeks' wages. Xiaowen squeezed the envelope and feeling its thickness said, "Thank you, Elder Sister Zhang."

"How many months have you been pregnant?" asked Zhang Hui.

"About two."

"Do you intend to get rid of it?"

Xiaowen shook her head.

"You must think clearly," said Zhang Hui.

"I have."

"If you don't get rid of it, it'll be obvious to the customers in another two months, which means you have two more months to make money. I've worked it out for you and the money you make will only be enough for check-ups and tests. But what about the hospital stay after the baby is born?"

"There's also Changchi's wages."

"His wages are enough only for rent and food, right?"

"At best I won't stay in the hospital and will have the baby at home like in the village."

"Can you guarantee the safety of mother and child? Can you guarantee there won't be complications? Didn't you come to the city so that the child would get city treatment?"

"What should I do?"

"You figure it out."

Xiaowen left without uttering a sound. She entered the lift and descended to the ground floor and went through the main entrance of the hotel, and only then did she remember that Wang Changchi was still in the hallway on the second floor. So she got back in the lift and returned to the second floor and told Wang Changchi that they were leaving.

"We've just got here and now we're leaving?" said Wang Changchi. "Aren't you working tonight?"

At that moment, Xiaowen came to herself and said, "I thought I was already finished."

Wang Changchi felt her forehead.

"Are you feeling all right?" he asked with concern.

"It's nothing," said Xiaowen, "I'm just a little upset."

"If that's the case, then don't stay and give any massages."

"If I don't work, how will we take care of the baby?" said Xiaowen, suddenly raising her voice. "If you can't provide for the baby, why do you want me to have it? You knew we were coming to the city, so why were you in such a hurry to have a kid? Why couldn't you control yourself from the very beginning?"

"It's all my fault for underestimating the difficulties."

"All you can do is criticise yourself and not come up with a solution."

"I have been thinking about it."

"What kind of solution have you come up with?"

"Lots of them – selling a kidney, robbery, theft and swindling, but only one of them is possible."

"Which?"

"Selling a kidney."

"Who would buy one like yours?"

"My kidneys have the virtue of youth."

"People would probably be afraid of being contaminated, of becoming poor after receiving your kidney. And you haven't considered, can a part from an oxcart be used in a car?"

Wang Changchi was stunned, never imagining that Xiaowen could be so mean. That was the meanest thing he had ever heard since he was old enough to understand human speech. He wanted to lash out and slap her, but thinking of the child, he gritted his teeth. Xiaowen slapped her hand over her own mouth and said, "Sorry, I was never like this before. My temper is getting worse."

"Poverty is the mother of calamity."

Xiaowen lowered her head and bit her lip for a while.

"Changchi," she said, "since we haven't prepared, why do we want to have a baby?"

"Don't be like that. I'm already attached to him. I've even thought of a name."

"What's that?"

"Dazhi."

"Can we save it for the next one?"

"No. The sooner we have the baby, the sooner we'll enjoy happiness."

"Did having you make your dad happy?"

"At least I gave him the illusion."

"But I have no illusions."

"Believe me, believe the child."

"What can you give me that I would believe?"

"I'll swear an oath."

"Swear what oath?"

"I swear the child will have enough to eat and wear, will get a good education, will go to college, will have a job and position, and that he'll be nothing like his dad."

"What guarantee can you provide?"

"Money."

"Where's the money?"

"I'll make it."

Xiaowen was convinced that Wang Changchi was just boasting again. After all, he'd bragged like this more than once. But bragging for the sake of bragging did not affect the way Xiaowen thought. Xiaowen was reckoning accounts every day, almost every moment. She calculated what it would cost for the child's food, clothing, education and medicine... and the more she calculated, the less confident she was. So one afternoon she decided to go to the hospital and have an abortion.

When Wang Changchi got to the construction site that day, he felt nervous, as if something bad were going to happen. Nothing was right, even the air smelled sour. When Xiaowen was eating breakfast at their place, his legs felt weak to the point he almost fell off the scaffolding at the construction site. When Xiaowen was washing the dishes, he was losing his temper at work, criticising a co-worker for not laying the bricks levelly, but the co-worker answered back. When Xiaowen took out the money at their place, he felt a pain in his chest, but the pain was like an electric shock and passed as quickly as it came. When Xiaowen picked up her bag and left their place, his mouth felt parched, as if he had placed his tongue on burning charcoal, where it hissed, giving off smoke. He wanted a drink of water but was too lazy to climb down off the scaffolding. When Xiaowen arrived at the First Hospital, he suddenly felt dizzy, and everything went black. He fell from the scaffolding, as did a pile of bricks, almost all of which landed on top of him.

When Xiaowen arrived at the obstetrics and gynaecology department, a queue of pregnant women was waiting at the office of the doctor on duty. Xiaowen's turn came more than half an hour later. She told the doctor what she wanted, the doctor filled out some forms and got her to pay first and then have a check-up. When she arrived at the entrance hall to pay her fee, an ambulance arrived with its siren blaring. In a fit of anxiety, she turned to see the ambulance pull up at the entrance. The ambulance door opened and Old Andu and three workmen pulled Wang Changchi out and rushed him to the emergency department. Xiaowen's legs gave out and she sat down on the floor. But she managed to take a breath, got to her feet and followed the trail of blood left by the stretcher. Before she could finish calling his name, tears gushed from her eyes. Wang Changchi finally heard her crying, the only crying he had heard since his accident, and it was the only crying in the entire city that had anything to do with him. He knitted his brow and his eyelids twitched as if he were trying to open his eyes. But he seemed to lack the strength to open them. His lips moved as if he wished to speak. Xiaowen pressed her ear close to his lips and heard his voice, faint as a buzzing mosquito, "We're going to have money, please don't get rid of the child. If you do, the Wang family will have no descendants."

He fainted again after speaking. Xiaowen saw that the lower half of his body was a patch of fresh blood: the crotch of his trousers and bloody flesh were stuck together.

二十九 · TWENTY-NINE

THE MEDICAL EXAMINATION SHOWED THAT WANG CHANGCHI had no broken bones, just injured flesh, but the trouble was that his penis had been smashed like a cucumber by a brick and his left testicle had been crushed like a clove of garlic. The doctor inserted a catheter, removed the mashed testicle, pulled the skin together, and stitched him up, at least preserving the functional appearance of his penis. After the anaesthetic wore off and he regained consciousness, he unconsciously reached for his crotch with his right hand, but each time he reached, he was prevented by Xiaowen, who was watching at his bedside. In his mind, there was suddenly an empty space between his legs, as if everything had been torn out by the roots or forcibly demolished or that he was now a eunuch, so he urgently wanted to test and confirm. Finding his right hand restrained, he tried with his left, only to have it restrained as well.

"Is it still there?" he asked feebly.

"Yes," said Xiaowen.

He breathed a sigh of relief as if he had retained his dignity, although it had already been destroyed.

"This is definitely a reaction," he said. "The weak legs, chest pain, dry mouth and dizziness are reactions. Heaven was using its special method to force me to come here to stop you from having an abortion."

"Then Heaven is too cruel," said Xiaowen.

"But it helped us save a life."

"One injured, one going to give birth, the burden is like that pile of bricks."

"There's always a way out."

"It's over, I have moved further and further from the life you talk about."

"Even though the child's life has been saved, we still have to accept the punishment. Not everything is perfect."

Xiaowen sighed. Other than sighing, there was nothing else to do.

"Bad things can sometimes become good things," said Wang Changchi in an attempt to comfort her, but even more to console himself.

"It's been a long time since I saw anything good."

"Perhaps... they'll give me some workman's disability compensation."

"From the very beginning, even your classmate Huang Kui refused, so why do you think they will?"

"I said perhaps."

"Oh..." With each sigh, Xiaowen sounded more despondent.

However, a few days later, Old Andu brought the manager of the construction site to the hospital. They brought a bouquet of flowers, said a lot of nice things and left a paper package. Before they had vanished down the hall, Xiaowen could no longer restrain herself. She grabbed the package and tore it open. Inside was twenty thousand yuan. Incredulous, Xiaowen pulled out a note and held it up to the window to examine it. Seeing the head portrait and the anti-counterfeiting strip in the light, she shouted out in surprise, "Changchi, the money's real."

Wang Changchi smiled and said, "Twenty thousand is more than you could get for selling a kidney."

Xiaowen didn't seem to hear him, and she carefully tried to reinsert the note in its original place. Since the stack of money was bound with a paper band, it took her quite some time. Once the note was back in place, she rewrapped the package but still couldn't get it right. After several tries, it was either too loose or warped. She just couldn't get it to look the way it did.

"Don't wrap it," said Wang Changchi, "just take it to the bank and deposit it."

Xiaowen refused to give up. She tore the package open and rewrapped it, but it still wasn't right.

"It can only be wrapped so tightly by someone with years of experience," said Wang Changchi. "You only saw it once, so how can you expect to do it as well as them?"

All Xiaowen could do was put it down, raise her head and say, "With this money, I won't have to go and massage feet, will I?"

"I said I'd see to it that you lived like a city person."

Xiaowen almost said thank you, but the moment she opened her mouth, something seemed amiss as if she had discovered a startling secret, and her expression changed.

"Did you do it on purpose?" she asked.

"Do what on purpose?"

"Fall and hurt yourself."

"You think I'm mad?"

Regardless of how Wang Changchi tried to explain things, Xiaowen remained sceptical and assumed he had done it deliberately, otherwise his previous oath would be hard to explain. He earned a trifling five hundred yuan a month, so where was he going to get more?

"Who cares if it was on purpose or not?" said Wang Changchi. "Getting the money is the only thing that matters. The boss said it all. Who cares if a cat is black or white, so long as it can catch mice?"

Xiaowen saw the logic and thought it was better than selling a kidney, so she saved the money.

Although Wang Changchi was insistent, he soon developed doubts of his own. He recalled the circumstances of his accident over and over again. At first, he was sure he hadn't done it intentionally, and every detail confirmed that. However, the idea of having done it on purpose began to take hold, overwhelming the idea of "unintentional". The more his memories departed from the facts of the matter, the more ashamed he became of himself. He even began to suspect he had intentionally loosened his fingers on the night Xiaowen had to prise the key from his hand to let her go and make money. But the facts said otherwise. How could fact become fiction in memory? How was he able to convince himself? Because he needed money. There were no facts for someone without money. Intentional is intentional, he consoled himself, if it hadn't been intentional, then I wouldn't be able to stay in the city. Thinking and consoling himself this way, his injuries improved by the day. While Xiaowen was looking after Wang Changchi, she slipped off to the obs and gynae department for an ultrasound test.

The doctor said, "The foetus is normal and it's a boy."

When Wang Changchi heard the news, he was overjoyed. "A boy, that's perfect."

From then on, he wouldn't let Xiaowen come to look after him and told her to go back to their rented rooms and rest and calmly concentrate on the baby, drink more chicken soup or bone soup, and devote herself to producing a genius. Xiaowen refused to leave, so he refused to eat.

"So you really want me to leave?" asked Xiaowen.

He kept his eyes wide open until Xiaowen picked up the clothes he had changed out of and left the room. Only then did he manage a smile, take the food from the head of the bed and begin to eat. He could already get up and walk around, and though he still ached, he could look after himself. All he had to do was order food and water and someone would bring it to his bed. The bathroom was only five metres from the door to his room, and he could use it by leaning against the wall for support. His urinary tract still hurt when he relieved himself, though. At intervals, Xiaowen would arrive at the hospital bringing clean clothes for him. Before uttering three sentences, she was yawning constantly, as if the world owed her sleep.

"What's wrong?" asked Wang Changchi.

"I had no idea sleep was so addictive," she replied. "The more I sleep, the more I want to sleep."

"All pregnant women are that way. The better you sleep, the healthier the child will be."

Late one night, Wang Changchi had a chest pain that woke him from his sleep. Similar to the pain he felt at the construction site before he fell, it was like an electric shock that went as quickly as it came. He tossed and turned and couldn't go back to sleep, so he got up, grabbed his crutches and left his room. With each step he took, it pulled below his hips, and with each pull, it hurt, as if a joint was out of whack. Gritting his teeth, he entered the lift, got out on the ground floor and headed towards the main entrance. A biting wind chilled his hip, and the pain gradually seemed to freeze. He stopped a cab and hurried home. Quietly opening the door, he thought he saw Xiaowen sound asleep, but never expected to find the bed empty. Xiaowen wasn't there. He sat down on the edge of the bed, picked up Xiaowen's pillow and sniffed, breathing in a heady perfume. He turned off the light but sat for a while longer. Afraid of frightening Xiaowen when she returned, he stood up and turned on the light again.

The light shone directly downwards from above, imprinting his shadow on the floor. He looked at the slippers at the foot of the bed, at the wooden chest in the corner of the room, and a bit farther off at the cupboard, umbrella, dinner table and the thermos on the table... As he stared, all the objects became empty, a dazzling white surface, without focus, centre or objective. After what seemed like a long time, he saw a small dot moving in the ultra-whiteness, and so he adjusted his focus only to discover it was a cockroach. Slowly it climbed up the thermos, circled the cap, descended directly to the dining table, where it made a circle, and then descended the table leg to the floor. It made its way towards him until it reached his toes. It seemed to probe but also to hesitate. He sat motionless. The cockroach climbed up on his instep, and with each step it took, the skin of his foot itched. He remained absolutely still, afraid of scaring the insect as if it were a friend of the night. It stopped at his ankle, apparently considering whether to go up his leg. He held his breath and didn't blink, waiting for it to decide.

Suddenly the door made a noise, startling Wang Changchi. In the doorway stood Xiaowen, her eyes popping out in amazement. She tightly clutched a small cloth bag with both hands. Inside the bag was a solid object, which she rubbed with her fingers. She wore a cream-coloured jacket and a pink scarf. She was lightly made-up, but with a heavy application of lipstick, so heavy that it threatened to flatten her full lips at any moment.

"You're back," said Wang Changchi.

She replied with a grunt before entering and closing the door, taking off her leather shoes and changing into slippers. It was then that he realised she had been wearing high heels. In the few days he had not seen her, her appearance was that of a city girl, if not downright fashionable.

"Have you gone back to massaging feet?" he asked.

"What's wrong with that?"

From the cloth bag, she took out a stack of bills and tossed it on the bed.

"The money I made tonight is equal to what you make in a fortnight," she said.

"Who's that generous, giving you so much for a massage?"

"It's called a tip. If you give a good massage, the customer will sometimes give as much as a hundred or two hundred, sometimes only ten yuan."

She opened the chest as she spoke, taking out another pile of money and tossing it on the bed.

"This is what I've made recently," she said. "Altogether more than two thousand yuan."

"That amounts to about two hundred a night. Isn't that a little too easy?"

"What do you mean by that?"

"Nothing."

"Some people make more than I do."

"Don't we already have twenty thousand in compensation?"

"You think too much money will bite?"

"The problem is the child's dignity."

"Can you have dignity without money?"

"That depends on whether the money is clean or not."

"You stage an accident and it's clean, but the money I make massaging feet is dirty?"

"You made all of this by massaging feet?"

"What else can I do?"

"How should I know?"

"Then don't slander others."

Regardless of how resolutely and decisively Xiaowen spoke, Wang Changchi still detected a shred of hesitation in her eyes. That hesitation only confirmed his belief that she was lying, but he didn't want to ask again because tears were at that moment welling up in her eyes, and the hesitation had become a look of being wronged. Although he didn't want to hug her or comfort her, he still betrayed himself. He thought hugging her would be like hugging his child that she was carrying.

"In another month, I won't be able to conceal my condition any longer," she said. "If I want to make money, I only have a couple of weeks or so left."

"You have to stop at once or someone will die."

"Why so mean?"

"Who isn't capable of murder and arson?"

"OK, then I won't concern myself with making money."

"You just concern yourself with having the baby."

三十 · THIRTY

ONE AFTERNOON, XIAOWEN BROUGHT HIS CHANGE OF CLOTHES. From the moment she entered the door, her face was expressionless, neither speaking nor replying, as if she were still angry at not being allowed to go and make money. Cautiously, he sounded her out like the cockroach that once stopped at his feet. He even told a joke.

"A turtle injured itself and asked a snail to go and buy some medicine," he said. "Two hours later and the snail still had not returned. The turtle swore, 'Fuck your mother, if you don't come back soon, I'll die.' Suddenly, from outside the door, the snail was heard to say, 'If you swear again, then yours truly won't go'."

When he finished, he expected her to laugh or at least her face to relax a bit, but it seemed covered with a layer of wax. He laughed to provide himself with a way out of the awkward situation. She sat down on the edge of the bed and lowered her head, looking at the floor. Neither one of them spoke. The air grew tense as if stretched to breaking point.

Finally, the man compromised and asked, "Where do you feel uncomfortable?"

"I'm bleeding down below," she said, "so I feel bad all over."

He sat up quickly and asked, "Are you miscarrying?"

"That would be OK, so it won't have to suffer with us."

"Nonsense."

He grabbed his walking stick, determined to take her for a check-up.

Shaking her head, she said, "Perhaps I'll be fine in a couple of days."

One said go, the other no, the two of them were at it again.

"All pregnant women in the city get a check-up once a month," he said. "A miscarriage is no simple matter like taking a piss. If the position of the foetus isn't right, it can cost two lives."

She was silent. Leaning on his stick, he went out and called a nurse.

"A small amount of blood is considered normal," said the nurse, "but it would be best to see the doctor."

"Is bleeding normal?" Xiaowen asked.

"A small amount is," said the nurse.

"Then I'll go and have it checked," she said.

Wang Changchi breathed a sigh of relief and said, "I'll go with her."

She refused.

"I'll go as far as the door of obs and gynae," he said.

After the examination, the doctor poked her head out into the hall for a look. Wang Changchi hurried over. The doctor told him to come in and shut the door behind them, and then berated him.

"Are you the father or a beast?" she asked.

Wang Changchi didn't understand when suddenly a light went on in his head.

"If you keep poking like that," said the doctor, "there's no guaranteeing the foetus will survive."

Wang Changchi finally understood.

"I've been injured so how can I poke around?" he said.

The doctor didn't understand as her eyes swept over his face. Xiaowen's face flushed red, all the way down to her neck.

"When you say poke," asked Wang Changchi, "do you mean... the life of husband and wife?"

"What do you think I mean?" asked the doctor.

"Starting today, I won't poke any more."

"It's strictly prohibited."

"Strictly prohibited," repeated Wang Changchi, "strictly prohibited."

"I know the two of you don't have any sort of spare-time fun, but you can't enjoy yourselves at the risk of the child's life."

"Of course not, no."

The doctor slapped the table and said, "You know better, so why did you insist on doing it?"

"Some things I didn't know before," said Wang Changchi, "but now I do."

The doctor's chest was pounding as if she were the one who had been insulted. She wrote a prescription and handed it to him. He took it, bowing at the waist.

"A pregnant woman should rest in bed for a month," she said, "and not be overly active."

"Is the foetus safe?" asked Wang Changchi.

"That depends upon whether you fuck or not."

"Will the child's health be affected?"

"If she keeps the foetus, no."

"*Amituofo*," intoned Wang Changchi, "what a relief."

The doctor turned and looked at Xiaowen. "If your old man fails again to respect you," she said, "just dial 110 for assistance."

Xiaowen nodded. Wang Changchi thought she had some nerve to nod.

Wang Changchi took care of the paperwork so he could leave the hospital early and devote himself to looking after Xiaowen. Leaning on his stick, he went to the shops, cooked, did the laundry and mopped the floor, all to make sure that Xiaowen didn't need to worry about any of the housework. Xiaowen tried to explain things several times, but he covered her mouth. The only topics he talked about were the weather, the price of food, clothes and the latest entertainment news in the paper. He never touched upon anything sensitive. Xiaowen found it unbearable and secretly stamped her feet. She didn't understand his attitude, nor did she wish to be tortured by his phoney affection, but she didn't know where to start. Late one night, she couldn't take it any longer, so she slapped him awake. She wasn't sure if she had slapped him awake or if he hadn't slept for the last few nights.

"We have to talk," she said.

"Do we have to?"

"I'm about to go mad, so we had better."

"As long as you guarantee you won't get angry, cry or get excited, otherwise, let's not."

"Holding it in is worse than letting it out."

Wang Changchi sighed.

"Let's get a divorce," said Xiaowen.

"We can't divorce while you're pregnant."

"Then I'll have an abortion, and then we'll get divorced."

"You can't get an abortion at five months."

"Then I'll induce it."

"If you still have any feelings for me, then you'll keep it."

"Do you hate me?"

"No, that's nonsense."

Xiaowen suddenly burst into tears.

"Don't give your sadness to the child," said Wang Changchi. "Be a little happy, so that the child will be positive. Don't you want him to have a sound mind?"

Xiaowen choked back her sobs.

"Actually," she said, "I did it to make us a little more money, and to take some of the burden off you."

"Who was he? Who were they?"

"One was named Huang, one Hu, and there was a Mr Jia and Director Xie of the Mozong Company."

"I'm going to take them to court."

"How? I took my knickers off willingly."

"Are you that cheap? That much in love with money?"

Xiaowen started crying again.

"Fuck your ancestors!" said Wang Changchi. "Crying like this is murder, do you understand?"

"If you don't want me to cry, then don't curse."

Wang Changchi pulled out some tissues and handed them to Xiaowen.

As Xiaowen wiped away her tears, she said, "It's all on account of poverty, poverty made me do it. Even though I did it with them... there's only one I love in this life..."

Wang Changchi pulled out some more tissues and passed them to her.

She didn't take them and asked, "Are you really rich?"

Wang Changchi knew she was reluctant to use the tissues, so he stuffed them back in the box one by one. He smoothed out the tissues so that it was not obvious they had been pulled out.

"Wang Changchi," said Xiaowen, "you are so stingy, you won't even let me use some tissues. And you still want me to have your baby?"

Wang Changchi quickly pulled out the tissues again, even more than before. He held them in front of her, but she still refused to take them.

"You make so little money and you're so extravagant and wasteful. Who could live with you?"

He stuffed the tissues back in the box again.

"You don't love me any more," said Xiaowen, "why should I bear you a child? You love the baby, not me."

Wang Changchi tossed the box of tissues on the bed.

"Since you don't love me," continued Xiaowen, "why should I have your baby?"

"Did I say I didn't love you?"

"If you loved me, you wouldn't just hand me tissues."

"Then what should I do?"

"The one who loves me would wipe away my tears."

Wang Changchi never dreamed she could become so wily.

Was it on account of the environment or because she was pregnant? Maybe it was neither and it was her clients who had taught her. With this thought, he began to consider giving it all up, but suddenly he saw Wang Huai carrying a cane and coming over hill and dale to beat him. So he softened and was no different from his limp, injured dick. He pulled out some tissues and wiped away Xiaowen's tears.

"So you still don't love me?" asked Xiaowen.

The hand he'd used to wipe away her tears stopped in midair.

"Didn't I wipe away your tears?"

"The one who loves me would wipe more gently."

He gently lowered his hand and carefully wiped Xiaowen's face.

"You don't love me, do you?"

"I'm not wiping gently enough?"

"I wouldn't need to remind the one who loves me."

Wang Changchi couldn't bear it any longer and threw the moist tissues against the wall before they fell in bits onto the floor. The floor was littered with bits of paper. Xiaowen got down off the bed, dressed, put on her shoes and headed for the door.

"Where are you going?"

"To the hospital."

As she spoke, she reached for the door lock. Wang Changchi walked over and blocked the door. She shoved him. He latched on to the doorframe, not to be budged.

"You don't love me," she said. "You're using me. You pretend you tolerate me, but as soon as the baby is delivered, you'll dump me."

"To love a child is to love its mother."

"I don't believe you."

"How can I convince you?"

"You just can't convince me."

"Can I swear an oath?"

Xiaowen lowered her head.

"If you have the baby," said Wang Changchi, "I'll love you

forever. If I abandon you after you have the baby, may I be run over by a truck, crushed by bricks, squashed by a falling tower block, die from cancer, be bound up and killed by a rebar..."

Xiaowen cried and fell into his arms.

三十一 · THIRTY-ONE

AFTER A MONTH'S REST, THE SPACE BETWEEN Wang Changchi's legs recovered to superficially normal. That meant the skin had healed, he walked without a limp, and there was no pain when urinating, but the fact of the matter was that he could not get an erection. The other function of his penis had not returned. Fortunately, Wang Changchi did not need this function for the time being because Xiaowen was protecting the foetus.

Xiaowen's mood was basically stable, but she was frequently dizzy. Everything felt like being on a boat: the bed, buildings and streets. It was like being at sea, but she didn't know how to swim, so any sign of disturbance made her nervous, even wobbly. Every time she seemed to feel the boat roll, she would immediately latch on to whatever was at hand, sometimes the bed, the doorframe, or someone's shoulder, occasionally she would even clutch the rice straw that was used to wrap eggs. As long as she could hold onto something, she could steady herself.

Wang Changchi wanted to take her to the hospital for a thorough check-up, but she shook her head.

"I just need something to do so I won't get dizzy," she said.

So Wang Changchi let her go out to buy groceries, cook and mend clothes, but these chores couldn't distract her, so she frequently put her hand to her forehead and sat down, waiting for the dizziness to pass like a typhoon. Wang Changchi repeatedly tried to coax her to get help and finally persuaded her to go to the neurology department. The doctor rubbed her palms, squeezed her fingertips, and had her close her eyes and raise her arms level, but he was unable to find anything out of the ordinary. After everything else, he suggested she get a CT scan.

When she was told the price, she said, "I need to go to the

toilet."

Then she vanished. Wang Changchi waited in the hallway for a long time, but seeing she did not return, he asked permission to check the women's toilet and found no trace of her. Angry, Wang Changchi returned to the place they were staying, where he found her busily occupied with cooking as if they had never gone to the hospital.

"You can avoid debts," he said, "and you can avoid people, but you can't avoid illness."

Forcefully slicing a cucumber, she asked, "Why don't I get dizzy when I massage people's feet?"

"Yeah, why is that?" Wang Changchi also thought it strange.

"Because I had an income every day."

Thinking back, Wang Changchi felt she had a point, so he took the account book from the trunk and placed it in front of her.

"Have a good look," he said. "The amount we've saved is in five figures."

She picked up the sliced cucumber and threw it in the wok where it sizzled.

As she stirred, she said, "It's just going out and not coming in, so regardless of how much there is, it'll all get used up."

"Don't worry," he said, "I'm going back to work tomorrow."

Wang Changchi went to see Old Andu, who arranged for him to lay bricks. That evening after work, Wang Changchi headed home carrying the boxed meal from the cafeteria, when he decided to buy something to make Xiaowen happy. It was the first time he had had such a thought since arriving in the city, but his pockets were shrivelled, and he discovered he had not brought any cash. His eyes grew sharp, and everything seemed to grow luminous before him. The trees along the street, the cars, clothes, food and all the stalls became more than twice as eye-catching, even the litter on the ground stood out to his eye. As he walked, he noticed a bunch of roses that had been discarded on the roadside, so he bent over and picked them up, discovering that most of them had wilted, but two looked fresh. So he carefully plucked out the two good ones, afraid of knocking off the petals.

He entered with one hand behind his back and walked straight over to Xiaowen before whipping out the roses. Smiling and with eyes shining, she received the flowers and excitedly smelled them as if she were going to inhale them. But almost at once she detected that something wasn't quite right with the fragrance and that the petals were wrinkled.

She looked downcast and asked, "How much for one?"

Seemingly proud of himself he said, "Take a guess."

She flung the flowers on the table and said, "Fool, you were cheated by the flower seller."

"Really?"

"You're blind, the flowers are old."

Wang Changchi picked up the flowers and sniffed and felt that while the fragrance wasn't exactly fresh, it wasn't old either.

"I found them," he said.

Smiling once again, Xiaowen snatched the flowers from him, sniffed them and then put them in an empty vinegar bottle, which she placed by the bed. For a moment, the room seemed brighter.

"Are they no longer old?" asked Wang Changchi.

"Normally nothing is old if it's free."

Because of two long-stemmed roses, Xiaowen ate an extra half bowl of rice. After eating, she sprinkled a little water on the flowers. It had been ages since Wang Changchi had seen her so happy. After the happiness had passed, Wang Changchi wondered why she had been so cheerful. Certainly it was not because of the roses, but rather because they had come at no cost. After this, on his way back every evening, he'd bring something home, such as an empty cardboard box, some twine, a half bottle of glue, a brick-layer's trowel, concrete paper, or even a ping-pong bat missing its rubber surfaces. Each of these things that he picked up or walked off with only increased Xiaowen's appetite and made her laugh. To prolong her happiness at getting something for nothing, his range gradually expanded. He scanned every nook and corner on the street and carefully examined every bit of rubbish at the construction site. Sometimes he even considered stealing things, but the idea vanished as quickly as it came like brilliant fireworks in the night sky. The sight of a cigarette glowing in the dark of the night, brief as it was, excited his mind as if he really had stolen something. If he couldn't pick up anything, he'd spend a little money and buy slippers, pins, a sugar canister, a cloth doll, a toy truck, a piggy bank, a baby bonnet or a milk bottle. He never came home empty-handed. Whatever he bought, old or new, he always said he found it or someone had given it to him. Xiaowen's mood improved, she put on weight, and her dizzy ailment ended up with someone else.

One evening, Wang Changchi brought someone home with him. It was Liu Jianping, who had hauled mortar with him at the construction site in the county town. Through an introduction, he had transferred to the construction site where he happened to run into Wang Changchi. They patted each other on the shoulder for half an hour and then Wang Changchi brought him home. Hearing him use the dialect of her old home, Xiaowen accepted him as her brother, prepared two extra dishes, and hauled out a case of beer. They ate and drank, drank and chatted. And as they chatted, the maple tree of home came up.

"I'm from Dingguanchang," said Liu Jianping, "just below your village on the mountain. Normally when we look up we can see that tree in the gap. That tree really is huge – you can see it from more than ten *li* away. Once, just as I was passing by, it started to rain, so I took shelter under it, and I didn't get wet at all."

"Really?" cried Xiaowen.

Wang Changchi continuously rubbed his hands in excitement. He gulped down a full glass of beer and wiped his mouth.

"In the winter," he said, "when I went to primary school in the neighbouring village, everyone carried a brazier, and when we arrived under the tree, we'd all pile the fallen leaves inside. Because the leaves were damp, and the coal in the braziers wasn't burning vigorously, the leaves wouldn't catch fire but simply smouldered. The smoke became thicker and blacker, and then everyone set off at a run with their braziers, leaving long trails of smoke, like a train spewing steam.

"Every time I left home, I would look back when I reached that tree as if there were a public order on it. When I was returning home, I started to jog every time I reached that tree, hoping to get a glimpse of my folks all the sooner. After being away for a semester, one second more or less didn't make any difference. Jogging just felt like a sort of urgency."

As he spoke, Wang Changchi's eyes grew moist.

Xiaowen's eyes also grew moist. "Shame on you!" she said.

Liu Jianping's eyes grew moist after he spoke. The three of them actually began crying over a tree.

The number of empty beer bottles beside the table increased, the men talking with ever more animation. Talking and talking, Wang Changchi brought up his workplace injury. After listening, Liu Jianping suddenly raised his hand. At that moment, Wang Changchi and Xiaowen noticed that his little finger was missing a joint. They felt it was strange they hadn't noticed it before.

"I accidentally sawed it off when I was working as a carpenter for a rich bloke," said Liu Jianping. "At the time I was just going to put up with it, but I talked myself around. Why should I always be the one to do that? So I asked the boss for compensation. To tell you the truth, his words were sharper than those of the famous writer Lu Xun, each word an attack. In a right state, I stayed put and refused to budge. His frightened wife gave me ten thousand yuan, but I didn't leave. Her husband took out another ten thousand, but I still didn't leave. Think about it, ten thousand today, another ten thousand tomorrow. To tell you the truth, I thought I would just stay there forever. But they made a living, how else did they have that much money? On the third day, they called a policeman. The cop said, 'If you scarper, I'll get them to compensate you another ten thousand.' I figured half a pinkie was worth thirty thousand. You know, in the village, a whole life isn't worth that much. So I had to give the cop some credit."

"Thirty thousand? Half your bloody little finger is worth more than Changchi's dick," Xiaowen burst out.

"So you've got to have the nerve to occupy your boss's house," said Liu Jianping.

"He paid the medical bills," said Wang Changchi, "and gave me twenty thousand without a murmur. Everything is OK now, and I want to go back to work, so how can I ask for a handout?"

"You can't even get it up," said Xiaowen. "You call that OK?"

"If you really can't get it up," said Liu Jianping, "then you've made a pile. Don't you read the papers? The court has already ordered the first compensation for mental anguish. You can make the same case for your injury."

"How much for mental anguish?" asked Xiaowen.

"Tens of thousands," replied Liu Jianping.

"Then ask for compensation," said Xiaowen.

"I couldn't get the better of Huang Kui," said Wang Changchi, "so how am I going to beat a big boss?"

Liu Jianping slapped Wang Changchi on the shoulder, knocking him sideways.

"If you agree," said Liu Jianping, "leave it to me. To tell you the truth, it's what I do now."

"You get compensation for people?" asked Wang Changchi.

Liu Jianping nodded with self-satisfaction as if it were something to be proud of. Wang Changchi looked sceptical as if didn't make sense.

"Someone cut his finger off on purpose to get compensation," said Liu Jianping. "Another person tricked someone else into a mine, hit him over the head with a shovel and later told the mine operator that it was a relative."

"Isn't that really bad?" asked Wang Changchi.

"They were bad first," remarked Liu Jianping, "so we followed suit. In this world, we only need to remind them that we have bones in our bodies and can still be a thorn in their side."

Crash. Wang Changchi threw the beer bottle to the floor.

"You agree?" asked Liu Jianping.

Crash. Wang Changchi threw the second beer bottle to the floor.

Xiaowen trembled with fright. "Ancestor! Don't break any more, otherwise the kid will grow up to collect beer bottles."

Crash.

4
OVER THE EDGE

三十二 · THIRTY-TWO

"Do you know what you can do with fifty thousand?" said Xiaowen, shaking Wang Changchi awake and holding up one hand. By the dim light coming from outside, he could vaguely make out a fan shape and then saw five fingers. Since Liu Jianping had been there, Xiaowen had been going on about mental anguish, and wouldn't give it a rest, even late at night.

"Isn't Liu Jianping going to take twenty thousand of it?" asked Wang Changchi.

"Even just thirty thousand," said Xiaowen, extending her thumb and forefinger horizontally and leaving her other fingers standing straight up. "With thirty thousand we could build a two-storey concrete house at home and have enough for our child to go to school from kindergarten to high school."

It was as if Wang Changchi's mind were jolted by an electric shock because Xiaowen had said exactly what he had been thinking, which was to encourage the child to study and build a house in his old hometown. But still he hesitated, his right hand unconsciously feeling his private parts.

"Perhaps it's just forgotten what to do," he said, "and it might remember in a few days."

"Nonsense. I've pinched it for you a thousand times, and there's still no reaction."

"Don't you hope it will get better?"

"What good is hope? It takes actual strength. You were discharged from the hospital a month ago, and if you don't seek compensation, your boss will forget about it."

"What happens if it gets better? Won't that make me a swindler?"

"Can cotton become steel? An opportunity like this may never come again, so you have to seize it."

An injury became a business opportunity, and Wang Changchi didn't feel good about it. He turned his back, incredulous that he was so soft. He had never been very positive about getting compensation as if by not seeking it, he was leaving an avenue of hope. But if he were to seek compensation, and was successful, he would for shame's sake never get hard again. Regardless of how Xiaowen cajoled or pressured him, he didn't seek money for his injured organ from his boss but went to the urology department several times. The doctor wrote a bunch of prescriptions for Western medicines. He kept the medicine hidden and took it on the sly behind Xiaowen's back. He felt ashamed each time he took it as if he were failing to share some culinary delicacy with Xiaowen. After a couple of weeks, it was still as soft as cotton. Despite being upset, he didn't give up and went to see a Chinese doctor, who wrote a bunch of prescriptions for Chinese medicine. The Chinese medicine had to be boiled in water, which didn't escape Xiaowen's notice. Every night after dinner, he'd boil the medicine. Its smell bubbled out of the cooking pot, filling the whole room and permeating their bedding, pillows and clothes.

Holding her nose, Xiaowen asked, "Will this medicine really cure you?"

"Why would I take it if it wasn't going to cure me?"

"They just want your money," sneered Xiaowen.

This had occurred to Wang Changchi too, but if he saw every doctor as a swindler, and all medicine as snake oil, then there'd be no hope left for him. He took the Chinese medicine for about two weeks but it had no effect on his private parts. But he still had hope, guessing that the problem wasn't the medicine, but rather the dosage. Hearing him gulp down the medicine gave Xiaowen goosebumps as if she were drinking it herself and not him. Each time before drinking the medicine, he'd tell Xiaowen to cover her ears so she wouldn't get upset. She would remove her hands from her ears only when he finished. During the day, he'd pour the medicine into a plastic container and take it to the construction site. Seeing him drinking the medicine, Liu Jianping patted him on the shoulders.

"Making all that noise when you drink the medicine won't make it more effective," he said. "It's time to seriously go after some compensation."

Wang Changchi shook his head until the bones in his neck creaked.

That day, Wang Changchi received a money order for a thousand yuan from Wang Huai. It was sent from the post office in the county town. The thin slip of paper weighed heavily and painfully in his fingers. Since arriving in the city, he hadn't sent a penny to the village, but now the village was impinging on the city. What an irony! He hid in a corner of the construction site and wept silently before sending the money back, along with an additional thousand yuan.

Ten days later, Second Uncle replied, "A month ago, your mum and dad left the village in the valley saying they were going to the provincial capital to live with you. Only after receiving your letter and the money order did I realise they weren't with you..."

This came as a cruel blow to Wang Changchi, worse even than his fall from the scaffolding. That night he returned empty-handed to where they were staying, having forgotten the boxed meal from work along with his medicine bottle. Xiaowen thought it was strange, so while he was in the bathroom, she went through his pockets, where she found the letter from Second Uncle. She read it over twice and after getting the gist, went and knocked on the bathroom door. The door was not locked. Wang Changchi was just standing there apparently in a daze.

Holding up the letter, Xiaowen said, "I know where they are."

Wang Changchi had not originally planned to tell her about it and even less expected her to have an answer. Coming out of the bathroom, he snatched the letter away from her.

"You can't read, so what do you know?"

"They've got to be begging for money in the county town."

Wang Changchi covered her mouth.

She didn't close it but continued, "Begging is the only way they can make money."

"Nonsense."

Xiaowen knew she had said too much when Wang Changchi pulled a long face. But she couldn't restrain herself any more than if she discovered someone else's dirty secret.

"Actually," she said, "there's nothing really wrong with begging. At least they can support themselves, which is better than staying uselessly at home waiting for manna to fall from Heaven."

Wang Changchi said, "Maybe they're selling tofu? You know my mum's tofu is white and soft."

"Where would the money for that come from?"

"Borrowed."

"They didn't borrow any from Second Uncle, so who would they borrow from?"

Shit, what a disgrace, thought Wang Changchi. I have so many classmates and teachers in the county town, and if they see them begging, they won't be cursing them, but their descendants. No wonder my ears have been burning recently – they've all been cursing me.

Unconsciously, Wang Changchi rubbed his ears which felt like they had been burned. After dinner, his ears still felt warm, as if all the fingers in the world were poking his spine. He found a soft bag and packed a few clothes, planning to go to his home county for a short visit.

"What can you do even if you go there?" asked Xiaowen.

"Find them and take them home."

"You can't make any money at home, and without money, you can't build a house."

"Don't we have money? Enough for a two-storey house."

As he spoke, he opened the trunk and took out the account book.

"If you take the money," said Xiaowen, "what'll be left for the child?"

"You could always let me deliver it myself, right?"

Wang Changchi rubbed the account book between his fingers. His fingers got hot as did the book and both trembled. After hesitating for a moment, Wang Changchi returned it to its original place.

"If you don't send them money," said Xiaowen, "what good will it do to go home? As soon as you come back to the city, they'll go out begging again."

"Then what do you suggest I do?" Wang Changchi paced back and forth.

"I have a solution."

Wang Changchi stopped pacing. "What solution?"

"Send them the money in the account, but when you get back, ask for compensation from the property bloke. That way we can build a home in the village and still have money to have a baby in the city."

Wang Changchi thought it was a solution, but deep down he rejected it. In addition to being unwilling to accept physical defeat, he was also afraid of suing. He had never had the confidence to sue a wealthy, powerful person. Perhaps this was the real reason he had been taking medicine, clearly knowing it would have no effect and could delay the need to take legal action. He stood in front of the trunk for a long time, not daring to reach out his hand, afraid that the account book was still hot.

三十三 · THIRTY-THREE

RETURNING TO THE COUNTY TOWN, WANG CHANGCHI set about looking for Wang Huai. He checked all the busy places: the bus station, cinemas, shopping areas, restaurants and the wharf. Even the rubbish bins, tree stumps and telephone poles came under his scrutiny, but he didn't find any trace of him. The less likely he seemed to find him, the happier he was, believing that Wang Huai had not become a beggar and that the Old Man in Heaven would give him a different answer. But on the morning of the third day, approximately ten metres from the gate of the Second Primary School, he spied a prostrate figure, the shape of which was all too familiar. What was once noble, big and tall, courageous, safe, kind, wise and hard-working was now more like a dead dog curled up on the ground. His clothes were filthy and in tatters, his hair long and dishevelled, his face and hands soiled. A metal spittoon, which was bent out of shape and with half the paint missing from its surface, was placed in front of him. Most of the parents of schoolchildren passing by looked away but a number of the young students made their parents take out some change and throw it in the spittoon. The paper notes landed silently, the coins with a clang. He tensed with each clanging coin, even though he was standing across the street and couldn't really hear them.

Given the large number of people on the street, Wang Changchi didn't have the nerve to approach any nearer. He hid under a tree and watched from a distance, gritting his teeth to control himself, but his tears refused to comply and rolled down his face. As they rolled, he wiped them away, making him wish he could also wipe away the entire scene in front of him. As if in response, Wang Huai lifted his head and looked in Wang Changchi's direction. Wang Changchi saw that his unshaven face was black and thin, his eyes smaller and his eye sockets deeper. Wang Changchi banged his head against the tree trunk, once, twice, three times, until the old bark came off. After looking for some time and finding nothing out of the ordinary, Wang Huai lowered his head once again. The class bell rang from inside the school, and the stream of people on the street diminished. Wang Changchi wiped away his tears, came out from behind the tree, walked over to Wang Huai and tossed the twenty thousand yuan into the spittoon. It wouldn't fit into the spittoon and toppled over and fell to the ground next to Wang Huai's hand. Wang Huai's hand trembled as if he had been poked by a needle. Slowly he raised his head, looking up, stupefied, as if he were gazing into a bright light. As tears welled up in his sunken eyes, his whole face twisted, unsure whether to laugh or cry. When his face was no longer contorted, the tears flowed from his eyes, but solidified halfway down his face, like parched earth that had not received a drop of rain in ages. Seeing the scrawny, dry and cracked face in front of him, Wang Changchi found the eyes he had just wiped dry filling with tears again. He squatted and embraced Wang Huai and cried out, "Dad..." The cry seemed to break the dam of Wang Huai's tears. The tears swooshed down, flowing over mountains and fields.

"And Mum?" asked Wang Changchi.

Wang Huai pointed to the small lane opposite. Holding Wang Huai, Wang Changchi crossed the street. He never thought Wang Huai could weigh so little, almost like a child. He never thought he could be so small, like an infant. The smaller and lighter Wang Huai seemed, the more troubled and pained Wang Changchi felt.

They had rented a ten-square-metre hovel in the lane. A row of bottles sat on the windowsill facing the street. The bottles were filled with seven different coloured fluids, red, yellow, blue, green, black, white and purple, using discarded colourings. The bottles could have been flowers, beautiful and luxuriant, like a window decoration. Several wind chimes were suspended on the door which was hanging open. They were all rusty, and one look showed that they had been picked up somewhere. Inside was a bed, next to which sat a wheelchair. The kitchen stove stood near the window and in the corner, cardboard boxes and other rubbish were piled up. Placing Wang Huai in the wheelchair, Wang Changchi turned to see Liu Shuangju standing in the doorway. She blocked ninety per cent of the incoming light, which bristled around her silhouette like ears of grain. As the room was suddenly thrown into darkness, neither one of them could clearly make out the other. "Mum," he called. She was stunned and the mesh bag dropped from her hand. He picked up the bag. She wiped the corners of her eyes. He placed the bag on top of the cardboard boxes.

"You're back," she said.

"Yes."

She kept wiping away her tears. He handed her several Kleenexes. She pressed them against her face, and they at once came apart in her hands. He led her inside and had her sit on the edge of the bed. She blew her nose, wiped the paper from her face and carefully sized him up.

"Your face looks yellow. Are you ill?" she asked.

"No."

Pinching his hands and arms, she said, "You haven't been injured, have you?"

"No."

"How's Xiaowen? She has two more months to go before the baby is due. There's nothing wrong with the baby is there?"

"No."

"As long as there's nothing wrong, that's good. Ma will fix you something to eat."

As she cooked, Liu Shuangju said, "Coming here to beg was all your father's idea."

A month before, Wang Huai had sold all the chickens on the sly. When Liu Shuangju came back from the fields, she thought they had been stolen. She had lit three sticks of incense in front of the chicken coop, burned some paper and was preparing to put a curse on the perpetrator. This was an old custom. The villagers believed that by lighting a few sticks of incense and adding a curse, the thief would suffer retribution. The retribution Liu Shuangju had in mind was nothing more than the thief suffering a stomach ache, not so bad that he'd have to go to hospital, but enough to make him realise the wrong he had done, and to quietly bring back the chickens. But before Liu Shuangju opened her mouth, Wang Huai took out a wad of banknotes, twelve times the value of one chicken. Seeing this, Liu Shuangju knew what had happened.

"If you want to sell them, go ahead," she said, "but why sell them all?"

Wang Huai gazed off into the distance. The mountains were streaked with green, flocks of birds cut through the sky, and the setting sun was a patch of gold. Liu Shuangju put out the incense.

"Are you mute?" she said.

Wang Huai didn't turn to look at her. It was as if he were scanning an interior world of ideals.

"I sold them," he said, "because I wanted to send some money to Changchi and Xiaowen."

The moment he said he wanted to send them money, her heart went soft.

A week later, Wang Huai sold two young pigs. Liu Shuangju cried at the sight of the empty pig pen. "Is your next step going to be to sell me?" she asked.

"Look at my legs," said Wang Huai.

She looked and saw that his legs had shrunk considerably, and his calves and thighs could be encompassed with one hand. Although she looked at his legs for quite some time, Liu Shuangju was unable to work out the reason for selling the pigs.

"Where did my legs go?" he asked. "They evaporated with time. Where did the time go? I wasted it. If I don't act, I'll die in this godforsaken dump. The grain here isn't worth anything, the animals here aren't worth anything, even the people here have no value. I don't want to waste another minute here."

Accustomed to his grumbling, Liu Shuangju assumed it was just another one of his obsessions. She didn't think it would amount to anything until he wheeled himself around to pack his luggage. His clothes, ID and money were all stored in a wooden chest, which for his convenience was placed on the floor beside the bed. After he started packing, Liu Shuangju placed the chest on top of the square cabinet and changed the lock. He couldn't reach the chest without Liu Shuangju's help, much less open it to remove things. His spittoon, toothbrush and other unimportant items were placed in a soft bag but important things such as his clothes, ID and money were not included. Every day, Liu Shuangju continued going to the fields to weed. She had no other way of making a living except by working the land.

Wang Huai asked Liu Baitiao and Wang Dong separately to come and take the chest down. They shook their heads.

"Liu Shuangju made it clear that anyone who helped you get to the city was intentionally harming you," they said, "depriving you of food and clothing and living a life worse than that of a dog or a pig."

Sneering, Wang Huai said, "No wonder you are poor, knowing so little. I'm going to the city to share in Changchi's good fortune – he's rich and has prospects."

Regardless of how much he boasted about Wang Changchi, Liu Baitiao and Wang Dong refused to get the chest down. Wang Huai figured he'd have to do it himself rather than ask others. He got a bamboo pole with which he slowly pushed the chest, a little bit each day, confident that the day would come when he would be able to push it down. But with all the pushing, he encountered a problem. Even if he succeeded and managed to prise open the chest and get the money, it was still just the first step in a ten-thousand-mile journey. He couldn't make it to the road unless someone carried him. And even if he got to the road, and Liu Shuangju refused to accompany him, he'd still have a difficult time.

So he changed his strategy.

"Counting on my fingers," he said, "I see that Xiaowen is in her fifth month. This will be their first child. They are still children, who not only need money but also help."

This time, it was Liu Shuangju's turn to gaze off into the distance. She looked over the mountains and seemed to see Changchi, Xiaowen, and even the grandchild in the womb.

"Even a dog knows how to teach its offspring to bear and rear their young," he said, "which is more true with human beings.

Xiaowen has never been a mother, so you have to go to the city and teach her."

Liu Shuangju was silent for three days. Wang Huai brainwashed her every day.

"We can't change fate, but there is hope for the grandchild," he said. "If the birth goes smoothly and the child grows up healthy, it would be worth even picking up rubbish for a living."

Hearing this repeatedly, Liu Shuangju unlocked the trunk. She turned over the corn and the new shoots in the field to Second Uncle and his wife and set off with Wang Huai for the city. The day they left for the city, Second Uncle and Liu Baitiao walked ahead carrying Wang Huai, with Liu Shuangju carrying a basket on her back bringing up the rear. Liu Shuangju kept looking back the whole way, even when the village had vanished from sight, while Wang Huai, who was sitting on an uncovered bamboo sedan chair, never once looked back. It seemed he had no qualms as if his home were in front of him and not behind him.

At the county town, Wang Huai's plan came into being. He held on to the money, taking tight control of the finances, not allowing Liu Shuangju to go to the provincial capital or go home. Liu Shuangju suddenly felt as if she had been abducted and sold, and cursed Wang Huai as a cheat.

"Did you really think Changchi has got rich?" asked Wang Huai. "Going empty-handed, the two of us will not be able to help them, but would become a burden."

"Then why did you force me to leave the village?" asked Liu Shuangju.

"I figured it out. Xiaowen still has three months to go before giving birth, and in that time we can make a little money in the county town–"

"Your father has lost face for the Wang family, the Liu family and the He family. Every day he goes down to the street where everyone seems familiar, and I feel so ashamed that I have to bury my head in the crotch of my trousers," complained Liu Shuangju as she cooked.

She was so upset that she forgot to put salt on the vegetables.

三十四 · THIRTY-FOUR

WANG CHANGCHI HAD TO USE A WHOLE BAR OF SOAP to wash Wang Huai clean. Perhaps Wang Huai wasn't that dirty, but Wang Changchi felt a whole bar was necessary to restore his identity. After bathing him, he dressed him in clean clothes and wheeled him out of the door.

He asked questions continuously: "Are you taking me to the bus station? If we're going to the bus station, why aren't you bringing your mother? Did you want to invite me for a drink? Are you wheeling me to the crematorium? Why did we make another turn? So you are taking me to buy clothes? It doesn't seem so. Are you taking me to the police station? No, not that either. You're taking me to see Huang Kui's dad?"

Without uttering a word, Wang Changchi wheeled Wang Huai straight to the barbershop on Little River Road. When he saw the sign, Wang Huai shouted for him to stop.

"Changchi," he said, "I'll do whatever you ask, just don't cut this hair of mine. It's like an actor's face or a product trademark. If you cut it, I'll have no income."

"So you're planning on being a beggar for the rest of your life?" asked Wang Changchi. Wang Huai pulled on the wheelchair brake, making it screech to a halt while leaving two black skid marks on the pavement.

"You know given the shape I'm in, I can't make any money in the village." Wang Huai lowered his head.

"Who told you to make money?"

"I can't count on you, and in this way, I can lighten your burden a little."

"On the contrary, you just make it heavier. What did you teach me when I was a child? That starving to death was preferable to begging."

"In those days, I could still talk about dignity, but now–"

"And why not now? Don't you have food to eat?"

"I refuse to admit that I'm crippled... I want to earn my own living."

"No matter how bad, you can't make a living by kowtowing."

"That's... what I wanted to tell you."

"Then why are you refusing to get a haircut?"

"Because I can bear the fact that I am a good-for-nothing, but I can't accept that my son has no dignity."

"I can take a thousand hardships, but I can't let you lose even the tiniest bit of face."

Wang Huai suddenly lifted his head, his teary eyes fixed on Wang Changchi. Only then did their eyes meet. Just before that, one had kept his eyes on his crotch, the other on the river's surface, fearful lest their eyes meet. But now each longed to look at the other, hoping to see the pure heart behind the pitch-dark face.

"Changchi," said Wang Huai, "you have prospects."

Wang Changchi scooped up Wang Huai and carried him into the barbershop. Strangely, his pace slowed to such an extent that it was like a slow-motion scene in a film. Was it out of hesitation or did he wish to hold Wang Huai a little longer?

After the haircut, Wang Huai regained his former appearance and looked more like his old self. He apologised the entire way back.

"Changchi, I lost face for you," he said. "Not only am I sorry for the Wang family ancestors, but also sorry for our unborn descendants."

His apologies went on for the length of the road. Previously it had been Wang Changchi who had apologised to Wang Huai, but now the roles were reversed, as if Wang Changchi had subjugated Wang Huai. But Wang Changchi felt no delight in the conquest, knowing full well that those who apologise feel easy, while those being apologised to actually feel more responsible. He had something of a guilty conscience, of not feeling right, so he quickened his pace to push Wang Huai back to the rented room.

Lost in thought, Liu Shuangju was still sitting beside the cardboard boxes, as if she hadn't moved an inch since they went out more than an hour before. Only after Wang Changchi had called her several times did she come to herself and say, "Changchi, do you really intend to force us to go back?"

"Do you mean you want to stay and lose face?"

"Despite all the complaints, I've grown accustomed to it."

"Accustomed to scavenging through rubbish?"

"I can make more in one month here than I can working hard for a year in the village. See these cardboard boxes, bottles, magazines, newspapers, and this lampstand, rice cooker, clothes, cotton padding and television set, they can all still be used."

"Nobody has any use for them, it's awful."

"If a fly liked cleanliness, wouldn't it die of hunger?"

"You're my mum, not a fly."

"I more or less live like a fly."

"Then I'm the descendant of flies."

"Nonsense, you're clean. Look to your future, not to us."

"I'm part of you, how can I not be concerned?"

She was shaken by what Wang Changchi said. She turned to look at Wang Huai.

"Let's go back," said Wang Huai. "Being a farmer sounds better than being a beggar."

"But a farmer's income is not necessarily higher than a beggar's," said Liu Shuangju.

"It's not simply a matter of money, you have to consider integrity and reputation. Changchi is filial and has honour. Do you think you'll suffer from hunger and poverty?"

Sighing, Liu Shuangju said to Wang Changchi, "I never thought that when we brought you to the city you'd end up rejecting us like a city person."

"You should be satisfied," said Wang Huai. "No amount of money can buy a filial heart and honour."

They took care of the stuff they had scavenged, packed their luggage and, after returning the key to the landlord, hurried off to the bus station.

Just before boarding, Liu Shuangju asked, "Won't you come home and have a look?"

Wang Changchi shook his head. But that wasn't what he was

really thinking. He wanted to return to the home that was always on his mind and have a look at the old house, vegetable garden, pig pen and Second Uncle, and at the maple tree, the mountains and fields, and even eat his fill of home cooking. But he didn't have the courage to go home, fearing that the villagers would see through his father's lies and might work out that his parents had been begging. With a whoosh, the bus door closed and Wang Huai, who was sitting in his wheelchair, was blocked from view. Liu Shuangju's face was still visible, pressed so closely against the bus window that her nose was flattened as if it were going to burst. The bus honked several times and slowly got underway. Wang Changchi watched its rear end disappear in the distance, his heart grieving.

Coming out of the bus station, he arrived at the gate of the car repair shop and sat down on the same stone where he had rested the previous year. The mechanic was the same, but he no longer recognised him. Wang Changchi looked at the road where it entered the mountains far away and imagined the bus passing Ma Village, Jiali and the township government. He imagined Liu Shuangju getting an uncovered bamboo sedan chair from her cousin Genying's home and having Wang Huai carried past the reservoir, Taishang, the tea plantation, all the way to the door of their house. He imagined Liu Shuangju fumbling in her pocket for the key and unlocking the rusty lock.

Gradually it grew dark, the car repair shop closed, and the street lights went on, resembling two rows of candles. When the mechanic left, he gave him several questioning looks, but Wang Changchi made no response. Wang Changchi arrived in front of the place they had rented and saw the colourful bottles still sitting on the windowsill and the rusty bells chiming in a melancholy fashion. He could detect the smell left behind by Wang Huai and could see Liu Shuangju's footprints in front of the door. He walked around the place, breathing deeply, and then placing both hands against the wall, pushed for all he was worth. The wall collapsed and dust rose from the ground. He thought, If they hadn't left, the hovel would have fallen down sooner or later. If I hadn't knocked it down, they would have come again to beg. Perhaps this wasn't the reason he had pushed it over. Had he thought to bury this unsavoury history? Perhaps he had hoped to erase his own memory.

At that very moment, Wang Huai was already seated in the main room at home. Second Uncle and his wife, Zhang Wu, Zhang Xianhua, Wang Dong and Liu Baitiao had all come to visit, even Guang Sheng from the neighbouring village had turned up. They asked about things in the outside world. "How much money does Wang Changchi make? Is Xiaowen going to have the baby soon?"

Liu Shuangju poured wine and tea for them and offered cigarettes and confectionery. After a few glasses of wine, Wang Huai's face and neck were red. Excitedly, he loosened his belt, pulled out two wads of cash and tossed them on the table. Everyone's eyes suddenly grew fixed, and the room fell silent.

Liu Baitiao was shocked. "How did you come by so much money?" he asked with a broken voice.

"It's from Changchi," said Wang Huai.

Exclaiming with admiration, they asked, "Is Changchi a big boss?"

Wang Huai drank without saying a word and smiled until his face was a mass of wrinkles.

三十五 · THIRTY-FIVE

WANG CHANGCHI DIDN'T REALLY WANT TO MAKE a big deal out of it and quickly put it out of his mind. Every day he showed up at work to lay bricks, hoping to go on in this way, ideally with no changes and with no end to the building. As long as he could hold a trowel in his right hand, a brick in his left and inhale the choking smell of mortar, he'd feel that life was as dependable as cast rebar. But Liu Jianping just kept slapping him on the shoulder, accusing him of being a turtle with its head pulled in, or a worm or an ant, those small creatures without backbone or nerve. Every time Liu Jianping belittled him, his mouth would spout a world of animals. At lunchtime on the construction site, Wang

Changchi would take his meal and go and hide in some deserted corner, where he would gulp down his food alone. But Liu Jianping seemed to have some innate ability to locate him, wherever he went. Besides belittling him, he also took pity on him.

"An opportunity is like a fart," Liu Jianping said. "It won't stink forever."

"Are you so sure of yourself?" asked Wang Changchi.

"I've done it three times, and for over ten thousand each time."

Wang Changchi didn't believe him. Of course, he had reasons for his disbelief, because when he first started to work in the county town, Liu Jianping had been a wimp who followed him around to scrounge a little food. Had he now undergone a genetic mutation? Liu Jianping handed him several wrinkled pieces of paper. Wang Changchi unfolded them and saw that they were written notes demanding compensation and giving power of attorney to Liu Jianping, complete with signatures and fingerprints, all looking like the genuine article. After reading each page, he handed them back and asked, "Why do you want to do this?"

Liu Jianping said they had been forced to do it. At every construction site, wages were in arrears. It had happened to him at least five times, and he didn't have enough money to buy *mantou*, so he went directly to the bosses and threatened them with fist and club. The bosses were in the wrong, and all they had to do was get tough and they'd pay out the wages. At first, he just followed along and reaped the benefits, but after a couple of times, he became braver. Because he also had stamina, and because for centuries people had abided by the rule of "a life for a life" and "borrowed money had to be repaid", why was it that these days the creditor feared the debtor? The more he talked, the more excited he became, as if he possessed the key to success. Wang Changchi had no choice but to treat him with increased respect. That evening, he established a power of attorney and the following day he went with Liu Jianping to the hospital for proof that he was impotent. After acquiring two sets of documents, Liu Jianping disappeared from the construction site, saying he had some important business to attend to. Wang Changchi continued going to work every day, but he frequently dropped bricks and they would break on the floor. The brick walls he laid were not straight, and each day he grew slower, fearing that something was about to happen.

Sure enough, Old Andu called him to the site office.

"You'll have to stop or get out of here," he said.

His legs went soft, and he pissed himself in fear. Old Andu saw the steam rising from the bottom of his trouser legs.

"Since you're a coward," he said, "why d'you want to cause trouble?"

"My wife's going to have a baby soon, and we don't have the money for the hospital stay, much less the money for the baby's milk."

"Weren't you recently given twenty thousand in compensation?"

"I gave it to my parents."

"You can't even blackmail."

"Is twenty thousand enough to remedy my impotence?"

"Who says you're impotent?"

"The doctor." Wang Changchi took out a copy of the diagnosis.

Old Andu examined it and called in Rongrong, who was in charge of the phone, from next door.

"Give him a hand job," he said. "I want to see if he really is impotent or not." Rongrong and Old Andu were from the same hometown and were lovers. Hearing that she was supposed to give him a hand job, her face immediately looked as if it had been painted red.

"Are you going to do it or not?" asked Old Andu.

Rongrong shook her head.

"If you don't do it," said Old Andu, "don't bother coming back tomorrow. Every day you take from the boss, but when you're really needed, you're not there, and you think you can continue to work here?"

Rongrong sighed as if she wanted to sigh away her shame. She picked up a new pair of gloves and just as she was about to put them on, Old Andu snatched them away.

"These are too thick to make anyone hard."

Once again, Rongrong sighed as if to sigh away her weakness. She walked over to Wang Changchi. He was even more nervous and ashamed than her, and when she grabbed his crotch with both hands, he squirmed.

"If you're afraid of being checked," said Old Andu, "that means you're faking it."

"The doctor has already checked me," said Wang Changchi.

"Heck, these days you can get fake proof just by giving a pack of cigarettes. Who believes anything?"

"Then check again if you don't believe me."

So saying, Wang Changchi opened his trousers. Rongrong reached out. Wang Changchi dodged her.

"You're really going to do it?" he asked her. "We're all villagers, why not have a little sympathy?"

"Who said villagers have to show sympathy for one another?" said Old Andu.

Rongrong pulled open Wang Changchi's trousers, but he grabbed them before they could slide down. Rongrong's hand reached to his crotch. Wang Changchi screamed for dear life as if a white mouse had burrowed its way down there. The little white mouse was hot and ran all over. For Wang Changchi, the desire to get hard was there, but not the ability.

Ashamed, he lowered his head and said, "Old Andu, if I kill you one day, you can't say you didn't have it coming."

Rongrong kept working at him for a while and then removed her hand. Shaking her head, she walked over to the cistern and grabbed a handful of laundry detergent. She rubbed her hands together until the cistern was filled with soapsuds. Despite all the soapsuds, she still felt dirty, so she grabbed another handful of detergent. It was as if she couldn't wash away the filth unless she rubbed off a layer of skin. Wang Changchi hitched up his trousers and, unable any longer to bear the insult, walked over to Old Andu and shook his fist at the left side of his face, but just before striking, he pushed "pause" before hitting "reverse". He had never struck anyone before and still didn't have the courage to do so.

As he came out of the construction site, Wang Changchi felt an empty sensation between his legs, as if essential balm had been applied, and there was nothing there. He crossed one street and then another, his legs never quite coming together, leaving an unbridgeable gap. He walked without stopping, to make sure his legs kept working together. He walked and walked until he arrived at Liu Jianping's place. Knocking on the door, Liu Jianping turned out to be home. He invited Wang Changchi in. It was a two-room place of thirty square metres, along with a kitchen, bathroom and small balcony. The place was old, but the walls had a new coat of white paint. In the living room was a small bookcase in which stood a few dozen books, all on law. A vase of flowers sat on the tea table and, although the flowers were made of plastic, they had not collected any dust. The curtains consisted of two layers, one of gauze, the other of fabric. In the bedroom, the blankets were folded in nice, neat squares, and two chests stood on either side of the bed, a heavily thumbed book on law lying on top of the left one. Only then did Wang Changchi realise that Liu Jianping had moved on. He was not a simple labourer but had risen to be an expert on compensation. He went to the construction site not to work but to drum up business, that is to find out who needed compensation.

"You don't need to be envious, I've already paid the price," said Liu Jianping as he pulled up his shirt and rolled up his trousers, showing the scars on his arms, back and legs as he did so. "Knife wounds, broken bones and abrasions, I've had my share of all of them."

Wang Changchi rolled up his shirt and pointed at the knife scars on his belly and then patted his crotch and said, "My dad's two broken legs should also be included."

"All we have to do is take off our clothes and we're the same," said Liu Jianping.

Because of their similar wounds, Wang Changchi's trust in Liu Jianping increased immensely, and because of his law books, his admiration bordered on worship. He picked up a volume and flipped through it mechanically without taking in a word. Even the bouquet, even Liu Jianping were in soft focus, while his mind was filled with nothing but that recent humiliating scene.

"Your boss is as slippery as a loach," said Liu Jianping. "He's already escaped twice after being cornered. I'm afraid getting money out of him will be more difficult than plucking feathers from a flying bird."

"No matter how difficult, you've got to help me. There's no way back now."

"Jumping from the building will be the only way to get your boss to appear."

"My dad used that method to threaten an agency back then, but he achieved nothing except crippling himself."

"This is a big place and if you're lucky, a journalist will report it. Although the bosses like to boast, once they're exposed, they piss themselves."

"We have to come up with a different method," said Wang Changchi, shaking his head. "If I fell by accident, my whole family would be ruined. I've got aged parents and an unborn child, so it's too risky. Aren't you studying law? Why not give it a try?"

Wang Changchi held up a law book as he spoke.

Smiling sarcastically, Liu Jianping said, "Do you think I understand any of that? I keep them around to boost my courage. With my background, all we can do is cheat, simply punishing the cheats by cheating."

"Isn't there always a way to reason things out?"

"Sure, but you have to put up the money first, otherwise no one will give you the time of day. Even if you win in court, a few tens of thousands in compensation won't be enough to dig yourself out of a hole from a lawsuit. At the time you'll get a written verdict in your favour, but all you'll get for your trouble will be a statement with an official seal, which would be like winning a competition with no prize money."

Wang Changchi was silent. After a moment, he set the book down and softly asked, "Is there any other way?"

"Yes, said Liu Jianping, "but do you have the nerve?"

"Maybe."

"How about kidnapping."

After a period of silence, Wang Changchi said, "I don't have a gun."

"Even if you had a gun, you wouldn't dare. Do you know who your boss is?"

Wang Changchi shook his head.

"Lin Jiabo," said Liu Jianping.

"Him again? He owed us once at the county town."

"Do you know who killed Huang Kui?"

"Don't tell me it was him."

"The police never arrested him because of interference from his dad."

"Why did he want to kill Huang Kui?"

"Maybe because Huang Kui knew too much about him."

"Shit, I'm out of here." Wang Changchi raised his voice, which shocked Liu Jianping.

三十六 · THIRTY-SIX

IN THE MORNING WANG CHANGCHI WANTED TO HAVE A RARE LIE-IN, but his biological clock went off at seven. He couldn't go back to sleep, so he sat up gently. Normally at this time he would be rushing about, dressing, brushing his teeth and washing his face, one action after another. As if on relentlessly turning wheels, he'd roll out of the door until he got to the eatery downstairs where he'd buy two *mantou*, and then roll on until he got to the construction site. But now, he felt worn out from all the rolling and didn't feel like moving. His backside stuck to the bed sheet, and his upper body didn't move, as if he were frozen in the air.

An hour later, Xiaowen woke up. Wang Changchi was still sitting on the edge of the bed.

"What time is it?" asked Xiaowen. "Why haven't you gone to work?"

Unblinking, Wang Changchi seemed not to hear.

Xiaowen slapped her head and said, "See how dumb I am, I almost forgot about the idea of jumping off the building."

Wang Changchi still didn't move, as if his mind had come to a complete standstill. Only after Xiaowen got up and made some rice porridge, fried some eggs and called him several times did he get up off the bed, brush his teeth, wash his face and eat breakfast.

"Jumping off the building is just a gesture, to get the snake to come out of its hole," said Xiaowen. "Whatever you do, don't be like your father and actually jump."

Wang Changchi didn't make a sound.

"It's windy up there," Xiaowen continued, "so dress warmly, don't climb too high, don't stay there very long. Once you're up on the scaffolding, secretly tie yourself on with a rope, and above all, don't fall and hurt yourself."

Xiaowen took out a rope as she spoke. About a metre in length, it was coarse and strong with metal tips at both ends.

"Where did this come from?" asked Wang Changchi.

"I bought it," said Xiaowen. "People are always selling these at construction sites as well as selling placards with slogans like, 'I injured myself for you, you compensate me' or 'Refuse to pay what you should, and you'll cut off the children and grandchildren' or 'I am going home for the New Year, please give me my wages', or 'You who owe money – if you have the nerve, let's step outside' and so on. They have everything you'd expect and there are lots of buyers, so it's become a business."

The first thing that came to Wang Changchi's mind after leaving was that he'd like to tie up Lin Jiabo with the rope he was carrying, but that idea disappeared like the steam rising from the steamers at the *mantou* shop. He walked around the construction site for three days but never had the courage to climb up on the scaffolding. Every evening, he would listlessly return home, as if he had wronged Xiaowen. Although Xiaowen never rebuked him, there was clearly something wrong with the rapid and heavy sounds she made when cooking. She also put the dishes on the table more audibly, made a racket when washing up and ran the water more noisily than usual. Wang Changchi felt as if he were on tenterhooks and stayed at home as little as possible. On the evening of the fourth day, he once again lowered his head and returned home but discovered another person there. Who was it? He couldn't place him. Thinking deeply for a while, he suddenly realised it was Liu Jianping.

"Are you going up on the scaffolding or not?" asked Liu Jianping.

"No."

"If you don't climb up, how will you ever get compensated?" asked Xiaowen.

"I have to be different from my father," said Wang Changchi.

"All other methods are fraught with potential problems," said Liu Jianping. "Either someone gets hurt or there's no money to be had. If not done right, you'll break the law. Jumping off a building is tantamount to suicide although no one else gets hurt. At best, you just want to force the boss."

"Bosses these days all have guts," said Wang Changchi. "Someone jumping off a building isn't going to scare them."

"Then I'll climb up with you," said Liu Jianping. "There's strength in numbers."

"I don't want to copy my dad."

"Some things you have to do even if you don't want to," said Xiaowen. "You can't avoid it any more than you can refuse to bow and burn incense for your ancestors."

"Coming up with new ways of getting compensation is hard," offered Liu Jianping. "It's best to follow tradition."

"I don't want to do it all over again."

A few days later, Wang Changchi finally came up with a way that was different from his father's. That made him extremely excited, and he couldn't sleep all night. Throughout his life, everything he did had been influenced to some extent by his father, and only now did he feel entirely free. Perhaps he felt elated simply because he was different from his father. Of course, his method didn't arise out of thin air but was arrived at after thorough consideration and putting the pieces together. First of all, he got the company's phone number from the wall of the construction site, after which he passed himself off as a big client and called the company from a phone booth, asking for the address and how to locate it. Speaking in dialect, he claimed to be someone from Lin Jiabo's hometown who wanted to see him, but he was stopped by the security guard. Two days later, he arrived at the company claiming he had business to take care of. The security guard asked him what business and for a moment he couldn't answer, and so he was again stopped at the gate. The third time, he said he was looking for Old Deng who worked at the company. The security guard asked for Old Deng's full name and he replied with "Deng Dezhi", a name he made up on the spot. The security guard checked and said there was no such person and pushed him out. After these attempts, the security guard remembered him and made it impossible for him to try again.

He stayed in the vicinity of the company where he squatted and kept watch. He discovered that every morning Lin Jiabo arrived at work in a black saloon with the licence plate 88888. When the saloon passed, he was no more than five metres from Lin Jiabo, but they were separated by window glass, just like two different worlds that couldn't touch, as if one was inside the TV and the other was outside. They were at their closest for a moment, for a second, for half a second. The entrance to the company was blocked by a guarded barrier, clearly preventing anything from being accomplished there. He walked five hundred metres back in the direction from which Lin Jiabo had driven and found a junction where the Dongbao Road Police Station stood.

At 9.12 am, Wang Changchi fell like a corpse from the sky and landed with a thud on the bonnet of Lin Jiabo's saloon, forcing it to stop. His nose hit the windscreen, and the pain felt as if his temples were going to burst and his eardrums were pierced, so much so that he didn't want to go on living. Fortunately, the pain passed quickly. Pedestrians gathered around to look, blocking traffic. Two policemen came running out of the police station, one to direct traffic, the other to Wang Changchi. Sitting on the bonnet of the car, Wang Changchi held a placard that read

"Injured on the job, compensation demanded". The number of onlookers increased and their shouting, whistles and the sound of their horns grew louder.

Pointing at Wang Changchi, the policeman said, "Get, get, get down off that car."

"It's really hard to catch him," said Wang Changchi. "If I get off, he'll run."

"Don't make things difficult," replied the policeman, "just let the traffic pass."

With both hands, Wang Changchi latched on to the bonnet for all he was worth. The policeman grabbed his legs and pulled. He slid off the bonnet and hit the ground, his chin striking first the bumper and then the surface of the road.

"Get up," said the policeman.

Wang Changchi held the tyre with both arms, his face pressed against it, the same way he had first embraced He Xiaowen, distorting the flesh of his face. The policeman kept pulling him. Each time he pulled, the car would rock and sway. His shirtsleeves were torn. The onlookers pressed closer, calling the policeman rough, saying he had no sympathy for the poor. With veins popping, someone even rolled up their sleeves. Seeing the crowd around him, the policeman's cold and aloof expression turned gentle and amiable.

Squatting, he said, "Friend, all you have to do is get up and I'll help you straighten things out."

Wang Changchi didn't believe him and looked askance at the policeman as if to determine how much water his words held.

"All you have to do is get out of the way," said the policeman, "and I promise you I won't let him slip away."

Wang Changchi still had his doubts.

The policeman offered him a traditional salute, saying, "This is such a great honour!"

As he expected, Wang Changchi released his grip and stood up. The policeman brushed the dust off him, the same way his mother had done when he was little. His hard heart melted at once.

"I had to act this way as a last resort," he said. "I don't like to make trouble – he forced me to do it."

The policeman knocked on the car door until the window slowly rolled down. The policeman indicated that the car should be driven to the police station, but Lin Jiabo stepped on the accelerator and the saloon shot forward like an arrow as if he had not deigned to notice the policeman's gesture. Wang Changchi thought it was over and that his plan would come to nothing.

Lin Jiabo's car was led to the police station by a police motorcycle with its lights flashing. With the help of Officer Wu, Wang Changchi managed to sit down face-to-face across a table from Lin Jiabo. This was the first time they were able to properly size each other up at close range. Lin Jiabo was thin, with a pale complexion and a pair of black-framed glasses sitting on his nose. He sported a crew cut, had small eyes, was dressed in a suit and snow-white shirt, had a long, thin neck and was effeminate-looking. Wang Changchi's skin was dark and coarse, his hands scraped from handling bricks and his clothes and hair were dusty from the street. What Lin Jiabo found most difficult to accept was that Wang Changchi had large eyes with double-folded eyelids, normal features with bushy eyebrows and straight teeth... Lin Jiabo thought if he hadn't been born in the wrong, wretched place, he'd be a model man. Wang Changchi thought, So, a swindler and murderer is very elegant. Lin Jiabo thought, Regardless of how good-looking or ugly they are, they swindle with the same attentiveness and methods. Wang Changchi thought, A book cannot be judged by its cover, the sea cannot be fathomed, the meat eater is cruel, when he washes his hands at the pondside the fish die, and when he passes through green mountains the grass withers. Lin Jiabo thought, By jumping off buildings and crashing into cars at the slightest provocation, you have made society chaotic. Wang Changchi thought, You have destroyed all prestige. Lin Jiabo thought, You have a negative impact on the overall quality of the Chinese people. Wang Changchi thought, You have squeezed all the energy and profit out of us. Lin Jiabo thought, You spit, shit and piss all over. Wang Changchi thought,

You give and take bribes, and keep a mistress, and government officials and businessmen collude with each other. Lin Jiabo thought, You are the dregs of humanity. Wang Changchi thought, You are a snake, a scorpion. Lin Jiabo thought, Your shoes stink. Wang Changchi thought, Your cologne smells so bad it makes me want to puke...

Speaking in dialect, Wang Changchi was the first to break the silence. He thought using dialect would move Lin Jiabo but didn't expect that he wouldn't even bat an eyelid. Wang Changchi stated his charges and what he wanted, and placed the written accusation and proof of his injuries on the table. Without uttering a word, Lin Jiabo turned and looked out of the window. Wang Changchi stared at him, audibly clenched his fists, and considered striking him several times, but restrained himself. Lin Jiabo waved through the window. Officer Wu entered.

"Sir," said Lin Jiabo, "please inform him that it's not that I refuse to compensate him, it's that I don't want to compensate him for no reason. Even if he is due compensation, it must be done in accordance with the law, through the proper department and not because of these savage actions of his. We are a law-abiding nation, in which each person must respect and obey the rules. If everyone wanted to resolve issues through extortion, that would be the end of the law."

"I don't have the money to sue," said Wang Changchi, "so why talk about law and order?"

"I'll lend it to you," said Lin Jiabo.

"Can you lend me fifty thousand?" Wang Changchi raised one hand.

"You don't mean it."

"I don't mean it because I can't sue you and win."

"You haven't tried, so how do you know?"

Wang Changchi was stunned. Clearly, he wasn't going to get his money by force as Officer Wu would intervene. Going to court was not the poor's strong point. He looked at Officer Wu and could see the outcome. Officer Wu was very embarrassed because he couldn't force Lin Jiabo to do anything and he couldn't help

Wang Changchi, so he looked away as if the solution was hanging in the tree outside the window.

"Actually," said Lin Jiabo, "there is another way that doesn't require any money, which is to go to the Labour Bureau and let them mediate. I'll pay whatever they decide."

Wang Changchi knew that every one of these words was false, but he couldn't come up with a reasonable response, and he watched as Lin Jiabo walked out.

Officer Wu patted Wang Changchi on the shoulder and said earnestly, "Have faith in the law and that most people in the world are good."

Suddenly, Wang Changchi was all goosebumps.

二十七 · THIRTY-SEVEN

THE CITY WAS AS COMPLICATED AS A RADIO CIRCUIT BOARD, the roads resembled wires and the buildings capacitors and resistors. Wang Changchi had no idea where the wires went, nor did he know the functions of the capacitors and resistors. But determined to get compensation, he did locate the Labour Bureau. The person he met was a female section chief by the name of Meng Xuan. She was about forty, with elegant features, a lithe body, and her voice was gentle and warm. After carefully reading the documents Wang Changchi had brought, she agreed to help him. But in two weeks of making dozens of phone calls, she was unable to contact Lin Jiabo, and her noble desire to help gradually cooled. Every day, Wang Changchi arrived, filled with hope, while at the same time bolstering Meng Xuan's morale. If there was someone in her office, he'd wait out in the hall until she was free, and only then would he timidly enter. Meng Xuan would smile wryly when she saw him, would push the buttons on her desktop speakerphone and then successively make three calls, one each to Lin Jiabo's office, the company office and to Lin Jiabo's older brother, but in all three cases the same message would play: "The party you are trying to reach...". Each time the message played, Meng Xuan would shake her head with regret, as if the disconnected phone number was hers and not Lin Jiabo's.

Clearly knowing there would be no result, Wang Changchi continued to show up for the simple reason that if he didn't, where else would he go? If he stayed in their rented place, he would have felt guilty. He couldn't resign himself to looking for a new job, and even if he did find one, he wouldn't be paid right away. Afraid that the workers would change jobs, the bosses only issued wages once every three or six months. If Xiaowen were to go into labour, he'd still find his hands empty, leaving him entirely powerless to act. So he had no other choice. Only by standing there did he avoid feeling guilty towards Xiaowen for running away or abandoning things. Sometimes he would bring Meng Xuan a gift such as a roasted sweet potato, a small bag of oranges or sweets. Xiaowen roasted the sweet potatoes, while he bought the oranges or sweets. The moment he placed these gifts on Meng Xuan's desk, she would break out in smiles, thanking him over and over again. When Meng Xuan was away attending a meeting, he came as usual and was more punctual than a public employee, the only difference being he didn't punch a timecard. He leaned against the wall in the hallway, his unblinking eyes on Meng Xuan's office, like a dog waiting for its master. Meng Xuan was away on business for ten days in a row. When she returned, she saw Wang Changchi still leaning against the wall in the hallway as if he had never left and were part of the wall.

Feeling sympathetic again, Meng Xuan took Wang Changchi to Lin Jiabo's office. Tipped off by security, the employees all vanished when they saw Meng Xuan and Wang Changchi coming as if they were contagious. Some fled to the toilet, some to a meeting room and others down the emergency corridor. Office door after office door closed, but Meng Xuan managed to stick her foot in one that was a little slower than the others. Meng Xuan passed her letter of introduction through the door, which opened a tad wider perhaps out of embarrassment, and out poked a face Wang Changchi had once hated. He Gui was the "registered trademark" of that face, the foreman at the construction site in the county town who once owed Wang Changchi money. The position on his ID was now deputy director-general.

Deputy Director-General He took out his keys and personally opened Lin Jiabo's office. The room was filled with so much dust that they left footprints with each step they took. Meng Xuan wondered if it had not been cleaned intentionally for her benefit. Wang Changchi wiped the desk with his hand, leaving a streak.

"Lin Jiabo hasn't been to the office for a month," said He Gui, "nor can he be contacted by phone."

"Where does he live?" asked Meng Xuan.

"He drives himself home. He's never given his address to anyone."

Meng Xuan told He Gui he should represent the company in discussing workman's compensation with Wang Changchi.

"I'm not a legal representative," said He Gui, "just a worker, so there's no way I can represent the company."

Meng Xuan had seen plenty of attempts like this to shift off responsibility. Brow furrowed, she told He Gui to contact Lin Jiabo immediately.

"I'll try," said He Gui, who nodded and bowed before leaving, never to return.

Meng Xuan and Wang Changchi sat waiting in Lin Jiabo's office as if by doing so he would appear. The office was so quiet they could hear each other breathing. Meng Xuan breathed calmly and lightly, Wang Changchi heavily and rapidly. Not a sound could be heard in the hallway. The employees had vanished as if they had gone up in smoke. Dust floated in the beams of slanting sunlight shooting through the window as if it was the only active element in the room. Everything else was still. From the window, the crowns of the trees could be seen below. The sound of the traffic drifted up sporadically. Meng Xuan looked out of the window for a while, then closed her eyes and leaned back on the sofa, as if she were preparing for a protracted battle, while Wang Changchi's eyes were open wider than ever. He started sizing up the office. The sofa was real leather. The desk was huge, at least the size of a single bed. The pencil holder on the desk held red, blue and black pencils, each one of which was sharpened to a fine point. A silver-coloured phone stood next to the pencil holder. Next to the phone was a desk calendar on a wooden stand, and next to the calendar was a desk lamp with a green shade. Next to the lamp was a pile of newspapers and letters. Those on top were faded, indicating age much like tree rings. At the back of the office stood a row of brown bookcases in which were arranged books about management and some famous works of literature. Wang Changchi remembered these famous works from his high school textbooks. Seeing the titles, he thought back to his school days and of his parents who sent him to study. Several small sculptures, stones and photos stood among the books. The photos were of Lin Jiabo smiling and standing in front of various backdrops. Wang Changchi glowered at the photographs as if to incinerate them with his eyes.

"Comrade Changchi."

Startled, Wang Changchi turned to look at Meng Xuan. It was the first time he had heard someone address him in that way, and he was so moved that his eyes became moist.

"The bureau is not all-powerful," said Meng Xuan, "and perhaps all I can do is sit and wait with you this afternoon."

"So he's not the least bit afraid of the bureau you work for either?" asked Wang Changchi.

"As long as he doesn't show up," said Meng Xuan, "there's nothing I can do, and even if he did show up, I can only try to reason with him. The bureau has very little power and perhaps ultimately your problem can only be solved in the courts."

This talk left Wang Changchi cold. A ferocity took hold of him.

"Section Chief Meng," he said, "don't waste your time by staying here, please go ahead and leave now."

Looking at her watch, Meng Xuan said, "I have to wait until it's time to knock off work, that's my principle in life."

When the time came to finish for the day, Meng Xuan stood up. Wang Changchi didn't move.

"So you're not planning to leave?" she asked.

"I'm going to stay rooted right here until Lin Jiabo appears," replied Wang Changchi.

"It won't do you any good."

"I promised Xiaowen that the baby would be born in hospital. There's no time to waste."

"Even if Lin Jiabo appears, what can you do?"

"If he doesn't compensate me, I'll strangle him."

"That's a crime!" said Meng Xuan, sitting down again, a look of disappointment on her face.

"Why can he break the law and I can't?"

Meng Xuan took a deep breath as if she had been hit in the chest.

"Abide by law and order," she said quite calmly, "but whatever you do, you must not resort to violence."

"This has nothing to do with you," said Wang Changchi.

"I'm the one who brought you here. If you two strangle each other, won't I be implicated?"

"But I'm at the end of my tether."

Wang Changchi couldn't be any more pessimistic. Meng Xuan took out a pen and a notebook. She busied herself in writing a name and contact details, and then tore out the page and handed it to him.

"This is Zhang Chunyan of the People's Court," she said. "Give the complaint directly to her. Only those who know how to use the law are smart."

Wang Changchi took the note in his trembling hand.

Rather than claim that Meng Xuan managed to convince Wang Changchi, it would be more accurate to say he now possessed a ray of hope for a lawsuit. They left Lin Jiabo's office ten minutes later. As they left, Meng Xuan closed the door and then pushed on it forcefully to make sure it was locked. They went downstairs, through the entrance hall and out of the door. The two of them wanted to say goodbye as this might be their final farewell. Suddenly Wang Changchi recalled that in his shoulder bag he had a bag of sticky rice dumplings, or *zongzi*, that Xiaowen had made. With her big belly, she had gone to the market to buy rice, meat and chestnuts, all of which she had carefully selected. After returning home, she inspected the rice to make sure there was no grit in it. She measured the rice for each *zongzi* with a cup to make sure that they were all exactly the same size. She had done her best to add as much meat and chestnuts as possible to each one and just the right amount of salt. She used a timer when cooking the *zongzi*. When the timer went off, she turned off the heat, not a second more and not a second less, making a science of *zongzi* making. She hoped her diligence would lead Meng Xuan to help Wang Changchi receive compensation. Meng Xuan had done what she could. Wang Changchi took out the *zongzi* and gave them to her. She accepted them with a smile and, as usual, repeatedly said thank you.

Wang Changchi headed off to the right, while Meng Xuan went left. After taking a few steps, Wang Changchi stopped as if he couldn't let go of something. In fact, this was the first time he had met a good person since arriving in the city. He wanted to look at her again, so turned around and watched her depart. Back upright, Meng Xuan walked in a straight line carrying her handbag. She could be described as slim and graceful. Not only was she pleasant, but also pretty. Seen from behind, the view of her back grew more impressive than that of the rickshaw puller in Lu Xun's short story *An Incident* and more moving than the sight of his father's back in Zhu Ziqing's essay *The Silhouette of His Back*. To avoid offending her, Wang Changchi hid behind a tree. Meng Xuan glanced back and seeing Wang Changchi nowhere in sight took the *zongzi* from her bag and threw them in a rubbish bin beside the road. Feeling as if he had been stabbed in the chest, Wang Changchi rushed from behind the tree towards the bin. Hearing footsteps, Meng Xuan turned to look, extremely embarrassed. Wang Changchi retrieved the *zongzi* and looked at Meng Xuan.

"I'm sorry," she said. "I shouldn't accept gifts, but if I don't, then I'm afraid you won't believe that I'm willing to help you."

Smiling derisively at himself, Wang Changchi peeled a *zongzi* and took a big bite. As he ate, the *zongzi* tasted salty, because as he ate, he tasted his own tears.

三十八 · THIRTY-EIGHT

ZHANG CHUNYAN HAD LIN JIABO SUMMONED to court. Since it was only for a paltry fifty thousand, Zhang Chunyan wanted to settle the matter without going to trial and so tried to reach an agreement with Lin Jiabo.

"If I give in to one," argued Lin Jiabo, "he'll be followed by a whole bunch more. Unless compensation is made more difficult, it will be hard to operate a business normally. There are many more like Wang Changchi. There's no end to labourers working on public projects who break a finger, have a stomach ache, asthma, a cough, haematuria, have a shadow on their lungs or who have an immune deficiency. Can they all be accommodated?"

"When an egg hits a stone," said Zhang Chunyan, "I feel sorry for the egg. What's more, there is the media, and if we go to trial there's no doubt you will lose."

Lin Jiabo opened his arms and said, "Bring it on."

Unable to afford a lawyer, Wang Changchi took the plaintiff's seat with the materials Liu Jianping had prepared. A group of reporters arrived, all of whom had been notified by Zhang Chunyan. She hoped to give the case more notoriety in order to strike fear into "shirkers" like Lin Jiabo. Xiaowen, Liu Jianping, Old Andu and Rongrong all came, as did a group of workers. Most of the workers sat down but a few had come directly from the construction sites and dared not take a seat. They stood behind the final row of seats, too embarrassed to even lean against the wall. Their clothes were spattered with mortar, and they were afraid of dirtying the seats and the wall. The judges had all sat down, and only the defendant's seat was empty. Wang Changchi was anxious, certain that Lin Jiabo was not going to show up. The clock on the wall ticked audibly, with only one minute remaining until the trial commenced. The crowd grew impatient, with some turning their heads and others looking at their watches, some fidgeted, others scratched in agitation, and even the judges seemed to slip away. The clock struck the hour and the start time had arrived. Wang Changchi was disappointed in the extreme. Suddenly a saloon screeched to a halt at the door, and all heads turned in that direction. The car door opened and Lin Jiabo, dressed in a slick, well-cut suit stepped out, tugged at his clothes, shrugged his shoulders, and walked forward with the slow-motion pace of an actor in a film. Finally, he had arrived. A clamour, if not an uproar, arose from the public seating.

As the presiding judge, Zhang Chunyan's investigation and presentation of evidence all went as smoothly as Wang Changchi could have imagined, and everything seemed to be going well and the situation developing in his favour. The only thing, like a fish-bone stuck in his throat, was that throughout the proceedings, Lin Jiabo looked up at the ceiling at a 45-degree angle, as if he were an awe-inspiring hero. He looked straight ahead disdain-fully, believing himself not of the same ilk or class as those sitting there. Wang Changchi thought, The arrogant will pay the price for their arrogance. Xiaowen finally understood the difference between the poor and the rich, which was when the poor lose, they look at the ground, while when the rich lose, they look at the sky. Zhang Chunyan thought that money made one headstrong. In the courtroom, only Old Andu and Rongrong appeared slightly sad, while everyone else was jubilant. However, when it was time for Lin Jiabo to make his statement, the atmosphere changed at once.

"Although the hospital has diagnosed Wang Changchi as being impotent," he said, "the diagnosis does not prove when he became impotent. Perhaps he had long been impotent and not just after coming to work at the construction site."

The public seating was thrown into a commotion. Wang Changchi raised his hand to rebut.

"If that's the case," he said, "then how could my wife get pregnant?"

As he finished speaking, Xiaowen stood up, thrusting out her belly and rubbing it with her hands, as if she were polishing a prize medal, and awaiting with satisfaction the judges' ruling. She was beaming with pride, even showing off.

"Does a pregnant wife prove that a husband isn't impotent?" asked Lin Jiabo. "Lots of wives have children with other men."

The courtroom was filled with laughter.

"I fuck your dad," said Xiaowen.

The laughter was even louder.

Zhang Chunyan struck her gavel and said, "Quiet."

The courtroom grew silent.

"Did some other bloke get your wife pregnant?" asked Wang Changchi.

"My wife has nothing to do with this case," said Lin Jiabo.

"Let me tell you that this child is absolutely mine," said Wang Changchi.

"Where's your proof?" said Lin Jiabo.

"If you doubt that, then I doubt the Earth is round and that you are not your mother's son."

"A paternity test will confirm it."

"I don't have the spare cash for that."

"I'll pay for the test. If the child is yours, I'll pay the compensation down to the last fen."

"Is that necessary?"

Wang Changchi turned to look at Zhang Chunyan. She turned to look at Lin Jiabo.

"Is that necessary?" she said.

Looking at the ceiling, Lin Jiabo said, "Of course. What if he's using a congenital disability to defraud me? These days there is no end to such people. I must defend myself."

Wang Changchi clenched his fists and stood up, intending to rush over and hit him, but then he remembered he was in court and that any rash action on his part could be used against him. Even though each word Lin Jiabo spoke was like a glob of phlegm spat on his face, what he wanted now was not dignity, but rather compensation, and the money for Xiaowen to have the baby in a hospital. Experience told him that when one flaunts one's superiority, one has to be prepared to lose everything. A person once said, when someone hits the right side of your face, offer them the left; if someone wants your underwear, then give him your outer clothing as well; if someone forces you to walk a mile, then walk two with him. Wang Changchi gritted his teeth and swallowed his anger.

"You're just hoping to use the process to stall for time," he said. "You might stall for the first day, but not for fifteen."

"I'll believe the evidence," said Lin Jiabo.

"Not just the evidence, you've already said you'd pay for it," said Wang Changchi.

"OK," said Lin Jiabo, "as soon as the court authorises a legal determination of paternity, I'll pay the costs."

"By then, I'm afraid you'll have vanished like smoke again."

"Let the court supervise. If I run away, then I'll concede defeat."

When he had finished speaking, Lin Jiabo left a telephone number with Zhang Chunyan. After sitting there apparently distracted, Zhang Chunyan announced that the court would go into recess. It was as if her mind had gone blank.

A legal paternity test was undertaken. Like an election, it was calm and tranquil on the surface, while secretly everyone had their doubts. The day Wang Changchi and He Xiaowen went to the hospital to provide samples, they were followed closely by Zhang Chunyan, the court doctor and Lin Jiabo. Even the department where an amniotic fluid sample was taken from Xiaowen remained open so that Lin Jiabo could keep his eye on things. After providing the samples, they were sealed in front of the plaintiff and the defendant by the court doctor, who also affixed an official seal. It was just like during an election when the empty ballot boxes were held up before voting to prove to voters that they were empty, after which they were securely locked so tightly that not a drop of water could enter.

Ten days later, Zhang Chunyan summoned Wang Changchi to the court. In order to calm himself, Wang Changchi paused outside her office two minutes before entering. It had been a long wait of ten days, which felt more like ten years. With victory so close and in sight, he was determined to be in control of himself. He pretended to be calm, low-key and nonchalant in front of Zhang Chunyan.

"What is this?" demanded Zhang Chunyan, as she slapped the test results down on the desk.

Wang Changchi looked, and his scalp immediately went numb, followed by his whole body, even his nerve endings were paralysed. The DNA test had determined that the child was not his! A few seconds later, despite these results, Wang Changchi suddenly recalled that distant afternoon when he and Xiaowen had made love, and could even recall the scent of his semen. Wang Changchi became alert a few seconds later, wondering if it wasn't all a plot.

"It's a mistake," he said, "you made a mistake."

"The entire paternity determination process was under my supervision. How can there be a mistake?" said Zhang Chunyan.

"If there wasn't a mistake on your end, then the lab got it wrong."

"An Yaping is an expert in the field. He signed his name, and that indicates he's willing to take legal responsibility."

"But lots of people would cheat the law for money."

"Is it your view then that anyone can be bought?"

"If he wasn't bought, how do you explain the ridiculous results?"

"All such talk is pointless without proof."

"Then I ask for another test."

"That's your business. The court-authorised testing is done."

Zhang Chunyan got up and locked the test results in her filing cabinet and turned around.

"Clearly the results are not in your favour," she said. "Indeed, they actually help Lin Jiabo. Even though the inability to father a child is not the same as impotence, sex and bearing a child are not completely disconnected. You must clarify the relationship between the two, which is no more difficult than telling the difference between a black cat and a white cat. For unless you can prove that you were sexually functional in the past – for example, did you rape someone or make someone pregnant or had your picture taken in some compromising way – I cannot rule for Lin Jiabo to compensate you."

"This is too much," muttered Wang Changchi. "I've heard of people changing their name, their age, their ethnicity, their personal file and their sex, but I've never heard of a person changing their DNA."

"Science can sometimes be cruel."

"This is not science, but morality."

"What you mean is–"

"That the test results are fake."

"Is that possible?" Zhang Chunyan re-opened her filing cabinet, took out the results and re-examined them. "Why are you always sceptical?"

"I know the seed I've sown," said Wang Changchi.

"You trust your wife that much?"

"We were in the village when she got pregnant, and we were more or less inseparable."

"If that's the case," said Zhang Chunyan, "then I support you to lodge a complaint about the test, but before doing so you must have proof."

"Then I'll be retested, and you'll have proof, right?"

"You're the smartest worker I've met, bar none, but the lab you choose must be more reputable than the one here."

That means I have to go to a big city, thought Wang Changchi.

三十九 · THIRTY-NINE

"First, I have to borrow money and then see how I can convince Xiaowen," said Wang Changchi.

Liu Jianping took out two account books, neither of which contained more than three hundred yuan.

"After subtracting rent, water, electricity and living expenses," he said, "you have almost nothing left over each month. The spare money you make you send home."

He decided to see Xingze. When he saw him, Xingze was so

happy that he patted him on the shoulder, offered him some tea and encouraged him to stay for a meal. But the moment borrowing money was mentioned, Xingze's face clouded over.

"Over the last two or three years," he said, "my wife and I have managed to scrape together a little money, but the boy is going to kindergarten soon. As I don't have a city residence permit, I have to rely on other people's backdoor connections to get him into a kindergarten. It means offering real money."

"Approximately how much?" asked Wang Changchi.

"For a good kindergarten," said Xingze, "I'll have to cough up fifty to a hundred thousand, for a second-rate one, at least ten to twenty thousand."

Wang Changchi never dreamed it would cost so much to get into a kindergarten. It was awful. He didn't have the heart to bring up money again with Xingze, but there seemed no better alternative, so he steeled himself.

"I'll pay you back when I win the lawsuit," he said evasively.

"One lawsuit leads to another," said Xingze, "just like the Russian Matryoshka dolls my son plays with. Even if you manage to win, you can't afford to fight. In tears our parents brought us to the city, they didn't want us to reason with them. Being reasonable, we can't get the better of them. Strength is what we have going for us, which means we use our strength to get out the money in their pockets. Be more realistic and find another job laying bricks and don't think any more about a lawsuit which you can spend time and money on with no guarantee of success."

Bracing himself, Wang Changchi decided to visit Zhang Hui. Zhang Hui calculated using her fingers.

"Let's start with the closest place, which is Guangzhou," she said. "Roundtrip tickets for two are four hundred yuan, taking the samples will cost at least two thousand, the tests another thousand, and then there's the cost of food and lodging. A single trip will cost you at least four thousand, and that doesn't include any unplanned expenses. The hospital is huge, and the patients are as numerous as ants. You can't just go in and have samples taken when you want. You'll have to queue and wait. Who can say how long it will take? Each additional day you wait means one additional day of expenses, all money spent for nothing. For determining paternity, you'll have to pay around five thousand, and that's even before the case goes to trial. Goodness! Can you pay all that back? For this lawsuit, you've already wasted one month, and if you'd spent that time working, you'd have made four or five hundred in income. If we add in your lost wages, that'll make a total of five and a half thousand yuan. And what about court costs and lawyer's fees? Should those be included? If so, then you won't profit from the case. Who can say how long the lawsuit will go on? You couldn't hold out for a month or two, much less a year or two. Also, Xiaowen is seven months pregnant, so would she be able to take that kind of stress? If there were an unexpected mishap on the train, wouldn't that be an irreparable loss?"

Those who are unwilling to lend money are exceedingly eloquent. Two days later, Wang Changchi was still ruminating over the lectures of Xingze and Zhang Hui. They were so sincere, so trustworthy and so considerate in their attempts to persuade him. Wang Changchi had to stop on the big West River Bridge and think about life. He thought that if they didn't get retested, it amounted to accepting the results. What ridiculous results! Wasn't he the father of Wang Dazhi? If I'm not, who is? For a few seconds, he felt wronged and irrationally doubted himself and doubted Xiaowen, almost going so far as to believe the filth, but he couldn't bring himself to do it. Even if he admitted to such falsehoods, he could not be afraid of a few flaws.

The sun was already sinking in the west. The rays of evening sunlight set the river shimmering. Hazy were the distant green mountains, the buildings and walls along the river were pleasingly jumbled. Amid the roar of the cars crossing the bridge, the ringing of a bicycle bell was occasionally heard. The bridge trembled slightly each time a bus passed, pedestrians went by constantly, raising a cool breeze to waft against the back of Wang Changchi's neck. Looking down at the river below the bridge, he suddenly had the urge to jump. All he had to do, he thought, was grit his teeth, close his eyes, lift his legs, loosen his hands, and in a matter of seconds, he would raise a splash, putting an end to it all. Then Wang Changchi thought of Wang Huai, about his father who had slipped and fallen from the third-storey railing of the Bureau of Education, and suddenly life was glorious and jumping shameful.

Returning home, he found that dinner was ready. He smiled and talked as he ate with Xiaowen. But she knew his smile was forced. Over the last few days, his smile had lost its past openness, much like the sun penetrating foggy mist or grit finding its way into rice. A forced smile concealed much that was best left unsaid.

"No news from the court?" asked Xiaowen.

Wang Changchi nodded in confirmation.

"What I said had an effect, right? It's better to rely on yourself than on others. If you had jumped from the building, we'd probably have the compensation by now."

Wang Changchi bit his tongue and remained silent.

"If it goes on like this," said Xiaowen, "not only will there be no money to have the baby, but even eating will become difficult. Didn't you notice there is less and less meat in your bowl?"

"How much money do we have left?" asked Wang Changchi.

"If you count the one-mao and one-fen notes, all together we have 927.68 yuan. I count it each day and each day there is less, slipping away faster than water."

Wang Changchi tapped his forehead, stood up, collected the dishes, washed them, scrubbed the pots and swept the floor.

While he was doing the housework, Xiaowen bathed. Wang Changchi got Xiaowen to sit on the edge of the bed, while he sat down on a small bench opposite. Facing Xiaowen's belly, he said, "I want to sing for Wang Dazhi."

It had been ages since the last time he had given the child any prenatal education. Apparently out of practice, he opened his mouth and started a number of times, but no song emerged.

"Dazhi," he said, "can you hear what your dad is saying?"

Xiaowen giggled and said, "He just kicked me."

"Dazhi, if you can hear me, kick one more time."

"He kicked again," said Xiaowen, rubbing her belly.

"Dazhi, if you want to call me Dad, kick twice."

"Ow-ow, he really kicked me twice."

"If you are really my son, kick three times."

"What does that mean?" Xiaowen slapped Wang Changchi on the head.

"Did he kick or not?"

"No."

"If he didn't kick, that means he's not my own flesh and blood."

"Then whose little bastard is he?" Xiaowen slapped him on the head again.

"Dazhi, if you really are my son, then kick three times."

"Ow-ow-ow..." Xiaowen clasped her belly, her features twisted.

"What's the matter?"

"He kicked me very hard, and it really hurts."

"How many times did he kick?"

"Three times."

"My son, my very own son!" Wang Changchi pressed his face to Xiaowen's belly, tears covering his face.

"Why all this piss and nonsense?" asked Xiaowen.

Wang Changchi then told her what the paternity test had established. Furious, Xiaowen trembled all over, making the bed bounce up and down.

"We have to be retested to save my good reputation", she said.

"Then we'll have to spend a lot of money."

"Whatever it costs, otherwise what will people say about me?"

"There's no way I'd believe them. I know this is a plot."

"All the more important to counter their plot with facts and shut them up." Xiaowen pushed Wang Changchi aside, stood up, and walked over and opened the trunk by the wall.

"I've got two thousand yuan of my own put away," she said. "Is that enough?"

Wang Changchi snatched the money and pushed it to the bottom of the trunk.

"When we have to use the money," he said, "whatever we do we can't fall into their trap."

Xiaowen's anger was still unabated, and her chest seethed.

"I've scrimped on food and clothing," she said, "and saved such a little amount with difficulty. I thought, so long as nothing life-threatening happens, I wouldn't spend a fen, but to relieve my anger, I'll give it to the lab. Tomorrow you will take me to provide a sample, otherwise—"

As she said, "otherwise" Xiaowen froze with her mouth hanging open. Wang Changchi latched on to her and called, "Xiaowen, Xiaowen..."

"Oh no," said Xiaowen, "I think the baby is coming."

Wang Changchi touched Xiaowen's legs and found her trousers all wet. Her waters had broken. Holding her, he made his way towards the door.

"We can't go," said Xiaowen. "We don't have the money for a hospital stay."

"I'll figure something out," said Wang Changchi.

"Put me on the bed and I'll give birth to Dazhi on my own."

"I said you'd have the baby in hospital and Dazhi would be born in the delivery room, and you would enjoy being treated as a city woman."

"Neither of us was born in a hospital and we're alive all the same, aren't we?"

"It's premature, and if anything goes wrong it could be fatal."

"Even premature, I won't go. Put me down. I'd rather die like a dog than be insulted by them."

Ignoring Xiaowen's pleading, Wang Changchi took her directly to the obs and gynae department at the hospital. The whole way, Xiaowen beat his back with her fists, and each blow was like a knife thrust to the heart. He held her tightly, and their clothes were soaked.

"You only have enough money to stay two days," said the doctor.

"I beg you," said Wang Changchi, "admit her now, and I'll borrow more money tomorrow."

Xiaowen gave birth at midnight. Although Wang Dazhi was just a little ball of flesh, everything was normal. The nurse carried him out of the delivery room and when she passed Wang Changchi, she said, "Hurry and have a look at your son."

Wang Changchi dashed over, and that pair of tiny eyes opened for a moment before closing again. Perhaps he wasn't accustomed to the light, or he didn't have the strength to keep his eyes open any longer. However, the instant they were open, Wang Changchi was certain he was his son as both couldn't wait to see the other. Afterwards, Wang Dazhi was placed in an incubator, which meant that Wang Changchi would have to pay even more money for care. Wang Changchi thought, What is money in the face of life? You spend your money only on those who love you, and the deeper the love, the more you spend. Wang Changchi smiled.

四十 · FORTY

THE FOLLOWING MORNING, WANG CHANGCHI looked at Wang Dazhi in the incubator, brought Xiaowen her breakfast and then left the hospital.

Before leaving, he said to Xiaowen, "I'm going to borrow some money, so I might be back a little late. When it's time to eat, the nurse will heat some chicken soup for you – I've already told her."

Xiaowen nodded, her eyes moist. On leaving the hospital, Wang Changchi wasn't sure where to go. He didn't know who would be willing to loan him money. He walked and walked until he reached Liu Jianping's place.

When Liu Jianping saw him, he asked about the case.

"If we were to sue An Yaping of the testing lab," said Wang Changchi, "how would he try to worm his way out and defend himself?"

Liu Jianping shook his head.

"He'd claim that the specimens were improperly handled and blame an assistant," said Liu Jianping. "If he manages to falsely turn his assistant into a part-time worker, you'll get nothing, not even an apology. So, there's no point in suing An Yaping. Your goal is to get compensation, the focus of which is still Lin Jiabo. When the rich are involved in a lawsuit, they pay lip service to justice. The poor, on the other hand, must get straight to the point."

Liu Jianping spoke exuberantly, spraying saliva, covering Wang Changchi's face. Listening and listening, Wang Changchi felt that it was a distant matter unrelated to him, and whoever was speaking owned it. Listening and listening, Liu Jianping grew distant, minute and hazy as if separated by a layer of glass, his voice growing faint until he could no longer be heard. Wang Changchi was in a dreamland. Liu Jianping thought he had closed his eyes to concentrate better, so he kept talking on and on. That is, until he asked a question, then he began to have his doubts. He asked the same question three times, but Wang Changchi failed to respond, so he shoved his shoulder. Once roused, he opened his eyes and said that Lin Jiabo is the focus...

"I've been through it all five times, and you still stop where you started," said Liu Jianping, seeming slightly disappointed.

Wang Changchi yawned a long yawn and said, "In order to refute Lin Jiabo, we have to first refute the test results. In order to refute the test results, we have to be retested. Getting retested will take money. Is that what you're saying?"

Liu Jianping handed him a box of essential balm. Wang Changchi opened it and applied the balm to his temples and nostrils. The balm burned and was sharply pungent, forcing tears from his eyes. He sneezed several times and his mind cleared.

"How can you be so absent-minded with such an important matter?" asked Liu Jianping, lamenting Wang Changchi's bad luck and angry at his passivity.

"Sorry," said Wang Changchi, "please repeat what you just said."

Looking at the ceiling, Liu Jianping seemed to be rewinding and after about one minute he said, "The problem is that the court won't accept the test results you provide as reliable."

"Then let them do it again," said Wang Changchi.

"Do you want another slip-up in the same place? If the

machines are off, there won't be any change in the results even if you do it a hundred times."

"So it's a trap?"

"There's definitely more than one involved," said Liu Jianping, tapping on the tea table. "You were injured at the construction site, you have proof of your hospital stay, and you have a written diagnosis. These three proofs ought to be sufficient to make Lin Jiabo pay compensation. As for a congenital disability, that is obviously Lin Jiabo's invention and Zhang Chunyan is actually in on it."

"So they were in it together all along."

"Before calling for a recess, didn't you see how Zhang Chunyan paused for some time? She was hesitating to see how those in the court would take it. It turned out that not a peep was heard in the courtroom."

"So that made her bolder."

"I didn't respond at the time either, otherwise the people in the courtroom would have shushed her."

"Jianping, what you are saying is true. Do you think this case can be won?"

"Theoretically, yes, but not necessarily in practice. Think about it, if they are actually willing to alter the test results, what won't they do?"

Wang Changchi grew silent. The room was as quiet as the wide-open countryside, except for the constant dripping of the bathroom tap, making it seem like there was a third party in the room.

"From the very beginning, I was opposed to you bringing this lawsuit," said Liu Jianping.

"I thought I'd be different from my dad. I never dreamed I'd be the same," said Wang Changchi, sighing. He gulped down the cup of water on the tea table, then got up to leave.

Liu Jianping followed him out. They walked along the pavement together, neither one spoke, as if by speaking they would leak air and lose heart. Sometimes Wang Changchi walked ahead, sometimes behind. Neither one said where they were going, but they both knew. Along the way, Wang Changchi wanted to turn and even looked back, but as soon as the idea struck him, his mind was filled with that little ball of flesh in the incubator, or Xiaowen weeping. He couldn't stop and even if his legs felt weak, he had to pretend he was tough.

They arrived at the construction site.

"I'll climb up with you," said Liu Jianping.

"You have to stay below in case I happen to fall to my death," said Wang Changchi. "The baby, Xiaowen and my parents will need your help."

Liu Jianping felt such words were inauspicious and spat several times, during which time, Wang Changchi climbed the scaffolding. Liu Jianping stood below, watching. Each time Wang Changchi reached up, a rope tied around his waist was exposed. That was the short rope with two metal ends that Xiaowen had once prepared for him. Which shows that before going to visit Liu Jianping, he already had the idea of jumping off the building, otherwise, why would he bring along a rope? Liu Jianping noticed that when they left, he had stuck the box of essential balm in his trouser pocket. If you want to talk about difference, this is where he differed from his father. His father had made no preparations to jump, but he was prepared. He was half a head taller than Liu Jianping, so Liu Jianping always thought he was big and tall and strong. But from a distance he found him small and pitiful, like a spider carrying a piece of steel, climbing upward against the massive pull of gravity. Gravity made his arms and legs look like thin plastic straws, in danger of breaking at any moment. He did not climb alone, he had four others on his back. Liu Jianping joined his hands and muttered a prayer for the bodhisattva to protect him and not allow him to lose his grip.

Gradually, Wang Changchi was able to see the Tai'an Building, the tops of the trees in the People's Park, the big West River Bridge and the West River itself. It was the first time he had looked down on the city and it really did resemble the integrated circuit board of a radio, criss-crossed, with highs and lows, and the big and the small. Some of the roofs were red, but most were grey. Some were planted with vegetation while others were covered with solar panels. His view broadened and he looked ever farther across mountains and rivers until he seemed to see his hometown, his father and mother bending over a land of bountiful harvests and a new building rising from the place where he was born. The maple tree above the village was clearly in sight. The black and white busts of Second Uncle, Zhang Wu, Liu Baitiao, Daijun and the Wang Dongs flashed before him, like those of martyrs. The head of the County Bureau of Education was burned to death; Lin Jiabo was shot to death; Meng Xuan became an immortal maiden; the spy Zhang Chunyan was apprehended... The whole city was a white canvas enlivened with green, black and red. He saw splotches of colour not unlike those he saw when he was exceedingly hungry during his study days, so he applied some essential balm to his forehead and tied himself to the scaffold with the short rope. The metal was cold, the wind was cold, only that little ball of flesh Dazhi was hot. He was right in front of his nose, his tiny pea-sized eyes blinking and his soundly sleeping face suffused with a smile. Wang Changchi suddenly recalled one thing he had forgotten to tell Liu Jianping, which was that Xiaowen had given birth, that he was a father, and that he had not had a wink of sleep all night long.

People started gathering below. Some laid out mats, others looked up. More and more assembled and soon the vehicles coming and going were unable to move and there was a cacophony of horns, vying with one another. Wang Changchi was sorry for those busy people and all the drivers stuck there. I have not only affected your work but also alarmed you, made you curious, indisposed you, caused a minor car accident, made people stamp their feet in frustration and caused the blood pressure of some to rise. However, if I weren't at an impasse with a child in an incubator who needs to be saved and aided and blessed and protected, and Xiaowen who needs to recover, and Lin Jiabo who refuses to pay compensation, I wouldn't resort to this even if I were shot in the head. In some cases, we have a choice, in others things are forced upon us, please pardon me.

Using a megaphone, a policeman shouted something like, "Don't harm yourself, value life, think of your family. Whatever problems you have, the police can help you resolve them. Since you are not afraid of death, why are you afraid to live? We must all die sooner or later, there's no reason to be in a hurry..."

Amplified by the megaphone, these profound truths were like fluttering sparrows, some of which entered Wang Changchi's ears, while others rose only to fall out of the sky, and the rest fell to the ground without taking flight. Regardless of what he shouted, Wang Changchi did not respond. Several reporters pushed their way through and after taking pictures of the area, they turned towards the sky and shot pictures of the entire scene, medium shots, close shots, and super close-up shots that showed Wang Changchi trembling, and in one shot he was missing a shoe. He was like a domestic fowl resting on a branch used by a wild bird, his face tense and frightened. Liu Jianping wanted to tell the policeman, If you shout his name and ask about his grievances, then he might not jump. But Liu Jianping didn't dare. He knew that if he made such a suggestion, the policeman might suspect him of being involved, and Wang Changchi's plan for making demands would come to nothing again.

The policeman sought out Old Andu in the construction site duty office.

"Why did this man choose your building site to try and commit suicide?" asked the policeman. "Does he owe anyone money?"

Old Andu started by saying he didn't know why, he didn't know the bloke, but later, unable to resist the policeman's interrogation and threats, finally mentioned Wang Changchi's lawsuit, but he emphasised that it was just to stir up trouble.

"Go and get Lin Jiabo for me," said the policeman. "Otherwise if someone dies, I'll take you into custody."

Wiping away his sweat, Old Andu made several phone calls, but couldn't get in touch with Lin Jiabo. The policeman was unable to contact him as well, so sent someone to the company. After receiving Old Andu's phone call, the company was all locked up. The police were helpless. All they could do was get the traffic moving and disperse the onlookers.

The traffic started moving again and the crowd slowly broke up. The sun shone a little, and Wang Changchi started to feel warm. No one shouted any longer. Wang Changchi felt that this was not very encouraging and wondered how long he could hold out. His arms and legs were numb, he was hungry, and he was shaken by fatigue.

四十一 · FORTY-ONE

"Changchi…" Vaguely, he heard a warm voice. But his eyelids felt like they weighed a ton and were as impossible to open as if they had been sewn shut. "Changchi…" The voice was so familiar, but still he couldn't open his eyes. His tears flowed first. Goodness, I actually went to sleep. If I hadn't tied myself to the scaffolding, I might already be flat on the ground.

"Changchi…"

The shout began to rouse him. Another shout roused him a bit more. His stiff body felt like a thawing glacier, and his numb flesh again felt pain. He straightened his neck with difficulty. A gold light shone before him as if a bodhisattva were sitting there like a red sun shooting sparks in all directions when he blinked his eyes. Gradually the haze dispersed. He saw Wang Huai sitting in the caged platform of an aerial ladder. He thought, The bodhisattva sent my dad to save me. If I don't wake up, then I must really be dead. And so he shouted, "Dad…"

"Changchi, don't move."

"Dad…" Wang Changchi's face was wet with tears, "you're a grandfather."

"Boy or girl?" Wang Huai wiped his moist eyes.

"It has a little wee-wee."

"Then your mum won. She dreamed that Xiaowen gave birth prematurely, so we came to the city early."

"Where's Mum?"

"Down below watching the luggage."

"Dazhi really looks like her, especially when he smiles."

"The house is ready, just waiting for you to come home for the New Year."

"Xiaowen is fine."

"Believing Xiaowen had given birth, the whole village sent gifts. Your mum's pockets are heavy."

"Dad, we don't need money."

They reported the good news, not the bad, each trying to comfort the other, afraid lest the other suffer a mishap. Gradually, the wind dried their tears, and their features returned to normal. Wang Changchi saw that Wang Huai had a crew cut, was wearing new clothes and that he was clean-shaven.

Wang Huai said, "Let's go home, Changchi."

"Don't worry, I wasn't really going to jump, I just wanted to frighten them."

"You're the only one who'll come to grief. You won't frighten anyone else. Your dad is a lesson."

"So I shouldn't reason with them?"

"Let it go."

"I'm not going to give up."

"Just think of Dazhi and you will, just like I think of you all the time. With my legs reduced to this state, why should I want to linger? Everything has been for you. If it weren't for you, I would have died ages ago."

"Dad..."

"You have to raise Dazhi, watch him grow up, see that he gets an education and has prospects, a pretty wife and smart kids. Otherwise, you're not qualified to jump from here."

"I climbed up here for Dazhi."

"Regardless of how much worse things get, you can't shame the child. Don't let him bear that burden. The time he learns that his father jumped in exchange for his first mouthful of milk will be the time he vomits it up."

"I have shamed Dazhi."

The aerial ladder moved forward slightly. Wang Huai grasped Wang Changchi's hand. The two trembling hands resembled a swaying arched bridge, growing firmer and more stable as it trembled, until it no longer moved.

"Changchi," said Wang Huai, "your hand is warm. Rub your left leg, now your right leg. Are they numb? If so, keep rubbing like this."

As he spoke, Wang Huai demonstrated.

After rubbing for a while, Wang Changchi said, "Dad, my legs are no longer numb, and my hands are no longer tired."

"Now slowly untie the rope."

"It's done."

"Now grab hold of the horizontal bar of the platform, right, hold it like that," cautioned Wang Huai.

"I feel a little unsteady. Dad, don't be nervous."

"Cross your right leg over first, now your left leg."

As the platform shook, Wang Huai grabbed Wang Changchi in his arms.

"Child, you nearly made me piss myself with fear."

Wang Changchi tightly embraced Wang Huai and could smell the sharp odour of urine. It doesn't need to be said that this was an odour from home that he hadn't smelled in ages.

The aerial ladder slowly descended against a backdrop of the setting sun.

Three hours earlier, just after leaving the bus station, Liu Shuangju had pushed Wang Huai towards this place. They were attracted by the crowd. At first, they didn't know that it was Wang Changchi who had climbed up above but listening to the people talking and the police shouting, their awful premonition was confirmed. Wang Huai shouted Wang Changchi's name up into the air a couple of times. Liu Shuangju did the same. But, tired and exhausted, Wang Changchi had already fallen asleep while clutching the scaffolding. Nervously, Liu Shuangju paced around. Wang Huai looked on helplessly.

"What is his relation to you?" asked the policeman.

"My son," replied Wang Huai.

"How could you raise someone who isn't afraid of death?"

"He must have been forced by someone. Otherwise, he wouldn't do this."

The policeman handed him the megaphone. Wang Huai lifted it and was about to shout but lowered it.

"If I shout, I might jolt him," he said.

"What do you suggest?" asked the policeman.

"Can you get me up there?"

The policeman called the fire department and said, "Send a ladder truck."

While waiting for the truck, Wang Huai went to a nearby barbershop for a haircut and a shave, then he put on new clothes. The ladder truck arrived, but they didn't know how to attach Wang Huai. Wang Huai suggested tying a chair to the platform and then tying him in. As they were tying the chair, Liu Jianping noticed them.

He quietly told Wang Huai, "All you have to do is go up and Wang Changchi's plan will fall through."

"Plans can't keep up with changes," said Wang Huai. "That year I wanted to frighten some people, but I still ended up falling. If I don't go up, Changchi won't be able to hold out."

Wang Huai was tightly bound to the chair.

Pulling out a wad of money, Liu Shuangju said, "Take this up with you and tell him his boss has compensated him."

"There's no need," said Wang Huai, "he's not doing it for the money."

"He's doing it precisely for money," interjected the policeman.

"Even if he's doing it for the money," said Wang Huai, "I can convince him. I want him to know that some things in the world are more important than money."

A fireman wanted to accompany Wang Huai up. He refused.

"I can handle my son," he said.

And so, Wang Huai was lifted high into the sky on the aerial ladder until he was just one metre away from Wang Changchi.

When the aerial ladder was brought down, the policeman gave Wang Changchi a scolding.

"Do you know how many policemen were tied up in this

thing?" he asked. "You disrupted traffic, alarmed people, wasted taxpayers' money, and if I didn't feel sorry for your father, I'd throw the book at you for disturbing public order."

Rebuked, Wang Changchi's face flushed red, and lowering his head, he held his breath like a child who had done something wrong. Wang Huai apologised repeatedly.

"It's not that I'm not sympathetic," said the policeman, "but too many people like you threaten to jump off buildings, and to scare who?"

Wang Changchi thought, If I had a speck of hope, would I be here now? Not a chance. But seeing that the policeman had wanted to save his life, he didn't want to respond. He braced himself and listened until the policeman was tired of talking before he wheeled Wang Huai away.

Liu Shuangju complained the whole way.

"You fool, how could you be as daft as your father?" she said. "What kind of pigsty could produce this kind of pig, and what kind of father produces such a son? You're so stupid! If you don't have money, you can make some, but when you end your life, you don't get another one. Even by becoming a beggar, you don't play with your life. Do you have any idea how I suffered when I was pregnant with you? I puked up bile, not to mention being on tenterhooks all the time, worried you might be born without an arm or a leg. Do you think that your life is yours alone? It's also mine. It's a good thing I had a premonition and had that dream, otherwise we wouldn't have run into you today. That means you're lucky. If we hadn't run into you, you wouldn't have been able to hold out and, loosening your grip, we'd be without a son, and Dazhi would be without a father. You should thank your lucky star."

"If you and Dad hadn't met, would I still be here?"

5

TWISTED

四十二 · FORTY-TWO

WANG DAZHI SPENT A MONTH IN THE INCUBATOR. It took one month to cure his asthma and two months for his prickly heat. In that time, his care used up nearly all the money his grandfather, Wang Huai, had brought. How did Wang Huai come up with that apparently unlimited supply of banknotes? Everyone avoided the topic as if it was a dirty word and speaking it would injure his self-respect. But Wang Changchi and Xiaowen both knew exactly where it came from. Wang Huai earned the money by kowtowing on the streets, otherwise there wouldn't have been so many one-mao notes and coins. Wang Changchi had always been opposed to Wang Huai begging. Now he not only had to spend his banknotes but there wasn't a moment when he didn't feel awful, the shame of selling himself, the fear of rotten corruption. Even worse, he felt like someone who had been caught stealing money and was trussed up and paraded without a stitch of clothing through the streets for all to see. His shame increased with each fen spent, and with each mouthful of food eaten, he felt the urge to vomit. To his very soul, he felt entirely covered in chicken shit, mouldy and with an unbearable stench. So each time he held Dazhi, he would first scrub his hands clean, even under his nails. He shaved himself smooth and gargled with warm water.

He found another job, still laying bricks, at a construction site on Liberation Road. Laying brick after brick, he grew absent-minded and felt he was still working for Lin Jiabo, often playing back the scene of his fall. The more he replayed it, the more he hated Lin Jiabo, and the more he hated the bloke Lin, the cleaner he felt. Hatred released the psychological pressure and diminished his feelings of humiliation. He didn't allow Wang Huai to venture outside, afraid he would make a fool of himself. He also didn't allow Liu Shuangju to go out and collect recyclables, to keep the house from smelling. The only thing Xiaowen, Wang Huai and Liu Shuangju did was look after Dazhi or cook. The meals were very simple, sometimes rice porridge with pickles and *mantou*, sometimes a big bowl of rice noodles, sometimes a plate of stir-fried meat and one of vegetables. There was less and less to do. And when there was nothing to do, the three of them would look at each other and the room grew very small.

Finding the inactivity intolerable, Liu Shuangju would sneak out and collect recyclable waste after Wang Changchi left for work. But she had to sell it the very same day she collected it and dared not bring the tiniest bit home. Since so many people were out collecting, Liu Shuangju never came up with anything big and even on a good day she only made a pittance. Making so little did not sit well with her since she and Wang Huai had made good money before. As beggars, the most they made was dozens of yuan, so what she picked up wasn't recyclables but rather loneliness. At first, she would return to the rented room before noon; later on, she went farther and farther until she forgot or was just too lazy to return home. She was reluctant to spend money and so skipped lunch and went hungry. Going hungry didn't matter, but not going home did, because Wang Huai had no way of going to the toilet. Sometimes he had to go so badly that his face turned blue.

Unable to bear the sight, Xiaowen would say, "Dad, do you want me to carry you to the bathroom?"

Wang Huai would shake his head as if he were guarding his last shred of dignity. He thought his only contribution to the family at present was being able to hold it in. To make holding it in bearable, he drank less, ate less and talked less. By doing this, Liu Shuangju was not only able to save the family the cost of one meal, but also Wang Huai cut the cost of his food and drink by thirty per cent. Saving this way allowed diligent and frugal house-hold management, increasing income and decreasing expenditure. What head of the family wouldn't want to do so? Thinking about it this way, Wang Huai was able to squeeze out some pleasure and stir himself.

But no matter how Wang Huai held back, he couldn't increase the family's productivity. Relying solely on Wang Changchi's income was a strain for a family of five.

Talking it over with Xiaowen, he asked, "Can you keep a secret?"

Xiaowen recalled how in the valley Uncle Zhang Wu had also asked, "Can you keep a secret?" before he explained the source of Zhang Hui's income. At that time, she was totally enraptured by the city, her head filled with boundless fantasies as dazzling as sunlight, as beautiful as rosy clouds, and a riot of colour like mountain flowers.

"... Are you listening?" asked Wang Huai.

Coming to herself, Xiaowen said, "Yes, I'm listening."

"All you have to do is keep one eye open and one closed," said Wang Huai, "and I can earn money for the family every day."

"Changchi will blame me."

"If you don't say anything, he won't know."

Xiaowen nodded in tacit agreement. From then on, Wang Huai, Liu Shuangju and Xiaowen shared another secret. The moment Wang Changchi left, Liu Shuangju and Xiaowen would carry Wang Huai along with his wheelchair downstairs. Xiaowen would stay at home and care for Dazhi while Liu Shuangju would push Wang Huai to go begging. They went to the square, the train station, the bus station, the entrance to the school, cinemas and department stores. Wherever there were bound to be lots of people, that's where they'd push their way in. Before the end of the workday, Liu Shuangju would push Wang Huai and fly back. Sometimes, as they tried to make it back on time, Liu Shuangju's shoulder bag would be lifted by the wind and the cap Wang Huai used for begging would be blown off his head. Each day on his return from work, Wang Changchi would find the four of them at home in good order, in much the same position as he had left them. They resembled baby birds in a nest waiting to be fed, the only difference was that they were all smiles. With the same scene repeated on a daily basis, Wang Changchi felt the place was too crowded, felt like heaving a long sigh and wondered why they didn't go out for a walk. Even by going out to pick up the recyclables and begging, they would breathe more freely than by just keeping still and doing nothing.

One day, Wang Changchi left work early because the boss was happy having signed a big contract and gave all the workers a half day off. When he returned to their place, he saw only two of them there and the other two were not in their usual spots. The half-empty room made him more anxious than a full house.

"Where are Mum and Dad?" he asked.

"They went out to enjoy themselves," said Xiaowen.

He bathed and then played with Dazhi on the bed. Xiaowen threw the account book to him.

"The rich can fritter away a fortune," she said, "why not poor folks like us?"

Opening the passbook, he said, "What a joke, but I'll be paid in a few days."

"Isn't there a saying," said Xiaowen, "something about before it rains?"

"Weaving before it rains, which means taking precautions before it's too late. I taught you that at the county town, and you still remember."

"Your wages are just enough to keep the family in food and drink."

"What do you have in mind?"

"Can you guarantee no one will get sick? Besides, we have to put some money aside for Dazhi, otherwise how will he go to school?"

Wang Changchi sighed, his first since the arrival of Wang Huai and Liu Shuangju.

"The only solution is to let me go out and work," said Xiaowen.

"What about Dazhi?"

"Doesn't he have a grandmother and grandfather?"

"They'd make a beggar out of him."

"And I'd make an illiterate out of him."

"You want to massage feet again?"

"That's the only thing I know how to do."

"Are you comfortable using that kind of money to send Dazhi to school?"

"Is there a stalk of corn that isn't fertilised with pig shit? Is there one flower that doesn't grow from the mud?"

Wang Changchi did not argue, seemingly convinced by Xiaowen. He stared dumbly at Dazhi as if he were a stalk of corn or a flower. Dazhi had normal features, his eyes and ears were large, and when he smiled two dimples appeared on his face. Not only was he a handsome devil in infant form, but looked like someone who was destined to be well off. At only a little more than three months, his eyes knew how to communicate with others. Whenever Wang Changchi moved his eyes, he would follow. When Wang Changchi looked to the left, so did he; when Wang Changchi looked right, so did he. If an adult started talking about something serious, he'd control his crying until they had finished speaking before starting again. The moment Wang Changchi sang, especially one of the songs he had sung as part of his prenatal education, then his ears would prick up and he would wave his two small fists to the music as if keeping time. He really was a joy to watch.

A shout came from downstairs. Xiaowen responded immediately and went out. Then came a "dong, dong, dong" as they were heard carrying Wang Huai upstairs. Turning his head to look at them, Wang Changchi noticed that their expressions were a bit strange, especially Wang Huai, who seemed to do everything possible to avoid making eye contact.

"Did you lot go out begging for money?" he asked.

Wang Huai shook his head.

"We just went to the park," said Liu Shuangju.

"If you went to beg for money then you are not fit to be Dazhi's grandparents."

"If they said they didn't go begging," said Xiaowen, "they didn't go. Why are you making wild guesses?"

By speaking up for them Xiaowen only increased Wang Changchi's suspicions.

"Since you didn't go begging," he said, "do you mind if I search you?"

Raising both hands, Wang Huai said, "Go ahead and search."

Wang Changchi went over to him, squatted and went through all of Wang Huai's pockets, but found nothing but half a hard *mantou*. Wang Changchi fixed his eyes on Liu Shuangju.

"So you suspect me too?" asked Liu Shuangju.

Wang Changchi went through her pockets but found nothing other than a bunch of paper towels.

"Do you believe them now?" asked Xiaowen.

"You have to be role models for Dazhi," said Wang Changchi, "and not spend all day doing things that lose face."

Xiaowen knew that he was in fact referring to her.

"What do you mean by losing face?" she asked. "Being poor?"

At midnight, Wang Changchi was sound asleep. Liu Shuangju lightly tapped Xiaowen. Mother-in-law and daughter-in-law quietly pressed close to the window and counted the money. One yuan, two yuan, three... a total of 22.75.

"When he was searching you, where did you hide the money?" asked Xiaowen.

"In my shoes," replied Liu Shuangju.

"He almost figured it out."

The two of them laughed aloud at their lucky escape. Wang Huai, however, found it no laughing matter. He stared wide-eyed at the ceiling, feeling conflicted, just the same as Wang Changchi had felt.

四十三 · FORTY-THREE

XIAOWEN WENT BACK TO WORK AT ZHANG HUI'S PHOENIX FOOT SPA. She left every day after dinner and returned at two or three in the morning. Before leaving, she would do her makeup and when she got home she would remove it. She applied it hastily and carelessly and removed it very quickly, never spending more than ten minutes. But it was precisely during that brief ten minutes that the entire household held their breath, listening closely to her every movement. She did her best to make herself as insignificant as possible. She dared not speak loudly or show any anger, she walked softly and carefully closed the door, anxious to reduce herself to the size of an ant or to become transparent.

Unable to stand it any longer, Wang Huai said, "Xiaowen massages feet, so why does she have to wear lipstick?"

"Why can't she wear lipstick?" Wang Changchi retorted.

"It is a blessing that she is massaging feet," added Liu Shuangju enigmatically.

"If she's not massaging feet," Wang Changchi said, "what is she doing?"

Liu Shuangju thought that Wang Changchi would catch her drift and didn't expect such a reply.

Somewhat stunned she asked, "Do you really not understand or are you playing dumb?"

"I really don't understand," replied Wang Changchi.

Liu Shuangju turned to look at Wang Huai. Wang Huai cleared his throat.

"If Xiaowen really is going to massage feet," he said, "then applying lipstick once would be enough."

"How do you know she applies lipstick more than once each night?" asked Wang Changchi.

"Don't you have eyes? Sometimes when she leaves, she is

wearing red lipstick but comes back wearing purple. Sometimes she leaves wearing purple and comes back wearing orange."

"She drinks water and talks. Can't she retouch her makeup?"

"Then how do you explain this?" Liu Shuangju held up a condom. "I found this in her bag when I searched it."

"With five people squeezed into this room, she has to keep some personal things on her. We can't very well ask you to mind your own business, can we?"

Wang Huai slapped the arms of his wheelchair but held his tongue.

"Since she is keeping it for you," said Liu Shuangju, "I was wrong about her."

"Of course you were wrong about her," said Wang Changchi. "She married into our family at a very difficult time, and never enjoyed any happiness in those tiring and miserable days. Do you think that was easy? Other women have dressing tables, but she has to sneak off to the bathroom to put on her makeup. To avoid waking us, she sometimes doesn't even turn on the light when she comes home and has to wash in the dark. She doesn't want to make any noise when she washes, so she only turns on the water a little bit. She could use taking care of Dazhi as an excuse not to work, but she doesn't. Instead, she goes to massage people's feet at midnight. She massages so many feet, but no one has once massaged hers. Why does she have to torture herself? Doesn't she do it all for the sake of this family? How is she related to us? If she hadn't had Dazhi, there wouldn't even be any blood ties. Sometimes I really don't know why she doesn't just get up and leave. Why doesn't she run off with someone with money?"

One night, someone pounded on their door, waking everyone. Wang Changchi turned on the light and opened the door to find Old Xu from downstairs. He sold odds and ends and ran the telephone business in the block.

"Has your wife had an accident?" asked Old Xu. "Otherwise she wouldn't call at this hour."

Wang Changchi threw a jacket over his shoulders and went downstairs with Old Xu. Picking up the receiver, he heard

Xiaowen crying. She said she had been arrested and was now squatting in the foyer downstairs from the Phoenix Foot Spa and that he had to bring five thousand yuan and get her out of there. The money was in the coat with the checkered lining. Wang Changchi was dumbstruck and stood there motionless. Although she had already hung up, he remained there holding the receiver. Only his jacket broke the mood and slowly slid to the ground.

Picking up the jacket, Old Xu asked, "What's the matter with you?"

Only then did Wang Changchi come to himself, take his jacket and run back upstairs.

He opened the trunk and found the coat with the checkered lining, with two thousand, eight hundred yuan in the pocket.

He asked Wang Huai, "Do you have any money?"

"If it's a matter of life and death, I have some," said Wang Huai, "otherwise don't even think about taking it."

Without replying, Wang Changchi counted the money once and then again as if by not stopping he could double the amount.

"What the heck is going on?" asked Wang Huai. "Why do you need so much money?"

Embarrassed to say, Wang Changchi counted the money to avoid replying with the truth.

"Was she caught without her clothes on during a vice raid?" asked Wang Huai.

As he counted the money, Wang Changchi's hands shook, and several notes fell to the floor.

"We can negotiate," said Wang Huai, "don't take so much money just to waste it."

"How do you know we can negotiate?"

"Zhang Wu was arrested once in the county town," said Wang Huai, "and was going to be fined five thousand yuan. He turned out his pockets and said he only had a thousand from selling an ox. 'In just five minutes I can give you an ox. Won't that be enough?' he said. The vice police wouldn't agree and were going to hold him. In tears and with his nose running, he said that he had his old mother and a child to think of, his mother was blind, his child was crippled and his wife had cancer... He cursed three generations of his family. The vice cop said, 'Since your family is so miserable, how could you think of fooling around with prostitutes?' 'My wife has uterine cancer,' he said, 'so it's been years since I did it, so I wanted to remember what it's like. You young men have no idea that the older a person gets, the more he likes to remember.' The vice cop went soft-hearted, confiscated his ox and let him go. If someone like him with money and who isn't miserable can elicit so much sympathy, people like us who really are poor and miserable ought to be able to get even more. Or you can take me with you so they can see my legs and I'll help you by crying. I'm sure they will come down."

Scolding him as shameless, Wang Changchi took off, clutching the two thousand, eight hundred yuan.

Looking at his departing back, Wang Huai shouted, "Fool, are you that well off? Are you too poor to think about the money?"

Wang Changchi arrived outside the foyer and saw a row of men and women squatting, guarded by several vice cops. The men wore only their underpants, and the women's clothes were in disarray. Eyes fixed on the door, they resembled a bunch of orphans waiting for someone to claim them. Wang Changchi waved through the window.

"My man is here," said Xiaowen.

"Get him to come in," said a cop.

Xiaowen beckoned him inside. Wang Changchi waved her outside. The two seemed to be in a waving competition.

"Big brother," said Xiaowen, "my man is a bit embarrassed, so let me go out and get the money."

The vice cop beckoned him forcefully several times through the window. Wang Changchi had no choice but to enter under their gazing eyes. He felt like he was walking on nails and wished the electricity would go off at that moment.

"What is your relationship to He Xiaowen?" asked the vice cop.

"Husband."

"What's your name?"

"Wang Changchi."

"According to article thirty of the Public Security Administration Punishments Law, there is either to be a) a fine or b) detention. Which do you choose?"

"Are you asking me?"

"Ask her, your wife."

Pointing at Xiaowen, the vice cop said, "Did you make her do this?"

"Would you let your wife do this?"

"If my wife did this, I'd shoot her."

Wang Changchi trembled as if he had been shot. Xiaowen kept winking and shaking her head, trying to hint at something. Wang Changchi didn't understand, nor did he speak to her. He pulled out the cash and placed it in the vice cop's hand.

Counting it, the vice cop said, "You're short two thousand, two hundred."

Wang Changchi turned out the pockets of his jacket and trousers. The four pockets hung there like shrivelled breasts.

"Even if I dug down three feet," he said, "that's all there is, so you may as well lock her up. Detaining her for fifteen days would mean a saving of two thousand, eight hundred, which works out to more than a hundred and eighty yuan a day. As a bricklayer, I can't make that much in a day."

Looking him over from head to foot and seeing his trousers spattered with mortar, the vice cop figured his wallet must be pretty thin, so he said, "You two can go now, but don't do it again. Poverty is no excuse for having no dignity."

Wang Changchi turned and left, quickly walking out of the main door. Xiaowen stood up and rubbed her numb legs, then set off, limping after him.

They walked through the streets late at night, one in front and one behind, separated by a distance of about five metres. If Xiaowen walked faster, Wang Changchi walked faster. If Xiaowen slowed down, Wang Changchi slowed down, always maintaining the same distance.

"I have something to say," said Xiaowen. "Can you slow down?"

Wang Changchi did not slow down.

Xiaowen shouted in the street, "You dummy, why did you hand over so much money?"

Although there were few people on the street, her shout did startle the residents, and several windows and doors were heard being pushed open. Wang Changchi had to slow down.

Catching up with him, Xiaowen said, "Didn't you see me winking and shaking my head?"

"Who knows what that was all about?"

"I meant you shouldn't hand over that much money."

"On the phone, you said five thousand, but I only found two thousand, eight hundred, about half, which was enough."

"They forced me to say five thousand. Before you arrived, a mother who really had no money came for her daughter and paid only eight hundred."

"It was dirty money anyway, and I felt better getting rid of it all."

"Is the money your dad makes clean?"

"Cleaner than yours."

"Clean is what I want too, but can you support the family? If you can support the entire family, I'll buy a bottle of alcohol to kill the germs and from then on be a happy person, cutting firewood, feeding the horses, travelling around the world, facing the sea as the spring flowers bloom."

Wang Changchi was startled. He had no idea she could memorise poetry. As he recalled, he had never taught her those lines, so where did it come from? A customer, it had to be a customer who liked reciting poetry and who taught her the lines as they fooled around, fooled around as he instructed her. How ridiculous! The more he thought about it, the more bitterly disappointed he felt, so he quickened his pace, once again lengthening the distance between them.

四十四 · FORTY-FOUR

WANG HUAI AND LIU SHUANGJU DIDN'T SPEAK TO XIAOWEN, making a pantomime out of communicating. Whether it was handing a nappy, washing clothes, mopping the floor, going shopping, cooking, giving Dazhi a bath or applying talcum powder, everything was done using looks and movements. No one was willing to be the first to break the silence. Xiaowen felt that if she spoke first, it would be tantamount to admitting she was wrong. Wang Huai and Liu Shuangju felt if they spoke first, it would mean that they forgave her. One was unwilling to admit she was wrong, two were unwilling to forgive, and the three of them lived a life without language. Only when Wang Changchi returned from work was the place filled with the sound of human speech. On the surface, they spoke to Wang Changchi, when in fact they were speaking to the other side. Wang Changchi was nothing but a medium or a platform. They didn't even need an answer from him, all they needed was for him to act as a deflector. So they chattered on and on and Wang Changchi said nothing.

"Changchi, a man can't swallow that sort of attitude."

"Nor can a woman, Son."

"Wang Changchi, don't force yourself, and it won't get caught in your throat."

"Changchi, if word of this gets back to the village, your mum and I won't be able to hold our heads up for the shame, but will have to hide our faces in the crotches of our trousers."

"Some mothers are forgiving, but this one is not, Son, consider that!"

"I don't care what others say. I, He Xiaowen, only care about your views, Wang Changchi."

"Wang Changchi, do you realise that if this had happened in the evil old society, the husband would write a letter casting off his wife?"

"It's what is now called divorce, Son."

"If you want to get a divorce, let's get a divorce. Who's afraid of whom? All you have to do, Wang Changchi, is suggest it, and I'll do the paperwork at once."

"Changchi, there's no need for any paperwork. At the time, all we did was invite some people over to celebrate. There's no marriage certificate."

"Have a little backbone, Son. What woman would look twice at a bloke with such a hangdog look?"

"Are you mute, Wang Changchi? Stand up and speak up for me. Who did I act in such a shameful way for? For myself? If I had married a rich man, or had another way to make money, do you think I'd go out and do this? It's the same as your dad begging. We were all forced to–"

"Changchi, I didn't force her."

"Son, who would force her to do such a thing?"

"It's all because of that bloody Lin Jiabo," roared Wang Changchi.

He leapt to his feet and grabbed a cleaver. "I'm going to hack him to pieces."

The three of them were stunned. Wang Changchi walked towards the door, waving the cleaver. As the room was so narrow, he almost cut Xiaowen's nose, Liu Shuangju's arm and Wang Huai's wheelchair. Soon he was out of the door, waving the cleaver.

"Stop," shouted Wang Huai. "What does this have to do with Lin Jiabo?"

"If it's not him, then who is it?"

He spoke as he headed downstairs.

In hot pursuit, Liu Shuangju pleaded with him, "Son, are you crazy? Don't you think this family is messed up enough?"

Wang Changchi turned and waved the cleaver in the direction of Liu Shuangju. She recoiled in fear. Wang Changchi swore and swung with the cleaver as if the air he hacked was his enemy. He hacked all the way to West River Bridge before he stopped and then began to hack away at the concrete railing. Because he struck with such force, his hand went numb, the blade bent, and the concrete railing pitted. He fumed as he hacked. Wang Changchi, in this wretched situation, someone sleeps with your wife and you hack up a railing. Someone cripples you, and all you can do is swear at his mother. You have no bloody skill to muddle along in the world, so why did you want to come out of your father's balls in the first place? You relied on your mum and dad to beg for the money to pay for your wife's hospital stay, are you even human? It would be better to end it head down... He looked down from the bridge and then threw the cleaver away. It was ages before he heard the kerplunk of the cleaver hitting the water. He trembled.

In the past, Wang Changchi had more or less run back to their place from work in his desire to see Dazhi, thinking all the while about Xiaowen and worried about his parents. But now after work he dawdled, reluctant to leave the construction site and his mates at work. Only after dark when the street lights went on and his mates picked up their rice bowls did he saunter home. Even after returning to where they were staying, he'd just pull a long face and not say anything, and when Dazhi cried, he seemed not to hear.

Unable to suppress her irritation, Liu Shuangju asked, "What's your view about all this?"

"I don't have one," he said.

"You have no view about something so important?" asked Wang Huai. "Even the weakest person would complain, showing their approval or disapproval as a warning. If you can't talk tough, get your to mother teach you."

"Shut up, all of you." Wang Changchi said. "Let this be the end of the matter, this includes Xiaowen, so stop going on. If you want to blame someone, blame me, blame me because I didn't get into college, blame me for being useless, blame me for being poor."

Xiaowen began to weep and immediately cooked an extra dish.

Pointing at the dish, she said, "I made this especially for Changchi. No one else can have any. He spends the whole day working hard at the construction site, so he should have a little more to eat."

In the end, nobody ate the dish. Wang Huai and Liu Shuangju

agreed with what Xiaowen had said. Wang Changchi didn't eat any because he thought Xiaowen treated him and his parents differently.

Wang Huai, Liu Shuangju and Xiaowen all stopped working and did nothing but sit indoors all day long, as exemplary models. Liu Shuangju couldn't stand just sitting there, so she decided to wheel Wang Huai out for some fresh air, but it was impossible for her to get Wang Huai and his wheelchair from the first floor to the ground floor by herself. Watching what was going on, Xiaowen pretended not to see a thing, waiting all day with her ears pricked up for Liu Shuangju to ask her for help. Unwilling to ask Xiaowen for help, Liu Shuangju hit upon a solution. First, she carried Wang Huai down on her back and placed him at the bottom of the stairway, then she went back upstairs and fetched the wheelchair. Each time she went downstairs or upstairs, Liu Shuangju had to carry Wang Huai and his wheelchair separately. Even though Xiaowen was right there, she didn't lend a hand. The mover and the moved were filled with resentment and felt that Xiaowen had changed, that she wasn't so kind any longer. From beginning to end, Xiaowen's attitude remained cold and was intentionally teaching her parents-in-law a lesson.

Returning from the construction site in the evening, Wang Changchi saw two familiar figures on the dusty roadside. Their heads were turned towards the exit to the construction site. Perhaps they had gone numb from looking so long, as even when Wang Changchi appeared before them, they didn't react. They resembled statues, one of which was modelled after Rodin's *The Thinker*. *The Thinker* was Wang Huai, his head wrapped in a towel and his face and hands covered with bloodstains.

"Who did that?" asked Wang Changchi.

"A beggar did," said Liu Shuangju. "We had no idea that beggars in the city have territories. If two policemen hadn't shown up, your dad would've been beaten to death."

"Who asked you to beg?" asked Wang Changchi.

"I said no begging, no begging, but your mum said we weren't doing anything anyway. If I oppose her, she won't take me to the toilet or carry me upstairs. Going upstairs or downstairs is no big deal, but if I can't go to the toilet, I have to go in my trousers."

"He's filthy," said Wang Changchi, eyeing Liu Shuangju. "He's covered with blood, why didn't you take him to hospital?"

"Why waste the money? The wounds will heal in a couple of days," said Wang Huai.

Wang Changchi wanted to open Wang Huai's hand and look at his wounds, but he refused.

"It's nothing, just a small injury," he said.

"It's so dusty here, why did you come to the construction site?"

"We wanted to have a 'meeting' with you," said Wang Huai.

"Go back to our place."

"If we do that, it'll be an enlarged meeting."

Turning away, Wang Changchi took several deep breaths.

"OK, what the hell is it?" he said.

Wang Huai did not reply at once but was trying to set the mood and find the opening remarks for the "meeting". He pointed at the construction site with his other hand and said, "Are you willing to spend your whole life in this kind of place?"

"Where else is there to go?"

"I've been thinking nonstop about this for days. I think if you go on this way, you'll only be able to make enough to live on but not change your fate."

"Isn't being able to pick up someone else's rubbish already doing pretty well, without trying to change fate?"

"It has to change, otherwise even Dazhi will be a goner."

"You've gone from the village to the city, but two generations of father and son have done nothing but cripple themselves and changed nothing."

"That's because you don't work hard enough."

Wang Changchi stretched out both hands, saying "Look, my fingers are all misshapen. You don't call that hard work?"

They looked at his hands and his bent, black and swollen fingers covered with innumerable cracks. Like brothers unable to get along, they would never come together in good order. Looking at them, Liu Shuangju's eyes grew moist. But Wang Huai was unmoved.

"You still haven't bored through the wall to borrow someone else's light," he said. "You haven't studied by moonlight, you haven't tied your hair to a beam and jabbed yourself with an awl, you haven't–"

"But I studied until I saw stars and passed out in the classroom."

"If you don't die in the process, that can't be called working hard. Can you study again for the university exams? All you have to do is get into college, become a cadre, and only then will you be able to be reborn, otherwise, you'll always just be a labourer."

"Only with bricks and cement. I can hardly hold a pen any more."

"Didn't lots of educated youth and workers in those days grit their teeth and get into university? You have sound limbs, a nose and a mouth. Others can do it, why not you?"

"Because university is missing from my genes."

"Then you'll eat dust all your life."

"Since it's my fate to eat dust, why should I ruin my brains to be a cadre?"

"That's wrong. How old are you? You still have time."

"You couldn't do it, so why should I be able to?"

Wang Huai was exasperated, sorry for his hardship and angry at his unwillingness to change. He felt Wang Changchi was like mud too soft to plaster a wall, like a wildcat trapped in a fire. Blood rose to his brain, his scabbed wound grew inflamed, his towel grew moist with blood again and his palms felt cold. He bled with disappointment.

四十五 · FORTY-FIVE

XIAOWEN RETURNED FROM SHOPPING TO FIND THE PLACE EMPTY. Before she had gone out, Wang Huai, Liu Shuangju and Dazhi had been playing on the bed, but on her return no one was there. Her chest suddenly felt congested and sweat inexplicably appeared on her forehead. Unconsciously, she looked to the corner of the room and saw that the cloth bag Liu Shuangju had brought back from the countryside was gone. A letter with a key placed on top of it was sitting on the dining table. With one look she knew that it wasn't good news. Xiaowen opened the letter but didn't really understand it, so she took it to see Wang Changchi at the construction site.

Wang Changchi read the letter.

"They've taken Dazhi back to the countryside," he said.

"Why did they take my son away?" asked Xiaowen.

"Because they feel I don't have any ambition and that you are likely to degrade yourself," explained Wang Changchi. "For them, this family is like a tin of paint which will even turn a white child black. If we want Dazhi to get out of the filthy muck and not be contaminated, to remain stainless, hollow stems shunning vine and branch, scent growing purer with the distance, upright and in peace, the only way to do so is for them to take him back to bring him up."

"Nonsense," said Xiaowen. "If they can raise a genius, what are you doing here?"

Pointing to the letter, Wang Changchi said, "He says at least he has learned from his failure."

"Can failure be used as a justification? Aren't you afraid he'll fail again?" Xiaowen stamped her foot in irritation.

"Perhaps... perhaps he can produce a miracle."

"He can't even take care of himself, so how do you expect him to produce a miracle? I can tell you're all mad."

"Then what do you suggest we do?"

"Hurry up, we can't let Dazhi be taken away."

They ran downstairs and out of the construction site, flagged down a cab on the street and sped to the eastern station. Inside, they were told that the bus to Tianle County had departed ten minutes earlier. The ticket collector confirmed that a man in a wheelchair and a middle-aged woman carrying a baby were on the bus. Paralysed, Xiaowen sat down on a bench, as if her son had been abducted and sold, tears running from her eyes.

"Why are you crying?" asked Wang Changchi. "If you're upset, we can buy two bus tickets to the countryside and bring Dazhi back."

"Go and buy the tickets," said Xiaowen.

Wang Changchi walked towards the ticket window, but after taking a few steps walked back.

"Are you sure you want to buy the bus tickets?" he asked.

Wiping away her tears, Xiaowen said, "What do you reckon?"

"Let me think," said Wang Changchi, sitting down. "My first thought was that Dazhi is too young and too delicate. Will he be able to adjust to the village environment? The village doesn't have milk or hospitals and the electricity often goes off, the pigpen and cattle pen are close to the house, and there is a steady stream of fleas and ants. The floor is dirt and mixed with the droppings of chicken, oxen and dogs. If he's hungry all he'll have is rice milk, and when he's thirsty he'll have to drink untreated water. The only time they boil water is when making tea. When he sleeps at night, can he survive without a mosquito net? When he crawls, he'll be covered with dirt, if he's lucky, if not, he'll be covered with shit. Can a person of genius be raised in such an environment? No one within a kilometre speaks Mandarin, nor is anyone ever heard reading. The steps leading to the house are earthen. Who's to say he won't fall? And if he does happen to fall, who can guarantee he won't be crippled, made dumb or even killed?

"But, I too grew up drinking rice milk and I can lift fifty *jin* with one hand now. Isn't that strong? The floor is a bit dirty, but I believe that when Dazhi crawls, they'll put down a clean mat for him. Drinking untreated water doesn't matter because the water there comes from a mountain spring and is cleaner than city water. When it comes to the sound of reading, rest assured, my dad has nothing to do, so he'll read Tang poetry and Song lyrics to Dazhi every day. In the letter he left behind, he mostly quotes the Song dynasty writer Zhou Dunyi's *Ode to the Lotus*. Unbelievably he can write *Ode to the Lotus* from memory! I'd nearly forgotten it. He's showing off his memory and perhaps even directing and encouraging me. In other words, since it'll be some time before

Dazhi goes to kindergarten, let him be the trustee. Young working women these days all leave their kids in the village for grandpa and grandma to look after, freeing workers to be productive. Even more, the love of grandparents for their grandchildren is greater than that of parents for their children and is even more indulgent. Haven't you noticed how my dad holds Dazhi with so much care all day long as if he were holding a basket of eggs? Many times he fell asleep holding him, unwilling to let him out of his hands for a single moment. Why did he hold him like that? Because he's lost all hope for me. He's placed all his hopes on Dazhi. So, I think he's safer in their hands than in ours."

Xiaowen wiped her eyes. "Then why did he say I'm likely to degrade myself?"

"He made a mistake."

"That's not what you really think."

"Then what do I think?"

"You think the same as them."

"My thoughts are more complicated than theirs."

"How complicated?"

"Too complicated to be explained simply. First, this is what I think... the lower half of my body is no good, so if I don't let you go out with other men, then sooner or later, we'll end up getting divorced. Even though you are with other men, that doesn't mean the fate of our marriage is decided, but at least it can be mitigated. My strategy is to live one day at a time, at least until Dazhi is a little older. That's why I'm reluctant to buy the bus tickets. Sooner or later, you're going to leave me, and I can't work and take care of Dazhi, so ultimately Dazhi will have to be cared for by his grandpa and grandma. If we don't let them try their hand at it now and let Dazhi get used to them, it'll be too late for them to lend a hand when you suddenly leave. I know what you do when you go out at night, but I put up with it and even cover up for you and never bring up the subject. When you come home at midnight, though my eyes are closed, I am still awake. Sometimes I lie awake all night long, recalling the night sky at home filled with stars. It's so beautiful... sometimes I secretly say a prayer for you that you don't catch some disease and that nothing bad happens to you. I'm a man, your husband, and I have a strong sense of self-respect and need respect. If you're going to do it, just do it. Why insist upon being caught red-handed?"

"Then I won't do it any more!"

"Go ahead, but you'd best not do it for money. You're still young. If you find someone to your liking you can leave, but it would be best to say something first so that I won't be too shocked."

"I did it, but that was business, and I was angry. I felt bad every time I did it. I had to imagine they were you so I could stand it. Whoever they were, in my heart they were all you."

"I never thought anyone would be my substitute."

"Who told you to be so spineless?"

Wang Changchi thought of Lin Jiabo and felt that all his difficulties had been caused by him. He was very anxious to kill him. But thinking about it over and over, he also dug deep into his own soul. He asked himself if the injuries he sustained in the fall were intentional. At the time, Xiaowen had been seduced into doing wrong by Zhang Hui and wanted an abortion so she could make money for a few years. In wanting to prevent Xiaowen from getting an abortion, and being so concerned about money, did he fall on purpose intending to get his boss to pay compensation?

At this point, Wang Changchi paused for quite some time, as he often did when things got difficult and before an important decision needed to be taken. He came to a negative conclusion. Who would trade their whole life's happiness for several tens of thousands of yuan, especially since he had previously tasted his boss's dirty tricks? Was there any guarantee he would be compensated for the fall? Only in a fairy tale. This made him hate Lin Jiabo even more. Wang Huai took courage from hope, but Wang Changchi needed hatred to sustain what he was capable of.

四十六 · FORTY-SIX

WANG DAZHI HAD CRIED EVER SINCE THEY RETURNED TO THE VALLEY, and when he slept he twitched constantly as if he were still badly shaken. His crying sounded like a horn, like the roar of a car engine, like music, like singing, like the purr of a refrigerator or air conditioner, like a bicycle bell... It was as if he had brought all of the sounds of the city with him, making the once quiet village quiet no more, making the villagers who had for ages gone to bed and dreamed peacefully now lose sleep and even hallucinate. When she wasn't feeding him rice milk and milk, Liu Shuangju was burning incense before the ancestral tablets, praying that the ancestors might accept the grandchild.

All the lactating women thought he was hungry. Zhang Xian-hua, Wang Dong's wife, Bao Qing's wife, Jiang Po's wife and Yi Long's wife, among others, came one after the other and anxiously lifted their tops, took hold of their firm, white breasts and stuck their pink or brown nipples straight into Dazhi's mouth. But Dazhi did not suck and, without exception, spat out the nipples. Even though he wouldn't buy it, the women remained as enthusiastic as ever. They revealed virtues of good-ness, sympathy and pity, while quite possibly showing off their full breasts and copious reserves of milk, but even more likely hoping that this little city mouth would accept their nipples. After being rejected several times, they would rip off their tops that had tightly covered those chests that no one had caressed in a long time and ask, "What is there not to like? Both your dad's and mum's feet and legs were spattered with the mud here, their mouths stuffed with the local vegetables, so how is it that a Silkie chicken can so quickly become a phoenix?"

At night, tired from crying, Dazhi nuzzled in Liu Shuangju's bosom. Unconsciously, Liu Shuangju took out her shrivelled breast and stuck it in Dazhi's mouth. Dazhi did not reject it but actually began to suckle until Liu Shuangju was numb all over, sucking on it until she forgot her age and generation and was once again filled with a mother's pride. The following day, she made a pot of chicken soup for herself just like the one Wang Huai served her during her one-month lying-in. A few days later, her shrivelled breasts began to swell slowly, Dazhi finally suckled some milk and stopped crying. For Wang Huai, it was as if he saw Wang Changchi born a second time. Heaven has finally given me another chance, he thought.

"I will raise him to be a university student," said Wang Huai to Liu Baitiao.

"I want to raise him to be a cadre," said Wang Huai to Zhang Wu.

"Being a cadre, he can be a leader," said Wang Huai to Daijun.

"Being a leader, he can make the Wang family famous," said Wang Huai to Second Uncle.

"Being famous, he can allocate money to build the village a road," said Wang Huai to someone else.

Everyone contained their laughter and felt Wang Huai was obsessed and exaggerating things. How could he raise a university student? If he wanted to raise a cadre, why not start with Wang Changchi? But Wang Huai had his own plans. Late one night, he nudged Liu Shuangju awake.

"What are you twitching about this time?" mumbled Liu Shuangju.

"I heard footsteps," said Wang Huai. "Go and see if it's a thief."

Startled, Liu Shuangju held her breath, but she heard nothing except the chirping of the insects in the night. Wang Huai thought she was still half asleep and that her sense of hearing wasn't altogether there. Liu Shuangju would have none of it, so she listened carefully but heard nothing except the neighbours snoring.

"It's like taking a long-distance bus ride," said Wang Huai. "You have to go to the toilet even if you really don't need to, and only then can you be at ease."

"There are only some worthless bundles of firewood outside," said Liu Shuangju.

"Aren't you afraid they'll steal our Dazhi?" asked Wang Huai.

Liu Shuangju turned back the blanket and Dazhi was at her

bosom. Wang Huai held Dazhi and squeezed him tightly and then with eyes wide open looked out of the window.

"Can't you sleep?" asked Liu Shuangju ·

"I keep feeling there's someone outside," said Wang Huai.

Liu Shuangju threw on some clothes and got out of bed, took the torch, and went around the house checking all the doors and windows before returning to bed.

"Are you sure there's no one outside?" asked Wang Huai.

"Can't you stop for a while? I have to work in the fields tomorrow."

"Since no one's listening, I'll tell you my plan."

Showing no interest, Liu Shuangju lay down and went to sleep. Wang Huai gave her a shove and woke her again.

"They all doubt my ability to raise Dazhi, and think I'm short-sighted," said Wang Huai.

Yawning, Liu Shuangju just wanted to go back to sleep.

"This is such an important matter," said Wang Huai. "Can't you just stay awake?"

With her right hand, Liu Shuangju felt around beside her pillow for the essential balm. Opening the jar, she applied the essential oil to her temples. This time she seemed fully awake.

"For his primary school education," said Wang Huai, "I plan to teach Dazhi myself. I have all the textbooks. For junior high school, we'll send him to the village. Although they say the village doesn't produce anyone talented, still we'll have double insurance. During the day, when he goes to class, I'll go with him and sit at the back and study what he studies, like studying with a prince. The teacher will teach by day, and I'll teach by night, covering each class twice, which will allow him to recite something backwards fluently. Using this method, he'll certainly be able to get into the senior high school in the county town. I'll also accompany him there, again teaching him each class twice. When the time comes, he'll have no problem getting into Tsinghua or Peking University."

Rubbing her eyes, Liu Shuangju said, "Goodness, how did you come up with such a good idea?"

"It's the same as our account book," said Wang Huai. "Don't tell anyone else, otherwise they'll all do the same, and we'll lose our competitive advantage."

"Do you think I'm that daft?"

"Each time I turn this plan over in my mind, my head spins like a super typhoon which can carry off a person along with his wheelchair."

"The blind rely on their ears, and the lame rely on their heads. I'd no idea you'd become so smart since the lower half of your body became useless."

"When was I ever stupid?"

Dazhi cried again. It wasn't because he was hungry, but because his whole body was covered with red bumps, breaking out all over his arms, back, bottom and legs. At first, Wang Huai didn't take it seriously and figured it was just flea bites and that a little essential balm would take care of it. He didn't expect that when he applied the essential balm the bumps wouldn't shrink but actually increase in size as well as join the irregular red blotches into a solid patch of fiery red. Wang Huai tried decoctions of herbal medicine and chicken bile, all of which were ineffective. Dazhi's whole body was red, like a pile of burning embers. If he was placed under a blanket, it would grow hot. Holding him would make a person painfully hot. He cried until he was hoarse, until there was only his breath left in him. Liu Shuangju was beside herself and urgently asked Guang Sheng from the neighbouring village to come.

Guang Sheng's principal occupation was as a spirit medium, and he concurrently ran a small business. A spirit medium is the same as a ghost master or shaman, someone who communicates with the spirits. They stand in both the worlds of Yin and Yang. Sometimes they represent this world, or the Yang world, seeking answers from the ancestral spirits, sometimes they represent the ancestral spirits, relaying their commands to this world. Their principal function is to repair relations between later generations and their ancestors as well as to dispel evil spirits and ghosts for the health and peace of the living.

On a square table, Liu Shuangju arranged the offerings which included a live rooster, a bowl of white rice, a piece of cooked pork shoulder and a bottle of rice wine. Once everything was arranged, Wang Huai lit the incense and burned paper spirit money. Smoke and paper ash danced in the main hall, the smells of cooked meat and live chicken mixed, the aroma of rice wine, incense and spirit money blended. Sitting in front of the spirit tablets, Guang Sheng consulted the oracles, which are consulted to seek the cause of something. The subject in this case was, "Why are the bumps all over Dazhi's body so red?"

Was it because no one had looked after the ancestral graves in a long time? Or because no one burned joss sticks and lit the lamp before worshipping? Or

because someone defecated in an inappropriate place such as in front of a temple or next to burning incense? Had someone offended some kind of spirit or pulled down a bridge or dug up a road to frame someone? Had bad words been said about a particular ancestor? Guang Sheng asked everything from north to south, from black to white, to which the oracles had always replied "no", which made Guang Sheng anxious and his head sweat.

"All professions and occupations advance with the times," offered Wang Huai. "Has yours progressed?"

Getting the point, Guang Sheng asked, "Has a leader been offended? Was someone's tyre punctured resulting in an accident? Was money made illegally or fake goods made and sold? Was a river polluted or trees felled? Is it on account of a mistress? Is it on account of a child born outside the state plan or for cursing the government or seeking an audience with higher-ups? Is it because of using drugs, prostitution, or visiting prostitutes?"

The oracle responded in the affirmative, indicating that the last question was the right question. The villagers who had been watching the busy proceedings were stunned, and the whispering rose and fell like bursts of rain.

With his fist in his palm, Wang Huai said, "Everyone out."

But no one wanted to leave, just like a cinema audience glued to their screen as the film reaches its climax. Guang Sheng got up and cleared the hall and barred the main door, leaving only Wang Huai, Liu Shuangju and Second Uncle inside. Guang Sheng once again began to consult the oracles to determine whether it was using drugs, prostitution or visiting prostitutes. He had to ask about each in turn, but on the second question the oracle said "yes". Finally, Guang Sheng found the cause, but finding the cause was not the final goal. That was to ask the Wang family ancestors to indicate a solution to the problem. He picked up the rooster and walked around the place three times, bit off a small piece from the rooster's cockscomb and spat it in front of the spirit tablets, and then sat down on a bench, closed his eyes and mumbled as his legs moved incessantly... He resembled a courier racing on a horse towards the Wang family walled compound in the nether world. Sweat rolled from his forehead, and his under-clothes were soaking wet. He was in this state for a quarter of an hour before returning to the world of men, when he suddenly opened his eyes.

"Your daughter-in-law's body is dirty," he said. "Her body is dirty so her milk is dirty. Her dirty milk has polluted Dazhi. Because Dazhi carries something dirty on him, the moment he entered this house, the ancestors were angered. The one who is angry is none other than Dazhi's great-grandfather, Wang Huai's father. Your father wants you to slaughter a piglet and offer it at the family graves, also pour some rice wine, burn spirit money, and take Dazhi along and say some nice things. In life, your father was concerned about reputation, so you must also set off fire-crackers and create a little activity to make him happy. He only needs to be happy and he'll pardon Dazhi, and Dazhi will get well."

With Guang Sheng's business complete, Wang Huai turned to discover the throngs of heads at the windows and at the cracks in the door.

四十七 · FORTY-SEVEN

"DAD, IS YOUR HEART MADE OF STONE?" asked Wang Huai. "Are you mad, how could you not dearly love such an adorable great-grandchild? For forty-eight hours, I have offered the pig and wine, burned spirit money, and set off firecrackers, but not only have you not reduced Dazhi's swelling, you have actually made more bumps grow and made them harder. Now he even has them on his neck. Do you intend to hound him to death? Have you no sympathy? Do you know who your closest relation is? I am your snot-nosed son, Dad, do you still recognise me? Do you still remember... I think you are confused and do nothing. For so many years I have put up with it and waited, thinking you'd protect me, never imagining that you'd forgotten me, casting aside the person most filial towards you. Are you so busy? Look! Can you see what I've become? My legs are no good, I can't work, I failed to raise Changchi into something, and I've placed all my future hopes on Dazhi. But you not only failed to protect him, you are also angry with him and punish him. He has only been in this world a few hundred days, so why should he be responsible for his mother's sins? He is as spotless as a sheet of white paper, as cute as your little snot-nose was in his day, so why not give him a chance?

"Truly, you're ever more unreasonable, and nothing like my father. When you were still my father, if someone gave you a cookie, you'd hide it in your bosom until it was soaked with sweat, but you wouldn't eat it. Why did you treat your children with such affection when you were alive, and after death want to create such difficulties for your descendants? Have the prevailing winds of time blown to the nether world of Yin? You told Guang Sheng you wanted a pig, which surprised me at the time. Do you know the difficulties facing our family? And still you want a pig. Isn't that like openly seeking a bribe? So be it, anyway, I do miss you and wanted to take this opportunity to express my filial devotion. But you've taken the pig, the wine, the spirit money without helping me to solve the problem. That's not your style. That is unless you are some sort of high official in the nether world and have become corrupt. Have I not given enough? Must you receive gifts before you cure your great-grandchild? It's really a case of refusing to have anything to do with one's kin.

"I am still confused after a lot of thinking. I can't eat nor get a good night's sleep, so I've crawled three *li*, making a special trip to rebuke you. If you don't believe me, look at my bloodied hands and torn trousers. To offer you praise I can get someone to carry me here, but to rebuke you I sneaked out secretly. This is not something to show off, and I don't want others to know we are quarrelling. If you still recognise me, your son, and remember how I wore mourning clothes for you and knelt till my knees ached, then please cure Dazhi of his bumps at once. Otherwise, I'll have nothing more to do with you, I'll ignore you at the Tomb Sweeping Festival. If it should come to that, I'd rather go and worship at someone else's grave, at those solitary graves of forgotten ghosts than worship you. Did you hear all that? Wang Shangcheng, I'm not asking you to advance me as an official nor make me wealthy. I'm just asking you to help your great-grandchild."

After giving this rebuke, Wang Huai did not leave at once but sat by the grave for half a day. Wang Shangcheng was apparently left speechless by his rebuke. Clouds drifted across the sky and floated away, occasionally passing directly overhead, shrouding him and the grave in a cold shadow. The watery paddy fields in front of the grave had already been harrowed and resembled panes of glass. The anger seething in his chest gradually subsided. He finally heard the insects chirping all around him like a drizzling rain. From time to time, grasshoppers took flight amid the grass. A snake swam quickly through the paddy field, leaving a wake of ripples. This was the spring that folks long for in the winter, with green grass, colourful flowers and birds winging through the sky. But the spring was real and not a metaphor or symbol. Wang Huai had to crawl back by the same route. Crawling, crawling, he saw the tracks he had left when he came, two long, unbroken lines made by dragging his legs, like two pieces of wood, erasing the footprints on the road.

That night, Dazhi spat out white foam and his temperature shot up.

"If we wait any longer to take him to the village clinic," said Second Uncle, "I'm afraid his life will be at risk."

It was pitch black outside. Wang Huai got Second Uncle and Liu Baitiao to fasten his wheelchair quickly to two poles. Carrying Wang Huai, they set off with traditional and electric torchlight. Liu Shuangju had planned to carry Dazhi on her back, but Wang Huai wouldn't allow it. Clasping him tightly, Wang Huai could monitor his body temperature and breathing constantly. He was warm as an oven at his bosom. Wang Huai kept shouting the whole way, fearful that Dazhi might go to sleep and not wake up.

"Dazhi, oh, Dazhi," he said, "your granddad died once before, but the King of Hades sent him back. He sent me back because I didn't want to die. If a person doesn't want to die, he won't. It's said that life is tough for the Wangs, so if you are a Wang, just push this illness back. Dazhi, oh, Dazhi, whatever you do, don't fall asleep, you still have to take the university exams and you still have to be a cadre, as well as allocate money to build a village road. If there were a road, your Second Great Uncle and Great Uncle Liu would find it easier, and it would be easier for the people of our village to visit the doctor. Dazhi, for the sake of the road, you have to hang on..."

The traditional and electric torches made their way slowly along the pitch-black and winding road. The night wind set the grass and trees along the road rustling while making the traditional torch flicker. The sound of their footsteps silenced the chirping insects. Though he shouted, he actually fell asleep. The moment the poles tilted, he would wake up, rub Dazhi's chest and check his nostrils. He still had a fever and was still breathing. Alarmed, he broke into a cold sweat, wondering how he could have fallen asleep. He felt he had only slept for a matter of seconds, but he had a dream right there, sent to him by his father.

In the dream, his father had asked, "How could you rebuke me like that? You can't freely rebuke your father even if I am high-handed, imperious, corrupt, lustful and avaricious. You just have to lump it and say nothing. Who told you to be my son? Who told you to come out of my urethra decades ago? Dazhi's illness is worsening as punishment for you rebuking me. At one time the Wang family had dignity, everyone possessed etiquette and a sense of shame, but now how have you all ruined it? Some beg and some sell their bodies. If you do not mend your ways, I will cut off the head of the Wang family. When one arrives it will get sick and when one is born it will die."

Wang Huai dimly recalled arguing in the dream, saying something like, "I, too, want to live a dignified life, but reality is like a sharp knife at the neck, forcing us to behave in ways we don't want to."

"I don't care about your difficulties," his father had said. "All I'm concerned about is that you don't let our ancestors down."

Wang Huai felt as if he were being attacked from the front and rear and broke into a sweat on two sides. It was all sweat, but at the front it was hot while at the back it was cold.

They arrived at the village clinic to find the door locked and no lights on inside as if there were no patients. Second Uncle knocked on the door, but with no response from inside.

"Pick up a stone and bang on the door with it," said Wang Huai, "otherwise they'll pretend they can't hear anything."

Second Uncle picked up a stone and pounded on the door. Suddenly, the door opened.

Dr Ma stood at the door and gave them a tongue-lashing: "What are you doing? Are you here to vandalise or steal?"

"The child is in a bad way," said Wang Huai. "I beg you, please hurry and help him." Dr Ma squatted and carefully examined the door.

"You broke my door, and you still ask for help? Is your child more important than my door?"

"We need your help right away", said Wang Huai. "I'll pay for the door."

"First pay five hundred yuan," said Dr Ma.

Without the slightest hesitation, Wang Huai pulled out five hundred yuan. Dr Ma took it and counted it. He looked at each note under the light to make sure none was counterfeit and only then did he show any interest. He had been at the village hospital for over twenty years because he didn't want to give any gifts to the leaders, so every year he made his report but was never transferred back to the county town.

"Can you hurry up a little?" asked Wang Huai.

Only then did Dr Ma come to and slowly took Dazhi's temperature, listened to his heart, looked at his tongue, took his pulse and examined his pupils. Wang Huai continuously asked questions, while Dr Ma made no reply, a silent scientist. From doing the examination to writing a prescription to getting the medicine, shaving the boy's head and giving an injection, he did everything himself at the same uniform speed. Wang Huai was so anxious that he wanted to curse his mother. Finally, he got rid of all the bubbles in the IV tube by tapping it and it looked like he was going to pick up the IV needle, but unexpectedly turned and went to the toilet. Returning from the toilet, he washed his hands and spent more time washing them than he had spent in the toilet. Finally, he lifted the needle toward Dazhi's head and tried to insert it. Owing to his poor eyesight, he tried eight times before getting it into the vein. Wang Huai groaned each time as if the needle had been stuck eight times into his own heart.

"Now you're in a hurry to have him treated. What were you doing before?" asked Dr Ma finally.

Wang Huai didn't reply for a while, which gave him a chance to go on talking.

"At first it wasn't a serious illness," Wang Huai said, "just a few flea bites."

"Flea bites are just part of being a village child."

"But this child is not a village child."

"Even if he was born in New York," said Dr Ma, "such a severe case would be unlikely. If he had taken medicine in time, his whole body wouldn't have had an allergic reaction."

"There's no other medicine but essential balm in the countryside."

"Then why didn't you bring him to the village clinic sooner?

By not bringing him sooner for treatment you've ended up with his whole body being affected and his immunity decreased, high fever and pneumonia. If you had waited any longer, it might have cost his life."

"My legs are bad and making the trip is not easy, so I thought I would take care of it out in the countryside."

"Did you take care of it? No. In the end, didn't you just kick the ball to me? I suffer from insomnia, and then you show up."

"I apologise."

"Are you his father?"

"No, I'm his grandfather."

"Oh, so he's not yours. I fuck your mother's grandfather. Even if he's not yours, isn't a life still a life? You don't cherish him in the least. If I were your son, I'd slap you so hard that you'd end up in the Pacific Ocean. In all the world can there be a grandfather who treats his grandson like you? You've got to be one of a kind."

Dr Ma dumped a bellyful of anger on Wang Huai as if he had upended a dustbin over his head. As long as Dazhi got well, Wang Huai couldn't care less about the complaining and was even prepared to put up with the cursing. Each time Dr Ma drifted off to sleep, Wang Huai would push him awake. If Dr Ma wasn't cursing, Wang Huai would remind him by saying, "Should I have brought Dazhi here sooner?" Dr Ma would then repeat the same diatribe once again. The two of them spent a foul-mouthed night together, one cursing and one being cursed.

四十八 · FORTY-EIGHT

AFTER RUNNING THE IV FOR THREE DAYS, Dazhi's condition had failed to improve. His temperature remained elevated, the bumps on his body were as red as ever, and he coughed more frequently than he had before going to the clinic. Frowning, Wang Huai asked Dr Ma if he could really cure the illness. As he was always more or less successful in the village clinic, Dr Ma didn't take this sort of paediatric case all that seriously, but it was a fact that the high fever had not abated.

Looking ashamed, he said enigmatically, "Just think about it. In ten years, the higher-ups have not allocated any funds to the village hospital. A medical school graduate would rather work in a private clinic in the city. Even to sell medicine, they still won't come to this place to work. The new blood won't come, and the old blood gets transferred out with connections. Only an old fool like me still stays. Look at the hospital in the county town. New buildings going up, new equipment being added, awards given, red envelopes accepted, how can the village compare? They're as different as fingernails and toenails."

Although this complaint of Dr Ma's had nothing to do with Dazhi's condition, nor had he replied whether or not he could cure the illness, Wang Huai did understand the insinuation. After paying the bill, he picked up Dazhi and told Liu Shuangju and Second Uncle to put him on the bus.

Dazhi was admitted to the paediatric ward of the County Town Hospital. There, he received an IV and the same medicine, the only difference being that the ability to insert an IV at the county town was clearly superior to that of Dr Ma. Each time, Wang Huai had to groan only twice before the nurse managed to get the needle in. Something else was a little different and that was that the fees were far higher than at the village clinic. After five continuous days of IV treatment, Dazhi's condition had not improved, which led Wang Huai to have an argument with Director Lu.

"Are you not taking Dazhi's treatment seriously because I didn't give you red envelopes," asked Wang Huai, "or do you simply not care whether a poor person lives or dies so that's why you are using fake medicine? How come after five days Dazhi is still running a fever? Was the diagnosis wrong?"

Director Lu immediately organised a group of doctors to do an examination. The five doctors frowned but couldn't ascertain the cause. Ashamed, Director Lu tucked Dazhi in bed and then patted Wang Huai on the shoulder.

"The County Town Hospital sorely lacks qualified doctors able to treat difficult illnesses," he said. "The equipment isn't the best, and there are insufficient drugs. You'd be better off transferring him to the Provincial Hospital."

Holding Dazhi, Wang Huai along with Liu Shuangju got on the long-distance bus to the provincial capital. Wang Huai made a baby sling out of a sheet to hang at his chest in which he placed Dazhi. In this way, the jolting of the bus would not disturb Dazhi's sleep and also ensured that Dazhi wouldn't slip from his hands if he dozed off. Watching for a distance and then sleeping for a distance, Wang Huai felt there was a change in Dazhi's temperature, he seemed cooler and no longer feverish. He got Liu Shuangju to take his temperature with a thermometer and found that it had dropped half a degree. After another hundred kilometres, they checked again, and it had dropped another half degree. Dropping one degree in two hundred kilometres, why would they need a hospital? From that day on, all those who suffered from a fever could just take a long-distance bus. Wang Huai and Liu Shuangju wondered if something was wrong with the thermometer. Wang Huai shook it until the mercury had dropped below 30C before placing it under his armpit. After five minutes, the thermometer read 36.7C. He wasn't convinced, so he checked Liu Shuangju and got a reading of 36.5C.

Placing the palm of her hand on Dazhi's forehead, Liu Shuangju said, "Even if you don't trust the thermometer, you can still trust your palm."

Wang Huai pushed aside Liu Shuangju's hand and placed his own palm on Dazhi's forehead. It was the first time he had doubts about his palm.

When they reached the paediatric ward of the Provincial Hospital, Dazhi's temperature was normal, his lungs sounded fine, the red bumps on his body were half gone and those that were still there had shrunk to small red dots and no longer formed patches. Wang Huai requested that they take X-rays of Dazhi, but the doctor said it was not necessary. Wang Huai again requested it, and the doctor acquiesced. After the X-rays, the doctor said there were no shadows on Dazhi's lungs and no obstructions in his trachea. Wang Huai couldn't figure out why Dazhi's illness was cured when he arrived at the Provincial Hospital.

"Perhaps it's a case of failing to acclimatise to a new environment," suggested the doctor.

Wang Huai wondered if that could happen in only one generation. It really was a matter of forgetting one's roots, simply a betrayal. He was familiar with cases of people forgetting their origins and betraying, but nothing so quick. If the doctor's explanation was tenable, then Dazhi was allergic to the countryside and couldn't live there with them. They had to return him in good condition to Wang Changchi and Xiaowen. So their newly burgeoned second chance of being parents had been nipped in the bud. And the happiness that Dazhi brought to their hands and bosoms and the joy to their senses of hearing and smell would vanish. When they came out of the hospital, they didn't go directly to where Wang Changchi was living but rather sat stupefied in the park, like those who cling to power and refuse to give it up, dragging out the process for as long as possible. Wang Huai had taken Dazhi to raise him as second to no one, his first duty being to take him away from the filth. Wang Huai felt there was nothing as filthy as Xiaowen's profession, but from Dazhi's side, nothing was dirtier than a bunch of fleas. Wang Huai refused to throw up his hands and surrender so quickly.

"The sun's setting," said Liu Shuangju. "Let's go."

Wang Huai didn't move.

"The street lights have come on, let's go."

Still, Wang Huai didn't budge.

"The park's closing."

Only then did Wang Huai move his wheelchair. When they arrived at the entrance to the flat, Wang Changchi and Xiaowen were watching television. Hearing Liu Shuangju shout, they hurried downstairs, one took Dazhi while the other helped Liu Shuangju carry Wang Huai upstairs. As soon as Dazhi landed in Xiaowen's bosom, he impatiently took her breast and suckled as she walked from downstairs all the way up to their room. Like a blood-sucking leech, he clung to her breast. The scene thoroughly upset Wang Huai's concept of right and wrong. Wang Huai realised that the sweetest thing to a child's mouth was its mother's milk, regardless of what she did. Before letting them catch their breaths, Wang Changchi showed them around.

"This is a colour TV," he said, "this is a gas stove, this is a water heater, so from now on there's no steam when you're cooking rice. When you bathe there's instant hot water. If you get bored you can watch TV."

Liu Shuangju was sceptical. Wang Changchi carefully showed her how to turn on the gas stove and with a "poof" a ring of blue flame shot up, and with another "poof" it vanished. Liu Shuangju was so frightened, she stood in front of the stove, not daring to move.

"Oh, where did all these red bumps come from?" asked Xiaowen, as she lifted Dazhi's clothes.

Wang Changchi's expression changed, and he asked, "What exactly happened?"

Liu Shuangju then related everything about Dazhi's illness. As she listened, Xiaowen's face went from red to the colour of pig's liver. Wang Changchi could scarcely breathe.

"You neglected him till you almost cut off the Wang family line," he said. "I've never told you that as a result of my injury, I can no longer have kids. Dazhi is my sole son and the only one left in our bloodline."

Wang Huai gasped as if his lungs had been frozen. "Why didn't you tell us how serious your injury was?" he asked.

"I'm telling you now, aren't I?" said Wang Changchi.

Liu Shuangju burst into tears. She cried for Wang Changchi's pain, for how pitiful he was and for her inability to help him.

"Don't cry," said Wang Huai, "don't cry. The more you cry, the more it will think we're easily browbeaten."

Wang Huai used the word "it" to indicate fate, as well as Heaven, as well as the lineage of Wang family ancestors. He always felt "it" was opposing him, otherwise one family wouldn't have produced two cripples.

Even after all the bumps had disappeared from Dazhi's body,

Xiaowen could still not forgive Wang Huai and Liu Shuangju. She didn't smile.

"She gives all her smiles to her clients," said Liu Shuangju.

Xiaowen moved around unnecessarily and made a lot of noise. Returning from shopping, she banged the vegetables down on the table. When she chopped vegetables, she held the cleaver twice as high as usual. When she cooked, she intentionally struck the wok. When she ate, she chewed noisily, as if each bite was cucumber. Even when she returned at midnight, she turned the tap on high. Sometimes the water splashed outside the bathroom onto the faces of Wang Huai and Liu Shuangju, who were sleeping on the floor. Pots, pans, tubs and ladles were the tools to express her anger. Hands, feet, eyes, nose and mouth all relayed her dissatisfaction. But Wang Huai and Liu Shuangju held their noses and bore it. They bore it because they wanted to talk to Changchi and play with Dazhi on the mat. They also bore it because they had no money coming in. With no income, they had no right to speak, with no income, they had no concept of right or wrong, nor moral superiority for that matter. The big things they enjoyed – the TV, water heater and gas stove – had all been purchased with the money Xiaowen made. On the surface, they stayed respectful, but inside they cringed, terror-stricken by Xiaowen's body and words.

Xiaowen had left for the night shift.

"Changchi," said Wang Huai, "can you take off your trousers and let your dad see?"

Pretending not to hear, Wang Changchi thought, What kind of talk is that?

"Take them off," said Liu Shuangju.

She also wanted to see how he had been injured. Wang Changchi thought, Why must I suffer such shame?

"Just let me see it, and I can tell you if it can be fixed," said Wang Huai.

"What are you afraid of? Your mum and dad watched you grow up. We used to be able to see, but now we can't?"

Clearly, Wang Changchi didn't feel comfortable.

"I've put up with everything in silence here," said Wang Huai, "because I want a chance to see your injury. I won't be at ease until I can see it. I can only go home reassured after I've seen it. You are flesh of our flesh, we suffer your pain, we suffer your injuries."

Suddenly Wang Changchi stood up, dropped his trousers, and in what was close to a roar, shouted, "Then take a look..."

As he spoke, he banged his head against the wall, his whole body shaking as if he had malaria. Wang Huai and Liu Shuangju looked from a distance. Wang Changchi's dick trembled. Liu Shuangju came over and helped him pull up his trousers, the same way she did when he was a child and fastened them.

"It looks like it's in good shape," said Wang Huai. "Does it hurt when you urinate?"

Wang Changchi shook his head.

"Then it's not an illness," said Wang Huai, "but just temporarily frozen from shock. Remember, as long as you draw breath, never give up."

"I've lost everything, what is there to give up?"

"Raise Dazhi well," said Wang Huai.

四十九 · FORTY-NINE

WANG HUAI AND LIU SHUANGJU HAD RETURNED to the countryside. Xiaowen was working the night shift. Only Wang Changchi and Dazhi remained at home. Before Dazhi fell asleep, Wang Changchi talked to him, although he didn't necessarily understand. But after Dazhi fell asleep, Wang Changchi became mute. He turned off the light and lay in bed with his eyes wide open, wondering what Xiaowen was doing, who she was speaking to or if she had already... Or, every time he thought "or" he would close his eyes. He shut his eyes until they ached. "Or" was "or" and those dreadful images filled his mind, and he could do nothing to get rid of them. He had turned the light on and off many times, and got out his high school textbooks to revise, thinking he might retake the national college entrance exam in the hope of changing his present situation. He thought if he held Dazhi while answering the questions he would increase the likelihood of his success, because when the newspapers announced the successful candidates, most came from adverse circumstances. Some of them had terminal illnesses, some were missing arms or legs, some had passed out at their post, and some were from broken families, deserted by wife and child. Wang Changchi possessed more than the necessary qualifications but had missed becoming a useful person. But as he revised and revised, the words in the textbooks leapt off the page to become drops of water, bricks, gravel, even becoming Wang Huai's eyes, and finally nothing but a blur. Reading the textbooks, the only thing he wanted to do was sleep, but as soon as he lay down in bed, he found himself awake. Either way, he couldn't win.

Returning from work at night, Xiaowen didn't seem satiated. After washing, she teased Wang Changchi as if she had not eaten her fill at a banquet and wanted to have a bowl of noodles at home. The ways she teased him grew more numerous, but the lower part of his body did not respond. So ashamed, he dared not open his eyes but believed she was well-intentioned in trying to stimulate him. But he also felt these were her customary actions, nothing more than transferring them from body B to body A. Or was this her way of expressing her regret? Perhaps it was sympathy? Sometimes while teasing him, she'd fall asleep. He pushed her leg off his body as if it were a piece of wood. He wondered, Will I be tormented this way my whole life? I can deceive myself, but how can I deceive Dazhi in the future? Should I get a divorce? Should I take Dazhi and leave before he has any memories of his mother? Would that be too cruel? But if I can't be cruel, this bad background will stick to him like an advert pasted on a telegraph pole that can't be torn or rubbed off. If not dealt with properly, he could turn out to be a bad character. Considering this, Wang Changchi itched to get up and just leave and make a clean break. When he went to push himself up with his arm, he found he had no strength as if his body was too heavy, and that "getting up" was nothing more than an idea. He thought, If I leave now, a rooster with a baby chick, I won't be able to make any money. I can't very well take Dazhi with me when I go to lay bricks, can I? The foreman would never agree to it, and even if he did, I couldn't take Dazhi to that lousy place. Never mind that the sound of the mixer is hard on the ears, or that falling bricks and rebar are dangerous, the dust alone would be enough to suffocate Dazhi...

Tossing and turning, Wang Changchi discovered that every road he considered was blocked, not only impassable but also a headache. Holding his head he thought, Just doing what's needed, who wouldn't fall short? But the more he fell, the more beautiful it would be, the more thrilling. All he had to do was cast his dignity aside like so much spit and lower his hopes for Dazhi, then he could get by. Really? Wang Changchi couldn't resign himself to it.

He shook Xiaowen awake and asked, "Can you change jobs?"

Half asleep, Xiaowen said, "Sure, if you can get on top of me."

Xiaowen was already asleep before the words were out of her mouth, leaving Wang Changchi adrift in his thoughts.

Several days later, Wang Changchi again talked to Xiaowen about changing jobs.

"I'm serious," said Wang Changchi.

"I'm serious, too," said Xiaowen.

"What are you serious about?"

"What I'm serious about, is stopping all talk of me changing jobs unless you can get on top of me. I'm a human being, and I need a normal married life."

Wang Changchi broke into a sweat.

"If you won't change jobs," he said, "let's get a divorce."

"Whatever you like," said Xiaowen.

He hadn't imagined Xiaowen would be so casual about it and not even bat an eyelid.

"Then you really agree to a divorce?" asked Wang Changchi.

"Aren't you the one who brought it up?"

"I thought you'd be reluctant."

"Who could be that reluctant?"

"Then sooner or later we'll have to divorce."

"I thought you meant right away."

"If we divorce, Dazhi comes with me," said Wang Changchi.

"Anyone is OK, except his mother," replied Xiaowen.

"So you never loved him?"

"You tell me."

"How would I know?"

"You have the advantage, so why bring it up and use it against me?"

"So I'm the one who's wrong again."

"Don't you just want to show off how clean you are? I admit I'm dirty and not fit to be Dazhi's mother. Does that make you happy?"

Wang Changchi was upset. Xiaowen was upset. Both of them had a bellyache and even walking they were always angry. He was the one to bring up the matter of divorce, but he thought it was too soon. As if he knew what was going on in his mind, Wang Huai sent him a package. He opened it and found it filled with Chinese herbal medicine and containing a letter:

Changchi,

These medicines were prescribed by Guang Sheng. I worry that herbal medicines might be harmful and ineffective, so give it a try for two months. I tried it for you and unexpectedly found that my body responded. It actually worked on the lower part of my body. Afraid that you won't believe me, I've had your mother sign this. She says it's good, it really is good. This is our family saviour. Take it with confidence, I guarantee you'll see results in two months.

Also, your grandfather sent me another dream. He told me to tell you to get Dazhi away from his mother as quickly as possible, otherwise, there'll be a disaster.

Take care!

Your dad, Wang Huai & your mum, Liu Shuangju

Beside his mum's name was a red fingerprint. Looking at the fingerprint, he couldn't help but think it was Wang Huai's, like some advert for snake oil. The medicine from the provincial hospital had no effect, how could something from Guang Sheng work? Guang Sheng was no stranger to him. Since he was a child, he had seen him fool ghosts, and now he trying to fool him. Wang Changchi dumped the box in a corner of the room.

From the television, he got the address of a psychiatrist.

"Your illness is not physical, but mental," said the psychiatrist. "The greatest obstruction is that you despise Xiaowen for being unclean, rejecting her psychologically."

"Can it be cured?" he asked.

"Yes."

"How?"

The psychiatrist made him lie down and close his eyes. Now, not only did he reject Xiaowen, but also the psychiatrist. The psychiatrist asked him to name as quickly as possible what he believed to be the ten dirtiest things.

"Shit, snot, dust, fleas, corruption, directors, Lin Jiabo, mud, hands, Rongrong, smelly feet, villages..."

He listed twelve things without pausing. The psychiatrist told him to stop and then asked him to list as fast as possible the ten people to whom he was the most grateful.

"Dad, Mum, Dazhi, Xiaowen, Second Uncle, the teacher in charge of classes, Liu Jianping, Zhang Hui, Liu Baitiao and Zhang Xianhua."

"Subconsciously," said the psychiatrist, "you don't find Xiaowen dirty, but consciously you reject her. Your conscious mind is not your true intent but rather imposed on you by your external environment or collective consciousness. Just think of Pan Jinlian in *The Water Margin*. On the surface, everyone shouts and beats her, but everyone wants to sleep with her. What about the 'Eight Beauties of Qinhuai'? If they were around today, they would all be goddesses. Do you know about Du Shiniang, the one who sinks the jewel box in anger? If you were to summarise, you would discover that all those in that profession are honourable women. All of them had integrity, except for Pan Jinlian, who was a seductress. It was a vocation for all of them rather than a profession. So, first of all, you must get rid of the idea that Xiaowen is impure. There is a way to do that, which is to think of your son breastfeeding. Don't you think such a scene is beautiful as well as holy and pure? When a baby nurses, he doesn't ask the reputation of the person feeding him. A baby's perspective is the most fundamental human perspective."

Although the psychiatrist couldn't convince Wang Changchi in one visit, he continued to come and listen to his irresponsible talk. Later, because of the cost, Wang Changchi stopped seeing him. One night, Xiaowen was teasing Wang Changchi, as was her habit. Of course this was just some habitual play and not warm and concerned behaviour. Perhaps because she was half awake, Xiaowen thought she was still at work. Unexpectedly, Wang Changchi responded. Not only was Xiaowen taken entirely by surprise, but Wang Changchi's head seemed to explode. After the explosion, colourful banners waved, drums sounded to Heaven and firecrackers popped.

"Now can you change jobs?" he asked.

Xiaowen bit her lip in silence. Wang Changchi grew rougher and rougher. He thought, If you don't answer, I won't soften. Xiaowen could take no more and parted her teeth and groaned. She groaned more loudly and resonantly.

"OK," she said, "I'll change, isn't that enough?"

After three nights at home, Xiaowen could stay put no longer. Counting on her fingers, she went through the accounts with Wang Changchi saying how much was being lost each night. Wang Changchi said that her word was worthless.

"The matter of greatest urgency right now is to make money and not talk about reputation," she said. "Human life has stages, each coming after the next. You can't just jump to the top. Reputation is important, but it should never come before money. This job depends on physical appearance and if you don't grab it when you're young, it'll be gone in a flash. After I make enough money, there's still plenty of time to change jobs."

"How much money would be enough?" asked Wang Changchi.

"Enough for Dazhi to go to college and for us to buy a place in the city."

Wang Changchi mentally calculated that to make that much money, Xiaowen would have to sell herself her whole life. Now he understood that given the difficulties facing them, it was not a matter of him being on top of her, but money. It was so simple, but he needed a semi-literate to open his eyes.

五十 · FIFTY

WANG CHANGCHI LEFT THE MASONRY JOB and paid a thousand yuan in tuition fees to study at the Painters Training Class. Every day after class, he would shoulder a bag full of stuff and return. After Xiaowen went off to work the night shift and Dazhi went to sleep, he'd take out bottles, cans and various-sized pieces of wood, which he'd set up in the room and paint. At first, all he could do was paint the pieces of wood in different colours, later he could paint various patterns on the wood. He repainted the trunk in the corner of the room. It was no longer the same trunk. It looked like an antique and at the same time bigger than before. He painted the door and the window frames and the room was filled with the smell of paint. The landlord smelled the paint and ran upstairs to the first floor to look. He sniffed and nodded his head, and then had Wang Changchi paint all the doors and window frames up to the fourth floor. In under ten days, Wang Changchi painted more than twenty doors, more than twenty window frames and more than twenty bathroom doors, and made what he used to make in a month as a bricklayer.

Handing the money to Xiaowen, he said, "We're going to get rich, how about changing jobs?"

Xiaowen took the money and counted it. "You call this getting rich?"

"Look at how quickly I made it, not just the amount."

"The speed? You earned it that quickly?"

"You can't just be concerned about the speed. You have to smell it too."

Xiaowen smelled the money.

"Doesn't it all smell like paint?" she asked.

"Smell it again."

"What are you trying to say?"

"Never smelled it? The money you make all smells like sperm."

Xiaowen forced Wang Changchi down on the bed and twisted one of his ears. Wang Changchi cried out in pain.

Grinding her teeth, Xiaowen said, "Shooting off your mouth, eh?"

"Not me, I wouldn't dare."

"Swear it."

"If ever I dare make fun of your profession again, may my head sprout pimples and my feet ooze pus."

"Try harder." Xiaowen gave his ear another vigorous twist.

Wang Changchi cried out in pain. "If I do, may I be shot dead..."

Only then did Xiaowen loosen her grip.

Rubbing his painful ear, Wang Changchi said, "Dazhi, your mum is very aggressive and strong-willed."

Dazhi raised both arms and let them drop, and broke into a smile as if he had understood. From time to time, Wang Changchi and Xiaowen would fight, always caused by Wang Changchi's freezing irony and burning satire. At first, Xiaowen was really angry and would come down on him with a heavy hand. Wang Changchi's ears, nose and backside were all bruised. But slowly, the fighting became a form of entertainment. Discussing Xiaowen's profession became a hot topic of conversation for them. At first, it wasn't quite appropriate, sort of like a husband and wife talking about farting, but as they talked more freely, it became natural. If Wang Changchi hadn't discussed it for a while, Xiaowen would initiate it herself. She discussed the status of her clients, their embarrassments and even what they liked. As she spoke, Wang Changchi would get sarcastic. It was like a pair of sparring boxers, with one willing to hit and one willing to be hit.

The more vicious the sarcasm, the more she enjoyed it, like drinking a bowl of hot and spicy ginger soup when suffering from a cold... And Wang Changchi's sarcasm was just sarcasm. He was actually no longer angry like in the past. When he was not angry, Xiaowen was not only unhappy, but she also felt lost.

Wang Changchi went to work as a painter at an antique reproduction furniture factory. He had to wear a mask because the paint fumes were so potent. Sometimes he'd go half the day without wanting to say a word. Silently he squatted among the furniture, painting with great care. Those morticed joints often made him think of the beams at home and of Carpenter Mao and Carpenter Fan. Seeing beautifully patterned wood, his mind would go back to the floorboards in his house, the woods in front of the village and behind his house, the big maple tree in the gap and the sound of wood burning in the pit. Sometimes he would imagine the furniture as fellow villagers, each piece having its own name. One was called Wang Huai, the others were called Liu Shuangju, Jianping, Xiaowen and Dazhi. It was great not to talk. He could project into the distance to where there were no boundaries, he could think about things he had never seriously considered before. Shutting his mouth, his mind developed. He discovered he had become intelligent.

The first intelligent thing: he left his job, set up a stall on the street and worked for himself. Although he didn't get work every day, when he was lucky, he could make around a thousand yuan a job. The second intelligent thing: he didn't dress too well, but was always clean, his hair neat, he wore a smile and never had a speck of paint on his fingers. He looked like a worker but was not dirty. The third intelligent thing: he made a copy of his ID and pasted it on a sample of his work, taking the initiative to be open about himself to dispel any customer reservations. As a result, whenever a customer showed up, nine times out of ten he'd be chosen. Many painters would sit for days and never be picked, while he would never go a day without being selected. He painted gateways, chairs, counters, beds, wardrobes, bookcases, sofas, desks, dinner tables, shoe racks and the like. He worked in meeting rooms, offices, cafeterias, shops, and for the Lis, Zhaos, Huangs, Zhangs, Weis, Zhus, Zhous and Hus... He made more and more money.

Late one night, apparently bothered by something, Wang Changchi sat on the edge of the bed blankly staring at Dazhi sleeping peacefully. Dazhi was already calling him "Dad". The first thing other children learned to say was "Mum", but the first word that came out of Dazhi's mouth was "Dad". Because of this, Xiaowen would often hold Dazhi and complain.

"I gave birth to you, fed you, loved you, but you appreciate nothing," she would say. "All you know how to do is suck up to your dad. For such a little fellow, you are more snobbish than an adult. One look and it's obvious you'll never show filial obedience to your mum."

"He said 'Dad' first," explained Wang Changchi, "because I sang him several dozen songs as part of his prenatal education."

Xiaowen would have none of it and said that despite being produced by her, Dazhi was the heir of the Wang family, and most members of the Wang family were biased against her. Wang Changchi said nothing. Xiaowen was disheartened until Dazhi learned to shout "Mum" and called for his mum more times in a day than for his dad. Only then did Xiaowen feel at ease. Not only was Dazhi shouting "Mum" and "Dad", but he could also say "Grandpa", "Grandma", hat and cup. Every time he made a new sound, Wang Changchi would feel inexplicably unsettled. Most parents want their children to grow up quickly, but Wang Changchi hoped that Dazhi would slow down.

The door opened with a click. Xiaowen was back.

"Why aren't you in bed?" she asked.

"I couldn't sleep," said Wang Changchi, "so I was watching Dazhi."

Dazhi was sound asleep, and his chubby face and white skin with its pink blush made him absolutely adorable. Xiaowen went to kiss him, but Wang Changchi pushed her away.

"Go and wash first," he said.

After Xiaowen had bathed, Wang Changchi asked to see the

account book to check the balance. Xiaowen added the total in her head and told him how much. Although she couldn't read, she was good at counting money.

"Is that enough to send Dazhi to school?" asked Wang Changchi.

"It's only enough for his high school tuition. He doesn't have a city residence permit, so each time he goes to a school, we have to pay a sponsorship fee," said Xiaowen.

"How much is the usual sponsorship fee?"

"With connections, ten or twenty thousand, without, eighty to a hundred thousand. I heard that when Xingze's kid went to kindergarten, they paid fifty thousand. If you don't pay enough, the child won't get in."

"That's so expensive. How can villagers like us afford to pay that?"

"That's why I'm making all the money I can."

"Even if you work like a dog and make a tremendous effort to send Dazhi to school, it still doesn't guarantee he'll amount to anything, does it?"

"Of course not, but if he doesn't get in, he won't have any chance."

"If he doesn't succeed, then he'll have to live like us."

"That depends on his fate."

"Actually, we can change from being passive to being active."

"How?"

"Give him to a rich person so that even if he doesn't succeed, he'll still be rich with a place in society."

"Absolute nonsense. Dazhi is my son. No one should even think about taking him away."

Xiaowen picked up Dazhi and hugged him tightly, afraid someone would take him from her.

"I've been thinking while I paint," said Wang Changchi, "and thought about this for six months before having the courage to say it."

"Anyone who can say something like that is not a man but a beast."

"But after doing so much painting, I've seen lots of rich people's houses and furniture. I'm envious and I'm angry. It's life all the same, but why so different? Don't I work hard enough? Or am I thicker than most people? No. There's only one reason. I was born in a rural village. From the moment I was conceived, I was finished. With great ambition, my father tried hard to change. I, too, gritted my teeth hoping to change, but you see the result. Can we change? Perhaps we can make a small measurable change, like making a little more money, but there's no way to make a change to the quality of our lives. An ox is an ox, a horse is a horse, but even taking it to Shanghai or Beijing won't make a phoenix of it."

Shaking her head, Xiaowen said, "You're mad. You must be mad. You wouldn't let me get an abortion but instead actually risked your life to jump off the scaffolding at the construction site. Now that we have put up with all these difficulties, you want to..."

"At the time I didn't know reality was so cruel," said Wang Changchi. "After fighting several rounds, I know that reality has killed me, just like the general Guan Yu when he slayed Hua Xiong. In those days I thought fate was tied up with working hard, now I think fate is tied up with using one's head, using one's brain, thinking, and shifting from physical strength to brain power. If you say you don't want to let him go, no one is more reluctant to part with Dazhi than I am. I want to keep him close to me, I want to help him pick the stars, but if you have an idea like this, you also need the actual strength to pull it off. You've already worked out that we are a long way from having that strength, and if we include birth, old age, sickness, death, finding him a wife and buying a house, then is our strength really strength?

"If Dazhi were sort of stupid and a little on the ugly side, then he'd spend his whole life painting with me, which I could accept, but he is so bright and good-looking, and to make him paint would be nothing less than a reckless waste. At this moment, perhaps you think I'm cruel, but if Dazhi could live a good life in the future, you'd admire me for wracking my brains. Being cruel now is only being cruel to ourselves, being cruel in the future means being cruel to Dazhi. Think about it, take advantage of the fact that Dazhi has no memories, and make a quick and firm decision."

Xiaowen started to cry, waking Dazhi and the two of them cried, the sound of one was deeply sad, while the other was clear and resonant. As he listened, Wang Changchi's nose began to tingle.

五十一 · FIFTY-ONE

Xiaowen didn't go back to work the night shift after that, and Dazhi was always at her side. Sometimes when Wang Changchi reached out to hold Dazhi, Xiaowen would unconsciously avoid him and watch him with alarm.

"I'm his dad," said Wang Changchi. "I'm not out to sell him. That was a bad idea, and I've been beating myself up over it for days."

Although she was sceptical, Xiaowen handed Dazhi to him. He pressed his nose against Dazhi's face and inhaled deeply, and his heart melted.

"Actually, rich people have their problems and poor people have their happiness," said Wang Changchi, "so we don't have to live the way they do."

"You nearly threw Dazhi away as if he were rubbish," said Xiaowen.

"That's not throwing away, it's throwing at a fixed point."

"What fixed point were you planning to throw him at?"

In silence, Wang Changchi stared blankly as if trying to remember.

"When I married you," said Xiaowen, "I thought you were a nice person. Now I see that you're rotten."

Wang Changchi stared straight ahead.

"If you want Dazhi to have a good life," continued Xiaowen, "as his father shouldn't you work harder? What rich person wasn't poor once? You're too much of a gambler."

Wang Changchi didn't dispute what she said and just put up

with Xiaowen's sarcasm. After all, he had been pretty sarcastic towards her, so now he let her dig away. It was payback time.

"The way I see it," said Xiaowen, "you're no better than my clients."

Her words were like a bludgeon, finally prising open Wang Changchi's mouth.

"First of all," he said, "I admit I'm no better than one of your clients. Who are they? Rich people. Penniless people like me want to save every penny, so how can we go out and fool around with prostitutes? But I must also make it clear that I am not rotten. As for the family I've found for Dazhi, the grandfather is an official, the grandmother a senior police officer, the mother an assistant professor and the father the owner of a business. They have power and money, and if Dazhi were to end up in their family it would be a blessing."

"Such a nice family, can't they have kids of their own?"

"The assistant professor can't have kids."

"How do you know?"

Wang Changchi did not answer. Xiaowen didn't ask again. She started working the night shift. Every evening when she arrived downstairs, she would slacken her pace, imagining that she would open the door and not see Dazhi, that he was already with the rich family. But each time she pushed open the door, Dazhi was still there, lying next to Wang Changchi, breathing regularly. Even though he was sleeping, he still had his little finger in his mouth. In the past, the first thing Xiaowen did after returning home was to bathe. Now the first thing she did was to look at Dazhi. Sometimes she would stare at him without moving for half an hour. She bought lots of new clothes for Dazhi, a new outfit each day. She threw away all the toys Wang Changchi had picked up in the past and bought new ones. She even bought the best powdered milk for him and the best buggy, so that he could live like the well-to-do second generation. Every day when she bathed Dazhi, she examined him very closely, the mole on the back of his neck, the shape of his navel, the hair on his head and how it grew, his little fingers and toes. She had silently committed it all to memory as if by doing so, no one would steal him away.

"Is their family really as good as you say?" Xiaowen couldn't help asking.

"Whose family?" replied Wang Changchi after hesitating.

"Take me some time so I can see."

"You're joking. D'you think it's like visiting relatives?" Wang Changchi finally replied.

"Since you think they're so good, why don't you take Dazhi to them in secret while I'm working at night?"

"Does that mean you agree?"

"Why must I agree?" Xiaowen roared.

"Then... I'll take him right now." Wang Changchi picked up Dazhi.

Xiaowen snatched him away.

"You can't make me watch him leave with my own eyes," she said.

Wang Changchi slapped his head, unsure whether to stand or sit.

"It's not that I've never thought about secretly taking him," he said, "but each time I got close to the door, my legs froze, and I couldn't move. I got a little farther each time. The farthest I got was West River Bridge, but he started crying, my heart softened, and I brought him back."

"Do you still want him to live a good life?"

"I do, but I can't bring myself to do it."

"Then let him spend his life painting with you, and just let him hate me my whole life."

"Perhaps he'll pass the exams and get into college."

"That's what your dad thought, but you didn't pass the exams."

Wang Changchi heaved a long sigh.

A week later, after Xiaowen finished work, she saw from a distance a figure standing downstairs. Her legs froze, and a sharp pain went through her chest, so painfully that she had to squat where she stood. The figure approached. It was Wang Changchi. He pulled her to his chest.

"I was planning to meet you at the Phoenix Foot Spa," he said, "but suddenly I felt the energy sucked out of me and I couldn't take another step."

Xiaowen lashed out and roundly slapped him, saying, "Wang Changchi, I will hate you for as long as I live."

6

DESPERATE DAD

五十二 · FIFTY-TWO

THREE MONTHS EARLIER, WANG CHANGCHI had got a job repainting old beds at an orphanage. The orphanage said the funding came from a donor who not only wanted to oversee the use of the funds but also wanted to choose the colour of the paint. As he stepped through the orphanage gate at the agreed time, Wang Changchi saw two women sitting beneath a vine arbour. One was Zhao Dingfang, the director of the orphanage and the other was Fang Zhizhi, the donor. They appeared to be on very close terms as they laughed and talked. In the oppressively hot weather, the vine leaves shone brightly above like shards of broken glass suspended in the air but appeared dark below. The grapes hanging under the arbour were still unripe. The heat bounced off the concrete and their foreheads were covered with small beads of sweat. A contract was lying on the concrete table. Wang Changchi wondered if all the formality was worthwhile for a mere thirty beds. It was rather like accepting Japan's surrender. But Fang Zhizhi looked serious and wanted Wang Changchi to read it over carefully, word by word. Twice while Wang Changchi was reading, she asked, "Do you understand it?" Having taken the university entrance exam twice, naturally he understood it. The contract was quite detailed, even specifying the brand of paint to be used, that the beds had to be painted outside in the courtyard, and that they had to be painted blue, no, sky blue. Zhao Dingfang said that the contract had been written by Teacher Fang and that the beds had to be taken outside to avoid harming the children with chemicals such as formaldehyde, heavy metals and toluene. Sky blue was chosen because she wanted the children to think of the sky, ocean, fish and even happiness. Wang Changchi suddenly felt ashamed because when he painted the trunk and window frames in their rented place, it had never occurred to him that the paint might harm Dazhi, and he actually liked its smell. Feeling so ashamed, he was also very touched.

"I'll offer a discount," he said.

"No," said Fang Zhizhi, "the cost is not an issue."

Wang Changchi and Liu Jianping moved the beds outside and lined them up. Wang Changchi made sure they were perfectly straight as if hoping to demonstrate how diligent he was to that diligent person. Liu Jianping was in charge of sanding while Wang Changchi did the painting. The two of them wore grass hats and masks. Dust flew under the scorching sun, and the smell of paint drifted in the air. Liu Jianping was the first to take off his mask because he was in the habit of talking while he worked. When he sought compensation for others and went to court, he relied on his mouth, so his mouth would never consent to be sealed by a painter's mask for long. It wanted to sigh over current circumstances, express anger, as well as complain about social inequality, frustrated talent, and finally pose the question, "Is this what we're going to do for the rest of our lives?"

"If not this, then what?" asked Wang Changchi as he too removed his mask.

Liu Jianping refused to back down, believing that he should at least be a lawyer, and even if he were completely down and out, he wouldn't want to be reduced to being a painter. Strictly speaking, he was not a painter, but at best a painter's assistant. So he fantasised about having a gun and leading a troop into the mountains. As that option was not available, he imagined he was Zorro driving out mischief-makers, protecting the people, killing villains and leaving a big "Z" on their bodies. The role he played changed constantly, if not a hero, then a leader, and when he got to the exciting part, he'd toss away the sandpaper and walk off while throwing out the line, "I'm bloody well not going to do this." Sometimes he took a few steps and came back, sometimes he'd walk away and not return for half a day. Wang Changchi slowly digested all his speech, believing that the roles Liu Jianping wanted to play were the same as those he wished to play, the only difference was he didn't have the nerve to say so himself. But there was a difference. Liu Jianping could wash his hands of it, but Wang Changchi had to stay and finish the work on his own.

When Zhao Dingfang had a free moment, she'd bring Wang Changchi a bottle of water, adding, "Master, you are working so hard."

When he took a break, Wang Changchi saw Zhao Dingfang working alone beneath the arbour.

"The donor who is paying for the painting is very pretty," he commented, by way of conversation.

Unexpectedly, Zhao Dingfang screwed up her mouth.

"Looks alone are not enough," she said. "One must also be able to conceive a child."

Feeling that he had spoken out of turn, Wang Changchi bit his tongue and thought, She's so pretty and with such a nice disposition. I bet she has a lot of money, but the Old Man in Heaven is such a prankster for not allowing her to have a child.

In his intermittent conversations with Zhao Dingfang, he learned that the donor taught English in college and that due to two abortions before getting married, her fallopian tubes were blocked. She had taken all sorts of medicines from East and West and seen all manner of fertility doctors, but her fallopian tubes remained blocked, and so she had come to the orphanage with the thought of adopting a child.

From time to time, people would come to the orphanage and adopt a child, even foreigners. As if purchasing merchandise, they would look them over carefully until they found the one they wanted, then do the paperwork and take the child away. While Wang Changchi was painting the wooden beds, five foreign couples came and adopted five children. While they were occupied with the paperwork, Wang Changchi stood by the door to watch and occasionally understood a few English words. He discovered that Zhao Dingfang had three important notebooks: in one she noted the particulars of the child; in another she recorded the contact information of the adoptive parents; in a thinner one, she wrote down what the adoptive parents were looking for. While Zhao Dingfang was busy, Wang Changchi took the opportunity of flipping through the thin notebook and saw written under Fang Zhizhi's name, "Male baby, healthy, blood type B", along with a phone number. The moment he saw "blood type B", his strength left him, and everything went black. He almost fainted and broke out in a sweat. To make absolutely sure, when he got back he took Dazhi's birth information out of the trunk. Fixing his eyes on the place listing the blood type, his hands began to shake, trembling as if he had Parkinson's.

What he had to do was get the details about Fang Zhizhi's family. That was going to be difficult because if he was too obvious about it, she would notice, but if he was too discreet, he might not get any details. He walked around the College of Foreign Languages at West River University where Fang Zhizhi worked. No one knew him and he knew no one there. If someone saw him from a distance they would probably avoid him as if he was a salesman or a thief. Once he secretly tailed Fang Zhizhi but lost her. At one point, he wanted to go for broke and directly place Dazhi in the orphanage but was afraid that by ill luck, Dazhi might not be delivered into Fang Zhizhi's hands. Although he didn't have all the details about Fang Zhizhi's family, based on her status and the way she dressed and talked he determined that her family was not bad, and besides she did have the money to do good works. The problem now was how to find Fang Zhizhi's address. He could make use of her phone number but would only use it as a last resort. For this reason, he had bet with himself and if he won, it was the will of Heaven.

Finally, he finished painting the beds. Neatly lined up in the courtyard, the beds were drying in the breezy sunlight. Some paint was left over and under normal circumstances Wang Changchi would have put it aside to use on another job. However, this time he didn't, but instead painted the ceiling of the orphanage bedroom sky blue. Afraid that the paint would dry too slowly, he brushed on a very thin coat and asked Zhao Dingfang to point several electric fans at the ceiling to blow it dry. As a result, by the time the beds had dried, so had the ceiling. Fang Zhizhi went to the orphanage to check on the work and when she learned that Wang Changchi had painted the ceiling at no charge, she realised how kind and honest he was and asked him to come to her house to paint the frame of a sofa. Startled, he shouted to himself, "Goodness, I really won?" The bet he had secretly made with himself had been whether or not Fang Zhizhi would ask him to her house to paint something.

Wang Changchi didn't go to her house, but rather to her parents' house. Her father was an official in charge of construction by the name of Fang Nanfang, and he had a passion for mahogany furniture. He loved the colour of mahogany and would never allow it to be painted, but with time cracks had appeared as well as some discolouration due to heat damage. Someone had suggested to him that applying only a thin coat of clear lacquer would renew the colour of his beloved mahogany and prevent it from cracking and discolouring. Fang Nanfang had long since latched on to this idea but had never had any time to act upon it, and now Fang Zhizhi recommended Wang Changchi to him. He nodded by way of consent.

Wang Changchi arrived at the Fangs' house. Lu Shanshan had taken time off from work and was there to oversee the entire job. Lu Shanshan was Fang Zhizhi's mother, held a civilian post in the police department and would retire in a couple of years. She followed Wang Changchi wherever he painted, superficially to put things away, but secretly to make sure that Wang Changchi didn't damage the furniture or steal anything. Wang Changchi checked things out as he painted. The place consisted of four rooms and two large central rooms. The large pieces of furniture were all mahogany, paintings and calligraphy were hung on the walls, and antiques stood on the shelves. The storeroom was filled with wine.

When he looked at the walls, Lu Shanshan said, "The paintings and calligraphy are fake."

When he looked at the antiques, she said, "They are fake, too."

When he turned and glanced at the storeroom, she said, "The wine is faker yet."

As Wang Changchi painted in silence, Lu Shanshan talked on and on about the difficulties they were having, about how Old Fang spent all his salary on mahogany furniture, and how they now had no cash. Although she told a sob story, Wang Changchi knew they were well off and that if Dazhi were able to join them, his happiness must be due to merit earned in a previous life.

After Wang Changchi finished painting the wardrobe, he turned to the dressing table, after the dressing table, he painted the desk, and after that he painted the bookcase. Inside the bookcase were several photographs, some of which featured Lin Jiabo. He was embracing Fang Zhizhi on the Eiffel Tower, in Venice, on Mount Fuji, in front of the Statue of Liberty... There was also a family photo of the four of them. He stood at the back, with a beaming smile. Never had he expected him to be Fang Zhizhi's husband. He suddenly felt muddle-headed. He thought, I can't very well give Dazhi to my enemy, can I?

五十三 · FIFTY-THREE

HE SPENT MORE TIME THINKING THAT DAY THAN ANY OTHER, but because he never stopped thinking, his brain seemed to solidify. The clock hands moved so slowly, they seemed to be painted on. That night at his place, he drank a half bottle of spirits on his own, going over his mixed feelings for Lin Jiabo countless times. The first time he thought, I did jail time for him. He cheated me of my wages. He had someone stab me, and I almost died from loss of blood. He did away with Huang Kui and shifted the blame onto me so that the police came to the village to arrest me, threatening everyone in the village until they lost sleep over it. I had a fall at his construction site and became impotent and he didn't compensate me for the mental anguish. Even when I stopped his car he didn't compensate me, and when I took him to court he didn't compensate me, and when I climbed the scaffolding he didn't compensate me. And he even disappeared on me. What is he? What kind of filth is he? It's no exaggeration to say that he destroyed my state of mind and ruined my life.

The second time he thought, I did jail time for him, but he paid me. He Gui, the foreman at the time evaporated into thin air while owing me three months' wages. Living in the workers' shed in the county town, I was so hungry that I was just skin and bone and dizzy. Being that hungry was like being without oxygen and I nearly started going through the rubbish. If I hadn't done his jail time, I wouldn't have made that thousand yuan, nor could I have sent money to my dad to pay off his debts. Because we owed money, people took away the lard, the hens, the chest and even Dad's coffin. From another point of view, could it be that he rescued our family? Right, the construction site in the county town was run by his company, so when He Gui owed me money it was actually him who owed me money. But I wasn't the only one owed money; lots of others including Liu Jianping didn't receive their wages. So I, Wang Changchi, wasn't the sole person being targeted. That was a county-government project, and the rumour was he owed us money only because the county government owed him, and to this day the building remains unfinished. At the time, he got Huang Kui to give me an additional nine large notes but on the condition that I disappeared from his sight. Several hundred workers never had that opportunity. I was the only one, so was his action entirely malicious? Whose world is this? Whose territory is this? How could he just tell me to disappear and then expect me to disappear? Perhaps it was a way out for him, or something said in anger after paying me. But I was young and hot-headed and had to insist on dignity first and didn't give him a chance. I wonder what made me do it? I even served jail time for him. I took off my trousers in front of Huang Kui, so there was no point in talking about dignity.

Today I wouldn't throw away my wages to have the last word or for what little dignity I have left. Only when you're poor do you understand the value of money, only when you experience loss do you understand how stupid you are. Only now do I understand how high the cost of maturity is. As for me being stabbed, there's no sense arguing about that. It was perpetrated by the men under Huang Kui. Huang Kui was behind it, so how can Lin Jiabo be blamed? That is the question, just like Hamlet's "To be or not to be". Perhaps Huang Kui acted on impulse, perhaps Huang Kui had been deceived and his followers had acted on their own. Lin Jiabo can be blamed for this, but he can also be blameless, depending on how you look at it. Didn't Huang Kui later break off with him? It's clear they were not indivisible or in league to the death, but each taking what he needed. All crows are black, but there are different shades of black, dark black, jet black, light black, and not every one of them can be considered an enemy. Some can be used, and some joined with. Besides, Huang Kui wasn't a good bird. He'd pull out a cleaver for anything and cut off a finger for something said that he didn't like. If he didn't die by his own hand, he'd have died by someone else's, just in a different fashion or in a car accident, or shot in the head, or by jumping off a building.

What's more, did Lin Jiabo do away with Huang Kui? That hasn't been confirmed and according to Liu Jianping, the police have no solid evidence. Why should I hate Lin Jiabo based on a rumour? I shouldn't be angry with Lin Jiabo on account of Huang Kui. In truth, they were all the same kind of filth, always supporting criminals. Also, the police had good reason to come to the village to arrest me. After all, Huang Kui and I were enemies, and I did have a motive. Who could guarantee that a low-level cop from the county town would be a match for Sherlock Holmes or the Black Cat Detective? They were under pressure and wanted to do a praiseworthy job, so it was natural to think of me. Only a fool wouldn't consider me the proper choice for a scapegoat. To tell the truth, if I were a cop, I'd think and do the same.

As for the matter of my impotence, when you think about it, he also had a point. The moment I went to the hospital, he paid for my treatment and hospital stay. Even before we had arrived at a compensation agreement, he got Old Andu to deliver twenty thousand yuan. Only because I had this large chunk of cash was I able to convince Xiaowen not to have an abortion, thus saving Dazhi. Goodness, he actually saved Dazhi, no wonder I keep thinking about giving Dazhi to them. It was the will of Heaven all along. Wang Changchi, just go along with it. Some who are injured at construction sites never receive any compensation. What is compensation for mental anguish? Moreover, your impotence is fake. Doesn't it get hard now? If he knew, he could countersue me for extortion. Even Xiaowen suspected that your fall was staged, why can't you? Of course, you could never admit to that, but the psychiatrist said all people have a subconscious. Can you swear that your fall wasn't subconscious? Perhaps he's not as bad as I made him out to be.

The third time he thought, Wang Changchi you are like day-old rice: sour. Thinking twice, you can turn a bad person good. What kind of timing is that? Maybe I'd feel better if it took me three tries to change my mind. I didn't expect you to give in after just thinking twice, that's faster than diarrhoea. Are you the same person? Why do I want to be the same? Didn't you learn your lesson deeply enough? Can you go any lower? And your face? Your backbone? You don't even want your own child. What prospects do you have left? I only want to give him away so that I can have some meagre prospects. If I keep him, that will be the start of despair. Even so, I cannot give him to an enemy. Is he my enemy? Of course! At least there is no one else I detest so much...

One afternoon as Wang Changchi was painting with his head down, Lin Jiabo suddenly opened the door and came in. They glanced at each other, but Lin Jiabo didn't recognise him. Wang Changchi thought, Perhaps it's because I'm wearing a mask, perhaps he just doesn't remember me. I got up close to his car, tried to jump off the scaffolding at his construction site for compensation, and raised such a ruckus and yet he still doesn't remember me? It was all useless and, now I think about it, so pointless.

Lin Jiabo turned towards the bedroom and shouted, "Ma, I brought two free-range chickens."

"Put them in the kitchen," said Lu Shanshan.

Only then did Wang Changchi notice that Lin Jiabo was carrying two plucked chickens. Being on edge, he hadn't taken everything in a moment ago.

"Are they for soup or for frying?" asked Lin Jiabo.

"Frying," replied Lu Shanshan.

Lin Jiabo walked into the kitchen, cut up one chicken and marinated it in wine and salt and placed the other in the freezer. Wang Changchi thought, What a good son-in-law. Would he make a good father? He continued mulling this over until Lin Jiabo closed the door and left. He thought, *Amituofo*, if I can get his address without much trouble, I'll give Dazhi to them. If I can't get it, or it's too much trouble, that means the Old Man in Heaven wants Dazhi to stay with me.

This time he lost. After painting the furniture and being paid, he had no reason to hang around. As he left, his whole body seemed to float, and he felt defeated and even rebuked Heaven for only going halfway and not helping through to the end, like killing a chicken but not cleanly with a single stroke of the knife. But he hadn't given up entirely. His pocket contained a slim hope. It was a photograph of Lin Jiabo and Fang Zhizhi sitting on a balcony. It was a spacious balcony with a round table and two cups of tea or coffee on it. Lin Jiabo was sitting in a chair and Fang Zhizhi was on his lap. He held her tightly with both hands, so tightly that her breasts were pushed out of place. One was wearing shorts and the other pyjamas, and both were smiling at the camera. Since the camera was positioned slightly above them, the trees and the artificial sports ground in the distance below were squeezed into the picture. Judging from the size of the tree trunks and the distance between the branches and the balcony, the balcony had to be five or six storeys above ground level.

The following day, Wang Changchi found the sports ground

on the West River University campus. Looking up, he noticed several low-rise buildings nearby. Based on the angle of the photo, he could work out where Lin Jiabo and Fang Zhizhi lived. The buildings were not on the campus, but the balconies on one side faced the campus, while the others faced the West River. That evening, Wang Changchi squatted and kept watch. Sure enough, he saw Fang Zhizhi return from work and go up the stairwell to the fourth floor before stopping. When he heard her take out her keys and open and close the door, Wang Changchi was elated. Watching the fourth-floor balcony from a distance, he was in suspense. The bet with himself had been to obtain the address easily, and now he had found it through skill. Was that going against the will of Heaven? No, he thought, if using a photo to obtain an address couldn't be called easy, then what could? So-called not easy should apply to his previous experience of trailing Fang Zhizhi, when he had followed her and lost her and followed and lost her again, experiencing many difficulties. He might have been discovered and the police called, or while following her he might have been hit by a car, or he could have followed her for two weeks and found nothing. The more Wang Changchi thought it over, the more he felt it was the will of Heaven. Once again, he had a bet with himself and said "*Amituofo*, only if Dazhi doesn't cry when I take him away."

五十四 · FIFTY-FOUR

"I swear by Heaven that Dazhi really didn't cry," said Wang Changchi.

But Xiaowen didn't believe him. Picking up a cleaver, she forced him to go ahead of her.

"Dazhi was sleeping at the time, and I picked him up off the bed," said Wang Changchi, repeating his actions as he spoke. "I picked him up like this and went to the door. I thought if Dazhi cried, I'd come back, but if he didn't, I'd just keep going. I stopped at the door for five whole minutes, but Dazhi didn't make a peep, as if he approved. So I walked through the door, holding him like this, and went downstairs and walked to the corner. It's darker here because some lout broke the street light, watch out, there's a step here, careful, don't trip and don't cut yourself with the cleaver. Sorry, but please put that cleaver away, otherwise you'll make people nervous. I'll take you to Dazhi because I miss him too and not because you have a cleaver. The most you can do with it is cut me or kill me. I don't even want to keep Dazhi, so why should I care about my life? OK, OK, OK, I'll stop talking so much and get on with it. Hang on, let me think. I stood here for five minutes, yes, it was right here, because I was afraid Old Xu in the general goods store might see me, so I stood here out of the light. The wind blew, and the cars roared by on the street, but Dazhi didn't cry. Before, all I had to do was get to the street and even if he was sound asleep Dazhi would always wake up and sometimes even cry. But that night he was totally quiet and his breathing regular, and he seemed to understand what was going through my mind. Since he didn't cry, I kept going until I reached the bus stop. You see, this is the stop for buses twenty-two, thirty-two, nineteen and seven. At the time, I didn't care which one came first and was just going to get on it. As I was thinking, a bus came, so without looking at the number I got on with Dazhi."

"Which bus was it?" asked Xiaowen.

Wang Changchi noticed that the cleaver was no longer in her hand.

He tapped his head and said, "I don't remember."

Xiaowen thrust her hand into her shoulder bag as if to pull out the cleaver again.

Wang Changchi cleared his throat and said, "Number seven, I remember, it was number seven."

They turned their heads to look, and a number 32 went past followed by a number 19. Finally, a number 7 arrived. They got on the bus and like that night, because it was late, there were empty seats.

"I sat in the fifth row, right, in this seat," said Wang Changchi. "As I sat down, the number five entered my head. I thought, This is the will of Heaven. The Old Man in Heaven was telling me I should get off at the fifth stop."

Xiaowen looked out of the window, and Wang Changchi looked out of the window, one looking left and one looking right. The street lights flashed by one after another, and the shops along the street were all brightly lit. Suddenly, outside the window on the left, the image of Dazhi's head seemed to appear faintly. He moved when the bus moved and stopped when it stopped. Wang Changchi looked away, but wherever he turned his eyes, Dazhi reappeared. He couldn't bear to look, so he closed his eyes. He sat thinking with his eyes closed...

Xiaowen stepped on his foot and said, "We're at the fifth stop."

They got off the bus beside the main gate of West River Park.

"At that time of night," said Wang Changchi, "lovers and people exercising occasionally came out of the park and others often passed the gate, so I put Dazhi down by the gate, right here. Then I sat with him for a long while. I said, 'Dazhi, don't blame your dad for being so heartless. I'm doing it as a last resort. If you stay with me, not only will you be poor all your life, you'll end up with "bent-neck disease". In other words, you won't be able to lift your head and look people in the eye. After a while, your neck will stay bent down. You'll live without dignity, be unable to get a city residence permit, or get into a good school, unable to afford to get ill and stay in hospital, or find satisfying work. Unable to cope, you'll become "returned goods", moving back to the village, and even becoming lame, impotent, committing crimes, and will be facing an early death. If you go off with someone else, it'll be like the television advert says: everything is possible. You might enjoy unlimited wealth and high rank, have lots of children and grand-children, and live to be a hundred years old. You might also serve as a high official or inherit property, live in a villa, drive a luxury car and marry a beautiful wife. Most important of all, though, you'll have honourable parents, and no one will dare pick on you, nor will you have to grovel to others. You'll be able to hold your head up. Although this is only a possibility, a possibility is better than nothing. The person who dares to take you from here will be capable and at least guarantee that you don't want for food and clothing. If you want to live a good life, don't make a peep. If you want to stay with your mum and dad, then cry. All you have to do is cry, even whimper a little, and I'll take you back at once.' But I waited one minute, two minutes, ten minutes, and Dazhi didn't declare himself. He seemed to understand what I said but pretended to be sound asleep, with a smile on his face. The little wretch didn't make a sound and gave nothing away. Why didn't you cry? Dazhi—"

"You're not so awful that you'd leave Dazhi here," said Xiaowen.

"Then where did I leave him?"

"All I want is Dazhi. I don't care where you left him."

"You can't have him back. He's happy now."

"Happy where?"

"In someone else's house."

"Where is it?"

"In a penthouse with floor-to-ceiling glass, a real leather sofa, mahogany furniture, a Simmons sprung mattress, a huge colour TV and even three bathrooms. Since Dazhi was adopted, two people look after him every day. They have a luxury car and a high-rise suite, but no children, so all their wealth will be Dazhi's in the future. Dazhi was born in the wrong place once, but now he has ended up in the right place."

"Take me there."

"Then all my previous work will be wasted. If I were Dazhi, I wouldn't want to come back."

"Are you going to take me or not?"

Wang Changchi shook his head. Xiaowen raised the cleaver. Wang Changchi placed his hand on the railing.

"Cut," he said. "Even if you cut off my hand, I won't destroy Dazhi's happiness."

Xiaowen's hand trembled slightly.

"If you're scared," said Wang Changchi, "then close your eyes and cut."

Xiaowen closed her eyes. The scene suddenly felt strangely familiar to Wang Changchi, rather like the time Huang Kui tried to bolster his courage as he placed his hand on the table for Wang Changchi to cut off a finger.

"Cut, cut and you'll feel better," he said.

Xiaowen closed her eyes and hacked, but she missed and struck the railing with the cleaver, which fell to the ground with a clang. The whole time, Wang Changchi didn't once move his hand from the railing. This made him different from Huang Kui. One hand flashed away when the cleaver fell, the other stayed as if intentionally awaiting the pain. Xiaowen shook all over with fright. Wang Changchi pulled her to his chest and hugged her tightly. Xiaowen cried.

"Just bring Dazhi back and I'll stop working nights," she said. "I'll make him happy."

"Impossible. Even if we worked twenty-four hours a day and retired at eighty, we couldn't give him what he has now."

As he spoke, Wang Changchi gently stroked Xiaowen's back.

"Dazhi, where are you?" sobbed Xiaowen, trembling. "Come back if you can hear me shout. Come back even if you can't hear me. Dazhi, Mum misses you and she's heartbroken."

Sometimes Xiaowen was in a good mood, sometimes in a bad mood. When she was in a good mood, she'd go shopping, cook and go to work at night. When she was in a bad mood, she would try to force Wang Changchi to take her to get Dazhi. Each time they set off, Wang Changchi would start from the moment he picked Dazhi up off the bed and, as he walked downstairs, he would tell Xiaowen what had happened. At the bus stop, Wang Changchi would be at a loss, unsure which bus to take. Xiaowen kept pushing, so they took the number 19 once and the number 22 another time, and on both occasions, they got off at the fifth stop. The number 19 stopped at a large shopping centre, while the number 22 stopped at a scientific research institute. At both places, Xiaowen burst into tears and sang Dazhi's praises.

"He's so young but he can keep time to music," she said, "and when he hears his dad's footsteps on the stairs he looks towards the door, and is all smiles when he sees his dad push open the door and come in..."

As he listened, Wang Changchi felt his throat tightening and his eyes grow tearful.

When he couldn't listen any longer, he said, "Let's go. Let's go and get Dazhi."

Wiping away her tears, Xiaowen followed Wang Changchi. As he walked, he thought, This will ruin Dazhi, this will harm Dazhi. So he randomly got on a bus with Xiaowen and didn't get off until the last stop.

"Where is Dazhi?" asked Xiaowen.

"I really can't remember."

One evening, Wang Changchi came in and found Xiaowen folding clothes on the bed, with a new suitcase standing next to it. The rice had not been cooked, nor had the food, and the room felt dreary.

"Where are you going?" asked Wang Changchi.

"Leaving." Xiaowen put the clothes in the suitcase.

"You've got to be going somewhere, right?" Wang Changchi closed the suitcase and sat down on top of it.

"I told you if you didn't bring Dazhi back, we're divorcing."

"I'm still strong enough to make money after getting divorced, but who are you going to rely on?"

"Of all the men in the world, you're the only one with strength?"

"Of course there are lots of men, but they won't necessarily treat you as well as I do,"

"You gave my precious darling away. Is that what you call good?"

"If you really want a child, then we'll have another one and call him Dazhi, too."

"I only want the original one."

However much Wang Changchi coaxed her, Xiaowen would not give in. Wang Changchi thought about the worst scenario but couldn't bear it. He thought, Xiaowen is uneducated and even if some bloke does marry her, there's no guaranteeing he won't browbeat her. Although she can make money washing feet now, she can't do that her whole life. The moment she gets old and her looks go or she gets some disease, who'll take care of her? This gave Wang Changchi such heartache. He thought of how she had looked after him at the hospital in the county town. He remembered how she married into his family without requiring any betrothal gifts, and what they had suffered together after arriving in the city. He thought, She married me hoping I would teach her to read and bring her to the city. If we separate, who'll teach her to read? She doesn't know the difference between 園 (garden) and 圓 (round) or between 坐 (sit) and 座 (seat). How will she ever get by in the city in the future? Wang Changchi had tried to harden his heart, but now it had softened, like an ice cube under the sun.

"Let's go and get Dazhi," he said, unable to bear it.

This time, Xiaowen carried her suitcase.

"If I don't get Dazhi back," she said, "I'm leaving."

Wang Changchi thought, She's burning her bridges. At the bus stop downstairs, she got on the number 32 without waiting for him to decide.

"Why the number thirty-two?" asked Wang Changchi.

"You took me on numbers seven, nineteen and twenty-two, but not number thirty-two, so you must have taken this one when you gave Dazhi away."

Wang Changchi thought, If she were educated, she'd be something, a master of inference. The bus proceeded west. One of them looked to the left, the other to the right. The buildings vanished from both sides leaving only the vast night sky. Only after crossing West River Bridge did the buildings reappear beyond the windows. Suddenly, Xiaowen stepped on Wang Changchi's foot.

"Let's get off," she said.

"This is only the fourth stop," said Wang Changchi.

"It's the fifth stop."

"The fourth."

"The fifth."

There was no arguing with her, so Wang Changchi followed her off the bus.

"Where is Dazhi?" she asked.

"Near the next stop," said Wang Changchi.

"Why are you telling me?"

"I'm afraid you'll leave."

Bursting into tears, she said, "I'm so upset. On the one hand, I miss him, on the other, I'm trying to convince myself to forget him. It's like writing characters and then rubbing them out. I want him back, but I also want him to live a better life. My heart has been torn in two. Tell me, which side should I listen to?"

"Let's listen to the Old Man in Heaven," suggested Wang Changchi.

"How do we do that?"

Wang Changchi took out a five-fen coin.

"When the coin hits the ground, if the national seal is showing, we'll go back," he said. "If the five is showing, we'll go and get him."

Xiaowen stared blankly at the coin, then gave a slight nod. Wang Changchi tossed the coin up high. Hitting the ground, it spun for a while before coming to a halt. Silence fell over the world, so quiet that even the sounds of the cars vanished.

"You can open your eyes," said Wang Changchi.

Not daring to, she said, "Tell me what it says."

"The national seal."

"Does it really?" asked Xiaowen, incredulous.

"It's the will of Heaven. You have to look. Otherwise, you'll cry and try to look for him."

Xiaowen opened her eyes and looked at the coin, then heaved a long sigh. "Oh, Heavens!"

五十五 · FIFTY-FIVE

But Xiaowen still left him. That was a week later. Wang Changchi came back to find the place empty, the suitcase was gone, and there was a note on the table. "Wang, every time you do it with me you wear a condom, you don't love me, you think I'm dirty, so I'm leaving. He." The words were scrawled quite large, uneven and crooked, like a facelift that transforms an oval face into a rhomboid. It was the first time Xiaowen had written such a long sentence. Wang Changchi looked at the note for a long time.

"I wear a condom because I don't want another child," he said. "We can't afford it, you fool."

He went to the Phoenix Foot Spa to find out where she was.

"She must have run off with a rich bloke," said Zhang Hui.

"She's made a mistake," Wang Changchi said, shaking his head.

Wang Changchi went to the police station to report He Xiaowen missing.

"We'll be in touch the moment we know anything," said the policeman.

With two people missing, the place seemed huge. The dining table was wide, the bed was wide, and the room seemed wider by two-thirds. Every night, Wang Changchi turned out the light and listened to the footsteps in the stairwell, hoping that Xiaowen would suddenly return. His sense of hearing grew more acute, and he could hear all the way down the stairwell to the street and catch the pedestrians whispering and forward all the way to the other side of the West River and catch Dazhi's babbling. His hearing reached to the streets, the square, the bus station, the train station, the hospitals, the schools... but after three months of listening, he still failed to hear the sound of Xiaowen. She was like a small pebble thrown into the sea, without even a splash. Previously, he'd had someone with him in the city to share their innermost thoughts and feelings, now there was no one. His only comfort was to go and see Dazhi. He often sat in the pavilion on the river, staring dumbly at the Lin family's fourth-floor balcony. Sometimes he would sit and talk to himself as if he were at home chatting with Dazhi, Xiaowen, Wang Huai and Liu Shuangju. Sometimes, he would gaze in silence until the lights went off in the Lin family home before getting up and leaving. Wherever he was painting and no matter how far from the Lins', the moment he got off work in the evening, he'd buy a boxed meal, impatiently take the bus and sit in the pavilion and eat and watch, unwilling to waste even a second. All he had to do was set eyes on the floor where Dazhi lived and, as if receiving a signal, he would feel reinvigorated however tired he was and would grow calm if he was agitated. Slowly the balcony became Dazhi for him, the building became Dazhi for him, the trees in front of him also became Dazhi for him.

Meanwhile, he received a letter from Wang Huai.

Changchi,

What has happened? Your mum and I haven't been able to sleep recently. We're nervous and have premonitions that something is about to happen. When you have time, send a piece of clothing that each one of you has worn recently, and I will ask for you. Is Dazhi well? Can he walk? Send some photos. We miss him.

Dad

Wang Changchi decided to visit home. He took the long-distance bus. When he arrived at the gap, he didn't hurry the way he had in the past, but on the contrary, some power stopped him. He dragged his feet as if at each step he was switching to a lower gear. It was in the afternoon and two hours before dark. As he didn't want to be seen, he slipped into the forest. He thought that anyone who couldn't even dare to go home in daylight was a loser among losers. As he sat in the woods, the scent of trees, green grass, rotten leaves and new flowers wafted towards him. The mosquitoes circled his ears, buzzing. The mountains were the same as before, but the village looked more run-down and deserted. That was especially true of his own house, though it had always looked askew and ready to topple in a gust of wind. The songs and chirps of the night-time insects rose slowly like the tide and the sky turned dark. The white kitchen smoke blended with

297

the night, the oxen returned to the village and the voices of those coming home in the evening were heard from the road. Relying on the meagre light from the horizon, Wang Changchi went from the forest to the tea plantation, and from there entered the backdoor of his house. The door was unlocked and creaked as he pushed it open.

"Who's there?" asked Wang Huai.

Without replying, Wang Changchi went directly into the room. They were in the middle of eating, and seeing Wang Changchi, they stopped chewing.

"What are you doing here?" asked Wang Huai. "Dazhi? Xiaowen? Why didn't they come?"

"First have a wash and I'll get you some rice," said Liu Shuangju.

Putting down his luggage, Wang Changchi looked at the two fir trees, stripped of bark, rising from the floor to the roof, supporting the large leaning roof beam. Wang Huai's eyes followed his eyes upward. Their line of sight met on the beam.

"It's OK," said Wang Huai, "it'll hold for another couple of years."

"Didn't I give you twenty thousand yuan to build a new house?" said Wang Changchi.

"We gave it back to you when Xiaowen gave birth."

"I thought that was money you made begging on the streets."

"Begging only provides for room and board."

Wang Changchi opened the suitcase and took out a pile of money.

"I made this from painting," he said. "Is it enough for a house?"

"Of course it's enough," said Wang Huai, "but I don't want to take your money. You have to pay rent, raise Dazhi and put some aside so he can go to school."

"No, there's no need..."

Wang Changchi had almost said, We don't have to raise him, but instead bit his lip and said, "I can make more."

Wang Huai sighed and said, "A family in the village and a

family in the city all depending on you, how can you bear such a heavy burden?"

"It's slowly becoming less weighty," said Wang Changchi.

Late at night, Wang Huai arranged incense, spirit money, pork shoulder, wine, white rice, a rooster and cymbals, among other things. In his wheelchair, he started to perform a ritual. The previous year, he had taken Guang Sheng on as his teacher and had become a shaman. He had hesitated before entering the profession, but when compared with all other possibilities, if he wanted to take on some responsibility for the household, though crippled in body but not in will, then his only choice was to become a shaman. He was better educated than Guang Sheng, so he made a better shaman. Nowadays when anyone from the village or outside had issues with ghosts, most would come and see him rather than Guang Sheng. Whenever he was needed, they would send people to carry him over and treat him with good wine, rice, food and tobacco. When they saw him, clients with a sense of humour would say, "Master Wang thinks of everything, he even brings his own seat." He rejoiced that there were professions in the world that didn't require a person to stand, otherwise, he'd have no way to make a living. When he finished a ritual, he'd receive some cash and could take the rooster from the ritual with him. The respect he received surpassed that shown to Guang Sheng and later that shown to Teacher Pang at the primary school. Each time he was carried to and from a ritual, he saw himself as the "ambassador of the nether Yin world stationed in the Yang world" and would recall the ancient words, "Poverty demands change, change demands development, permanence follows development."

Wang Huai muttered incantations, and his body swayed as if he were riding a horse to the nether world. He sweated, his clothes were damp and after about half an hour, he'd gradually become steady. Wang Changchi handed him a piece of Dazhi's clothing. He drew a symbol on the clothing and uttered a formula.

Then he opened his eyes and said, "Great wealth and honour, never will he worry about food and clothing."

Wang Changchi thought, It looks like he is with the right people. Wang Huai closed his eyes and re-entered the spirit world. Wang Changchi handed him a piece of Xiaowen's clothing. He drew and uttered an incantation for a while.

"Xiaowen is gone," he said.

"Can you find her?" asked Wang Changchi.

Wang Huai closed his eyes and rested his hand for a while on the mat. He seemed to see something and then thrust with his finger.

"What are you poking?" asked Wang Changchi.

"I see a paper window," said Wang Huai, "but can't break it no matter how hard I poke it."

"Is Xiaowen hiding on the other side of the window?"

Wang Huai nodded.

"Poke it harder, please break it open."

Wang Huai poked for more than ten minutes until he could no longer move.

"I'm out of energy," he said. "Forget it, child."

"Try again."

"It's the will of Heaven. You cannot use force."

Wang Changchi handed him a glass of water. Wang Huai took a mouthful of water and spat several times around and then continued. His face was covered with sweat and his clothes soaked through. Wang Changchi handed him a piece of his own clothing. He drew and uttered an incantation for a while. Doubt seemed to cloud his face, so he drew and uttered an incantation again. More doubt. Again, he drew and uttered an incantation and, like the sun appearing between parting clouds, he said, "Good, good, good, everything is great, a happy family and a long life."

After Liu Shuangju and Wang Changchi went to bed, Wang Huai sat up drinking alone unhappily. When daybreak came and Liu Shuangju got out of bed, he was still drinking.

"What's the matter?" asked Liu Shuangju.

Wang Huai got her to push him inside. In the bedroom, he told her to close the door. Liu Shuangju closed it.

"Can you keep a secret?" asked Wang Huai.

Liu Shuangju nodded.

"Last night when I looked at Changchi's clothes," said Wang Huai, "I saw a patch of blood. It was terrible as if the family had been broken up!"

Liu Shuangju went pale and asked, "Could you be mistaken?"

"I looked three times." Wang Huai held up three fingers.

"What can we do?"

"Don't let him leave home, keep him in the village."

"If he doesn't go back to the city, who'll take care of Dazhi and Xiaowen? You bamboozle people with ghosts, are you so sure you're right?"

"It doesn't matter. Just don't tell Changchi, otherwise he'll come to harm."

"Have you ever been right with other people?"

"Sometimes, sometimes not."

"Then it's only superstition."

"I wish..."

Actually, Wang Changchi trembled all night. As he lay in bed, his head was filled with nothing but the image of Xiaowen. She carried water, cooked rice, slopped out the pigs, washed clothes, swept and slept. Whatever happened in the household, she was involved, appearing again like in scenes in a film.

After lunch, Wang Huai asked, "Strange, why couldn't I open the window last night?"

"Perhaps you don't have enough power," said Wang Changchi.

"You can fool others with this game," challenged Liu Shuangju, "so now you're going to try it on at home?"

"My clothes were soaked through," said Wang Huai, "why should I make such an effort to fool someone?"

They were all sunk in thought, so they said nothing. After eating, Wang Changchi secretly slipped out of the village through the forest to visit Xiaowen's house. Xiaowen's mum, dad, brother and sister-in-law seemed to know something because they all frowned and didn't even offer him any water.

"Don't come here and bother me," said Xiaowen's dad. "If you do, I'll demand her back from you."

Wang Changchi had no choice but to slink back, dejected. On his return, he found the main room filled with villagers. Wang Dong was missing two fingers.

"They got cut off in a machine when I was working in Shenzhen," he said.

Liu Baitiao had lost at gambling again and wanted to borrow money from Wang Changchi. Zhang Xianhua had had another baby, exceeding the permitted number and had not only been fined but her husband was being sued.

"Zhang Wu has contracted some strange illness," said Daijun.

"What bogus strange illness?" said Second Uncle. "It's just venereal disease."

Wang Changchi thought, Zhang Hui makes money by selling herself and after making money sends it home to Zhang Wu, who in turn takes the money and fools around with prostitutes. That's just a vicious circle, isn't it? As they were talking, Zhang Wu arrived. Someone got up and offered him a seat, but in an exaggerated fashion, as if they were unwilling to sit with him because he might be contagious.

"How is Zhang Hui?" asked Zhang Wu.

"Fine," said Wang Changchi.

"How is Dazhi? Xiaowen?"

"They're all fine."

When he said they were all fine, his heart was filled with pain.

Wang Huai and Liu Shuangju urged Wang Changchi to stay, fearing if he left, he would never return. They urged him to stay because he seemed restless, and as soon as he got up, he made it clear he wanted to go back to the city.

"Xiaowen is there to take care of Dazhi," said Wang Huai, "so why are you in such a hurry?"

Wang Changchi didn't know why he was so impatient. He had given Dazhi away and Xiaowen had vanished, so why was he in such a hurry to get back? When he was in the city, he thought of home. When he was at home, he thought of the city. He was like a pendulum swinging back and forth, but not knowing where to stop.

"If you really must go," said Wang Huai, "then take a small bench."

Wang Changchi and Liu Shuangju didn't understand him.

"If you sit on a bench from home," explained Wang Huai, "wherever you go it'll be like home, and whatever danger you encounter, the ancestors will protect you."

Liu Shuangju understood, but Wang Changchi did not. Liu Shuangju tied a cord to the small bench. When Wang Changchi was leaving, she hung the small bench over his shoulder. Wang Changchi put down the bench, Liu Shuangju slung it on his shoulder again. Off it came, on it went many times until Wang Changchi hurled it away. Liu Shuangju started to cry. She knew Wang Huai wanted to use the bench to help explain the patch of blood he saw when questioning the ghosts, but Wang Changchi was unaware. Liu Shuangju couldn't tell him the truth, so she just cried.

"Changchi," said Wang Huai, "take the bench. It'll be like taking us and having family with you to give you a little more strength in a fight."

As he walked, Wang Changchi mulled over what Wang Huai had said. He thought about that time he left home carrying a chair. That chair accompanied them as they sat on the playing field at the Bureau of Education, and it went with him when he went to study at the county town. Wang Changchi suddenly missed it, so when he arrived in the county town, he went to see the head of classes. The head of classes still had the chair. Wang Changchi lifted it with both hands and got on the long-distance bus to the provincial capital.

五十六 · FIFTY-SIX

THAT NIGHT WANG CHANGCHI HAD WANTED TO TAKE DAZHI directly to the door of the Lins', but he began to hesitate at the second bus stop. He thought that a direct approach might alarm Fang Zhizhi, so he swung back and forth between "direct" and "indirect". As the bus passed another stop, he felt he could no longer hesitate as Dazhi might start to cry. So, gritting his teeth, he got off at the fourth stop and changed to bus 21, which went past the orphanage.

After Fang Zhizhi received Zhao Dingfang's call, she hurried over. She was entranced by the cooing baby in front of her. He had delicate features, his body normal and healthy, blood-type B, good hearing and a clear voice. He was well-nourished and dressed in clean clothes, looking nothing like a baby abandoned by a poor family. The thing that set her pulse racing most was that when she was about to leave, he grasped her ring finger and called out "Mama". She fell to her knees at once. However, she still had to go through the process of calling Lin Jiabo, Lu Shanshan and Fang Nanfang to come and judge. They came twice in one week and they all liked the child, so they completed the adoption paperwork. Fang Zhizhi named him Lin Fangsheng. The day they went to pick him up, Lin Jiabo drove while Fang Zhizhi held the baby. Lin Fangsheng kept his eyes open the whole way without crying.

Although Lin Fangsheng was weaned, Fang Zhizhi insisted that he should be breastfed. For this reason, she took three months of maternity leave and ate all sorts of lactation-promoting foods, took Chinese medicine and had injections of foreign lactation-inducing drugs, which eventually had the desired effect. Lin Fangsheng sucked greedily, and Fang Zhizhi freely supplied. Both of them had to determine their place in this supply-and-demand relationship. Slowly Dazhi's smell changed. They began to detect the scent of the Fang family on him. They went from holding him to nuzzling and kissing him. He became one of the family, and they often forgot that he had been adopted.

They bought him Italian clothes and English toys, gave him American powdered milk to drink and French bread and Swiss chocolate to eat. When he was three, Fang Zhizhi read English words to him, at four, she provided him with a piano teacher. Under the instruction of Fang Zhizhi, at five he could distinguish between alveolar and velar nasal consonants, and at six he could play Bach's Minuet in G Major. At seven, he entered the most prestigious primary school in the city. At eight, Lin Jiabo took him to play football. He was intelligent and liked to study, and he was always at the head of his class and won all the awards.

During his first year of junior high school, his grandfather Fang Nanfang retired, and Lin Jiabo lost all his scruples. He was often away on business and when he was home, he was busy with social appointments and seldom returned home before one or two in the morning. When she wasn't working, Fang Zhizhi looked after Lin Fangsheng, seldom asked after Lin Jiabo's business and had no idea that he was having an affair. The first to discover this secret was none other than Wang Changchi, who had been keeping watch across from the building for thirteen years.

For thirteen years, whenever Wang Changchi had any free time, he'd hang around near the building. Sometimes he paced outside the sports stadium, watching as Dazhi strolled with Fang Zhizhi or kicked a football with Lin Jiabo. Sometimes he'd go to the little shop at the bottom of the building to buy things where he'd occasionally run into Dazhi who came to buy snacks. On one occasion, he was unable to control himself and caressed Dazhi's head, scaring the child out of his wits so that he turned and ran, but had the presence of mind to stamp on his foot before he did so. Dazhi ran all the way to the fourth floor and Wang Changchi's hand was still hanging there in the air as if savouring, but also as if he were afraid that if he pulled his hand back, he'd crush Dazhi's head. Every time he saw Dazhi, his blood would surge, and he would feel so excited that he almost collapsed. He wanted to call out his real name and rush forward and hug him, but a voice would always say, "All your previous work will be undone, you'll ruin him." The voice sounded like Xiaowen's, also like Wang Huai's but also like his own. He knew that only by restraining himself could he obtain happiness for Dazhi, and like walking a tightrope while carrying a bowl of hot soup, there was no room for a misstep. He would eat the rice and oil that Wang Huai and Liu Shuangju bought for Dazhi and every time he ate it, he felt regret as if he had committed a sin. Could he take the rice and oil to Fang Zhizhi? Clearly he could not, he couldn't even celebrate the boy's birthday. Every year on Dazhi's birthday, he'd buy a gift, take it to the pavilion and wave it at the balcony, as if in this way Dazhi could receive it. Only by waving the present could the suppressed pain in his heart find release.

It was easy to deceive himself, but it became ever more difficult to deceive Wang Huai and Liu Shuangju. They wanted to see pictures of Dazhi, so Wang Changchi had to buy a camera and hang around the kindergarten and use a telephoto lens to get a close-up of Dazhi. They wanted him to bring the family of three home for the New Year, and every year he had to make excuses.

He said, "Dazhi is still too young. If he goes home, he'll be bitten by fleas and if not treated properly he'll end up back in hospital."

He said, "He has to practise the piano."

He said, "Dazhi has reached a critical point for getting into school, so he had to stay in the city to wish the school leader a happy New Year..."

They wanted letters from Dazhi, so he imitated a child's handwriting and wished Grandma and Grandpa well. They wanted to see Dazhi's exams, so he'd come up with the teacher's topic and then write the answer with a black pen, mark the paper with a red pen, and then post it to Wang Huai, always with a mark above ninety-five. When he saw Dazhi's exams, Wang Huai's extinguished hopes reignited as if they had been doused in petrol.

One year, before the Spring Festival, Liu Shuangju shouldered half a pig and pushed Wang Huai to below the building and shouted, "Changchi". Wang Changchi heard her shout but dared not open the door. Liu Shuangju carried the half pig to the door on the first floor, then went down and carried Wang Huai up, before going down and picking up the wheelchair. Wang Changchi heard the commotion outside the door and was so anxious that he wanted to jump out of the window. He knew that the door was his last line of protection, and once it was opened, all the hopes of Wang Huai and Liu Shuangju would be dashed. But the door had to be opened sooner or later.

They waited outside and chatted. In the room he saw the dusty kitchen, scattered piles of clothes, mosquito repellent strips littering the floor, and only then realised he had ignored the place for a long time, and it had been years since he had looked after it properly. The window curtains were streaked with mould. Why hadn't he noticed before? Two dead cockroaches were lying in the corner. When had they dried up? A line of ants was going through the wall on the right side. Sunlight broke through the kitchen window to shine on the slippers tossed randomly on the floor. Both ends of the fluorescent lamp were filled with dead insects, and there were a number of cracks in the ceiling... He wasted more time sizing up the place.

As she was anxious, Liu Shuangju pressed close to the window to see inside more clearly. Wang Huai knocked on the door as if he knew someone was inside. Wang Changchi thought, Oh well, they'll be disappointed, but better sooner than later. All I can do now is do my best to keep them from fainting.

Wang Changchi opened the door and invited Wang Huai and Liu Shuangju in. Their eyes swept over the room and doubt began to creep over their faces.

"What happened?" asked Wang Huai.

"We got divorced," said Wang Changchi.

"And Dazhi?"

Wang Changchi didn't utter a sound.

"Did Xiaowen take him with her?"

Wang Changchi continued to remain silent.

"When did you get a divorce?"

"The year I went home."

"Where do they live?"

"I haven't a clue."

"Didn't you post Dazhi's letters and exams to me?"

"I made up the exams and wrote the letters."

As he spoke, Wang Changchi took a stack of exam papers from

under the bed mat. Wang Huai snatched them, his hands trembling slightly, his face ashen.

"Where did you get the photos of Dazhi?" he asked.

Wang Changchi said nothing. Wang Huai threw the papers on the floor.

"You're not going to say the photos are fake too?"

"I gave Dazhi away."

"Who to?"

"Rich people."

Pow! Wang Huai slapped Wang Changchi. The room was entirely silent for several minutes.

Rubbing the slapped side of his face, Wang Changchi said, "If we can't give him a good life, why shouldn't we give him away? He rides in a luxury car, lives in a big house and goes to the best school. Can you give him those things? I understand there are two kinds of love, love in the narrow sense and love in the broad sense. Love in the narrow sense meant keeping him, and for his whole life he'd be like you or me or Liu Jianping, Xingze or Zhang Hui. In the broad sense it meant his happiness, allowing him to succeed and not grow hardened to life."

"But that means he calls someone else 'Dad'."

Wang Changchi's heart ached.

"Happiness has a secret combination, like opening a safe. Some people say, 'Open sesame' while others say, 'Dad'."

"Get him back or I'll disown you."

"It's like the stump of a banana tree. Soon it bears fruit, so there's no reason to cut it down. Isn't the life Dazhi is now leading exactly what you longed for? The streets are lined with flowers, none of which we've fertilised or watered, but can't we still enjoy the sight of them?"

"You're too clever for your own good. Where is he?"

"I won't tell you."

Wang Huai once again raised his hand, but this time he missed his mark. In a flash, Wang Huai realised that Wang Changchi was no longer a child. His face showed no fear, just resoluteness. Although he was not yet forty, his hairline was already receding, his black hair was sprinkled with white, and his brow was creased. Seeing the worry that weighed on him, Wang Huai felt desperately sad for him. But desperation was desperation and forgiveness, forgiveness. He slapped his own face instead.

"Liu Shuangju, let's go," he said. "If he doesn't bring Dazhi back, I don't ever want to see him again for as long as I live."

Liu Shuangju didn't move.

"Why aren't you coming?" asked Wang Huai. "You want to forgive him for such disobedience? I'm going even if you're not."

As he spoke, he opened the door and rolled himself out into the hall and over to the edge of the stairway. The wheels hung in the air when they suddenly stopped.

"Go," said Liu Shuangju. "You think going forward is a golden road, but all you do is go in circles. What'll come of it all? I've spun around until my knees hurt, and I can't walk any further."

五十七 · FIFTY-SEVEN

SEVERAL NIGHTS IN A ROW, a red saloon brought Lin Jiabo home and stopped downstairs. The car stopped briefly and left. Lin Jiabo watched it depart and only when it disappeared, did he go upstairs. Wang Changchi discovered that each time the red saloon arrived, the door didn't open immediately, but only after five to ten minutes would the door open and Lin Jiabo step out. Wang Changchi was curious to know who was driving the car. What were the people in the car doing for those few minutes? But he dared not get too near. One night, he brought a bottle of spirits and lay down at the side of the road, drinking and waiting. As expected, the red saloon pulled up and as it stopped, he staggered over. There was no response from inside the car, so he bent over the windscreen and peered in. He saw that Lin Jiabo was at that very moment kissing a woman. They froze in fear when they saw the man at the windscreen, then separated and glared angrily at him. He pounded drunkenly on the windscreen. But the car set off in a flash, leaving him to fall on his face.

"It's their family business, I'm not going to get involved," Wang Changchi warned himself, from time to time. But the more he warned himself, the more worried he became, much like watching someone else take a fall and not helping them up, but only looking back from a distance. He thought, Lin Jiabo is now Dazhi's dad, no, Lin Fangsheng's dad. Were his actions harming Dazhi and Fang Zhizhi? He thought he had found a model family for Dazhi and hadn't expected the dad to go off track. The father straying would impact the mother, which in turn would naturally impact Dazhi. It was no simple matter, but a tidal wave. Despite his anxiety, he had no plan. He wanted to get involved but was afraid of causing trouble for Dazhi. As a result, he painted the Zhaos' cabinet the wrong colour. When they saw it, the Zhaos' were so angry that they docked his wages and refused to reimburse him for the cost of materials.

They even pointed at him and said, "Peasant, cheat, you're blind, may you die without heirs, scoundrel, rubbish, scum, bastard, dog shit, pig brain..." A whole chain of insulting words to varnish him with. But he refused to back down and only when he placed the sample next to the cabinet, did he discover that the colour was different. He had never dreamed that anxiety could affect one's sense of colour. As he went down the stairs, he thought the Zhaos would stop him and pay for the materials or even give him a little food money. But it didn't happen, and a month's work was for nothing. He'd already paid out twenty large notes and was now angry enough to smash a brick.

Several days later, Lin Jiabo received a mysterious letter, which read,

You have a lovely wife, a cute son, for which many people envy you, but you want to waste it, turning your back on your wife to fool around outside. How rotten you are. For your own good, I encourage you to stop messing around, otherwise, someone will set you right.

Signed, "a Servant of Wu Song"

Lin Jiabo thought, Who's behind this? Who dares tell me what to do? No one talks to me like that apart from my father-in-law Fang Nanfang, not even my old man Lin Gang. He then considered all his friends who knew his secret but couldn't think of one who would get involved. Well, is Fang Zhizhi keeping an eye on me? He carefully examined the writing and found that it was not hers. Even if she had intentionally disguised the characters, her hand wouldn't be so unfamiliar. He took care to hide the letter and went home as if nothing had happened. There was no change in Fang Zhizhi's attitude towards him and Lin Fangsheng was in a normal mood. But he, on the contrary, seemed to be totally absent-minded. He forgot to close the door and turn off the air conditioner. Even when he drank some water, it seemed to stick in his throat. Since he had needed Fang Nanfang's help with his business for so many years, he had always acquiesced to Fang Zhizhi. If she wanted to take a trip, he went, if she went shopping, he carried the bags, if she lost her temper, he gave in. When she said she wanted to adopt a child, he consented with alacrity, like an obsequious secretary catering to the boss.

Sometimes he would ask himself, Am I really that good? No. I'm not really that good. I'm just pretending, but after a while you get used to it. Fang Nanfang doesn't really have any power now, so I don't have to pretend any more. But why am I still so irresolute?

The reason is that little son-of-a-bitch. He's so wretchedly well-behaved. All I have to do is open my arms and he comes running and calls me "Dad", as clear and crisp as biting into a cucumber. When I go away on business, he calls me every day and tells me not to drink. Sometimes when I'm drunk and return downstairs, all I have to do is call upstairs to Fangsheng and immediately I'll hear his footsteps in the hallway. Even after midnight, there's no delay as if he had been waiting and listening. It doesn't matter when I call him, he'll always respond. He comes running down and helps me upstairs, gives me juice to drink and wipes my face with a warm cloth. He's the first thing I see when I wake up. If he's not looking at me, then he's sleeping by my side, like a guard dog or a tame kitten. Taking advantage of me being drunk, he asked if I have a mistress, if I'll abandon him and his mother. I said, "Don't worry, I'll take care of you and your mum." He said, "That doesn't mean you don't have a mistress." I said, "No, I don't have one." He smiled and ran to the bedroom and reported to his mum, "He's had so much to drink, and he didn't confess, so it looks like he really doesn't have a mistress. Let him sleep in the bedroom." However, Fang Zhizhi would not agree as long as I was drunk, and she didn't want me in the bedroom. Sometimes, I thought, since she won't let me in the bedroom, why should I bother coming home at all? Simply because I'm afraid Lin Fangsheng will be worried? I know that if I didn't come home, he wouldn't be able to sleep.

When he was five years old, I was kicking a football and ran into someone. I injured my head and had to go to hospital. He came with his mum to see me. Seeing my bandaged head, he asked, "Dad, are you going to die?" I tilted my head to one side, pretending to be dead. He started to cry and tried to give me mouth-to-mouth resuscitation. His mouth was small, and his breath didn't have much force, but he tried until his face turned red and his neck swelled, putting all his energy into my mouth. At that moment, I didn't want to come back to life. His tears flowed down his face to my mouth. They were actually sweet. Seeing that I didn't come to, he slapped my face and said, "Dad, why did you die? Why didn't you discuss it with me or Mum before dying? If you die, I won't have a dad."

Ever since then, he has been afraid of me dying. Several times, he got up in the middle of the night and knocked on the bedroom door and asked, "Dad, are you still alive?" Every time I opened the door, I saw his face covered with tears, none of it dry, making me wonder if he was really a tearful son or that crying person in the legend. Crying, he came in and said, "Dad, I dreamed you died again. Why did you die so miserably?" Crying, he lay down on the bed and refused to go, insisting on sleeping between me and Fang Zhizhi. And though asleep, he kept twitching. Last week, he woke up in tears again, but this time when he knocked, he had his pillow with him. Fang Zhizhi said, "Fangsheng, Fangsheng you are in junior high and taller than your mum. Aren't you ashamed to come in here and sleep with us? You always dream about your dad dying, but never your mum, aren't you afraid of losing your mum?" He said, "D'you think I want to dream about Dad dying? After a dream like that, I feel weak and worn out for days."

"Never mind how well-behaved Lin Fangsheng is, he's not my own child," said Lin Jiabo.

When he said this, he and Fang Zhizhi were sitting on two chaise longues on the balcony. Fang Zhizhi seemed not to hear, her eyes fixed on the sports ground below, where Lin Fangsheng was playing football with a bunch of classmates. Although they were all wearing the same uniform, Fang Zhizhi could spot her son at once among the group. At that moment he was running with the ball, sweeping past a tall child, then a short one and then another short one, and nearing the opposite goal. He kicked the ball, which flew from the grass describing an arc through the air towards the upper left corner of the goal. Everyone fell silent. The goalkeeper jumped to meet the ball and knock it away from the goal. If they hadn't been talking about a serious topic, Lin Jiabo would have leapt to his feet and shouted for Lin Fangsheng. But at that precise moment, he seemed to be submerging a floating gourd underwater, suppressing an impulse, and sitting calmly on the chaise longue, as if the child who kicked the ball had nothing to do with him. Fang Zhizhi thought, Actually, my life is a lot like that ball. Clearly it was going in, but it was unexpectedly knocked away by a hand, not a hand, but rather by God's decree. To Lin Jiabo it was as if he had thrown a stone but never heard it land. He turned to look at Fang Zhizhi. Fang Zhizhi was looking at the football pitch. The two of them breathed cautiously as if the air were poison.

"You know, I've always wanted a child of my own." Lin Jiabo threw another stone.

"Then get a divorce." A reply finally came.

"We don't need a divorce. Couldn't we use a surrogate?"

"A divorce would be cleaner," scoffed Fang Zhizhi. "I don't want Fangsheng to have a rival mum."

"Thank you for your understanding."

"What's there to understand? I can't get pregnant, so whose fault is that? At the time, I wanted you to wear a condom, but you refused. So I had to have two abortions."

"That's why I've stayed with you all these years."

"You've stayed for my dad."

"He's your own father. You have your father, but I don't have a son of my own."

"You have to discuss it with Fangsheng first. I'll never be able to explain it to him. If you talk about divorce, he'll certainly do worse at school, and he could even end up traumatised for the rest of his life. If we pretend you died unexpectedly, he'll want to see the body before he lets the matter go. You know how sensitive he is."

"OK, I'll have a word with him."

"If you hurt him or reveal that he is adopted, then I'll declare war against you."

"I'll keep the harm to him to a minimum."

"Lin Jiabo, you are so cruel."

五十八 · FIFTY-EIGHT

AFTER THAT, THE MOMENT HE GOT HOME, Lin Jiabo would go to Lin Fangsheng's bedroom. He went in under the pretext of checking on his homework or exams, but what he really wanted to do was talk about the divorce. However, every time he saw those blinking eyes, his heart would melt, and he couldn't open his mouth as if it had been anaesthetised. Lin Fangsheng knew something was wrong but didn't think it was too bad, just that his old man had higher expectations of him. So, every evening before Lin Jiabo came upstairs, he'd already be doing his homework. Lin Jiabo silently watched Lin Fangsheng, sitting opposite him. He was quite good-looking, with large eyes and a high bridge to his nose, and when he pursed his lips, two dimples appeared. In all fairness, he thought, he is better looking than me, and the older he gets the more he resembles Fang Zhizhi. Where does the resemblance come from when he's not our own offspring? Physiologists would say that we grow to resemble those we worship. No wonder... when he comes across a perplexing problem, he knits his brows and grits his teeth, completely absorbed as if I were transparent. His quilt is folded tidily, his pillow neat and smooth. On the wall behind are the awards he has won over the years, all framed by Fang Zhizhi. There are no marks on the walls and not a scrap of paper on the floor. His polished football sits on the wastepaper basket by the door. His hair is short, he is clean, he has changed his clothes, his nails are trimmed, he is never late and never leaves school early, never asks for time off and always gets outstanding marks. Such a well-behaved child, it would be hard to find anything wrong. Does he have any shortcomings? Of course he does. His biggest is that he cries over nothing. He's sensitive and not very brave and is even startled when the wok lid falls on the floor.

One night after finishing a homework assignment, Lin Fang-sheng looked up.

"Dad, why are you still here?" he said. "Let me finish my homework and then come in, OK?"

What could Lin Jiabo say? His throat constricted and not a word came out, swallowing the words he was about to say like spittle. He left as quietly as he had arrived. The door locked with a click as he left. He had lost yet another opportunity to reveal his hypocrisy. For once he thought about abandoning the idea, feeling that a child of his own wouldn't necessarily be better than an adopted one and that it wouldn't be so bad for the three of them to continue as usual. But every time he returned to the county town, he didn't dare knock on his parent's door. Filthy rich as he was, he stood outside the door like the biggest debtor, his legs shaking because he knew that once he passed through those doors, his self-esteem would come crashing down. So he had to steel himself to enter. His mum would say, "I want to hold my own grandchild." His father would say, "The Lin family line must continue." His aunt would say, "You don't have any children, who are you going to leave all your money to?"

Finally, he came to a decision.

"Son," he said, "Dad wants to show you a contract."

Lin Fangsheng's eyes grew wide. On the table was a bilingual contract in English and Chinese. The first party was an Algerian agency, the second party was Lin Jiabo's company.

"Our company has been contracted to build a motorway in North Africa," said Lin Jiabo, "and I'll be taking people there in the next few days."

"How long will you be gone?" asked Lin Fangsheng.

"The soonest I'll be back is two years, and maybe as long as three to five years."

"Three years? You won't be back till I've left high school?"

"Several hundred miles of motorway through the desert will take several years."

"Does Mum know?"

"She doesn't mind."

"The road in front of the house needs fixing. Why do you have to work so far away?"

"I'll be making US dollars, so in the future you can study abroad."

"If I don't study abroad, would you still have to go?"

"I have to go because I must pay the workers their wages each month."

Falling silent, Lin Fangsheng continuously wiped his eyes, and his fingers were moist.

"When your dad signs a big contract, you should be happy," said Lin Jiabo.

Lin Fangsheng forced a smile, but it disappeared immediately.

"Dad," he said, "I want to be happy for you, but I don't know why I can't be."

His nose tingling, Lin Jiabo hurriedly reached out to wipe away his son's tears.

As he wiped away the tears, he said, "Sooner or later you must grow up. A man doesn't cry. Especially on the day I leave, you must definitely not cry. If you cry your dad won't be able to leave, and there'll be no one to build the road. Also, crying is not an auspicious sign when your dad is going far away. Remember, when you have problems, grit your teeth and carry on. Dad is putting you in charge of the house temporarily, so you must be brave and strong."

Lin Fangsheng nodded. "Since I can't cry when you leave, can I cry now?"

As he finished speaking, his shoulders heaved, and his face was covered with tears.

The day Lin Jiabo left, three strangers arrived. Each one took away a large trunk, which hung in the door frame for a moment, as if unwilling to leave. Helplessly, Lin Fangsheng watched without shedding a tear. Before leaving, Lin Jiabo hugged him and raised his thumb encouragingly. Lin Fangsheng wanted to accompany Lin Jiabo downstairs, but Lin Jiabo pushed him back and said, "This is our official goodbye." Lin Jiabo gently closed the door, and his footsteps grew fainter. Lin Fangsheng ran to the balcony and saw them place the luggage in a black Land Rover. The three strangers got in the vehicle, leaving Lin Jiabo standing by the passenger door. He looked up and gave a thumbs-up to Lin Fangsheng.

Lin Fangsheng waved and said, "Goodbye, Dad, bye."

Lin Jiabo waved, got in the car and shut the door before it rushed off. Lin Fangsheng waved until the car was out of sight. He turned around and discovered Fang Zhizhi crying in the living room. He took several Kleenex and gently wiped her eyes.

"Mum," he said, "Dad said not to cry when he left because it's inauspicious." Unexpectedly, Fang Zhizhi wept even more loudly. She was not crying over Lin Jiabo's departure, but because Lin Fangsheng was in the dark. Feeling frightened, Lin Fangsheng hurriedly covered his mother's mouth.

While eating dinner that night, Lin Fangsheng noticed that the food was saltier than usual. He hadn't imagined his old man going away on business would have such an effect on his mum's cooking. His dad had frequently gone away on business in the past, but why wasn't the food salty then? Was it because this time it was for longer, with more responsibilities and farther away? The food was saltier from one day to the next until finally it was so salty that he couldn't eat it.

"Mum," asked Lin Fangsheng, "didn't you want Dad to go to North Africa?"

"It's not that," said Fang Zhizhi. "He's always travelled a lot. I'm used to it, numb to it."

"Then why are you putting twice the salt in the food when you cook? If this goes on much longer, I'll become a saltwater fish."

"Really?"

Taking some food, Fang Zhizhi tasted it and said, "It's not salty. It must be your mouth."

Lin Fangsheng thought, Oh no, her sense of taste is all messed up, something big must have happened. Thinking back, he detected some things out of the ordinary. For example, when his old man left, why didn't his mum see him off? Why did she cry? She tried to be strong and would never cry in front of others. Also, why was her face so rigid? In the past when she spoke, her face was always quite animated, but now when she spoke only her mouth moved, and sometimes not even that. Her voice was flat and expressionless. Although she checks my homework every night, she is nothing like as strict as before. Even though I rub things out, she doesn't make me rewrite them. So what has happened?

In the middle of the night, Lin Fangsheng quietly got out of bed and slipped into Lin Jiabo's study. He turned on the light and closed the door, searching for an answer in the room. But the desk was unchanged, the drawers were the same, the filing cabinet was as orderly as ever, and the curtains were neat and tidy. He examined all the photos in the bookcase and even looked behind the mirror, but he found nothing unusual. In the photos, the three of them looked so close. Perhaps I'm thinking too much. He turned to leave when he noticed a crumpled scrap of paper in the wastebasket. He flattened the paper on the desk and found it was a letter. It was the one the "Servant of Wu Song" had written to Lin Jiabo, the gist of which was that Lin Jiabo shouldn't keep a mistress, otherwise the man would fix him. Lin Fangsheng's scalp tightened, and his mind went blank. He didn't know how long he had gone blank when suddenly he heard a knock at the door. He quickly thrust the paper into his pocket before going over to open the door.

"What are you up to?" asked Fang Zhizhi.

"I miss my old man," he said, "so I came to look at the photos."

Fang Zhizhi eyed him for a while, then looking at the study, asked herself, I wonder if he found something? But there didn't seem to be anything to discover in the study. So he really misses his dad? He's so filial.

"Hurry back to bed or you won't be able to get up for school tomorrow morning," she said.

"It's so late, why aren't you asleep?"

"I was, but the sound of your voice woke me."

Lin Fangsheng knew it was a fib because he could see that her eyes were bloodshot. She didn't look in the least like someone who had been asleep, and he had made no sound. But he didn't feel like pointing this out. He turned off the light and left the study.

"Goodnight, Mum," he said.

"Goodnight, Son."

Each went to their own room and gently shut the door, not wishing to disturb the other. Back in his room, Lin Fangsheng stared at the ceiling for a while but didn't feel the least bit sleepy. He calculated the time difference between Africa and China and knew that it was daytime in Africa, so he got out of bed, quietly opened the door, went to the phone in the living room and dialled Lin Jiabo's mobile number. He dialled several times but got only a recorded message saying that said the number did not exist. He wondered, How can it not exist? In the past when I rang him, I got through immediately, even at three or four in the morning. In the past whenever he went away on business, he'd always call. He's been away a long time, why hasn't he called even once? Once again, he slipped into the study and opened the lower right-hand door of the bookcase. Inside was a small safe with a combination lock used by Lin Jiabo. He thought, As long as the safe is still locked, Dad will be coming back. He took a deep breath and then exhaled, praying for the Old Man in Heaven's protection, then he placed his hand on the latch of the safe door. The latch grew warm under his hand before he turned it, expecting it not to open, but it opened with a click. It was empty inside. He thought, He's never coming back. He has abandoned me and Mum.

五十九 · FIFTY-NINE

LIN FANGSHENG WENT TO THE COMPANY IN SEARCH OF LIN JIABO. He Gui said the board chair had gone to Africa. Lin Fangsheng asked his maternal grandparents and they said, "We've told you so many times, why do you keep asking?" He called his paternal grandparents and they said, "He's abroad on business." He asked Fan Zhizhi, "Why doesn't Dad call?" Fang Zhizhi said it was because he was building a road in the desert and there was no signal there.

One afternoon, Lin Fangsheng bunked off school and went back to Lin Jiabo's company. Before heading upstairs, he caught sight of the car Lin Jiabo usually drove around in parked in the courtyard. Lin Jiabo's office on the second floor was locked. After waiting a while, Lin Fangsheng raised his hand, knocked and shouted, "Father". His shouting startled He Gui.

He Gui came running and said, "There's no one inside."

"I heard someone," said Lin Fangsheng. "My dad's inside."

"No, he's not," said He Gui.

Not believing him, he pounded his forehead against the door, each time harder, about to draw blood. He Gui had to get the key and open the door. Lin Fangsheng went in and saw that the desk and floor were covered with dust, the same as when his biological father Wang Changchi entered demanding money as if the office were intentionally kept dusty.

"Do you want to open the filing cabinets and have a look?" asked He Gui.

Not amused, Lin Fangsheng opened each of the filing cabinets and all the drawers.

When he pulled open the drawers, He Gui asked, "Is your dad that small?"

"Then why's my dad's car in the courtyard?" asked Lin Fangsheng.

"After he left the country," said He Gui, "the car was brought here for company use."

Lin Fangsheng pushed his bike out of the company gate, turned left, walked approximately a hundred metres, leaned the bike against a tree and sat down on the rear bicycle rack, swinging his legs. He had no idea that all his actions were being observed by Wang Changchi across the street. Wang Changchi thought, Back then, I stood under the very tree where he is sitting, eagerly waiting. Over a decade had passed and the trees along the street had grown tall, but the way the father and now the son waited was identical. He wondered what the Wang family owed Lin Jiabo from a previous life for two generations of them to be tormented by him.

At the end of the working day, the street filled with people and cars. Suddenly, the black saloon drove out of the company gate. Almost simultaneously, Wang Changchi and Lin Fangsheng saw that Lin Jiabo was driving the car. Lin Fangsheng shouted "Father" at the car, but it didn't stop. Perhaps Lin Jiabo didn't see Lin Fangsheng. Lin Fangsheng got on his bike and set off in pursuit, shouting for his father as he went, but the car sped up rather than slow down. Lin Fangsheng pursued him to the next junction, where he was hit by a red saloon. The car crushed the rear wheel of his bike, while Lin Fangsheng hit the street face up, unconscious. A crowd gathered. Wang Changchi squeezed through and shouted, "Dazhi". He pushed forward to check his pulse and breathing, picked him up and put him in a taxi. Since giving Dazhi away, he had not had the chance to hug him. Now, the Old Man in Heaven had used a car accident to fulfil his long-cherished hope.

At the Second Hospital, Wang Changchi carried him to the CT Room and then to his hospital ward. He was so nervous that his clothes were soaked through. The doctor said he had suffered a concussion and abrasions, but they were not life-threatening. Only then did Wang Changchi heave a sigh of relief and sit as if paralysed by the bed. He didn't know if it was real or a daydream. He opened Dazhi's collar and saw the mole on his neck. Still uncertain, he looked at the way his hair grew, the shape of his navel and his toes, and only then was he certain that it was the real Dazhi and not a substitute.

"Dazhi," said Wang Changchi, "let's go home. If you're willing, move your eyelids."

Dazhi's eyelids did not move.

"Even moving your fingers would be OK."

Dazhi's fingers did not move.

"Well then, wiggle your toes."

Dazhi didn't wiggle his toes.

"I said that on purpose because I know you can't move," said Wang Changchi. "If you really did move, you'd be a fool. My home is nowhere nearly as good as the one you have now. Son, this is the happiness from the virtue cultivated in your previous life."

As Wang Changchi was speaking, Fang Zhizhi rushed in, collapsed on the bed and cried out, "Fangsheng, Fangsheng..." She ran her hand from his head to his toes, fearful that something was missing. Wang Changchi quietly left the room. Standing beside her, the doctor and the nurse explained the diagnosis to Fang Zhizhi. It took them about half an hour to staunch her sobbing as if it were blood.

The doctor and the nurse left. Sitting outside in the hall, Wang Changchi stretched his neck to peek inside. He saw Fang Zhizhi's head squeezed against Dazhi's, like a mother dog and her pup. Her long, white fingers caressed Dazhi's head, from his forehead to his neck and to his ears. As she caressed him, she spoke to Dazhi. Her voice sounded like a gentle breeze and fine rain as she patted the unconscious Dazhi just as she had to soothe him when he was little until he went to sleep. She wasn't his birth mother, but better. At that moment her lovely face was more lovely than ever, her tapered almond eyes, the high bridge of her nose. Her mother's love so moved Wang Changchi that he wanted to cry. Half an hour, an hour, she did not move until Fang Nanfang and Lu Shanshan arrived.

Night was falling. Sitting on the bench in the hallway, Wang Changchi stared at the green door without blinking. Fang Nanfang and Lu Shanshan left with a meal box, leaving Fang Zhizhi as the only visitor. Wang Changchi dozed off on the bench and woke up again. When the doctor visited, he took the opportunity to peek into the room. Late at night when all was quiet, Fang Zhizhi thought about that stranger outside the door.

Taking an envelope, she stepped outside and asked, "Did you bring Fangsheng to the hospital?"

Fang Zhizhi thanked him and handed him the envelope.

"What's this?" asked Wang Changchi.

"Just a little something."

Wang Changchi gave the envelope back and said, "I was passing by, so I brought him here. I didn't know he was your son."

Fang Zhizhi was startled, "You are–."

"Teacher Fang, don't you recognise me? I did some painting for you."

"Oh, Master Wang, what a coincidence. Please take the money."

"I wasn't sitting here waiting for a reward but for your son to wake up. As I rescued him, I wanted to see how he was."

"It's nothing. The doctor said he'll wake up tomorrow."

"Hasn't the boy's father come here yet?"

"His father's away on business. Do take the money, otherwise I won't feel right."

"Heaven wouldn't like it if I took this money."

The two of them pushed the envelope back and forth and it fell on the floor.

"You don't want money," asked Fang Zhizhi, "so what exactly do you want?"

"I don't want anything," replied Wang Changchi.

"If you don't want anything, then don't stay here keeping watch. You're like some secret-service agent watching the door. It makes me uncomfortable. Is the money not enough for you?"

Picking up the envelope, Wang Changchi said, "If I take the money, will that make you feel better?"

Rubbing her chest, Fang Zhizhi sighed with a feeling of great relief.

"Let me know when the child wakes up", said Wang Changchi. "When he's better, my good deed will be done."

Fang Zhizhi nodded. Wang Changchi turned and walked away. Fang Zhizhi found his silhouette all too familiar.

The day after Lin Fangsheng awoke, Wang Changchi arrived at his hospital ward with a bouquet of flowers.

"Child," said Fang Zhizhi, "this is Uncle Wang who brought you to the hospital. You need to thank him."

Looking over at Wang Changchi, Lin Fangsheng asked, "How d'you know he brought me?"

"Uncle Wang told me," replied Fang Zhizhi.

"Aren't you always telling me never to trust strangers?" asked Lin Fangsheng. "He tells you he brought me here and you believe him? There are loads of swindlers these days. Did you give him any money?"

"How can you talk like that? If he didn't bring you, who did?"

"I think a policeman brought me in a police car," said Lin Fangsheng.

Fang Zhizhi turned and looked at Wang Changchi and asked, "Is that true?"

"Whatever the child says," said Wang Changchi. "I didn't want the money in the first place."

As he spoke, he took out the envelope from two nights before and placed it on the bed.

"Fangsheng," said Fang Zhizhi, "don't tell lies."

"I'm not lying," said Lin Fangsheng. "I remember now, this is the man who hit me. No wonder he's come to see me, he was afraid of being found out."

Fang Zhizhi turned to look at Wang Changchi again.

"What's really going on here?" she asked.

"You tell me," said Wang Changchi.

"No wonder you didn't want the money," said Fang Zhizhi, "no wonder you said Heaven wouldn't like it if you took it. You're a troublemaker, Wang, I want compensation."

Wang Changchi was in turmoil. He thought, Did Dazhi just falsely accuse me? He's no longer my son. For so many years I hoped he'd become theirs, and now finally he has been reborn, genetically modified and has changed from Dazhi to Lin Fangsheng. He has become theirs, and now he won't lose anything to anyone. The harder his heart becomes, the happier it makes me. Dad, we've succeeded, we've finally managed to plant a tree in the city. Wang Changchi suddenly laughed, laughed until Fang Zhizhi and Lin Fangsheng looked at each other in blank dismay.

六十 · SIXTY

WANG CHANGCHI CORNERED LIN JIABO IN THE TOILETS at the gym. Frightened, Lin Jiabo stopped in the middle of pissing and hoisted his trousers.

"Who are you?" he asked.

"D'you know your son's in hospital?" asked Wang Changchi.

"I've already called them."

"Why haven't you gone to see him?"

"What business is it of yours?"

"Out of sympathy, I'm asking on behalf of mother and son."

"Did they ask you to come?"

"I came on my own."

"Then take off those sunglasses, mask and hat, otherwise I can't trust you."

"If I take them off, will you go back? Will you go back and live with them again?"

"Take it all off and then I'll answer."

Wang Changchi did remove his sunglasses, mask and hat.

"So it's you," said Lin Jiabo. "Did you also write that letter?"

"Yeah, I wanted to keep you three together forever."

"If I'd known you were so caring, I'd have finished my piss."

As he spoke, he took a plastic cup from the sink, turned away and finished urinating. When he turned back, he held half a cup of bright yellow urine.

"If you drink this down," he said, "I'll do what you ask."

Wang Changchi grabbed the plastic cup and miserably downed it in a single mouthful. The stink rushed to his head, and feeling bad, he gagged several times.

"If you throw it up, it won't count."

His throat constricting, Wang Changchi forced it down, and it felt like swallowing his teeth.

"Only a real father could love his son so much," said Lin Jiabo.

Wang Changchi nodded.

Slapping the sink top, Lin Jiabo said, "Shit, you're such a parasite. You can have kids but can't raise them. Piss off, you scum. Look at you, you're not a man, you're not a ghost, you couldn't be a father to Lin Fangsheng. If you loved him, you shouldn't have got rid of him. You have the effrontery to warn me, as if you were so noble. If you are so noble, don't let me see you again. Just let this secret disappear so that Lin Fangsheng doesn't find out and have that nightmare for the rest of his life."

"If you're willing to return to mother and son, and you can guarantee that Dazhi will be happy for the rest of his life, then I'll disappear."

"How will you do that?"

"Any way is fine."

Lin Jiabo regarded the man before him with the angular face, dark skin and coarse, crooked fingers with increased respect. To be honest, he was rather moved, but also worried. He knew if Wang Changchi still harboured any love for Lin Fangsheng, he would be capable of doing any stupid thing. He could still follow me, Lin Jiabo thought, he could still follow Fang Zhizhi and Lin Fangsheng, and one day maybe even snap and snatch Lin Fangsheng away. If Lin Fangsheng left, then Fang Zhizhi couldn't go on living. If Fang Zhizhi couldn't go on living, then I'd be roasted on a spit for the rest of my life. I was the one who chased after her, got her pregnant before marriage and made her get abortions that blocked her tubes. Her inability to get pregnant again was all my doing. If she didn't have the emotional support of Lin Fangsheng, would she have consented to a divorce? For a woman without a child, getting a divorce is like committing suicide. What's more, having grown up in such a good environment, how could Lin Fangsheng accept this bloke as his father? If a hole is poked in that paper window, it would be like falling to Earth from heaven. Lin Fangsheng could end up mad or disturbed...

"I drank the piss, so you should keep your promise," said Wang Changchi.

Lin Jiabo came to himself.

"Look mate," he said, "you've touched me, so today I ought to treat you decently."

Learning from his long experience with Lin Jiabo, Wang Changchi pissed in the cup and held up half a cup of urine. The urine was both yellow and smelly and, compared with Lin Jiabo's, it made him feel inferior. It was two different worlds of piss: one bright and golden, the other yellow and murky. One of expensive natural foods and water, one of waste oil, hormones and elevated amounts of chlorine.

Wang Changchi extended the cup and said, "If you're not fooling around, then drink up."

Turning away, Lin Jiabo said, "Rest assured, I love them as much as you."

"You didn't answer my question."

"I promised you that I'd return to them."

"When will you go back?"

"Is the day after tomorrow OK? I have to pretend I rushed back from Africa."

"If I don't see you at the hospital the day after tomorrow, then I'll make you disappear."

Wang Changchi threw the cup on the floor, the urine splashing on Lin Jiabo's trouser legs.

"Are you that serious?" asked Lin Jiabo.

"You have no idea how much I suffer when he suffers," said Wang Changchi. "It's like when you raise a cat or dog, and it considers you its father. He's been unhappy since you moved out. In the past after lessons, he'd leave school laughing and talking with his classmates. After waving and shouting goodbye, they'd get on their bikes and go home. But recently he comes out alone with his head down and doesn't greet anyone. Even if one of his classmates shouts goodbye, he doesn't respond. When he rides his bike, he keeps his head down. You're the one who's made him slope his shoulders and keep his head down. If this carries on, he'll become a hunchback. He's thinner and his marks have dropped. He's near the bottom of the list posted on the school wall. In the past, he'd go straight home, now he turns and goes to West River Bridge from time to time to stare into the distance. Every time he stands there, I clench my arse and grit my teeth, afraid he'll jump. Even if he goes straight home, he doesn't stay indoors like he used to but stands on the balcony looking at the street waiting for a miracle to happen. Do you know what that miracle would be? To see you return home."

Lin Jiabo was filled with envy and hatred. He had a physical reaction and felt heartburn. It turned out that I never treasured being a father, he thought, but this is what being a real father is all about. How he wished he could say those words.

"He's my son now," he said, "so what are you worried about?"

"Since you accept him as your son, you can't abandon him."

"I just left temporarily."

"Then hurry up and return from Africa."

"I've already boarded the plane home," said Lin Jiabo and paused. "What was it you just said? Something like if I returned to mother and son and could guarantee his future happiness, you'd disappear."

"I can go back home and hide far away from here."

"But when you miss him, you might come to the city at any time."

"All you have to do is treat him well and I'll never show my face again."

"If you don't come back, how will you know if I'm treating him well or not?"

Wang Changchi was silent.

"Unless you disappear for good," said Lin Jiabo, "I won't go back to them. I don't want someone watching me raise a son, smiling in secret when he's happy and making criticisms when he's not, or even giving me a kick."

"If I disappear, who'll check on Dazhi's happiness? You could stitch me up completely," said Wang Changchi.

"I can guarantee it with money. Promises and feelings are not at all reliable."

"How can you guarantee it with money?"

"Before you disappear, I'll deposit ten million yuan for Lin Fangsheng. Won't he be happy for life with that kind of money?"

"It's not just money, he needs education, and he must go to university."

"You fool, even if he were an idiot, with a family like mine, he'll go to university. If I don't help him, his maternal grandfather will."

"How do you want me to disappear?"

"Stand on the railing of West River Bridge, and jump."

"But I still have to support my mum and dad."

"I'll give your parents another two hundred thousand, enough to live on for the rest of their lives."

Wang Changchi's eyes momentarily blurred, as if death was already showing in his eyes and his spirit that of a person just executed. The mountains and rivers of home appeared in his mind as did his parents, Xiaowen, Second Uncle, and his friends and relatives, even the yellow dog his mum had secretly sold...

"Are you willing to do it for the sake of your son's happiness?" asked Lin Jiabo.

"Must I?"

"If not, then no one can guarantee Dazhi's happiness. For a child with two dads, one slip-up could do immense harm. One of us must disappear. If I disappear, he'll suffer and not get any money. If you disappear, he'll never know, won't suffer, and he'll get ten million. It's so simple, you could understand it just by using your toes."

Wang Changchi's lips trembled slightly, then his whole body began to shake.

"Can I choose where I disappear?" he asked.

"No," said Lin Jiabo, "I have to see you do it."

"Let me think about it," said Wang Changchi.

"I'll be waiting for you at the hospital entrance the day after tomorrow."

As he said this, he threw the door open and left. Wang Changchi stood in the toilets for a long, long time, and never noticed the stink.

7
REBIRTH

六十一 · SIXTY-ONE

WANG CHANGCHI ARRIVED AT THE APPOINTED PLACE ten minutes early. He had been early all his life because in the end, he didn't want to be labelled as "late". His clothes were neat and clean, and he had had a haircut and a shave. He had considered buying a brand-new pair of leather shoes, but after working out that the five hundred yuan was enough to put a new glass window in his dad's farmhouse, he swallowed, wrung his hands and gave up the idea. He was wearing a pair of cloth People's Liberation Army shoes bleached out from washing and was standing at the railing in the middle of West River Bridge. It was the highest point above the water from which the loudest splash would be made if anyone happened to fall. After a lifetime, a person either disappears quietly or leaves with a bang, he must choose. The sky was particularly blue and the clouds were of the purest white, as if the sky were putting on its best just for him or to give him a final memento. The sunlight on the water's surface was broken by the wind into waves of varying intensity, blinding for an instant here, then there. The roar of the traffic was not as disagreeable as in the past, almost pleasant now, even the exhaust fumes seemed fragrant. Seeing the successive rows of orderly multi-storey buildings, he thought, Lin Jiabo is certainly hidden there behind a window, observing me and my every move through his binoculars...

Seventy-two hours earlier, Lin Jiabo had brought two hundred thousand in cash in a black plastic bag to Wang Changchi's rented room. He dropped the money on the dining table, which had been unsteady for years. The table shook and collapsed as if unable to bear the pressure. Wang Changchi felt the floor shake under its impact, with even a few aftershocks. Lin Jiabo looked for a bench to sit on, but each one looked like it would poke his backside. Having no choice but to stand, he opened his laptop and played a video. In the video, Lin Jiabo, Dazhi and Fang Zhizhi were squeezed together, smiling at the camera. Dazhi seemed the happiest, his dimples showing as he smiled. He held up an open bank account book. The camera slowly zoomed in, making the account book bigger and bigger, until it was as big as someone's backside, before stopping. Wang Changchi counted the eight digits in Dazhi's savings, a one followed by seven zeros.

"Can you see it clearly?" asked Lin Jiabo.

Wang Changchi nodded and thought, Dad, Mum, I've sold myself for a good price. This life of mine is probably the most valuable in our village, no, our township, no, our county. Your son is a success.

That afternoon, Wang Changchi went to the bank and transferred the two hundred thousand into Wang Huai's account. He had thought about going home, and Lin Jiabo had agreed to give him the time to go home to hug his parents and say goodbye. But he was afraid that after seeing his parents, he'd change his mind and break his promise. He was afraid the long delay might cause many hitches and that he'd go and ruin Dazhi's happiness, but he was even more afraid that in a moment of confusion, he would first wreak his revenge on Lin Jiabo. Every time he thought about the very end, he'd break into a cold sweat, upset that the time was so slow in coming.

Forty-eight hours earlier, he knocked on Liu Jianping's door. He hadn't bothered Liu Jianping in over a decade, and Liu Jianping had moved to a new place. But this time he had to steel himself and go to his door. It was He Xiaowen, his former wife, who opened the door. He had known about this for some time, so he didn't get upset and his expression remained neutral. But Xiaowen was so startled that her chin was nearly dislocated as it fell. She had never imagined that Wang Changchi would drop in.

Over a decade earlier, ten days or so after Xiaowen disappeared, Wang Changchi had sought out Liu Jianping. From downstairs he had seen the light in Liu Jianping's window, but when he got upstairs and knocked on the door, it was dark, making him suspect that the light had been broken by his knocking. He felt Liu Jianping had no reason to refuse to see him, perhaps he had been mistaken downstairs. So, he went downstairs to have another look up. Liu Jianping's window was black as if it had been painted over with a dark colour. It was snowing in his heart at the time, and his mood was at its lowest. He had given Dazhi away, Xiaowen had left, and he had hoped to go out and drink a few glasses with Liu Jianping to wash the bitterness away entirely. He had really expected Liu Jianping to be at home. In such a large city, Liu Jianping was the only one willing to listen to him pour out his heart. He stood there for a moment and then squatted by the roadside to wait, thinking that Liu Jianping might come home soon. But after waiting an hour, Liu Jianping had still not appeared. He stood up to leave, when he suddenly heard a window open upstairs, a sound that kept him there. He dashed to the foot of the wall and saw Liu Jianping stick his head out of the window, scan below the building and when he saw no one, pull his head back in. The light went on in the window. He thought, The guy is obviously at home, so why didn't he answer the door? Angry, he rushed upstairs and pounded on the door. Liu Jianping opened the door a crack and lifted his finger.

"Shh", he said, "I've got a girl here, right where I want her. Can you get lost for a few days?"

Putting his hands in his opposite sleeves, he left resentfully. A few days later he returned to see Liu Jianping, but the landlord said he had moved. After that, Liu Jianping vanished. A year later,

Wang Changchi went to a building site to paint the doorframes and discovered Liu Jianping leading a number of burly guys carrying banners and placards, his face red from demanding the wages owed to others. Wang Changchi pulled down the brim of his cap and put on his mask, and once they had dispersed, he got on the motorcycle he had recently purchased and followed him. Finally, he found his new address. At first, when Liu Jianping had moved without saying goodbye, Wang Changchi was confused, but following him now, his suspicions were confirmed. He Xiaowen was living with him. No wonder when Wang Huai "performed the ritual" he had said, "I see Xiaowen in the window but can't open it." A sheet of paper had separated him from Xiaowen. After hesitating for a while, he decided to keep silent and leave. His own household had fallen apart, and he didn't want to break up someone else's.

Xiaowen let Wang Changchi in. Liu Jianping brewed a pot of tea. The three of them sat in the living room just breathing, none of them willing to be the first to speak. The doors to the master bedroom and second bedroom were closed and there was a refrigerator in the living room and a washing machine in the bathroom, and brand-name soy sauce in the kitchen. Wang Changchi thought they must be living pretty well.

"Any kids?" he asked.

Liu Jianping shouted towards the second bedroom, "Qingyun, Zhishang, come on out."

The door opened and out bolted two fair-skinned children. The boy went to the mother and the girl to the father, and they timidly looked at Wang Changchi.

"Call him Uncle Wang," said Liu Jianping.

With one voice, the two children said, "Hello, Uncle Wang."

Their teeth were white and straight and their faces reddish, their expressions so cute.

"Jianping," said Wang Changchi, "could you get the kids to call me 'Dad'? I want so badly to hear the simple sound of children saying that word."

Liu Jianping looked at Xiaowen, Xiaowen looked at the children, the children closed their mouths, dark clouds passing over their faces. Wang Changchi took out a bank account book and placed it on the table.

"I made this by painting for more than ten years," he said, "and I'd like to leave it so the kids can go to school."

"You don't need the money?" asked Liu Jianping.

"I got rich."

"How?"

"Don't ask. Anyway, I, Wang Changchi, will never have to worry about money from today on."

Liu Jianping signalled to the children with his eyes.

"Go on, call him 'Dad'," he said.

The two children turned around and looked away. Xiaowen gave them a shove. They shook their heads.

"If someone wanted to give me so much money," said Liu Jianping, "I'd call him 'Dad'. If you don't want to, then we'll give the money back to Uncle Wang."

The two children turned around and shouted, "Dad Wang..."

Wang Changchi sighed with satisfaction, and his whole body seemed to melt into thin air. He closed his eyes, tears streaming down from the corners of his eyes.

"What about Dazhi? How's he doing?" asked Xiaowen.

"I'm here to tell you that Dazhi has succeeded. We don't have to worry about him. Just raise Qingyun and Zhishang to be the best they can be," said Wang Changchi.

"I think about him even in my dreams. I did wrong by him, and I hate you." Xiaowen wiped her eyes.

"You only hate me because you don't know how happy he is. You have kids now. What we are lacking isn't children."

Twenty-four hours earlier, Wang Changchi wrote two letters at his rented place, following which he went to the school to see Dazhi. Lessons were in progress, so the guard wouldn't let him in. He sat down in a rice-noodle shop across the street from the school gate.

"If you're not ordering anything, why are you sitting here?" asked the shopkeeper.

Wang Changchi took out some money and paid for a bowl of rice noodles, eating while turning his head to watch the gate. He had almost finished the bowl of noodles, but the school day wouldn't end for another two hours. Wang Changchi sat and stared blankly at the trees on the school grounds and the students on the playing field in their PE class. After a while, the shopkeeper came and tapped the table with his finger.

"You finished ages ago," he said, "so why are you still here?"

Embarrassed, Wang Changchi's face flushed red. He quickly pulled out some more money and said, "Give me another bowl."

The waitress brought another bowl of rice noodles. Having learned his lesson by eating the last bowl so quickly, he took his time eating this one, trying to drag out the time, hanging around in his seat. But despite eating the noodles one by one, it didn't take all that much time to eat. He finished the rice noodles in less than half an hour. He thought, I've already eaten two bowls of rice noodles, so he won't make me leave, will he? Unexpectedly, a half hour before school finished, the shopkeeper came over and asked, "Why are you still here?" Wang Changchi glanced around the shop and saw that the place was largely empty, but the shopkeeper wasn't going to let him just sit there. So he paid for another bowl of rice noodles. He slowly ate the noodles and then the school bell rang. Small groups of students came out of the gate. Finally, he saw Dazhi and two female classmates come out through the gate, laughing and talking. They patted each other on the shoulder at the gate before going their separate ways. On his guard, Dazhi looked carefully in all directions as if he had a premonition, his eyes finally alighting on the rice noodle shop. Wang Changchi felt their eyes meet, just as Dazhi had done the day he was born when he impatiently opened his eyes to look into Wang Changchi's. He went numb all over and, unable to control himself, shouted, "Dazhi". He wanted to stand up and rush out, but after having eaten three bowls of rice noodles, he couldn't get to his feet. Dazhi looked away, turned right, walked more than two hundred metres and got into a red saloon with Fang Zhizhi at the wheel. Since the boy had left hospital, Fang Zhizhi took him to school and picked him up, in case he had another fall. The car took off like a fish with a sweep of its tail. Wang Changchi thought, I've never consumed so much in my life. I've eaten my fill countless times, but I've only been this full twice, once when Xiaowen and I went to the county town and had our picture taken, watched dirty movies, and when I went to the police station to apologise. We had a plate of seasoned meat, two dishes of peanuts and cucumbers, a bottle of rice wine and four bowls of rice. But even then, I could still stand up.

It was now twelve o'clock sharp. The time Wang Changchi and Lin Jiabo had agreed upon had arrived. A clock somewhere struck the hour, probably at the church, but it also seemed to come from inside him, like the retort of a gun at an execution. Wang Changchi glanced back and climbed up on the railing.

六十二 · SIXTY-TWO

WANG CHANGCHI'S CORPSE WASN'T RECOVERED until the following day. When the police cut off his underwear, they discovered a small plastic bag which held a slip of paper with Liu Jianping's telephone number on it. The police contacted Liu Jianping and got him to identify the body.

Striking her breast, Xiaowen said, "Oh my goodness, so he came to say goodbye to us."

Liu Jianping and Xiaowen followed the policemen to the morgue and discovered that Wang Changchi had become size L and his skin was so swollen that it was about to split open. But regardless of whether he was an L or XL, Xiaowen and Liu Jianping still recognised him. They told the police officers his full name. After identifying the corpse, the two policemen took Liu Jianping and Xiaowen to the place where Wang Changchi lived. The door was locked. The police were going to call the landlord. Xiaowen took out the key she had left with years before. The police took the key, inserted it and turned. The door opened. In more than a decade, Wang Changchi never changed the lock, leaving the door for Xiaowen to open. Xiaowen looked over the place. It was still the same room but neater than it ever had been in the past, even the floor was mopped spotless. In the centre of the room stood the chair that Wang Changchi had brought from his old home in the country. On the chair sat a funeral urn on top of two letters. On one was written "To My Father, Wang Huai" and on the other "To Liu Jianping". The police told Liu Jianping to open the letter. His hands trembling, Liu Jianping tried to tear open the letter several times before finally succeeding. The letter read:

Brother Jianping,

Please, you must take me home and you must tell my mum and dad that I died in a fall at the construction site. Tell them that the two hundred thousand is compensation. Please, when I am cremated, incinerate this chair with me. After death, I don't want to have to stand, I want to sit, I am tired. Please. I'll thank you in the next life.

Changchi

Liu Jianping was the first to burst into tears, followed by Xiaowen. The police opened the letter to Wang Huai, and inside was a receipt for the transfer of two hundred thousand yuan.

"Where did he get that kind of money?" asked the police.

Shaking their heads, they said, "We don't know."

The two hundred thousand yuan stopped their crying. The police suspected that if Wang Changchi hadn't stolen the money, he had robbed someone. Swearing to Heaven, Liu Jianping and Xiaowen said that he wasn't the sort. The police didn't believe them, so they immediately opened an investigation. The focus of their investigation was the source of the two hundred thousand. After six months, they hadn't uncovered the source nor had anyone reported such a large sum of money being stolen or anyone being robbed. Then they agreed to allow Wang Changchi's corpse to be cremated. Representing the family, Liu

Jianping signed the papers. The workers pushed Wang Changchi, who had been in a freezer for six months, into the furnace. Liu Jianping placed the chair beside Wang Changchi. The furnace door was closed and with a whoosh the furnace flame blazed.

"Changchi," said Liu Jianping, "I burned the chair for you, sit down at ease and rest. Amen."

Liu Jianping, Xiaowen, Qingyun and Zhishang took Wang Changchi's ashes back to his home in the country. They arrived in the village at noon. A cold wind was blowing over the desolate land, and snow was vaguely visible on the distant mountain peaks. All the village dogs began to bark the moment they appeared in the gap. Hearing the wild barking, everyone opened their windows to see if it was a relative who had returned. Xiaowen held the hand of her son Qingyun, and Liu Jianping carried his daughter Zhishang in one arm and the funeral urn in the other. The farther they walked, the heavier their legs felt and the more their feet seemed to drag, as if they were stuck in the mud. Wang Huai and Liu Shuangju, one standing and one sitting in a wheelchair, were in front of the new two-storey house of Wang Changchi's family, gazing towards them from afar. Liu Shuangju's hair was almost all white and her face had almost twice the number of wrinkles of ten years earlier. Wang Huai was darker and thinner, and his legs were seriously atrophied so that they looked like two bones. They didn't know Liu Jianping, nor did they recognise Xiaowen. They assumed the four of them had nothing to do with them but remained gazing out of curiosity. To their surprise, they came closer and closer until they were standing right in front of them. Qingyun and Zhishang were the first to run to the arms of Wang Huai and Liu Shuangju, shouting "Grandpa" and "Grandma". It was only then that Liu Shuangju recognised Xiaowen. She hugged Xiaowen and cried out involuntarily.

When he saw the funeral urn, Wang Huai wanted to cry, but he had no tears. He had spent his whole life trying to improve the lot of the Wang family and his body had been consumed and dried up by time so that he had no bodily fluids left to express his feelings. Even when he took Wang Changchi's final letter from its envelope, he scarcely had the energy to tremble. Ever so slowly he unfolded the letter and read:

Dad, Mum,

The fate of the Wang family has been completely changed, so my duty is done. Dazhi has accomplished what generations of our family have been unable to do. He lives the life of an immortal, so you need not worry about him. Give the money you cannot use to Qingyun and Zhishang. If Liu Jianping and Xiaowen have no objections, consider Qingyun and Zhishang as your grandchildren. I am not a filial son, so please beat my backside.

On bended knees, Changchi

Wang Huai's head fell to one side as he fainted in his wheelchair. He only began to regain his strength the following day. Late at night Liu Shuangju placed white rice, a live rooster, a shoulder of pork, wine, incense, spirit money and cymbals on the square table in the main hall. In front of the burning incense, Wang Huai performed a ritual for Wang Changchi. His legs trembled and he mumbled an incantation. As he chanted, he scattered rice in the air and on the floor and poured out the wine. In half an hour, his forehead was covered with sweat.

Suddenly, he asked in a loud voice, "Where will Wang Changchi be reborn?"

Kneeling before the table, Qingyun and Zhishang replied, "In the city."

"Where?"

"In the city."

The question and answer were repeated a dozen times or so, but Wang Changchi's spirit continued to crouch in the funeral urn. Wang Huai scattered more rice and poured out more wine. He tore a piece of cockscomb and plucked some feathers from the rooster and flung them on the ground. This still failed to clear the impasse for the spirit or motivate Wang Changchi.

"Changchi," said Wang Huai, "I know you don't want to leave your mum and dad. I know you cannot bear to abandon us. You listened to your parents your whole life, so listen one more time. In the last generation, you were reborn in the wrong place and came to our family. We were poor and failed to provide you with a good life. In the next generation, you want to choose a good family and be reborn in the city. Qingyun and Zhishang are here, so you can depart at ease."

When he finished speaking, he mumbled more incantations.

He asked, "Where will Changchi be reborn?"

"In the city," replied Qingyun and Zhishang with resonant voices.

"Where?" asked Wang Huai, in a louder voice.

"In the city," shouted Liu Shuangju, Liu Jianping, Xiaowen and the aunts and uncles.

"Where?" asked Wang Huai again.

"In the city," they cried out.

"Where?" asked Wang Huai, his voice hoarse from shouting.

"In the city," came a chorus of shouts from outside.

Those were the voices of the villagers. The entire village helped to shout, "In the city". Wang Changchi's spirit was ready to move. Wang Huai banged the cymbals on the table. Wang Changchi's spirit suddenly took flight, passed over the roof and circled. Wang Huai hit the cymbals again. Wang Changchi's spirit flew towards the big maple tree, stopped on a branch and looked back, reluctant to let go. Wang Huai struck the cymbals once more. It was like the year he encouraged Wang Changchi to go and get tutoring or when he urged him to find work in the city. The sound of the cymbals reached the branch of the maple tree, and Wang Changchi's spirit took flight once more. It flew over the forest, the river, the motorway, the railway and buildings... straight to the provincial capital, it flew to People's Road, and on into the delivery room in the People's Hospital.

A cry was heard in the delivery room. Utterly exhausted, Wu

Xin finally gave birth to a baby boy. When Lin Jiabo, who was standing anxiously by the door, heard the words, "It's a boy," he was so excited he danced for joy.

六十三 · SIXTY-THREE

SEVERAL YEARS LATER, LIN FANGSHENG GRADUATED from the police academy and began work in the First Division of the Criminal Investigation Unit. Knowing there was something unusual about his background, Commander Gong didn't assign him any specific duties at first but allowed him to learn how things worked in the division. Intent upon doing an excellent job, as well as having read too much detective fiction, Lin Fangsheng would go down to the archives and go through the unsolved cases. Each time he looked through a file it was like reading a book with plot twists, a lot of room for the imagination and of course the opportunity for doing exemplary service. But after reading more than ten files, the hardest thing to forget was what he had seen first. Perhaps this was Heaven's will.

The first time he went to the archives, he wanted to examine that crime of passion case that had once caused such an uproar, but as he was passing the Number 2 filing cabinet, he felt someone tap him on the shoulder that so startled him, he moved to avoid it. When he looked around, no one was there, but there was a file on the floor, which he had knocked down as he moved away. He picked up the file and opened it. The first thing that caught his eye was a photo of a swollen corpse. Although the deceased was severely misshapen, he felt the person was in some way familiar, but couldn't remember where he had seen him. Leaning against the shelves, he read the file in detail. It was a nine-year-old case, and Lin Fangsheng knew there was something wrong. Officer Zhao, who had been in charge of the case, was only interested in looking for evidence of a crime committed by the deceased and never considered that the suicide had perhaps been murdered by another. A few days later, Lin Fangsheng handed the file to

Commander Gong. The commander glanced at the file and tossed it back.

"Don't you have anything better to do?" he asked. "You're interested in such a small case."

"Even so," said Lin Fangsheng, "it is a human life."

"Have you ever thrown stones in a river?" asked Commander Gong.

"Yes," replied Lin Fangsheng.

"First look at the stone that makes the biggest splash and most noise, not the one that doesn't make a sound or a splash."

Lin Fangsheng nodded, but he didn't want to give up. He wanted to use the unsolved case to test his own abilities.

Lin Fangsheng began to investigate the "Wang Changchi" file. He discovered that the man had not died, that he was still living and that he was the assistant director at a certain work unit. Lin Fangsheng thought that the names were perhaps a coincidence, but when he checked, he found that the birthplace, ID number, ancestral home and junior high school of the living Wang Changchi were identical to those of the deceased Wang Changchi. So, Lin Fangsheng paid a visit to Assistant Director Wang at his office. Clearly, Assistant Director Wang was not the dead man in the photograph. After several conversations, Assistant Director Wang dropped to his knees with a thud and begged Lin Fangsheng let him off the hook. Lin Fangsheng thought, Who says this is an insignificant case, isn't this a big splash? After investigating further, it turned out that Assistant Director Wang was actually named Ya Dashan, who had failed to pass the university entrance exam. Thanks to his father's interference, he switched his name to that of his classmate Wang Changchi. Wang Changchi's university admissions letter was withheld, and Ya Dashan took his place by assuming Wang Changchi's name. When he graduated, Ya Dashan, once again thanks to his father's intervention, got a position in a certain provincial work unit, where he finally worked his way up to the position of assistant director. At present, Ya Dashan's work was going well, he had a happy family, was in good health, and had a pretty wife and a son doing postgraduate studies. If Lin Fangsheng had not intruded, Ya Dashan would still be enjoying his stolen life with a clear conscience. Lin Fangsheng thought, for one person to destroy another person was an evil crime worthy of ten thousand deaths. He swore an oath that Ya Dashan would be punished according to the law.

He decided to pay a visit to Wang Changchi's old home, where he could perhaps find some clues to break the case. A road had been built, so Wang Changchi's home could be reached directly by car. Because the road's surface had not been metalled, the small car raised a cloud of dust. So as not to attract attention, Lin Fangsheng drove his own car, dressed casually and wore sunglasses. He saw Wang Huai, his bones as thin as sticks, sitting in his wheelchair and Liu Shuangju standing in the doorway, stooped over, her hair all white. Lin Fangsheng looked like any other cadre to them, and neither surprised nor curious, they imagined he was there to talk about family planning. Lin Fangsheng was startled when he saw several pictures of himself when he was little inserted in a picture frame in the main hall. At first, he assumed it must be another child who looked like him, but after rubbing his eyes and taking a second look, it really was him.

Pointing at the pictures, he asked them, "Why do you have his photos?"

Wang Huai's eyes brightened, he immediately sat up in his wheelchair, and he seemed to come alive.

"That is my grandson," he said. "His name is Wang Dazhi. Before he was born, he accompanied his mum and dad to the city, but because they couldn't provide for him, they gave him away to some wealthy people."

Looking closely at the photos, Lin Fangsheng suddenly went cold all over, his teeth chattered, and both legs trembled as if the weather had become frigid.

After returning to the city, Lin Fangsheng secretly investigated himself, but the more he dug, the more frightened he became. Late one night, he went to West River Bridge. The bridge was empty, and the street lights were reflected on the river's surface. He stood at the very spot where Wang Changchi had stood when he jumped into the river. He stood there for a long time until both his legs were numb. Later, he removed a file from his bag, as well as a stack of photos, and hurled them into the river. The file and the photos floated like fallen tree leaves. Lin Fangsheng's secret was buried from that moment on, and if he didn't give himself away, no one would ever know where he was from.

One morning, Wang Huai was staring at the picture frame when he suddenly shouted,

"Shuangju, what happened to Dazhi's photos?"

Liu Shuangju came out of the kitchen, looked up for a while, and discovered that of all the photos that were there, only those of Dazhi had disappeared. Was she losing her sight? Liu Shuangju put on her reading glasses but still did not see Dazhi. Wang Huai took Liu Shuangju's reading glasses and put them on and confirmed that Dazhi was nowhere to be seen in the picture frame. Dazhi had left without saying a word. Never again would they see their grandson. When they missed him, they could rely only on their memories. But their memories became ever more vague and unreliable. Sometimes, as they looked at themselves in the mirror, they recalled Dazhi. Because they vaguely remembered that Dazhi had his grandfather's eyes, his grandmother's nose and his father's mouth.

TRANSLATOR'S
AFTERWORD

The action of Dong Xi's novel takes place in a momentous period of recent Chinese history: the emergence of post-socialist China. The historical context is crucial for Dong Xi's narrative and yet may be unfamiliar to many readers outside China. After the death of Mao Zedong in 1976 and the launch of market reforms and opening to the outside world under Deng Xiaoping in 1978, China underwent dramatic changes that rewrote the lives of the country's citizens in a multitude of ways. With the gradual dismantling of China's system of centrally-planned socialism and other reforms, the economy took off, and China became the world's factory, raising living standards and reducing poverty. This economic miracle is the story most people are familiar with but not with many of the details behind it.

The reform and opening policy had profound consequences. As state and foreign capital poured into China, especially the urban coastal areas, the population swelled in the urban investment areas, with rural areas supplying the needed labour. Rural migrant workers could choose between low-paying jobs (or no job) in rural areas or better-paying, low-end jobs in a city. However, despite the new-found opportunities, restrictions and difficulties remained for these workers. The plight of these migrant or undocumented workers in post-socialist China is central to the mechanics of Dong Xi's story. China's rural-urban divide of the time is key to the novel thematically. We witness the breakdown of traditional values (associated with rural China) in the face of the new socio-economic order (emerging in urban areas), even a shaking of the very foundation of the concept of self.

One commonly encountered difficulty, for example, was the *hukou* (or household registration) system, the enforcement of which was not initially relaxed. By 1960, after agricultural collectivisation in the 1950s, the *hukou* system was strictly enforced by the government. The communist authorities took over the system from the nationalists, making it more extensive and effective. The household registration included extensive information about each member of the household and had to be kept updated by the head of household. The registration was on file with the police, from which they compiled lists of individuals of questionable political loyalty who needed supervision. Everyone had been assigned a rural or urban identity through the system. Ration cards and other resources were allocated according to the system. If a person was not registered in a location, they were not allowed to live there. This strictly restricted the free movement of the citizenry, allowing the government to transform Chinese society. People were prevented from migrating to urban areas.

Ultimately this led to the emergence of a socialist serfdom in rural areas. By the mid-1950s and throughout the Cultural Revolution, the policy was used to encourage people to relocate to rural areas or to forcibly relocate problematic elements. Disparities in access to education, healthcare and resources emerged between rural and urban areas. With the gradual dismantling of the centrally-planned system, beginning in rural areas, rural workers could earn more and wanted a larger share of other goods and services. But the *hukou* registration remained intact, at least initially. Thus rural migrant labourers left their registrations behind in the countryside, becoming undocumented workers in the urban areas. Without registration, they were deprived of benefits (health, education, housing, etc). Despite the difficulties, the country's urban population increased four-fold from 1980 to 2015. Between 1992 and 2006, the rural migrant labour population increased from fifty-three million to 115 million. Internal labour migration of this scale transformed the country. Eventually internal migration restrictions were relaxed, but for a time undocumented workers faced discrimination and exploitation and were considered second-class citizens by the state. However, even with the discrimination and growth of wealth inequality, most people felt optimistic that they could improve their lives and those of their children through hard work and sacrifice. In fact, more than 800 million people have been lifted out of poverty in China since the 1970s. This then is the milieu in which Dong Xi's characters operate.

This translation is based on the first edition of the novel published by the Shanghai Literature & Art Publishing House in 2015, while incorporating subsequent changes requested by the author.

I would like to thank the following individuals and institutions for their contributions to this translation. Thank you first of all to Dong Xi for his support and to the late Goeran Malmqvist and his wife Wenfen Chen for bringing us together. I would like to thank the Shanghai Literature & Art Publishing House for their financial support for the translation. I would also like to express my gratitude to Sinoist Books for publishing this title. In particular, I'd like to express my gratitude to Daniel Yang Li and my wonderful editor Susan Trapp. I'd also like to thank my wife Yingtsih for her assistance.

ABOUT THE AUTHOR

Dong Xi (1966-) is the pen name of Tian Dailin. Born in Guangxi Province, Chinese critics generally include him among the "New Generation" of writers. Notable works include the novels *A Resounding Slap in the Face, Record of Regret*, and *Fate Rewritten* as well as his *Collected Works* in eight volumes. His novella *Life without Language* won the Lu Xun Literary Award; *Record of Regret* won the 2005 Chinese Language Media Prize; and *Fate Rewritten* was the top-rated work by the Chinese Fiction Association and won the Huacheng Literature Prize for outstanding author. Many of his works have been adapted for television and a number have been translated into English, French, Korean, Vietnamese, German, Thai, Italian, Greek, and Japanese. Currently he is Writer in Residence at the Guangxi University for Nationalities.

ABOUT THE
TRANSLATOR

John Balcom is an award-winning translator of Chinese literature, philosophy and children's books. His translations have won numerous grants and awards, including an NEA Translation fellowship, the Science Fiction and Fantasy Translation Award, and the Northern California Book Award. Dr Balcom is Professor Emeritus at the Middlebury Institute of International Studies at Monterey, California and a past president of the American Literary Translators Association.

About **Sino**ist Books

We hope you found this story about the struggles and sacrifices of Wang Changchi moving.

SINOIST BOOKS brings the best of Chinese fiction to English-speaking readers. We aim to create a greater understanding of Chinese culture and society, and provide an outlet for the ideas and creativity of the country's most talented authors.

To let us know what you thought of this book, or to learn more about the diverse range of exciting Chinese fiction in translation we publish, find us online. If you're as passionate about Chinese literature as we are, then we'd love to hear your thoughts!

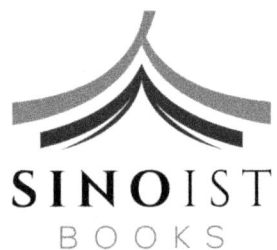

SINOIST
B O O K S